I0671801

Completely Out of Control

When Tyrbrand brought Kitten into the sitting room, Eirlin sat slumped in her usual chair staring at Fang, who lay on her worktable, trying to make himself seem as small as possible. "What are we going to do with you, my love?"

The Magician knelt in front of her. "Does something have to be done with him?"

She turned anxious eyes to him. "We have been concerned for months that he is too powerful and too willful. We worried that he would do something dangerous, and wondered whether he might need to be destroyed.

"When you gave him to me you broke the rules, Tyrbrand. No being should be given more Power than she can handle, and he is too Powerful. I...I can't handle him. I'm just not strong enough!"

Kitten could feel her hands shaking and the tears ready to break out.

"And now he has done what we feared. He cut Cuquita against my direct command. He has done her irreparable harm and played into the hand of the enemy as well. I've been waiting for you to come and tell me."

With her palms turned up, she reached out to Tyrbrand. "How can we avoid destroying him?"

The Cat with Many Claws

Sword Called Kitten #2

Gordon A. Long

AIRBORN PRESS
Delta 2013

The Cat with Many Claws

Published by
AIRBORN PRESS
4958 10A Ave, Delta, B. C.
V4M 1X8
Canada

Copyright Gordon A. Long

2013

Cover art by Dusty Hagerüd

All rights reserved, including the right to reproduce this book or any portion thereof in any form without the express written permission of the author.

ISBN 978-0-9921243-0-4

Thanks

To Cas Peace for her usual detailed and supportive editing, and to Dusty Hagerud for his artistry.

This is a work of fiction. All the characters and events portrayed in this book are fictional (except for the cat), and any resemblance to real people or incidents is purely coincidental. Except for the cat.

...oh, yes. And the dog.

...don't ask.

Contents

Prologue: Creation

The Magician patted the grizzled head, smoothed one tattered ear. "Don't try, boy. I know you can't get up." He gathered the wasted body, his weakened arms shaking with the strain. "Don't worry. All the pain will soon be gone."

He shouldered aside the door to the forge and laid the dog on a blanket folded on the workbench. The crooked tail thumped a few times.

Tearing his eyes away from his old friend, the Magician began his preparations. He stoked the forge high, pumping the bellows until the centre of the fire attained a clear, white glow. Satisfied, he opened the box that lay on the bench. The knife inside was tiny: the blade shorter than a child's finger, the tang a mere sliver of metal. The Magician laid out a set of long, fine tongs and a shallow metal tray. Then he began his mental preparation.

One hand caressing the dog's head, he choked down the sorrow that threatened to break his concentration. As if in understanding, the dog sent a weak lick across his wrist. Taking this as a final gesture of acquiescence, the Magician began to move into the dog's consciousness, blending his mind with the dim thoughts that stalked there. Then he reached out to the empty void that was the blade, forming the first tenuous bond between the two. The dog seemed to understand, the soul yearning from its pain-wracked body towards the clean new lair the Magician offered.

The dog's consciousness circled the blade as he would a new bed, willing but uncertain.

When the Magician felt that the animal's mind was ready, he quickened his pace, smoothly performing the actions he had rehearsed to perfection. The old dog was so intent on this new experience that he scarcely noticed the nick of the fine-honed blade to his throat.

Now the Magician had to be quick and sure. He pushed his own weakness and pain aside. As the dog's failing heart pumped blood into the pan, he used the tongs to lay the steel deep in the heart of the forge. The dog grew weaker and weaker while the blade glowed, first dull, then bright red, flaring towards white. At the same time, the Magician held the dog's mind firmly in his grasp, directing, soothing, dulling the pain. Tears streamed unheeded as the Magician prepared for his final move.

The moment came when the dog's heart scarcely beat, when the metal had reached a temperature it could barely withstand. The

Magician pulled the blade from the heat and inserted it into the pan of blood: first the curving edge, then, more slowly, the spine, and finally the tang. He did so blindly, his mind set on easing the last of his old friend's consciousness into the waiting sanctuary. Both subjects were in the ideal state of anticipation; the final words would seal the exchange. The Magician gathered his waning Powers and intoned the spell with careful diction.

"I name you Excisor."

There was a final hesitation, and the man's concentration was jolted by the feel of a wet tongue on his wrist. Then all resistance disappeared. The frail body in his left hand slumped, and the Blade in his right began to vibrate. There was initial puzzlement and confusion, but then a rush of joy as the old dog's soul was fused with the shining steel. A new Being had been Forged.

The long task had begun.

Dear Ecmund, Perica, Lord Delfontes, and of course, Kitten,

It is with some embarrassment that I write this letter. I was so pleased to be allowed to come to the Capital, so enthusiastic about what I might accomplish here. Unfortunately, things have not turned out quite the way I expected.

I hasten to reassure you that it is not Tyrbrand's fault. He has been endlessly supportive, and introduced me to some fascinating people. I have been able to make a certain amount of progress in my studies of Healing. However, politics smears its greasy fingers on even my simple profession; there has been resistance to my presence and the ideas I stand for.

Tyrbrand tries to help, but he is caught up with his duties to the king and with his Magician's undertaking, so he does not have time to tend to a country girl who would rather be at home.

We have decided that it would be better for me to return to Falkenby until he has finished the first stage of his task. Once that is done, he says he will need me back in Koningsholm, and perhaps the next time I will come better prepared to help him with his work.

For the moment, though, you should expect me close behind this letter. Once the decision is made, I see no reason to stay.

Except for Tyrbrand, of course, and I have resolved to be strong. If our feelings cannot endure a short separation, perhaps they are not as deep as they need to be.

In any case, thanks to the carriages of our King's new Post service, I will soon be home.

With Love,

Eirlin Bryghtwyn

1. A Puzzle

The three sat in the Overlord's workroom at Falkenby, the letter on the table in front of them. There was a long silence, until Kitten grew weary of it.

Four. A magic Sword of my intelligence and experience is an Entity worth consideration.

The four sat in the Overlord's workroom at Falkenby, regarding the letter.

Perica stood and paced over to the window, adjusting the tall, thick shutter to direct the evening sunlight so it cut the gloom of the unadorned granite walls. She shook her head, then tossed her dark curls back into place with a graceful flick of her wrist. "Ecmund, I don't understand. Your sister is a strong, confident person. She has gone to the Capital to study Healing as she longs to do. She is with Tyrbrand, a man who definitely interests her. Why would she want to come home? Could she be homesick?"

"She is more than homesick."

The two young people turned to face Lord Delfontes.

"I have been making some enquiries in the past month. I have discovered more of the lore of the Blood than I knew when I first came here."

"Which was basically," Perica flicked her fingers at her father, "nothing."

"As that may be. I have discovered that even now, almost two hundred years after the rule of the Blood of Inderjorne was taken over by our ancestors, the Maridon invaders, there always remains a leader of the Blood in each demesne, to whom everyone looks for support and strength. In the case of Falkenby, the obvious family is yours, Ecmund. Just as obviously, the true leader isn't going to be your uncle, because his personality is completely inappropriate. It won't be your cousin Jesco, because of his temper and his half-Maridon blood. That leaves you and Eirlin."

Perica's nose wrinkled. "When did you figure this out?"

Her father smiled. "I may not have the sensitivity that you two have, but I do boast some small experience in dealing with people. Why do you think I asked Eirlin to stay behind, that first day when the Village Council confronted me?"

Ecmund grinned. "The day you threw me in jail. Why didn't you think I was the leader?"

"Because those were not the actions of a leader. They were what you would expect from a man of action, a fighter. So I was interested to see what would happen after I had you removed. What happened? Eirlin. I could tell by the faces of the Council and of my own local soldiers that she was the one they all looked to. Once Eirlin stood up they all relaxed, as if the preliminaries were over and the real battle was now joined. They had done their parts, and they could watch from the sidelines."

"Eirlin is more closely connected to this area than others, so she is homesick?"

"I think 'homesick' is a rather weak word for what she is feeling."

"Well, she will be home soon."

Kitten puzzled this over. What was the problem? *Eirlin will come. Then she will be happy. Ecmund and Perica will marry, and we will all be happy.*

Ecmund stroked the Sword's hilt. "I wish it was as simple as you like it, Kitten."

Humans make things so complicated. You will see.

Eirlin arrived, a pale face peeking out from the darkness of the carriage, her back stooping to navigate the step. As her foot touched the packed earth of the village square, though, her shoulders straightened and she tossed her blonde braids back. "It is so good to be home!"

After a warm hug for her brother and a more decorous embrace for Perica, she looked around. "Albercas has been working on his inn." She pointed to the brighter thatch at one end of the roof, the freshly-painted casings on two windows.

Ecmund's anxious look turned to laughter. "Trust you to notice. Now that the King's Post stops here, he's been sprucing it up inside and out. I hope it meets your approval?"

She shrugged, grinning sheepishly. "I'm sure the innkeeper can make up his own mind about what his premises need."

Perica shook her head. "Ah, but someone has to approve. We can't have people just running around doing whatever they want, can we?"

Eirlin's brow furrowed. "I know you too well, Perica. What are you trying to say?"

The smaller girl merely nodded knowingly. "You know what I mean."

A glance to her brother showed that he was not going to help.

What's going on, Kitten?

Kitten brushed a light inquiry over the Healer's mind. There seemed no need for concern. She would figure things out on her own. *Welcome home, Eirlin. It is good to have you here.*

Ecmund laughed. "Kitten is learning discretion."

I have always known discretion. I merely choose to use it.

Eirlin shrugged and looked around the square again. A feeling of satisfaction welled from her. "It all looks very tidy. I'm so glad to be here."

"You already said that."

"And I'll be saying it again. Perica, has my brother organized a cup of tea for the thirsty traveller? If so, I make bold to ask you to join us."

"He certainly has. He's training up quite nicely, you know. Soon he might even be worth marrying." She trapped his hand in both of hers before he could swat at her. "And I imposed upon my cook to provide some appropriate treats, as well."

When they reached the cedar-shaked woodcutter's cottage near the edge of the village, Kitten could feel Eirlin's mood expand and lighten further, as she inspected the timbers and planks in the woodyard, commented on the size of the woodpile, noted the cleanliness of the plank floor, warmed her hands a moment at the fireplace and repeated her mantra.

Perica served tea in Eirlin's plain mugs and laid out a plate of baking.

"These are very fancy, Perica. They hardly suit our rustic table."

"They are appropriate to the occasion, I think. It is not often that a local leader returns to her demesne."

Eirlin laid her hands flat on the table. "All right, you two. Something is going on here, and you're going to tell me about it."

The two exchanged glances. Perica shrugged. "Father did some research into the Blood of Inderjorne. He found out about you."

"Found out about me? What about me? You're talking in riddles."

"He found out about the leaders of the Blood. Everybody knows it, nobody talks about it, but you're the head of the Blood in Falkenby. That's why you were so unhappy in Koningsholm. You felt the pull of the land."

Eirlin looked down at her hands, still spread out on the table. Then she looked up, but her right hand made an unconscious caressing motion across the scrubbed surface. "Whatever are you talking about?"

Eirlin the Intelligent has just revealed a huge hole in her knowledge.

The Healer stood and reached across the table, her hand slapping down on Kitten's hilt. "That is an insult, and you had better be ready to explain yourself!"

The mind of Eirlin the Exalted is powerful. Quivering in fear, I must obey.

"Now you are making fun of me."

Who, little me? How would I dare?

"Ecmund, will you control your Sword? Obviously her training has lapsed in my absence."

He laughed. "It's good to have you home, Eirlin. Sit down again, and tell me about the Capital. Is it as huge a city as they say? Are the buildings all of stone instead of wood?"

Eirlin began a frown, then thought better of it. "Whatever you are hiding from me, it will keep. My homecoming is too happy an occasion to spoil with an argument. Tomorrow, however..."

She sat again. "No, Koningsholm is not as huge as they say, but it is a very large city, by anything in my limited experience. And yes, the public buildings are made of stone, as are the residences of the Overlords and rich merchants. However, most people live in wooden houses. Some are three and four stories high, but many are the same size and construction as you would see if you stepped out of our door right now. So don't worry. There will be plenty of demand for the lumber from your new mill."

"I knew you would be able to tell me!"

Perica leaned forward. "Enough about wood and stone. What about Tyrbrand Ostersund, the handsome Magician?"

"What about him?"

"Oh, come on, Eirlin. It was perfectly obvious you two were interested, no matter how cool you tried to seem." Perica regarded her friend closely. "Obviously it didn't work out. Should I be preparing to scratch out some pale blue eyes?"

"No, no, nothing like that, Perica. He is always unfailingly polite to me."

"Unfailingly polite!" Ecmund rested his head his hands. "Death sentence. Even I know that."

Eirlin nodded. "I considered that, too. I was staying at the Ostersund ceasterhof, but I wouldn't see him for days, and I would start to think I had imagined our closeness. Then he would come and talk to me for hours: Healing, politics, magic, and we would have the most wonderful time. Then he would disappear again. He's a very busy man, what with the king's business and his own project.

"What project?"

"He didn't say, and I didn't think it was my place to ask. It had something to do with chemicals, though, and fire."

"Why do you say that?"

A cold chill ran down Kitten's blade. *Chemicals and fire? What has a Magician to do with fire?*

"Sometimes he would come home with the most awful smells about him, and he seemed to burn himself a lot." She sent Kitten a visual image.

Oh, no!

"What's wrong, Kitten?"

He's trying to forge a Sword.

"Oh, I don't think so, love. He's always said that he couldn't."

Eirlin, my dear, you are a wonderful Healer and you know many things. But when you start to tell a Sword about what a Smith looks like, I think you have gone a little outside your realm of experience.

"But..."

If he comes home smelling of fire and hot steel, with spark burns in his hair and along his arms, he's working in a Forge. Why else would a Magician work in a Forge? He's trying to make a Sword.

"But he always said he didn't have the Power."

Nonetheless. He's going to try, and he's going to fail, and it's my fault.

"It's not your fault, dear, and I doubt if that's what he's doing."

Ecmund shrugged. "Maybe he's making something else?"

What else is there? I don't think there's much of a market for magic Teaspoons these days.

Eirlin did not rise to the bait. "Whatever he's doing, it's taking a lot out of him, and I'm worried."

"Worried about Tyrbrand?"

"Yes. He is thinner, and his mind is often distracted."

The making of a Sword requires all from the Smith. Sometimes more than he has.

"What do you mean by that?"

The making of a magic Sword is a dangerous enterprise. Not all who try are successful.

"And is it a great problem if he fails?"

There is only one way a Magician can fail in making a Sword. He fails when it kills him. Then the Sword goes mad and has to be destroyed.

"Destroyed?"

Melted back down into a puddle of iron.

"Surely not."

Of course not, Eirlin. You know so much more than I do. I'm just making this all up for the fun of watching you worry.

Eirlin was on her feet again. "Don't mince words with me, you rusty piece of steel. If you know something I don't, you will tell me now. Have I made myself clear?"

Waiting is easy for a Sword. Waiting rarely does you harm, and it is very disconcerting for humans. Kitten waited.

"Kitten? I am speaking to you. What do you know that I don't?"

Definitely in love.

"What?"

What do you think, Perica?

"Oh, most definitely." The Maridon girl grinned. "Ears and eyeballs."

"Ears and what? What does that mean?"

Perica shrugged. "It's just an expression. You know what it means, because that's you. Ears and eyeballs in love."

Eirlin looked from one to the other. "A good try, but it didn't work. Kitten knows something, some danger to Tyrbrand, and she is going to tell me if she knows what's good for her."

Healers are such kind, gentle people.

"Healers sometimes have to cut to cure, and don't you forget it."

Oh. Then it clicked in Kitten's mind. *So that's it! Wonderful!*

"What? What's wonderful? Is this another attempt to distract me?"

No, Eirlin, it is not. I have just figured out what Tyrbrand is doing, and I feel a whole lot better.

"Well, what is he doing?"

If he didn't tell you, he has good reason.

"And now you're going to tell me."

Me, go against the Magician's wishes? Not in your lifetime. Not in several human lifetimes. Never, even in my lifetime. Not even when facing the ire of Eirlin the Terrible.

"Kitten..."

What are you going to do to me? Burn me? Break me over your knee? Throw me into a swamp?

Ecmund laughed out loud. "Sister, I think you have a little bit of learning to do about magic Swords. She isn't one of the local townsfolk you can bully into doing what you want."

"I don't bully anyone. What a horrible thing to say!"

"You don't bully because you don't have to. All of us do as you tell us. Kitten doesn't, and there's nothing you can do about it."

"But if Tyrbrand is in danger "

He isn't. I was wrong. He has every chance of success.

"But..."

Ecmund laid his hand on Kitten's hilt. "And for the moment, that is all there is to the story."

His sister looked at him. "There is something different about you."

He grinned. "Never should have left me on my own. Getting ideas of independence."

She smiled as well, and laid a hand on his arm. "No, I never should have left. But I'm back now, at least for a while."

"Is that a threat?"

"Take it as you wish. And Kitten?"

Yes, Eirlin?

"If you think of anything more about Tyrbrand, you will tell me, won't you?"

And I will try not to be too smug about it.

The Healer looked at her friends. "I am always interested to see how her sense of humour has progressed. Usually I don't like what develops."

Perica grinned and laid her hand over Ecmund's. "We are all changing, Eirlin. Let us hope it is for the better." She stood up.

"Come, Ecmund. It's time you escorted me home." She turned to the Healer. "Father would like to speak with you. Come up to the castle tomorrow afternoon, if you like. We can have tea and some talk."

My Dear Eirlin,

I am successful! The project I have been working on, which kept me from being a proper host to you, has concluded, at least the first stage. There is much more to do, but I am so pleased that I was able to complete the crucial opening steps.

Soon I will need you to come and make your most important contribution. I will let you know in plenty of time when I need you.

I have regretted the secrecy that kept me from telling you more, and many times I have questioned whether it was necessary. It will be so good to finally tell you all about my task, to be able to discuss it with you and receive your ideas.

It will also, of course, be wonderful to have you back here again. I found those brief times we spent together to be such a balm against the strain of my toil, and I look forward to more of the same pleasure soon.

Yours,

Tyrbrand

2. Business Not as Usual

Eirlin placed Perica's delicate china cup gently on the ornate tea table, smiled at her hostess in thanks and turned to the Overlord. "There is more news that we should talk about, Lord Delfontes."

He leaned back in his chair, smoothing his short, dark beard. "Yes, Eirlin?"

"My Post carriage was stopped twice on the way from Koningsholm."

His eyes narrowed. "Explain 'stopped,' please."

"In each case a band of riders in the livery of an Overlord waylaid the carriage and forced it to stop. Not that it was difficult. The driver didn't seem surprised. The riders required all the passengers to get down. They questioned each person, then allowed us to get back in and sent us on our way."

Perica frowned. "They can't do that. You were riding in a public carriage that carries the King's Post. Where did they get the right to stop you?"

Lord Delfontes raised a cautioning hand. "Did they say anything that would indicate why they had stopped you?"

"The second time, one of the men in the carriage was quite indignant. He asked the leader what right he had to stop the King's Post. The leader responded politely but firmly that we were on Lord d'Angelo's land, and any Overlord had the right to know who was passing across his demesne. The indignant passenger calmed down immediately. He nodded, even smiled a little, and didn't say anything more."

Delfontes nodded as well. "And that passenger was Maridon, was he not?"

"He had dark skin and hair."

Perica frowned. "How did you know that, Father?"

The Overlord's face was grim. "You know that we Maridon families have always kept to our original alliances, even though we've been here two hundred years. It makes it difficult for the king, I'm sure, ruling what must seem like two separate realms in one.

"Now it looks as if certain of the Maridon lords are pushing their boundaries, testing the king's resolve. While stopping the King's Post may seem a crime, no one has ever actually laid down what an Overlord may or may not do on his own land. The expansion of the Post route out to Falkenby meant that the king was extending his influence across new territories. Now they are pushing back."

"What can they want?"

Her father shrugged. "Who knows? But I'm afraid we're about to find out."

"How?"

He lifted a letter from his writing table. "This came by messenger yesterday. I have been invited to a 'meeting of like minds,' whatever that is. Now I can guess."

"You think the 'like minds' will all be Maridon?"

Delfontes turned to Eirlin. "Was there any indication that the soldiers were singling out 'Jornese, or those of the Blood?"

"The second group, from Lord Coelric, seemed to question the blond people more thoroughly. Except me."

Ecmund grinned. "I am the wind in the trees?"

She nodded. "I have learned something from Kitten. I just sort of faded, thinking as if I was not important, and they seemed not to notice me."

Perica turned to her friend. "You mean you can cloud men's minds, and make yourself invisible?"

Eirlin laughed. "Nothing that dramatic. I can make myself less important, that's all."

The Maridon girl looked up. "You are the tallest woman I know, your hair is bright blonde, and you can make yourself seem less important? That's an accomplishment in itself."

The Healer's training progresses.

Eirlin turned to the Overlord. "That's all I noticed. I believe they were paying more attention to the Inderjornese, and were more polite to the Maridons."

"What do you think they are after, Father?"

"We will soon find out. My best guess is that they want to get together to support each other, to influence the king on some policy or other."

"I see. There is nothing unusual in that, is there?"

"No. But combined with the stopping of the carriages, this sounds more serious than usual."

"You aren't thinking of a rebellion?"

Delfontes shook his head. "No, I see no evidence of that kind of unrest. Of course, I have been rather busy with my own problems. Anything could have happened in the Capital. Eirlin, you have been there most recently."

Eirlin smiled ruefully. "I'm afraid my attention was caught up in my own little affairs, my Lord. I didn't notice much else."

"But your affairs may be more important than you think. What was the political trouble you ran into in the infirmary?"

"Oh, that. I think it was more of a professional disagreement."

"Please explain."

"There is a division in the staff of the infirmary on methods of diagnosis. Some wish to use Powers such as mine more often; others wish to use the traditional methods of physical evidence."

"Traditional Maridon methods?"

"Yes, I suppose so."

"So you have a division in the infirmary on Maridon/'Jornese lines."

Eirlin looked at the Overlord in surprise. "You could see it that way."

"I'm afraid, given the general climate of the realm, we must."

Eirlin frowned. "That's horrible! A Healer must never put politics ahead of the good of her patient."

Lord Delfontes regarded her with raised eyebrows.

Finally she sighed. "I suppose you're right. It just bothers me, that's all."

He smiled. "But your information is useful to us."

Perica leaned forward, her face animated. "Right. There has always been a certain amount of tension between the 'Jornese and their Maridon conquerors. It should be getting better as time passes, but maybe it's not. Now there seems to be a cadre of Maridon nobility who are pushing for something. Probably more power. It always comes to that in the long run."

Delfontes glanced around the group. "It seems that no one disagrees."

"So, Father, what are you going to tell them at this meeting?"

"I don't know. It depends on what they ask."

Perica tossed her head. "I don't think it's much of a mystery. You have a group looking for more power. They gather together everyone who might support them. They present their case, they dangle their bait and ask for a pledge of support. If you don't support them, then you're lucky to make it home alive."

"A trifle melodramatic, dear, but accurate, nonetheless."

"So what are you going to tell them, Father?"

The Overlord rubbed his cheek. "I doubt it's a problem, Perica. If I turn them down flat, what will they do? I don't think they will be assassinating people on their way home, but I suppose some action could be taken against us. In spite of our recent success, you and I are not secure enough here to withstand serious trouble. But I don't..."

Ecmund cleared his throat, but did not speak.

Delfontes smiled at him. "What is it, Ecmund? I wouldn't have expected you to be shy."

"I hesitate to disagree, my Lord, but I suspect you may have understated the gravity of the situation."

"In what way?"

Ecmund compressed his lips a moment, thinking. "I get a feeling, and I don't know whether it's just me or if Kitten is adding to it, that there is a new level of tension between the Maridons and the Inderjornese. Not just a few lords and their men. All of us."

I show you what I see.

"Do you have any specific evidence?"

"That's the problem. I don't. It's just a general feeling that any Maridons I meet are edgier, more concerned with their rights and privileges. Perica, what did you make of that incident in the Inn yesterday?"

"I had considered it just another bothersome traveler from Koningsholm who needed a reminder that being from the Capital wasn't the ticket to getting his own way all the time. If I set the incident beside this conversation, he could have been an agent, testing the waters."

Delfontes leaned forward. "What happened?"

"I'm not sure of the details, my Lord. Rumour went around that some Maridon stayed in the inn and made a big fuss yesterday morning when he went to pay his bill, because of the service or the room or something. Innkeepers get that sort regularly. It's a part of their business, I always thought. However, in the light of this development..."

"Right. Next time you might find out more, now that we know what to look for and what questions to ask."

"I will do that, my Lord."

"The next question, Father, is who to take with you to this meeting."

The Overlord mused a moment. "There are few useful candidates. I can't take Ecmund, obviously. There's no point in having any more than my usual retainers. I would be outnumbered anyway. I would appreciate Kitten's help, though."

"Perhaps I could go along and take Kitten with me."

That is one of your stupider ideas, Perica.

"I heard that!"

"Heard what, dear?"

"Kitten. It was one of my sillier ideas."

"How about Jesco? He looks Maridon enough."

The Overlord raised his eyebrows. "Would Kitten come with him?"

For how long?

"How does the length of time matter, Kitten?"

I know he is your family, Ecmund, but too long in his company would not be good for my moral development.

"She would prefer not to spend large amounts of time with him, my Lord."

"Why is that?"

"It's hard to explain. Eirlin has done a lot of Healing, but Jesco's mind is still not...not quite normal. He carries a lot of anger in him."

"I see." The Overlord nodded. "Not a good milieu for the developing mind of a young Sword."

"Exactly."

"It will take three or four days. Perhaps I could carry her, and give her to Jesco if necessary."

Ecmund shook his head. "One thing I learned from Jesco. A swordsman must have his sword within reach, or he is useless."

Perhaps I should go. It might be interesting.

"Interesting?"

Yes. A hidden spy in the enemy camp. The idea carries a certain appeal. I might learn things Lord Delfontes misses.

"And you will risk the time spent with Jesco?"

Jesco has healed greatly. Perhaps I could affect him, instead of the other way around.

"What do you think, Eirlin?"

She laughed. "I'm hardly an expert on magic Swords, Ecmund. I don't see any danger. It would probably be very good for Jesco to spend time with her."

Perica tilted her head. "Has anyone thought to ask Jesco about this?"

Ecmund shared a smile with his sister. "Jesco will do what Eirlin asks. Besides, the last time he used Kitten, the results were spectacular."

"Ah. The epic battle with the Leute champion."

"Exactly. I'm sure he will be glad to go."

Delfontes slapped his hands on his thighs. "And Eirlin will ask him? Good. Then that's settled. Tell him to come and see me this afternoon. Plan to be gone about four days."

At that, the meeting broke up. Ecmund and Eirlin strode back down the hill to the village. "I'll go out to the farm this afternoon."

Eirlin smiled. "Why don't we check the tavern, first?"

"He doesn't spend as much time there as he used to, but we can try. I'll just pop in on our way through."

"Maybe I'll come with you. I don't go in there very often."

"For good reason. The barkeep wouldn't like it."

"Are you telling me I can't go into the tavern? Do you think I'm too delicate?"

He laughed. "No, I'm telling you that you're bad for business. You show your face in there and half the customers will start to feel guilty and go home to their wives."

"As they should!"

"Perhaps, but the bartender doesn't see it that way."

She sighed. "I suppose. Look, I'll make you a deal. You stick your head in. If Jesco isn't there, we'll keep going. If he is there, I'll come in and have a drink with you."

"You're serious."

"It's time I took a wider interest in the duties you have bestowed upon me."

Their arrival at the tavern prevented Ecmund from asking what that meant. It was a swaybacked, dingy building, crouched down between a smithy on one side and a tanner's shop on the other. Eirlin's nose wrinkled as they approached, but she said nothing. Then she stopped, a hand on her brother's arm.

"What?"

She nodded ahead up the street past the tavern, where a slight figure was approaching.

It is Wynna.

"What's she doing over here?"

Eirlin grinned over at her brother. "That's probably none of our business."

The girl neared the tavern, hesitating outside the door. When she saw the two approaching her she started, seemed about to leave, then turned back to accept their greeting.

"Oh...Hello, Eirlin...Ecmund."

He grinned, jerked his head towards the tavern door. "Just going in for a pint, were you?"

Eirlin jabbed her brother in the back, not gently. He had the grace to look guilty. "What she is doing is no business of yours, Ecmund. How are you, Wynna? Did you know that Johan the Pedlar was in the village? He came in on the Post carriage with me yesterday."

17

"Oh...oh, yes, I did, Eirlin." Her smile flickered and disappeared. "He always comes to our place first. We're his best customers. He has very good thread, you know. I'm not sure where he gets it, but we always buy...that is..."

Why is Wynna so embarrassed?

"Well, that's good. Ecmund and I were just looking for Jesco. Have you seen him?"

This change of topic didn't seem to help. Wynna's face went bright red. "No...no, I haven't seen Jesco. He's...maybe he's in there." She flapped a helpless hand towards the tavern. "I...I have to go now. I have to meet with someone for a fitting. A dress fitting, you know. I'll...I'll see you later. Bye, Eirlin...Bye Ecmund."

The two wished her a bemused farewell, and she hastened back up the street towards the centre of the village. Ecmund watched her go, a frown on his face. "She was certainly acting strangely. I'm sure she was headed towards the tavern. Why did she turn around and go back?"

"The obvious reason would be because she met us."

The girl with the little swords was upset to see you.

"Little swords?"

Not angry upset. She will try again tomorrow.

Ecmund glanced at his sister. "You don't think she's a secret drinker, do you?"

Eirlin smiled. "If she's a secret drinker, I doubt if she'd be going into a tavern in the middle of the day."

"Could you find out why, Kitten?"

She was relieved and disappointed.

"Kitten, you're not making any sense at all."

She will do better tomorrow.

Ecmund shrugged off his sister's puzzled frown. "When she gets like this, it's not worth trying to reason with her."

"Who, Wynna or Kitten?"

Ecmund spun her towards the tavern. "Now there's three of you I don't follow. I hope Jesco is having a drink. I need one myself."

Sure enough, Jesco was sitting at a table near the door, but there was no drink in front of him. He stumbled to his feet as Eirlin entered. "Eirlin! Welcome home. What are you doing here? Is there a problem?"

She smiled, and motioned him to sit. "No problem. Ecmund and I just thought we'd join you. You aren't drinking?"

He smiled, a bit abashed. "No, it's a bit early in the day for that. I was just thinking."

"You come to the tavern to think?"

He waved a hand at the room. "It's quiet in here this time of day."

In truth, there were only two other customers, both of whom nodded greetings before ducking their heads back into their drinks.

With a certain guilty air, Kitten couldn't help but note. *Ecmund is right, Eirlin. You are bad for business.*

She shrugged. "Well, if you're not drinking, Ecmund and I have something we need to discuss with you. Why not come home with us for lunch?"

They left the tavern, Jesco waving a casual good-bye to the glum barkeep. When they were in the street, he turned his attention to Eirlin. "What can I help you with?"

She outlined Lord Delfontes's problem.

"You want me to go along as his escort, take Kitten with me, and spy on the meeting?"

"Not spy. You're mainly there to protect him. We want Kitten there to see what she can pick up. Probably nothing, since none of the Maridons are sensitive."

"I see. He can't take a large escort, because that would look fearful or aggressive. If he has to give these people an answer they don't like, he might be in danger. If so, I have Kitten to even the odds. I like that."

Ecmund smiled. "Simple and straightforward."

"But you are not to find excuses for a fight, just to have another experience with Kitten."

Eirlin! How could you think that?

Jesco grinned. "Nice try, Eirlin, but I know you're only joking. I have too much respect for Ecmund, Kitten, and Lord Delfontes to jeopardize this endeavor," his right hand brushed past Kitten's hilt, "no matter how much fun it might be."

"So you'll go, then?"

"With pleasure. If what you fear is true, we need to get control of this situation as quickly as possible, or I'm going to get a whole lot more occupation for my sword than I need or want."

"You aren't looking forward to a good fight?"

"I have no argument against a good fight for a noble cause now and then. I do have a concern about the kind of damage a full-scale rebellion will cause to our realm."

"Well said, Cousin. I have high hopes for you."

To their surprise, the swordsman blushed. "Thank you, Eirlin. It is kind of you to say so."

Fortunately, they had reached their door and she turned to open it, leaving him time to recover his aplomb. There was no mention of the matter at lunch, and Jesco left soon after to obey the Lord's request.

As his footsteps retreated up the street, the two looked at each other. "I think Jesco is growing up."

"That Healing you and Kitten did certainly seems to have affected him."

Eirlin nodded slowly. "He is much better, but do not think that such a superficial Healing has removed scars it took a lifetime to create."

"In other words, expect the same old Jesco, at any time."

"Unfortunately, yes."

"I'll keep it in mind."

Ostersund Ceasterhof,

Koningsholm.

Maius ii

My Dear Eirlin.

It was a great pleasure to get your letter yesterday. I had just finished a most trying day with my task, and hearing from you allowed me to put it behind me for an evening of much-needed rest. It will be good to have you here in person soon.

This letter must perforce be short, because, while I basked in the glow of your regard yesterday, I must be diligent today.

Yours,

Tyrbrand.

3. The Lair of the Enemy

The next morning there was a short, uncomfortable ceremony in the street outside the woodcutters' cottage. At least, uncomfortable for Jesco.

"How do I treat her? Will she talk to me?"

Ecmund shrugged. "You'll know when she does."

Jesco's face darkened. "You're laughing at me."

Eirlin chuckled. "Of course we are. I've never seen you overawed before. You're a swordsman, Jesco. She's a Sword. I'm sure you'll handle it just fine."

"Oh, I can handle her fine. That's not what I'm worried about. Will she read my mind?"

"Nothing you don't want her to."

Yeugch!

Jesco frowned down at her. "Why did I just think of a cat spitting up a hair ball?"

Now Ecmund laughed, too. "She doesn't like people's minds. She says they are messy and clouded with warring emotions. Don't worry. Everyone has secrets, and she won't pry. If you need to talk to her, you can. She's always listening."

The swordsman reluctantly took Kitten's belt and strapped it around his waist. She snuggled in comfortably.

"She certainly feels light."

"She fits herself to you. Both physically and mentally. In a while, you'll forget she's there."

Jesco looked skeptical, but turned to his horse. Then he turned back. "I'm supposed to guard lord Delfontes, and keep my ears open. Is there something else you want me to do?"

Ecmund glanced at Eirlin, who shook her head. "We don't really know, Jesco. You and Kitten just be there, and do what you have to. We want to know what these people are planning, that's all. You don't have to take any action. Other than that, just do what Lord Delfontes says. He shouldn't be in any danger, but if they ask him something and he has to refuse, there's no telling how they might react."

"So I treat this as a standard escort mission: keep the usual watch but keep my eyes and ears open as well. I can do that."

"Exactly. Good luck, Jesco."

"Thanks." He mounted, nodded to Ecmund, and rode up the village street towards the castle.

Kitten had wondered what it would be like to be separated from her Hand. It had never happened in this manner before. As they left the village gate, she could feel the presence of Ecmund fading behind her, although she could still sense him. Them, actually. Brother and sister stood like a beacon of Power, which the Sword felt she could contact from a great distance. It made the separation far less disturbing.

She checked briefly on the thoughts turning in Jesco's mind, but decided to keep quiet. Time enough for contact if it was needed.

Lord Delfontes made only one comment as they were readying for the journey. "Is she speaking to you?"

"Not yet, my Lord."

Delfontes nodded, then continued checking his equipment. Jesco did the same.

Soon they were on the road, and Kitten fell into that half-thinking, half-dreaming state which served to while away long periods of inactivity. Jesco was riding beside the Overlord but they spoke little, each concerned with his own thoughts. Their escort, six men from the castle guard, were noisier at the start but soon quieted as well, and the troop jogged through the countryside, the clop of hooves and the jingle of harness their only accompaniment.

They made good time, and had passed through the demesne of Lord Peredes and were well into d'Angelo's territory when evening fell. They had decided to avoid contacting Lord Peredes, as he was a loyal supporter of the king and a sympathizer with the Inderjornese. So they found a small country inn and settled down for the evening.

Jesco drank little and spoke less. Kitten could tell that he was mulling something over in his mind, but refrained from prying. The farther she kept out of that seething brain, the better she liked it.

However, during the night she felt she must reach out. Jesco's dreams were unsettling, and it seemed to her that a restless night would detract from his efficiency on the morrow. So she calmed him, stripping the nightmares of their horror and pointedly ignoring their source, deep in the twists of his mind.

Searching for an alternative, she found something surprising. Up on the surface of his thoughts, quite open and easy to find, was what she could only describe as a warm spot. There was something in Jesco's life that eased him. Something that calmed him, but at the same time lifted his heart. Without intruding far enough to discover what it was, she bolstered that feeling, spreading the warmth over his nightmares, washing them away with...well, it couldn't really be called happiness, but for Jesco it was close enough. He settled, and his sleep became deeper and more healing. Satisfied, Kitten left matters there.

Her labours seemed to bear fruit, for he was up early the next morning, as cheerful as she had ever seen him. He joined in with the men's crude pleasantries and spoke more often to the Overlord.

"You seem to be in a good mood today, Jesco."

"I slept well, my Lord, and I am on a mission. It is good to feel useful."

"Don't you usually feel useful?"

Jesco mulled that over for a while. "It's hard to say, my Lord. A swordsman isn't useful very much of the time. He spends most of his life getting ready to be useful, if you see what I mean. In fact, if he has any kind of conscience, he hopes he won't have to be useful."

"I hadn't thought of it that way."

"I think a swordsman who takes joy in killing is on the edge of...well, I won't say insanity, but something very unpleasant. I love fighting. I love the challenge and the feeling that I'm doing something right. However, I don't kill unless it's necessary." He grinned. "That has been drummed into me since I was a child. 'Kill only to survive.' That's the rule of our people."

He jogged along in silence for a moment. Then he glanced wryly at Delfontes. "Besides, Eirlin wouldn't approve."

"You think a lot of Eirlin, don't you?"

Jesco shrugged. "Everybody does. You must have noticed."

"Everybody?"

"Pretty much."

"Is that normal for your people?"

"What do you mean?"

Delfontes glanced over at his companion. "A woman, and a Healer? It is not something that would happen in a Maridon community."

"Your loss, then." He thought a moment. "My Lord."

"Yes, I believe you have the right of it. She has great positive influence on her people. I am certainly glad to have her on my side."

"Which you contrived from the first, my Lord."

Delfontes shot another assessing glance at Jesco. "You notice more than people think, don't you?"

He shrugged. "Even a simple soldier has to keep his eyes and ears open."

"True. And that is all I expect from you at this meeting. Keep your eyes and ears open, and let me know anything that might be of importance."

"Ecmund tells me that this is some kind of gathering of powers. Could it approach treason?"

The Overlord glanced back at the soldiers, then lowered his voice. "It is possible, and if it is treason, I will have to extricate myself very carefully. If you hear me saying things that...well, shall we say things that Eirlin wouldn't approve of, then you can take that as a danger sign."

Jesco grinned. "A plan to follow, my Lord."

Delfontes nodded, and they rode on in silence.

After a while, Jesco reined his horse aside, let the soldiers pass, then followed at a distance.

"Um...Kitten?"

Yes, Jesco?

"Did you hear that conversation?"

Of course.

"Do you understand our duty?"

Yes, Jesco. I get information, I tell you, you relay it to the Overlord.

"Good."

And Jesco?

"Yes?"

You are going to have to learn to talk to me in your head. It will do wonders for your reputation to be seen talking to yourself.

"How do I do that?"

Think loudly.

"Think loudly." *Like this?*

Just like that.

Oh. That's easy.

Yes. You can contact me from quite a distance if you think hard enough.

"I don't plan..." *I mean, I don't plan to have you at any distance. A swordsman always keeps his sword within reach. That goes double with you.*

I like your attitude, Jesco.

Thank you, Kitten.

They reached Lord d'Angelo's castle in the late afternoon. This Overlord was, Kitten thought, an objectionably hearty man. He greeted Lord Delfontes personally and with enthusiasm.

"So, Sarza Delfontes da Falken. It is good to finally meet you."

"It is a pleasure to meet you, Lord d'Angelo. I have been too busy with the affairs of my new demesne for social calls, so this meeting serves a double purpose."

25

"Good enough, good enough. Next time, bring that pretty daughter of yours. Oh yes, we've heard all about her. We have plenty of young men of good Maridon blood who would be very interested. Plenty of them."

"I'll be sure to bring her next time. Thank you for the invitation."

'Young men of good Maridon blood?' Kitten sent Jesco the image of a taloned grey paw slashing across a dark face.

Calmly, Kitten. Ecmund has no competition in that regard.

'Good Maridon blood.' Phhht!

The two lords strode away and Jesco was left to get the soldiers bunked and the horses stabled. That took up his time until dinner. He had changed out of his riding clothes and was just beginning to wonder what to do next when a page approached him and said he was wanted. He followed the lad to the upper floors of the castle. There, he waited in a corridor with several others whose fighting gear bore the wear of much practice. Kitten scanned them all.

An interesting lot. Some of these men are very close to violence.

Jesco forced himself not to react. *Violence? Is there danger?*

I don't think so. They are just ready. Too ready. Trust none of them.

I never thought I would.

Soon, voices swelled and a door opened. Several well-dressed men came out, Delfontes in their midst. The escorts sorted themselves, each following at his lord's shoulder. Jesco swung into his position smartly and paced along.

Each Lord has his own guard.

Yes. Jesco's eyes scanned everyone, all his senses alert.

A trusting lot. Makes us less obvious.

True.

In the main hall, the personal guards turned aside at a lower level, and their lords took their places at the high table. Jesco commandeered a position where he could keep an eye on the room, disregarding another swordsman who had been headed for the same seat. The man glowered, but sat in a less desirable place.

Let them know you mean business, Jesco.

Of course.

It is good to be back in the company of swordsmen. Everything is so simple. The strongest takes the best and everyone else follows in line.

Do you always prattle like this?

Probably. Does it distract you?

Probably not, once I get used to it. Now, let's get to work.

Yes, your Lordship. I hear and obey. Ignoring his mental growl, she scanned the room.

26

It was pretty typical of the area. The main hall of a fortress from the old days, heavy and dark, with a hundred years or more of peace and Maridon gewgaws to destroy its utility but do little to soften the original harshness of its lines. She scanned its occupants, wondering if she would find a similar...

Then she scanned them more closely.

Jesco.

Yes.

There are open minds here.

What does that mean? Someone of the Blood?

They looked over the dark faces and hair. *Not likely.*

A Magician?

No, nobody that powerful. Several about the same as you, one stronger.

Can you find that one without attracting attention?

I am the dog, rustling through the rushes for scraps.

She sifted through the thoughts that permeated the room, easily centering on the mind that flamed brightly at the head table.

It is the tall man to the left of Lord d'Angelo. Do you know who he is?

No idea. Lord Delfontes will know him.

His mind is clear and very strong. I will watch him.

There were endless introductions, but it seemed all activities were social, and nothing of interest occurred until the meal was over and the speeches started.

It was apparent that the tall man was the guest of honour. Lord d'Angelo announced him as one who needed no introduction.

"Lord Fuentes da Baneza is a power in our realm, and is pledged to using his abilities for the weal of the realm and the good of us all."

Lord Da Baneza rose, and an expectant hush fell over the group. The Lord raised his flagon.

"I drink to the health and welfare of King Vetrorrillo da Marida." He drank deeply, and everyone in the room followed.

"My friends, that was no empty ritual. In this day, it is necessary to take that toast seriously. We are in a time of danger. Yes, real danger: to the power of the king, to the proper rule of this realm."

He paused to let the concerned hum die. He looked at each lord at the head table, then out to the minions in the rest of the room. "I know many of you think I exaggerate. Many of you think our kingdom is progressing as usual. You must drag yourselves out of your lethargy. You must become aware of the danger that lives within the heart of our dear land: the presence of a virulent disease that threatens our lives, our families, the very ideals upon which our realm is founded. You must believe me when I tell you that in recent years there has been a long, slow slide from the principles of our ancestors.

"Even now, these insidious traitors are working their way into positions of strength and influence in the kingdom. Their blond heads are showing more and more in the halls of power, in the chairs of justice. Oh, I know what some of you are saying. You think that we Maridons conquered a long time ago, and we have become mixed with the old society here. Over a century or so, they were bound to learn our ways. You might even think this is progress, that having two peoples, bound together by solid principles, will make our realm stronger.

"You could not be farther from the truth. The fact is, these traitors don't want to be bound with us for the good of the realm. They want to go back to the time when they were powerful. They want to return to an inept form of governance based on mumbo-jumbo and primitive magic."

There was another murmur in the room, which grew until Lord da Baneza cut it short with a sweep of his hand. "It is time for all forward-looking Maridons to say, 'Enough!' It is time for those of us who are right-thinking and loyal to group together in support of our monarch and our realm, against the rot that threatens to weaken us!

"And some of this is our fault, my friends. Of late our resolve has weakened, our strength has dwindled. We must rebuild our ranks, recruit those like us, grow our alliances, and teach our followers how to restore our beloved realm to the glory it once had.

"We must not shrink from this task, for this is our land, our realm and our Maridon heritage, which is our rightful treasure. Our rights, safety, and the well-being of our loved ones have fallen upon our shoulders. It will be our effort which stops our opponents who, in their arrogance, think their old way of ruling would result in a better realm."

He stopped and surveyed the crowd, his lip curling. "Better, perhaps, for them. Not for us.

"They have started a cowardly and underhanded campaign to take control of our institutions and our governance. They are in your demesne. They can control the minds of your subjects. Whether or not you believe in their mumbo-jumbo does not matter. The more susceptible of your subjects believe, and that is all they need.

"This is, at the moment, a relatively small group of malcontents. They must not be allowed to grow, to spread their pestilence to the rest of the population.

"Do not let their small numbers lull you. Some of them have achieved powerful positions, even into the king's inner cabinet. One of our main tasks is to make His Majesty see the danger he faces.

"But do not be dismayed, my friends. Many of us are now aware of the dangers, and our numbers are growing in leaps and bounds. We are asking you to join the fast-growing ranks of the movement. If you are sick of the dirty and corrupt practices of these traitors, then join with us.

"We must rise up, pledge our life, our arms and our sacred honour to ridding our realm of this plague of decadent rot. Are you with me?"

There was a wash of sound, as every man in the room bellowed out his support.

Stand up, Jesco.

What?

Stand up quickly. No one has noticed.

Oh. Of course. The swordsman rose to his feet, held his flagon high enough, and kept watching around him. Up at the head table, he could see Lord Delfontes doing the same.

Lord da Baneza watched and listened as the din increased. He then nodded in approval and sat. His face was calm, but Kitten read satisfaction in every line of his body.

That is one dangerous man.

Jesco merely caressed her hilt, but his mind was clear.

I don't think we're ready for that yet, Jesco.

The swordsman merely sat with the others, his eyes fixed on the head table.

After this uproar, everything else was anticlimax. Lord da Baneza, followed by a smug Lord d'Angelo, led the nobles to the private meeting room. The rest of the retainers settled in to enjoy a night of the lord's hospitality, and the private guards found themselves a table near the door, where they drank sparingly and gave away as little information as they could without seeming impolite.

Kitten entertained herself in the minds of her tablemates.

This is an interesting troop.

Jesco shrugged mentally. *I suppose so.*

It reminds me of what your training must have been. My sympathies.

That makes me feel so much better.

"Your name's Jesco, ain't it?"

He turned to the man who had spoken. A large man in his own version of the livery of Lord d'Angelo. In spite of the heat of the room, he was wrapped in a sheepskin garment that covered his body but left his weapons free.

"I'm Jesco. Who's asking?"

"I'm Vicen. I heard about you."

"Did you?"

"Yeah. Weren't you in some kind of battle with the Leute last summer?"

Jesco shrugged. "No battle. More of a ritual. In order to talk to their chief, first you have to fight his personal guard. We fought, then they talked."

"I heard it was a bit more than that. Some kind of epic swordfight, by the tales."

"He was a good swordsman. We had some fun, testing each other out."

"But you won."

Jesco grinned. "Things aren't as simple as they seem when there's politics involved. The winning of the battle has little to do with the skill of the fighters, and much more to do with how badly the chief wants to talk to the ambassador."

"You're kidding. You mean it's all a sham?"

"Oh, no. That was one superb fighter. If his chief hadn't wanted to talk, I'd have had to kill him."

"And could you?"

Jesco sized up the bigger man. "You never know until your point goes in, do you?"

The man's eyes held, then dropped. He covered with a grin and a slap on Jesco's shoulder. "That's when you find out, all right."

You handled him well.

It's all in the confidence. I usually have enough.

The more confident you are, the less you wave your point around.

Exactly.

4. New Duties

It was late on the following evening when a tired troop of horsemen trotted their sweating horses into the bailey at Falkengard. Perica was there to greet them, calling out for more torches, more hostlers, and somebody better get to the kitchen and start stoking the fires if they knew what was good for them.

Delfontes, high up on his horse, looked down on his daughter with fond pride. "What do you say, Jesco? Does she give orders well?"

The Swordsman looked around the bailey. "A lot of people doing what they're bid, my Lord. A good sign."

"You can't argue with results." The older man swung down off his horse and staggered a bit as his stiff knees took the load. "I'm for bed. That was a long ride in one day."

Perica planted herself before him. "No you're not. You're going to sit down and tell us all about it."

"Us?"

"Yes. Ecmund and Eirlin are here. We've been waiting since the sentry spotted you coming over the pass."

"Well, I suppose you had better come in, Jesco. You and Kitten will have some reporting to do as well."

They trooped up the stairs to Delfontes' private sitting room, where Ecmund and Eirlin rose to greet them. Jesco unbuckled Kitten's belt and held her out. "Here's your baby back, cousin, no worse for wear."

I am nobody's baby.

No, you aren't. We did our duty well.

I think so. It was a pleasure, Swordsman.

She felt a glow shoot through him that she had not sent.

Ecmund's hand polished her hilt, and she felt the world slide back to normal. "Any trouble?"

"She's very good for keeping a man sober."

"You mean her caustic comments, or her trick of clearing your head?"

"A little of both."

Perica bustled in, followed by two servants with trays of food and drink. "There you go, Father, Jesco. You can tuck in while you speak." She sat on the edge of a chair. "How did it go?"

Delfontes took time for a deep drink from a flagon. "Not too badly. We were able to get a lot of information, I didn't have to commit myself too deeply, and I don't think we aroused any suspicions."

31

They were pathetically enthusiastic to have him there.

Ecmund patted her hilt again. "Did you attract any attention, Jesco?"

"Kitten says not. I was recognized because of that duel with the Leute swordsman, but I downplayed my role, and it passed. Nobody noticed Kitten at all."

I am a plain old sword: nothing but dumb steel. Nobody I wanted to talk to, anyway.

"Was there anyone you could talk to?"

It was Delfontes who answered. "Yes, surprisingly. According to Kitten, there were several of what she calls 'open minds.' Perica, it seems you are not alone."

"Perhaps mixed blood, like Jesco?"

"In that assembly? I suspect not. Kitten says pure Maridon."

Eirlin leaned forward. "What an interesting situation. We had always assumed that the Power of the Blood was just that: a hereditary condition. Now we find a growing number of those with foreign blood who are developing the Powers. I will have to write to Tyrbrand and see what he says."

Lord Delfontes raised a cautioning hand. "I would be very careful how you word your question. The bad news I bring from this meeting is that there is definite trouble brewing. Political trouble. The main reason for the meeting was that Lord Fuentes da Baneza was visiting. He seems to be touring the realm, drumming up support for his alliance of Maridon supporters."

"What kind of man is he, Father? I have heard little of him, beyond his role as a leader of the extreme Maridon faction."

"He is a very dangerous one, Perica. Kitten says he is by far the strongest of those who have the Powers of the Blood, and he uses his talents to great advantage. You should have heard his speech. He had the whole crowd on their feet at the end, ready to protect the king from the blond traitors who want to undermine good Maridon rule of this realm."

"Is that what he said?"

"Basically, yes. Over and over. Kitten says he uses his Power to feed the emotions of his listeners, to work them together to produce a sort of frenzy. I tell you, he scared me."

Eirlin toyed with the end of her braid. "If he is using his Powers to stir up crowds, he scares me, too."

"Could Kitten do that?"

"Perica! What a thought!"

"There is nothing wrong with assessing our powers, Ecmund. If it became necessary, could Kitten use her Powers to whip up emotion in a group of people?"

Kitten held back a shudder as an old memory squirmed free. *Human minds are messy. Large groups of them are incomprehensible. And dangerous.*

Ecmund laughed. "We could feel insulted, but when she talks like that, it usually means she hasn't any idea of how to answer."

Lord Delfontes glanced from one to the other, trying to follow the conversation. "So she can't do it?"

I didn't say that. It is not something to play with.

Eirlin raised a hand. "But Kitten, when you do your 'I am the wind in the trees' trick, aren't you working on many minds at once?"

I suppose so.

"So you really can work your Powers on a group."

Did I say I couldn't? Sometimes I think I should go and talk to the trees. They listen better.

"Then it's just a matter of practice. You find out how you affect the minds of a group, and use that talent to increase the emotion you want them to feel. I presume from what I have heard tonight that there is some kind of piling on, so that they add to each others' emotion, and everyone feels it stronger."

Perica nodded enthusiastically. "That's what happens in any mob situation. People feed on each others' emotions until they all reach a frenzy."

Lord Delfontes frowned. "What do you know about mobs and frenzies, Perica?"

"Remember that tutor you dismissed because you didn't like his radical ideas? I found him very refreshing."

"Are you telling me that something you learned from Schonner is actually useful?"

"It seems to be."

"Hmph."

"Oh, don't be a curmudgeon. Most of what he said was complete twaddle, and I knew it. I just sifted through it for the interesting bits." She was interrupted by Jesco trying to stifle a huge yawn. "Oh, I'm sorry. You men have ridden hard all day, and here I am rattling on about my childhood." She turned to her father. "What did you have to agree to do, to help this movement?"

"Fortunately, not much. They are still trying to attract new support, so they aren't pushing anyone too hard."

She nodded. "That's how you do it. You ask people to do something that sounds easy. Once they have acted on your behalf, they feel committed. Then you ask for something harder, and if they accomplish that, they really are committed and they don't dare back out for fear of being exposed. Then you have them."

Delfontes himself yawned. "So, since there is no immediate disaster about to fall on us, is there any chance of excusing myself for a long, hot, bath and my bed?"

"Not at all, Father. The water is already steaming. Jesco, would you like to…?"

"No, no, my Lady. I'm for home and my own bed."

"You've just been riding all day, and now you're going to get back on a horse? I hardly think so. You can have a bath or not, as you like, but you're bunking down in the officers' quarters tonight. I've already ordered your horse put to stable."

Jesco pointedly ignored his cousins' grins. "Whatever my Lady wishes."

Ecmund laughed. "My! We should send Jesco on diplomatic missions more often. I think he's learning to be a courtier."

"Since I spent most of my time in the company of the personal guards of the other lords, I doubt I learned a lot of fancy manners."

"Nasty lot, that." Delfontes shook his head.

"I wouldn't call them nasty. Just businesslike men in a nasty business. And I didn't say bad manners, I said fancy manners. Swordsmen are always very polite to each other. It keeps them alive."

Eirlin shuddered. "I picture a very unpleasant time."

He shrugged. "It wasn't so bad."

They are very straightforward. You know where you stand with men like that.

"And where did you stand, Jesco?"

"I didn't push myself forward, but I didn't let anyone set himself above me. You tread a fine line if you have anything to hide in a group like that. Too strong, and you get challenged. Too weak, and you get put upon. Too much attention either way. Fortunately, fighters recognize those who don't want to be bothered, and leave them alone. As I said, I don't think I attracted any attention."

Ecmund nodded. "That's good, Jesco. Come around tomorrow on your way home and we can chat some more, see what you've picked up. Right now, go and grab the bed you deserve."

"I'll do that." The swordsman rose, stretched and strode out the door.

When he was gone, Lord Delfontes raised his eyebrows. "He's a good man. Much easier to get along with than I had expected. Taciturn but polite."

"Jesco has very good manners when he chooses to use them. He also has better control of his temper than you might think, and he would not do anything that would jeopardize your mission."

"I'm sure you are right, Eirlin. I was worried that he would stand out, but every one of them had brought a personal guard with him, so he fitted in easily."

Perica's eyebrows shot up. "Every one?"

"That's right. Each lord who came had a swordsman, chained to his left shoulder except for the most private of policy meetings."

"What does that tell you about them?"

"There is a lot of fear there. Ask Kitten."

Pitiful little men. They hide behind their bluster and their titles.

"Of course, anything she says about them could apply to me, as well."

I can tell the difference. Lord Delfontes had good reason.

"She says you had good reason, my Lord, and she can tell the difference."

Him, and one other.

"Who was the other one, Kitten? Lord da Baneza?"

That is correct. There is no fear in the man; he feels quite capable of defending himself. His guard was a superb fighter, I could tell from his demeanour. He was there to intimidate others, not to guard his lord.

Perica clapped her hands. "We are all tired, and need to finish this so we can go to bed. What are your marching orders, Father?"

"I am to seek out my allies, identify my foes, consolidate my powers and prepare myself to act on behalf of true Maridons everywhere."

Perica looked around the room. "As far as I can see, you have done the first three admirably."

"Yes, but I think I should sound out some of the minor lords around. I also need to pay a social visit to Lord Peredes. He cannot help but know that I passed through his demesne twice without acknowledging him. This is not a time for misunderstandings among potential allies. I think if I move carefully, I can 'consolidate my power' easily, but for my own reasons."

Perica nodded. "Eirlin, Ecmund, anything to add?"

They both shook their heads. "I'd say the only danger so far was that Jesco would be exposed." Ecmund spread his hands. "A very successful beginning to the campaign."

Eirlin shuddered. "Is that what you consider this? A campaign?"

Lord Delfontes made a calming gesture. "At the moment, it is only a political campaign, and with any luck we can help it remain so."

"I sincerely hope you are right, my Lord."

Delfontes grinned and rose to his feet. "There we have it. Eirlin has spoken, and our policy is set. Can I go to bed, now?"

A puzzled frown began on Eirlin's brow, but the lord forestalled her by taking her hand and making a mock courtesy to her. "I bid you good night, my Lady." He nodded to Ecmund and spun away. "See our guests out, my dear. I wish you all pleasant dreams."

He sauntered out, leaving the younger trio with smiles on their faces. "Your father is pleased."

"He should be. There was a great deal of possible danger, Ecmund."

"We knew that. I think he has a right to be pleased."

Eirlin lost her smile. "What did he mean, that last comment about 'Eirlin has spoken?' He wasn't joking."

Perica made a dismissive gesture. "My father isn't dense, and don't you pretend to be. He had you figured out from the first day we met you."

"What do you mean?"

"Eirlin, you stood in front of your new Overlord with a Sword on your hip, not a quiver of fear anywhere, and told him exactly his situation and how he was to deal with it. For certain, he was hoping you were the leader."

"Why?"

"Because if there was anyone stronger than you, he was in real trouble!"

Perica used the force of her laughter to close the conversation, and they tripped down the stairs to the bailey, talking of less consequential matters. There, Eirlin waited politely outside while Perica and Ecmund made a brief but intense good night. Then brother and sister strolled under the starlight down into the village.

"It's good to have you back, Kitten."

It is good to be back, Eirlin.

Ecmund rubbed her hilt. "How did you make out with Jesco?"

It was not as difficult as I thought. I did not intrude; he did not lose control. Actually, it was pleasant to be in the company of swordsmen again. They are a straightforward lot. Kill or die. No matter how you put it, that tends to simplify life.

"It's not that simple, Kitten."

Oh, don't go all 'maiden aunt' on me, Eirlin. Of course it isn't. They just think it is.

"What's this 'maiden aunt' business?"

You know what I mean. Unsufferably righteous.

"Ecmund, your Sword has just called me 'unsufferably righteous.' What are you going to do about it?"

"I don't know. Ask you to stop?"

"Hmph!"

"She also called you a 'maiden aunt.' Maybe I should marry you off. At least then you'd have someone else to be unsufferable to. Give the rest of us a break."

"Ecmund!"

Ecmund...

I know. He put his arm around his sister's shoulders. "Eirlin, you take all this much too seriously, then you get upset when we joke about it. How am I expected to deal with a sister who is the unofficial leader of the demesne? No, don't bother to deny it. Nobody talks about it, because that's the way of our people. That doesn't make it any the less true. If talking about it bothers you, I'll stop."

"It doesn't..."

"Yes it does. Especially joking about it. It's the one thing I know that can get a rise out of you." He walked along for a moment. "Did you ever wonder why that is? Why we have such a tradition of secrecy about our leaders? Perica and I were talking about it the other day. We think it has to do with the Maridon invasion. The true leaders of the Blood went into hiding and have remained so ever since."

"How can that help us in this new struggle?"

"Hard to guess, but it can't do us any harm. After all, it's not really a new problem, just a resurfacing of the same old one. We hid our leaders then and it was a successful ploy. So we'll use it again."

"But Ecmund, I don't want to be some sort of secret rebel leader. I've never hidden what I am. Not really. I don't want to try. It sounds like lying, and I won't do that."

He glanced across at her. "There may come all sorts of things that you don't want to do, Eirlin. Some of them, you may have to."

Ostersund Ceasterhof,

Koningsholm.

Maius xi

Dearest Eirlin,

I feel that it may be necessary to postpone your visit. The project is not going as well as I expected, and much though I would love to see you, I fear I would have even less time to enjoy your company that I did when you were here before.

About the matter you mention. I believe I understand what you mean, but due to the serious nature of the situation, it would be better to discuss this development in person. I will relay the information to the one who should be aware of it.

Hopefully I will be able to write you with better news soon.

Yours,

Tyrbrand

5. A Swordsman Off Balance

They were just sitting down to supper when there was a quick knock. Jesco entered before Kitten had time to announce him, or Ecmund to open the door. He glanced around the room, then stumbled to a chair and sat, his head in his hands.

"Eirlin, Ecmund, you've got to help me!"

Their eyes met across his bowed head.

"What's wrong, Jesco?" Eirlin reached out.

He shrugged off her hand. "Not that. I'm not sick. I'm in trouble."

"What kind of trouble? Have you been in another fight?"

He glanced up at her, his mouth twisting. "I'm in that kind of trouble all the time. Do I ever come to you for help?"

Eirlin sat back, folded her arms. "So what's the big mystery?"

Jesco's shoulders slumped again. "This is different, Eirlin. I don't know how to handle this one."

He looked up. The two just sat, waiting.

"It's Wynna. I don't know what to do with her."

"Wynna?"

The girl with the little swords.

Eirlin's mind was a jumble. "Wynna? Trouble? Jesco, you didn't...no, you couldn't have..."

"Not that kind of trouble, Eirlin. Worse."

Ecmund shook his head. "I'm tired of this guessing game. What is going on?"

Wynna Listens.

His cousin took a deep breath. "It's this way, Ecmund. After Wynna got into that trouble with those soldiers, I realized that she had a problem. I was as bad as everyone else, I guess. When we were kids we all teased her. Not in a mean way, of course. Not like the soldiers did, but still... We knew she was shy, so we'd draw attention to her. Then she'd go all red and we'd laugh, and that was all there was to it, really. It wasn't until I saw her so upset that day that I realized how she felt."

"I see. So what did you do?"

He shrugged. "I sent the word out to leave her alone."

"That's all?"

He grinned, one side of his mouth only. "Sometimes a reputation is convenient."

Eirlin smiled, patted his shoulder. "That was a really nice thing to do, Jesco."

I like Wynna. She is very careful with her swords. They always shine.

"Aye, but it didn't work. I noticed that everyone was staying away from her. I guess I scared them off too much. So all summer, every time I saw her, she was alone. And I knew it was my fault."

"But, Jesco..."

The swordsman raised his hand. "I know. But it was still my fault. So I got up my nerve and told her. I told her what I'd done, and that it was my fault, not hers."

"What did she say?"

"Well, she thanked me. So I asked her if it wasn't worse, her being ignored completely. She said, no, lots of people talked to her. But she was lying. You know how it is, Eirlin? When you just know?"

"All the time, Jesco. What did you do then?"

"There was nothing I could do. I didn't want to meddle some more, so I didn't do anything. Well, I did make a point of stopping and talking to her once in a while, hoping the others would take the hint, you know."

Eirlin laughed. "Why, Jesco. I think you're getting subtle."

He tossed his hands up. "Aye. Well, that didn't work, either. Now I'm in real trouble."

Eirlin shot her brother a grin. "I can't wait to hear."

"I was in the tavern the other day, sitting there having an ale, and I realized the place had gone dead quiet. You know the way it does when trouble just walked in the door? I suppose you wouldn't, Eirlin, but believe me, you can tell."

"How?"

"I don't know. There's a hush, with everyone sizing up the newcomer, then checking enemies and exits. Then the chairs all shift, edging towards a better view or a quick escape."

"Fascinating. And what was it this time?"

"I look up, and there she is."

"Wynna?"

"That's right. She looks around, spots me and traipses right over. 'Is anyone sitting here?' she says, just as calm as anything."

"Wynna walked into the tavern, alone? That took a lot of courage."

"Well, she was sitting a bit stiff and her knuckles were white. I knew she was scared, and I wondered what she was doing. But before I can ask, she waves to the bartender and he comes over. She orders ale, just like she's done it a hundred times before. He gives me a look, I shrug my shoulders, and he goes behind the bar.

"Then she turns to me and starts talking about the weather! After a while, Tamas comes back with the ale and she pays him, exactly the right amount. Slides an eighth across like she's done it all her life. 'That's for you, Tamas,' she says. Then she turns back to me, smiles, raises her mug, and knocks back a big swig."

Eirlin frowned. "She knew how to order, how to pay, how much to tip?"

"Well, sort of. She didn't really sound natural about it. Sort of more like she was reading from a book."

"What did you do?"

Ecmund laid a warning hand on Kitten, who was about to comment on Eirlin's hidden smile.

"What could I do? I stopped drinking. If she was going to drink a full mug of Tamas' strong ale, somebody had to stay sober."

Ecmund frowned. "Why did you let her, Jesco? Why didn't you send her packing?"

"I couldn't do that, Ecmund. I don't tell people what to do. What if I told her to go home, and she said, 'No'? Where would I be then?"

Why is that funny, Ecmund?

I'll tell you later.

"So you sat there and waited until she finished her ale?"

"Yes, and her chattering happily to me the whole time."

"What about?"

"I don't really remember. I was too worried."

"Worried about what? That your friends would come in and see you?"

"No, not that. I was worried how I was going to get her out of there."

"So how did you get her out?"

He shrugged. "Finally, when she's almost done, she looks over at my mug. 'Oh, aren't you finished?' she says. 'I'll get another one to keep you company.'" Jesco frowned. "Why are you laughing? This is serious."

Yes, why are you laughing, Ecmund? Why is Eirlin so red?

Ecmund straightened his face. "I'm sorry, Jesco. You have to admit it's rather funny."

His cousin glowered. "It wasn't so funny at the time, believe me. I said, 'No, no, I'm almost done.' I pretended to finish my ale and was about to suggest that we leave when she ups and signals Tamas for another round."

"You're joking!"

"No, I'm not. I waved him off and I got her out of there. She wasn't any too steady on her feet, but I got her out on the street and walked her around a while, then I took her home."

"And that was it?"

"No, that wasn't it. This afternoon she did the same cursed thing! I'm sitting there, minding my own business, and I look up and there she is. All cheerful this time, no nerves, already ordering a round before she sat down."

"So you drank with her, then took her home."

"That's right. What am I going to do, Eirlin? She's going to do it again, and I can't stop her."

Eirlin's face calmed. "Let me get this straight. She must have gone and asked somebody, so she would know exactly what goes on in a tavern. Then she had the courage to go in there, where she's never been, with all those men who used to tease her, and have a drink with you."

"That's right. And she's going to do it again, I just know it. How am I going to stop her?"

She shrugged. "That's easy."

"It is?"

"Of course. If you don't want to meet her in the tavern, meet her somewhere else. Take her out for a walk; that's what most courting couples do."

"Courting!" Jesco was on his feet, his hand on his sword.

Eirlin smiled up at him. "Of course. You're not stupid, Jesco. What else are you doing?"

"But...but...I didn't...she can't..." His face froze. "...courting?"

"Why not, Jesco? She has Blood as good as any one of us."

"She does? Not that it matters, but how do you know?"

"Her family comes from Visgard. They moved when her father got a post with the old Overlord. Then the father got sick, and she had to go out to work as a dressmaker. She's very good. She helped me with my blue gown for the Swearing In Cermony."

Ecmund frowned. "I don't remember them moving in. She's sort of always been there, you know."

"I remember when she came. She was so small and shy, and she made some kind of mistake the first day she came into the village school. Everyone laughed, she went all red and that was pretty much it." Eirlin frowned. "I'd always meant to do something about that, but I was too busy with my own affairs, I guess."

Ecmund smiled. "You can't fix the broken wings on all the sparrows, Linna. The girl seems to be doing fine for herself."

"Yes. Anyway, the Ceolmar family is well reputed back in Visgard. You could do worse, Jesco."

"But, I, but..."

Eirlin's voice lost all laughter. "Well, you think about it and make up your mind. Then you tell her, one way or the other. One thing you will not do…"

His hands came up defensively. "…No, no, Eirlin, I realize. I won't hurt her feelings. I couldn't do that!"

"That wasn't what I was worried about, but if you can manage not to hurt her feelings as well, that would be good."

Is Jesco going to marry the girl with the swords? That's a good fit.

Ecmund shook his head. "Wait a moment. What are you talking about, Kitten? What's this about swords?"

The other two looked at him, puzzled.

Wynna. She has swords. Wee ones. Very sharp and shiny. She treats them very well.

"I don't get it. She says Wynna has a bunch of little swords, all sharp and shiny."

Eirlin laughed. "Of course. She's a seamstress."

"Oh. Needles?"

Of course, needles. I'm not stupid, you know. Needles are like swords. If Wynna was a Hand, she would treat her Sword very well. Unlike some I could mention.

"She probably carries a packet of needles and pins with her. So Kitten likes her because she carries steel."

"Yes. And because she treats them with respect, keeps them in top condition."

"Well, there you go, Jesco. Your fate is sealed. In the mind of a Sword, the swordsman and the needlewoman are a suitable pair."

Jesco shrugged glumly. "Yeah, I suppose. I just wonder what Dad is going to say." Suddenly, he sat straighter. "What if we get married? I can't bring her to live with him!"

"Why not? She's obviously got more courage than anyone thinks. She's sort of like your mother was, you know?"

"She is?"

"Yes. Very quiet, never argued but tended, somehow, to get her own way. A sweet woman, your mother. Where do you think you get your soft spot?"

"What soft spot?"

"I've been in your head, Jesco. You can't fool me with all the bluster. You don't send all the broken-winged sparrows to me."

Her cousin slouched his weight onto his forearms on the table. "I don't know, Eirlin. Sometimes I wonder about that Healing job you did." He reached out, earnestly. "Don't think it was wrong. Not that. I know I'm happier now. But things are so much more complicated. I used to always know what to do. Now I have to think, then think again. Is it my old self reacting, or is it really a good thing to do?"

"And that's a problem for a swordsman, I suppose."

"It can be. But don't worry about it, Eirlin. I just have to learn to live with it. I'll be fine." He turned to Ecmund. "...And what do you think is so funny?"

"You think you're messed up now. Wait till you're in love!"

Many thoughts flashed across the twisting face of his cousin, who finally made an inarticulate growl and shoved to his feet. "I come for help and I get laughed at. Some family loyalty."

Eirlin smiled sweetly up at him. "You came for help, and you have been given your orders." Her smile disappeared. "Don't fail."

"Huh? Oh. Yeah. I guess I have. Thanks, Eirlin..." He seemed about to say more, but finally just shook his head and stumped out.

As the door closed and his footsteps faded up the street, Eirlin's pointing finger held her brother transfixed. "You. Will. NOT. Laugh."

Kitten watched with amazement as her Hand made a mighty effort and controlled himself.

That was very interesting, Ecmund.

He let out an explosive breath. "For me, too, Kitten. Poor Jesco!"

Eirlin smiled. "He'll learn to like it."

"What about Wynna? Do you think somebody better warn her?"

"About what? I'd say her mind is firmly made up. Do you want to be the one to try to change it?"

"Oh, no. Not me. I thought you..."

"I don't see any reason." Eirlin shrugged. "If we were ever going to find a match for Jesco, I can't think of anyone better."

"Jesco in love is going to be interesting."

"Well, I'm giving you your orders, too."

"I know, I know." He glanced pleadingly at his sister. "Can't I tease him, just a little?"

"Just don't hurt him. He doesn't deserve that."

"I'm not stupid, Eirlin."

"Fine. Prove it." She turned away into her bedroom.

"Why does she always get to have the last word?"

Because you give it to her.

6. Call for Help

Come on, Ecmund. Hurry!

"Eirlin, are you home?" Ecmund burst through the cottage door, his axe still in his hand.

Eirlin! Come quickly.

Eirlin jumped from her chair, her sewing scattering. "Is someone hurt?"

"No. It's Kitten. She says we must get everyone together."

"Everyone? Who is everyone? Why?"

Perica. We need Perica.

"All right. If we need Perica, we'll go up to the castle immediately." She threw her shawl around her shoulders as they hurried out of the cottage. "Do you have any idea what this is all about, Ecmund?"

"No idea. Kitten is too upset to tell me."

I am not too upset. I just don't know. I need more help. I can't hear him properly, and I need more Power."

"Hear who properly?"

I don't know. I can't hear him well enough, but someone is in trouble and I need more Power to hear him properly.

"I see. Do you think Ecmund, Perica and I will be enough?"

Jesco, if he is nearby. Anyone of the Blood we can trust.

"I think he's out at the farm this afternoon." Eirlin laid a quieting hand on the Sword's hilt. "Can you settle down and tell us what you need them for?"

Kitten tried to be calm. *I have been thinking about what you told me. About Lord da Baneza. About using people's minds together.*

"So you think there is a combined effect, when you have a group, that makes the strength of the group stronger than the sum of each person's Power?"

*I know that it happens. I have...*she shuddered at the memory. *I can make it happen, but it can be very dangerous.*

"How?"

It is too complicated to explain, Ecmund, even to my Hand. I do it by feel, not by thought. People are very strong when their emotions are involved, not so strong on practical things.

"Like listening to someone far away."

Exactly. However, in this case, I am sensing an emotion, so I should be able to tie his emotions to ours, and then we will feel what he is feeling. I sense him now, but it is fading. We must hurry!

They stepped out even quicker, panting at the effort. "Could that be dangerous?"

His call is very weak. It is either someone nearby who has very little Power, or someone very Powerful who is very far away.

Ecmund shrugged. "Or someone of medium Power, a medium distance away."

You understand the problem. PERICA! I have called her. She will meet us at the gate.

"But we only know one person who is very strong, and very far away: Tyrbrand. And his letters to me lately have not been optimistic about his project. In fact, he has put off the date of my involvement twice now, because he does not feel he is ready for me."

"You think he could be in trouble?"

She tossed up her hands. "I have no idea. He couldn't tell me anything about the project, so I have no idea what it is."

Yes, we do. Maybe he really is trying to forge a Sword. I didn't think he would be so stupid.

"Well, it could be that you were wrong."

Hmm...rarely, but it does happen. Where a Magician is involved...

"No one is blaming you, Kitten. It's just that..."

"And what has you two in such a rush that you arrive at my door breathless? Not too breathless to talk, I notice. Come in." Perica waved her hand impatiently, and the castle gate swung wider. "Kitten really shouted to me. Is it serious?"

"We don't know. Kitten is getting a distress call from someone, but it is very faint. We need your help and Eirlin's to strengthen her Power to listen."

"Of course. Any idea who it is?"

"We're afraid it might be Lord Ostersund. That secret project he was working on might have gone wrong, somehow."

Perica shot a glance at Eirlin. "Oh. The letters."

"Yes."

"Well, come in. Do we need anything?"

A quiet place.

"My sitting room. Come."

When they were all seated, the two women looked expectantly at Ecmund.

"Kitten was just explaining to us that we are not really trying to listen. We are trying to feel an emotion that this person is feeling. We are hoping that, since adding each person increases the Power of the group a great deal, once we connect with him his Power will increase the total to the point where we can get more information."

"Should we hold hands or something?"

"Kitten?"

It always helps if you touch my hilt.

They complied. There was silence, save for the distant hum of castle life.

"What do we do now?"

We were already doing it, Perica, until you interrupted.

"Sorry."

There was silence again.

Kitten lowered her sending to a soft purr. *That is good. Relax and don't try to do anything, to think anything. Simply experience whatever you are feeling. It's all right, Eirlin. I will shield you from what they are feeling for each other. Once they get used to it, they will concentrate on the task at hand.*

"Sorry."

Ecmund, please do not speak. Concentrate. There are many feelings in this group. This is unfortunately common in humans. Do not fix on any one feeling, or it will distract. I will try to find the emotion I have been listening to. It comes and goes, as the emotions of the sender rise and fall. Once I find it...there...it is getting stronger. Can you feel that? Despair. Terrible despair. This is worse than I thought, or maybe our Power is stronger. Let us all reach out, allow his feeling to seize us...

A wash of despondency suddenly overcame them. Kitten could feel their tears flowing, hear Eirlin's stifled sob.

Yes. It is Tyrbrand. Now we must send to him. Hold on. Do not let his emotion overwhelm you. Send him reassurance. Send him love, if you like. Feel what the others feel, meld it together, send it as one. There. Feel his despair dwindle? Feel the surprise? He is now aware of us. He is a Magician. He can probably identify us.

No, Magician. Do not pull away. Now is not the time for secrecy. Hold him. Keep sending those warm human feelings you love to wallow in.

Can we speak to him, Kitten?

I don't think so. Perhaps it is enough that he knows we are with him. We must go now. Send feelings of farewell.

Can't we stay longer? He needs us, Kitten.

I'm sorry, Eirlin. I tire. I must let him go. There. He is gone. Now please come back to yourselves. One at a time, take your hand away from me. Good. Very good. Now I must rest.

"Rest? Kitten, I've never heard you complain about being tired before."

47

A warm, Healing hand returned to her hilt. "Don't speak, Kitten, rest. I know the answer."

You do?

"I think so. Swords deal in emotions. They take them in, they store them, and they can give them back. What we just did took a lot of emotion. Where did it come from? A lot of it came from us, but I think most of it came from Kitten."

It is very difficult to keep all your minds focused.

"Can we help her?"

"I already am, Perica. She has shown me how to give energy to sick people, and I'm doing the same for her." Eirin was silent for a moment, and Kitten could feel the strength pouring into her.

Not too much, Eirlin.

"Don't worry, Kitten dear. Sometimes I feel drained after a long night of Healing, but this is nothing so hard."

Perica and Ecmund watched until they realized that nothing was going to happen.

"So what are we going to do?"

Ecmund shrugged. "That's obvious. Eirlin is going to Koningsholm. Kitten is going with her, because if Lord Ostersund has bungled a magic Sword, a true Sword will be of use. I'm going because of Kitten."

"And I'm going because neither of you knows a thing about the Capital, and if he's in political trouble..."

"Shall we take the Post Carriage?"

Perica shook her head. "I know you're proud of your success in getting the Carriage service extended out to Falkenby, my dear, but we need a larger party." Her eyes narrowed. "I will not be stopped by any Overlord who takes the whim!"

"I suppose." He shrugged. "When do we leave?"

Perica considered. "He knows he has our support, now, and that should help his mental state. He will be expecting us, of course. We will send a message by tomorrow morning's Post and leave the following day." She glanced at Ecmund. "We have business to arrange here, in case we are gone for a long time."

"We can't be gone for too long. The men building the mill need me to make decisions every day."

His betrothed gave him a sweet smile. "Then they will learn to make decisions for themselves, won't they? Perhaps it is good for them not to have you looking over their shoulders all the time."

"I bow to your superior experience."

"Thank you." She turned to the door. "I must speak with Father. What sort of escort should we take with us?"

"Escort? Why would we need an escort?"

"While I have all sorts of confidence in the ability of you and Kitten to protect me, a lady of my position does not travel with an escort of less than six men. It is just one of those things."

"All right. We'll take five soldiers."

Eirlin finished her work with Kitten and withdrew her hand. "Jesco might be a good choice. He is familiar with a different social level of the Capital, and he already knows the situation."

Ecmund nodded. "A good point. If there is trouble, it could come in many forms."

It did not take long to get the party ready. The following day there was a whole lot of riding around and making decisions on building and woodcutting, which Kitten found boring. The preparation and provisioning of the soldiers she found more useful. Finally, Perica declared herself satisfied.

"This looks like sufficient support for a lady of my station. Two swordsmen, four soldiers, and a lady companion."

"I am willing to braid your hair any time you need it, but you are going to be emptying your own chamber pot."

Perica's nose went up to a familiar angle. "In the places we will be staying, I'm sure there will be someone to take care of the essentials."

Eirlin turned to her friend, her levity gone. "I hope you can afford it."

Perica waved a dismissive hand. "In case you didn't notice, the early harvest has been particularly good this year. Cattle fetched more than usual, wool prices were up in the spring, and Ecmund has sold most of the wood in his yard. We can afford it." She turned seriously to her friend. "And even if we couldn't, we would still have to pay."

"Why would you do that?"

"Because that is how a lady travels. If I don't, people will ask why."

Eirlin shook her head. "I don't see it."

"Eirlin, half the nobility are in debt all the time. They run up huge bills on the strength of their name, then the tradesmen have a terrible time collecting."

"It is not the way my people behave."

Perica became very still, and her eyes seemed to focus past the wall of the room. "They don't? Now there is an idea."

"What?"

"I don't know. It just occurred to me that if the Maridon nobility are always in debt, and the 'Jornese are not, we might be able to apply some pressure. Buy up some loans, or something."

Ecmund had been listening idly, but now his head swung around. "How do you buy a loan?"

"Let's say you owe Eirlin a hundred golds. She needs the money back, but you can't pay her. I come along and offer her ninety golds in coin right now. She gets the money she needs, and I come around and collect from you when you have the money. I make the ten golds."

"But Eirlin loses ten."

"That's right. She never should have loaned you money she might need, and she paid the price."

"I get the idea. We buy up a bunch of Maridon loans, and then tell them they have to keep away from da Baneza's group or we'll demand payment."

"A trifle simplistic, but you have the gist."

Eirlin stood. "If we are ready to leave, why don't we go right now? I believe Tyrbrand needs us as soon as we can get there."

"Don't be so hasty. If we leave at this time of the afternoon we won't get far and we'll have an extra night on the road. Better to sleep well tonight and leave early in the morning."

Eirlin sighed. "As usual, your experience carries the day. We meet at the castle gate at first light."

"First light it is. That means I have some packing to do. Dear, will you inform Jesco and the soldiers?"

"Whatever you say, my Lady."

Eirlin strode to the door. "I know you two will be saying good night for a while yet. I'll see you tomorrow, Perica."

Kitten prepared to bask in the strong emotion shared by the two lovers, but soon Perica broke it off. "Eirlin was right, blast her. You have men to organize, and I have things to do. I'll see you at first light, my dear. Sleep well."

"Without you at my side, it is only a pale imitation of sleep."

"Hah! Some sleeping I'd get in your bed." But she turned her face up for one last kiss or two anyway.

Before the sun rose they were on their way. It was a grey day but dry, promising cool weather and hard roads. In spite of Perica's airs and graces, she rode as fast as the rest and they made good time. They stayed in the best inns and ate well, but the pace they set kept even the youngest soldier from risking too much drink in the evenings. They were on the road at dawn every day, and clattered into an inn yard to the light of torches most evenings.

On the border with Lord d'Angelo's land there was a newly built hut, and a soldier in livery stepped into the road in front of them. Perica merely kicked her horse to a gallop and rode straight at him. He got the idea.

Your betrothed can be very direct when the need arises.

Ecmund was too busy riding to answer with more than an affirmative.

By changing horses every night they always had fresh mounts, but after a few days the pace began to tell on the humans.

Ecmund.

"Yes, Kitten?"

You are tired.

"I am, a bit."

No, Ecmund. You are falling-out-of-the-saddle tired. You will make it to the inn tonight, but you are too tired to sleep well. So tomorrow you will start the day tired. Tired men make mistakes.

"I can manage."

Perhaps. But what about Perica? What about Eirlin? What about the soldiers?"

"No one has complained."

Perica is in charge. She will never give in. Eirlin rides to help her love. She will never give in. The soldiers are led by a woman. They will never give in. Jesco...is Jesco. The whole lot of you will ride until someone falls, or you are attacked because you weren't on proper guard, or any of a dozen troubles which can beset the careless wayfarer. And it is my fault. Well, partially.

"Your fault? You and who else?"

My fault and Eirlin's. She has been drawing on my Powers. She does that sometimes and doesn't even know it. I didn't realize it at first, but she has been using my ability to fuse the emotions of the group together.

"So now that you know, why don't you stop?"

It isn't that simple. Once the process is started, everyone feeds off everyone else. They don't need me anymore. I can't control everyone, and especially not Eirlin. Remember, I told you this was dangerous.

"Then what can we do?"

You have to make them stop.

"Me? Why me?"

Because you are the leader. You are the Hand. It is your responsibility. You are the only one who can solve this.

He sighed. "All right, Kitten." He rode in silence for a while. "Can I blame you?"

That is the coward's way, but go ahead.

That night at the inn, Ecmund glanced around the table. "Perica, you haven't eaten much tonight."

"It's all right. I'm just not very hungry."

"Just rode all day, and now you're not hungry. What does that mean to a Healer?"

Eirlin started. "Pardon?"

"What's the matter, Eirlin? Falling asleep at your food? Is that the symptom of anything you can think of?"

Perica slapped a hand on the table. "Ecmund, we're all tired. We had a hard day, and we have two more to go before we get to the Capital. Why are you picking a fight?"

"Three more."

"No, two. I ought to know."

"If we want to get there, we take three days. If we try to make it in two we're not going to get there at all, or we're going to show up in such bad condition that it will be us who need the help, not Lord Ostersund."

"We're doing fine. Look how much distance we made today."

"I appeal to the professional skills of the Healer. Look around the table, Eirlin. Look with your head, not your heart. What do you see?"

Eirlin's shoulders slumped. "I know. We've been pushing too hard."

"That's right. We're all on the edge, and it will only be luck that decides who falls over. I have a suggestion."

"I hope so. If you were just doing this for the sake of having an argument, I'd send you home to your sister and never speak to you again."

"A fine, loving response from my future wife, which shows how tired she really is. All right, don't throw your tankard at me, at least until you've finished your ale.

"Think. Why are we traveling so hard? To get to Lord Ostersund, because he needs us. But what if he doesn't? I suggest we try to contact him. Kitten says we should be close enough to talk. If he says there is no hurry, then we don't hurry. If he's in real trouble, we ride all night to get there. Whatever it takes. I just don't like to think we're risking trouble, perhaps for no reason at all."

"Where shall we do it?"

"You ladies have the biggest room in the inn."

"Right. Let's go."

"After you have eaten your supper, Perica."

"No, let's..."

"Perica, after you have eaten. You need your strength for this as well." He met her eyes for a moment. "All right, go ahead. If Kitten and I don't show up, what will you do then?"

Her fine, dark eyebrows lowered, and she glared at him. "If there wasn't such a good chance that you are right, you would be in serious trouble right now!"

"I take no credit. Kitten could keep me going long after you all wore out. She was the one who noticed what was happening."

"And she's the one who is going to solve the problem. Glad we brought her."

I love you, too, Perica.

"Of course you do. Everyone does. Now, see, Ecmund? Have I eaten enough of this glutinous stew? May we go now?"

"I thought it was rather good, myself. Plenty of meat." He held up his hands to ward off the loaf she was threatening to throw. "I believe we should retire to a more private spot for this discussion. Bring the bread if you like. We can eat it if you don't find another use for it."

This time the joining took less time, and the response was instant.

Eirlin? Where are you?

We are in Hernholm, Tyrbrand. We should be there in two or three days. Didn't you get my letter?

Yes, but I didn't expect you so soon. It's almost four days ride from Hernholm to the Capital.

How are you?

All the better for knowing you will soon be here.

How is your work going?

His feelings tightened up. *Better than before, but not as well as I had hoped. It is still too early for your part.*

We came because you needed us, Tyrbrand. Not for the project. You don't have to tell us anything. We were hurrying because we thought you might be in some kind of trouble.

A weak feeling of humour trickled through to them. *I am in trouble, all right, but it is all of my own making, and I am taking care of it. It will be good to have you here, though. Do not hurry, just knowing you are coming has made all the difference.*

Do you really mean that?

I am not used to having my veracity questioned.

Then don't put it at risk.

Again the wan laughter. *I deserved that. I must go, now. I find this type of communication draining.*

So does Kitten. We will contact you tomorrow night. As we get closer, it should be easier.

Good. Until tomorrow, then.

Sleep well, Tyrbrand.

You, too, my dear.

The feeling faded, and they were left looking at each other over Kitten's hilt in the dim inn room.

Ecmund sheathed his Sword. "That went well, I thought."

"Yes, but he seemed very...it's hard to tell, but...tired, I thought."

Perica nodded. "I agree. Kitten, what did you get from him?"

He is hiding his problems. The fact that he is too tired or weak to conceal them from me is telling.

"Do you think he is in danger?" Eirlin's face seemed gaunt in the candle's shadows.

I got no feeling of danger at all. I think he has taken on a very difficult task, and it is draining all his energy. Please do not talk to him for very long tomorrow. It is good for his spirits but bad for his strength.

"Of course, Kitten. It would be very selfish of me."

Ecmund stood. "But now that we are in contact, and he has reassured us that there is no immediate danger, we will take it easy tomorrow. Correct?" His eyes stayed longest on Eirlin, but she did not argue.

"I will order a warm drink, and with less to worry us we can all sleep better. We will depart well after sunrise, travel at a reasonable speed and stop when we feel tired. Does everyone agree?"

Perica sighed dramatically. "Isn't he wonderful when he speaks with such mastery?"

"Only when he's right. Otherwise, he just sounds like my little brother showing off."

They only become snarly like this when they feel they are losing control of the situation.

"Kitten! I heard that. Whose side are you on?"

Need you ask? I am on the side of right and reason, and my Hand, who can do no wrong.

Eirlin suppressed a huge yawn. "Exactly what I deserve for trying to argue with a Sword. I'm going to bed. Don't wake me up tomorrow," she held the door open, "unless I sleep late."

Ecmund made a brief farewell to Perica, and went to see about ordering the drinks and breakfast and informing Jesco of their decision. Soon the inn was quiet.

That went rather well, I thought.

"Yes, Kitten. Thank you."

The Sword uses her Power to assist the Hand in his enterprise. Thus it is written.

"Well, you used it tonight, and it all worked out."

Yes. You were very masterful.

"Don't spoil it by being sarcastic. Good night, wonderful Sword."

Good night, wonderful Hand.

7. Excisor

In spite of their resolve to rest, they continued to ride with serious intent and reached Koningsholm, tired but not exhausted, just at sunset on the third day.

"Now aren't you glad you brought me?" Perica rested her hands on her saddle bow and gazed around.

They had paused on the main street, which ran directly from the city gate to the central keep of the castle. It was wide and straight, but the roads leading away from it were a tangle of narrow alleys, broad residential avenues and crowded markets, bustling with people even this late in the day.

"And this is only the West Gate. The Koningsgata to the north is even bigger."

"This street always makes me feel like a little country cousin." Eirlin craned her neck to see around a highly piled cart that trundled past.

Ecmund nodded. "I knew the Capital was big. I didn't know it was so disorganized."

Perica waved a hand to indicate a rising swell of houses that swept up the mountain looming over the city. "There have been people living here for a thousand years. I was born over on that hill, where all the trees are." Her face saddened. "We sold the house when we left."

Ecmund patted her shoulder. "When we become rich and important, we'll buy it back."

Jesco nudged his horse closer in the crowded street. "There are places here you could get lost for hours. I did several times."

"Going back to your barracks from the tavern, no doubt." Ecmund was pleased to get a return grin.

Jesco smiles more.

Eirlin lifted her reins. "Let us keep moving. Perica, you said you knew the way to the Ostersund town home. I could probably find it," she waved her hand at a nearby building, "because I've been to the West Gate Infirmary over there, but I'd just as probably get lost."

"I can find the general area."

"If you can get us to the park with the waterfall, I know my way from there."

Eirlin.

"Yes, Kitten?"

Which direction is the Magician? Don't think, just point.

"Why, he's...he's...right that way." She pointed. "How do I know that?"

I don't know. It must be Magic.

Ecmund chortled. "So much for Magic. You just pointed straight through a large stone building. I think I'll count on our trusty local guide. Please lead on, my dear." He turned in his saddle. "Jesco, maybe you should take rear guard, make sure no one gets lost in the swarm. I'd hate to have to search the taverns for one of this lot." He stared at the soldiers, who showed him innocent faces.

Perica and Ecmund broke a path through the throng of people and the rest crowded behind. Just below the steep rise that led to the castle they turned north onto a less-busy boulevard that wound around the base of the hill. Stately mansions with high garden walls and wrought iron gates lined this street.

Ecmund gawked. "Does Lord Ostersund live in one of these?"

Eirlin laughed. "Not quite. His family ceasterhof fronts directly on the street, with a garden only at the back. It's very nice, though. You'll see."

Presently they reached a wide plaza where a tumble of water gushed from the hillside and spilled over the rocks into a stone-lined pool.

Eirlin pushed her mount forward. "There it is. We just turn down this street, and left at the second corner."

"Don't get in a rush. Your horse is tired, and these cobbles are slippery."

She glanced back at her brother, her face reddening. "I'm not hurrying."

The Magician is waiting.

"See? He's waiting." She kneed her horse into a faster walk.

Ecmund and Perica exchanged a smug glance.

I know what you're thinking.

"You always know what I'm thinking." Ecmund pushed his horse forward as well.

That's not what I meant.

"I know. Doesn't make what I'm thinking any less true."

She hasn't been this happy for weeks.

The Healer's joy did not last past the approach to the Ostersund ceasterhof, where the Magician waited in the street. Although Eirlin tried her best to hide her dismay at his condition, Kitten could tell from his wry smile that he knew.

She sent a tight message to Ecmund. *He looks terrible.*

Shh.

Ostersund seemed spry enough, directing servants to carry baggage and handle their horses. However, his voice had lost its deep resonance. In the light of the reception hall he was easier to see. Burn scars, newly healed, ran up his arms and pocked his face, and touches of grey lined his beard. Worse, though, was the way his robes hung on his gaunt frame.

What are we going to do, Kitten?

There are no secrets with a Magician, Eirlin.

Right. Might as well bring it into the open.

As they mounted the stairs to the private areas of the house, she laid a hand on his shoulder. "A good thing we got here. Whatever is wrong with Mistress Waldwine and her kitchen? You, my Lord, need a whole lot of fattening."

His smile twisted some more. "There is no blame on Mistress Waldwine. I have been a great trial to her. She makes her tastiest delicacies, but I seem to forget to eat them."

"We will deal with that. You sit here in the drawing room. Eowin and I will see to getting our guests settled. Then you and I," she stared him down, "are going to have a talk."

Kitten? The thought came almost silently.

Yes, Healer, right away. Gently, unobtrusively, she began to trickle energy into the emaciated body.

I know what you are doing.

"Fine. And you know you need it."

Dear Magician, with Eirlin there are times when it is best to be silent and obey.

Greetings, Kitten. I am very happy to see you.

I am not so happy to see you, my Lord. How could you treat your body like this?

The Magicians thoughts took a grim tinge. *You will see for yourself soon enough.* Sighing, he leaned back into the cushions. The darkness lifted from his mind and a softer smile edged his lips as he watched Eirlin bustling around.

"Ecmund, I have a favour to ask."

"Certainly, Eirlin. Whatever you need."

"Will you leave Kitten here with Tyrbrand? She might be useful."

"Of course." He laid her on the settee. "That is why I brought her."

"Thank you. Come. I'll show you to your rooms."

Ecmund smiled and motioned Perica to follow his sister out.

We are here, Magician. All will be well.

There was no response, but Ostersund's eyes began to close.

He responded quickly, though, when Eirlin strode back into the room, her face reflecting satisfaction. When her eyes fell on him, her happiness dimmed.

"Tyrbrand. What has happened? What is this secret project that has done you such damage?"

Please the Smith, tell me it has nothing to do with a Sword.

A touch of asperity jumped into the Magician's thoughts. "Of course there is no Sword. I still have some of my brains left."

"But you have created something."

Ostersund sighed once more. "I had hoped to make this presentation in a more formal way, with more success to show. However, we must deal with the situation as it stands." He struggled to sit upright, reaching inside his robe. "Eirlin Bryghtwyn, I have made you a gift."

"A gift? This project was a gift for me?"

"Yes, Eirlin. When you and I used Kitten's Power to heal Jesco, I realized that the lore of the magic Sword could be put to more peaceful uses as well."

I knew it.

"What did you know, my Lady Kitten?"

Eirlin said it herself. 'Sometimes a Healer must cut to cure.'

"Exactly." He withdrew his hand, revealing a dark leather sheath. "There he is. I have named him Excisor, for obvious reasons."

"A scalpel?"

"A Scalpel. With all the Power of a Sword, but created and trained only to Heal."

"Why, Tyrbrand, what a wonderful idea! So a Healer will be able to work like I work with Kitten?"

"No, my dear. <u>You</u> will be able to work like you work with Kitten. He was created for you."

Eirlin looked at Tyrbrand, opened her mouth, closed it again.

He is a Magician. There is no need to speak.

Ostersund passed a gaunt hand across his brow. "You must understand, when I created him I was thinking of all the uses you would put him to. I was trying to make the most powerful tool I could. And that is where I made my mistake. I think I made him too powerful."

"In what way? Is he dangerous?"

"Yes. At least he could be. At first he was easy, pliable. He learned quickly and was eager to please. But as he grew in strength and knowledge, his personality developed as well, and it is very forceful. As I forged him, I was concentrating on my technique, and I wasn't really thinking about the whole picture. I was thinking of how strong you are, and how you would love a powerful tool. Some of that must have seeped into his inner self. He is very young and still untrained. He becomes demanding at times and has no restraint if he does not get his way. That is where the danger lies."

"Has he done any damage?" She regarded the object, barely longer than his hand.

"Not yet. No, do not open the sheath. You are not ready for that yet."

Eirlin stared at him a moment, then shrugged. "Fine. Then put him away, and sleep. Kitten and I will begin your healing."

"I can't."

"What do you mean, you can't? You need sleep. It doesn't take a Healer to know that."

"But I can't sleep. I must be on guard for when he wakes."

"The Scalpel is asleep?"

Swords do not sleep.

"I don't know what else to call it. Sometimes he fades out, and I can only assume that he is resting. It is the only time I get some sleep myself, and it happens at irregular times."

"How else do you control him? Is he asleep now?"

"Probably."

"Probably?"

"He may be hiding from the new, powerful minds around him, but I doubt it. He is probably sleeping. This is all new to me as well. I discovered all the lore about Swords, but this is something original, with completely different problems."

"I see. What happens when he wakes? Do you have to keep watch on him all the time?"

"Not quite. Let me tell you about the sheath. The sheath has its own magic properties. It controls him, dampens his power on the world around him."

"So you can put him away when he's causing trouble."

"It isn't that simple. The sheath isn't powerful enough on its own." The Magician moved his hands helplessly. "He has to learn to abide by its rules. He has to learn to see the sheath as his safe place, like the den of an animal. If you leave him in there too long, he gets upset. If you use it too much, he will begin to hate it, and then it will no longer contain him."

"I see. Like any set of rules, the child must learn to live within their confines. If they are applied too harshly, eventually the child rebels."

"I knew you would understand."

"And now that we are here, you can go to sleep, and when he needs to, we can take him out of his sheath and...cope with him."

"I don't think so, Eirlin."

"Just rest, now, Tyrbrand. Relax."

He struggled against her soft pressure. "I can't, Eirlin."

"Don't worry. Kitten and I are here, now. We will take care of him."

The Magician smiled wanly. "I wish you could, Eirlin."

"We can. Don't worry."

He lay back on the divan and his eyes closed. "It would be a great relief, but I don't think you quite understand."

"Until you let us try, how can we know?"

His eyes snapped open, and the fierce pale blue gaze bored into her. "You know, I think you mean it."

"Of course I do."

The tension went out of his body, and he nodded. "All right. I can hear him mumbling around. He wants to come out."

"Is that what that feeling is? Like the room is too small? I wondered..."

"You begin to see the problem. Be ready." He groped for her hand, and she laid the Sword's hilt between their palms. With the other hand, he opened the sheath. "Here he comes."

"I'm ready."

I am ready.

...YIKE YIKE YIKE PEOPLE! YIKEYIKEYIKE FUN YIKEYIKE YIKEYIKEYIKE PLAY? YIKEYIKE NEWPEOPLE! YIKEYIKEYIKE LOVE YIKEYIKE WORRY YIKEYIKE YIKE PEOPLE YIKE YIKEYIKE LOVE YIKEYIKEYIKE ...

I can take care of this.

"Careful, Kitten. He is very young."

He is very rude, and needs to learn some manners.

...YIKEYIKE PLAY? YIKEYIKE YIKEYIKE YIKEYIKE YIKE...

YOU! Just what do you think you are doing? Who do you think you are, making the wonderful Magician so worried?

...YIKEYIKEYIKE YIKE yike yike...yike...CAT?

Yes, Cat. BIG CAT. With sharp claws. And you are a rude lit...

...oh! Oh! OH! OH!...

All right, little guy. Take it easy. I'm not going to hurt you.

...OH! OH! OH! OH!...

You're fine. The Magician is fine. He just needs to rest a bit. You need to rest a bit. Calm down. Calm down, now. CALM DOWN!

... OH! Oh, oh... whimper...

That's better. Now be still while I look at you.

"What was that all about?"

That was what is going on in his mind. Just a moment...yes... He thinks you love him completely and he can do no wrong. He also thinks he is in charge, and he is terribly worried because you are not happy, and he can't do anything about it.

"That's it?"

Among other things. Many other things I couldn't really make out. His mind is very messy.

"He is very young."

Eirlin pushed the Magician's head back down on the cushion and swung his feet up on the settee. "And you are very sick, Tyrbrand. How could you let yourself get this way?"

He batted weakly at her restricting hands. "Had to. Had to keep him under control. Crucial point, now."

"What crucial point?"

"Excisor. His strength increases."

"What can he do?"

"I don't know. He's like a baby. He doesn't know anything, doesn't know his own strength. He can hurt you without realizing it. Think of a puppy with sharp teeth."

And this puppy will keep his teeth under control, if he doesn't want to learn about teeth.

The Magician's head came up. "You are doing fine, Kitten. But please don't be too hard on him. It can have negative effects."

True. He is only a puppy.

"And you must get some sleep, Magician."

His smile flickered and died. "Yes, Healer. Whatever you say."

Eirlin looked around the room. "Then everyone has it straight. Tyrbrand will sleep. Kitten and I will watch. And Excisor will behave."

Oh, yes, he will. Did you hear that, little guy?

Yesyesyesyesyes!

Hmm. I hope so.

Kitten could feel the Magician's consciousness begin to slip. She sent a private tendril to Eirlin as the Healer soothed the man's ailing mind and body.

He is still tense. There, see? And there.

I see, Kitten.

Well done, Eirlin. Now he will rest and heal. Eirlin? All is well. He will be fine, and the new Weapon is powerful beyond imagining. All is well, Eirlin. Why are you crying?

He is so weak, Kitten. So sick. She stroked his brow, the wrinkles gradually easing under her tender fingers. *There is great damage. Some of it so deep I cannot reach it. I'm not sure he will ever recover.*

The Magician is powerful. He has just achieved an heroic deed. He has the best Healer in all of Inderjorne to Heal him, with her faithful Sword...

Mememememe!

"What?" Eirlin's surprise caused her to speak out loud, and she glanced down at Tyrbrand guiltily. He never moved.

Mememeheal?

"You? You want to help heal the Magician?"

Mememeheal!

"I don't think so, my dear. I don't know how to use you yet."

Nonono?

"No, little one. Not yet."

MememememehealhealhealMEMEMEHEALMEHEAL...

YOU WILL STOP THAT!

Oh!Oh!Oh!

Oh, quit crying.

Oh!Oh!Oh!OH!OH!

Ostersund stirred, his hands pulling into fists.

For the Hammer's sake, will you stop that? You're hurting my ears. If I had ears, which I thank the Smith I do not.

"No, Kitten. This way." Eirlin sent a calming wash over the little blade, and his cries died to whimpers.

That's better, dear one. Softly, now.

The Magician settled, and Eirlin wiped a hand across her brow. "I begin to see the problem."

So do I. He's a complete brat.

"No, Kitten, he's just young. He doesn't understand."

Right. He's a brat and he's ignorant as well.

Eirlin's hand closed firmly over Kitten's hilt. "Sometimes you aren't so mature, either, and don't you forget it. He has to be kept under control, but you can't be mean to him. It just makes him worse. Do you understand, Kitten?"

The Healer speaks. We listen and obey.

"And don't you get snippy with me, now!"

I'm agreeing with you! I meant it!

"I hope you did."

I did, Eirlin. You are right, as usual. I will find a time to argue when we do not have a young and impressionable mind nearby to learn bad habits.

"Wonderful. I'm stuck with two brats, now."

But you love one of us. That makes it easier.

"It does. And maybe some day I may come to love you, too. Wouldn't that be nice?"

I should know better than to start a fight with Eirlin the Fierce.

"Who?"

Eirlin the Fierce. The one everybody is afraid of.

"If that was a change of subject it was a good idea."

I am not without social acumen.

"You've been listening to Perica."

Yes. She has a fine vocabulary and a refreshing view of the world.

"You mean the view that the sun comes up each morning and circles around Perica, if it knows what's good for it?"

Are we going to keep this up all night?

"We may have to. You have a task to accomplish, and you need me awake."

I do?

"Yes, Kitten. You don't want to try to handle him by yourself. Now, don't get all pouty. Tyrbrand tried by himself, and look what it did to him. No, we're here for the night together, so let's settle in." She laid the Sword along the lounge beside the Magician. "Here, let's do a little bit of Healer work. Not enough to wake him up."

Of course, Eirlin. We are good at this.

Together they searched the surface of the Magician's mind, smoothing his worries, healing the wounds they found. As they worked, Kitten became aware of a presence. Warm, soft, loving.

Do you feel him, Eirlin?

"Is that Excisor?"

Who else?

"Isn't he sweet?"

Yes. He's quite... cuddly, isn't he?

Eirlin suppressed a laugh. "Cuddly? Am I listening to the 'Cloud Cat of the Leute, Afraid of None?' What do you know of 'cuddly'?"

I have never had a Hand who was quite so much in love before. Believe me, I am learning many new concepts.

"I'm sure you are."

Why does that bother you, Eirlin?

"What do you mean? I'm not bothered."

Eirlin.

"I'm not."

Eirlin, you can hide it from yourself, but you cannot hide it from me. You have a great emptiness. You have a terrible need. Must I go on?

The Healer's shoulders slumped, and she stared into space for a moment. Then she straightened, her hand unconsciously stroking the wrist of the man who lay in front of her. "I give solace to many, Kitten..."

But no one gives solace to you.

"I am a Healer. I take solace in knowing the good that I do." Her fingers pushed a stray lock off Tyrbrand's brow.

Do you love him?

"I don't know whether it's love or a magic bond of some sort created when we Healed Jesco last year. When I was here before, he was so caught up in forging Excisor that it took him away from me too quickly. That's why I came home, really. I know it sounds like I was running away, and maybe I was, but..."

What? Eirlin the Fierce running away? Never!

A wan smile crossed the girl's face. "Hard to believe, isn't it? But I did." She straightened. "But I'm glad I came back. We came back. We're needed, now."

Kitten indicated the small, warm presence that seemed somehow tucked between them. *Not right now.*

"Enjoy him while you can."

I know. Because I may want to sink my claws into him several times between now and sunup.

8. Civic Reception

For the next few days, the party from Falkenby spent their time close to the Ostersund mansion. Jesco and the soldiers found a tavern they could afford not too far away, Eirlin divided her role between training Excisor and Healing the Magician, and Perica went out to renew her social contacts. The third afternoon, she returned to Ecmund with a satisfied air.

"What makes you look like you just tasted a particularly dainty sweet?"

"Don't worry, I'm not going to ruin my figure on pastries. We," she drew herself up regally, "have been invited to a reception."

"Which 'we' is that?"

"All of us. You, me, Eirlin, Jesco if he wishes to go. Tyrbrand, of course. He probably already had an invitation and ignored it."

Eirlin glanced up from the scroll she was reading. "What sort of reception?"

"Oh, just one of those semi-informal things the City Councillors throw periodically to make sure everyone remembers how important they are. It's no great honour to be invited. Almost anyone can go, so almost everyone will be there. A good occasion to introduce you to Capital society."

"What are we supposed to wear?"

Kitten could hear Perica size up her friend's gown. *Fine homespun, but homespun nonetheless.* "Something a bit better than what you have, I think. What did you bring with you?"

"As you very well know, I only have one decent dress, the blue one from your father's Swearing In."

"Well, we don't want to create that much of a stir. Save that one for when you really want to impress someone. Since we don't have time to bring Wynna here for her special finery, I sense a shopping trip."

"Shopping?"

"Yes. I seem to recall a few tradesmen we might visit. I could have something thrown together as well, but I don't want to create too big a splash. Yes, we'll wander over to the Street of the Tailors first thing tomorrow."

"Is there time to have something made?"

"The reception isn't for three days. Plenty of time."

Eirlin looked dubious, but she had no basis for argument. "What about the men?"

"Oh, I suppose Ecmund could use a new tabard. Since Jesco is acting as my guard captain, he'll be wearing the new da Falken livery. Very impressive, if I do say so."

"Since you designed it, I suppose you should like it."

It is rather shiny. Ecmund will be completely overshadowed.

"I heard that, Kitten. Don't you worry. Ecmund will look just fine. Trust me."

In this matter you have all my trust, Perica.

"And so you should. Come, Eirlin. Fulfill your duty as my companion. Help me choose which one of my gowns to wear."

"I don't know, Perica. I was just..."

"...You have just been working too hard. I happen to know that Tyrbrand is playing with that toy of his right now, so they are both occupied. Come and have some fun with me."

"Excisor is not a toy, Perica."

"I refuse to believe that anything that tiny could be so much trouble."

Ecmund grinned. "Speaking from recent personal experience, I have found that the smaller they are, the more upset they cause."

Perica glared up at him with mock ferocity. "And you mind your manners, or there will be a whole lot more upset than you can handle!"

Ecmund turned a muscular shoulder to her fist. "Go play dressup with my sister. You're right. She needs to have some fun. Kitten and I have other things to do."

Kitten waited until the ladies were gone. *What do we have to do, Ecmund?*

"Now that you mention it, I'm not exactly sure."

You're not?

"No. I came in case there was physical danger. There is none. You are here to help with the new Scalpel. You have something to do. I don't."

So relax. Take a holiday when you can. Something always comes up.

They managed to keep boredom at bay for the next three days. On the fourth, there they stood – dressed in their formal best – in a straight row along the side of the vast, ornate reception room that formed the ground floor of the Koningsholm Guildhall.

Perica glanced around. "So what do you think, Ecmund?"

He looked up and about the room. "Fancy chandeliers."

"Hmm. I hadn't noted them especially. They are nice."

"Nice. Are you trying to impress us with your blasé attitude?"

"Of course. Is it working?"

"Most certainly. We're very impressed, aren't we, Jesco?"

"Very few people are armed."

Ecmund's hand slid to its familiar spot on Kitten's hilt. "I wouldn't be here without my secret advantage, and it would look strange if I was armed and you weren't. So here we are."

"Where's Eirlin?"

Perica winced. "She said she'd be along later, once she settled Excisor down."

Ecmund shook his head. "I don't think Tyrbrand really wanted to come anyway."

I could have settled the brat down.

Ecmund chuckled. "You could. And the moment we walked out the door, he'd be off and away again. You've got a lot to learn about youngsters, Kitten."

And you're the expert?

He laid his hand on Perica's shoulder. "Ask me in ten years."

She blushed and looked around for a reason to change the subject.

"Ecmund, there's someone I don't think I want you to meet just yet. Please entertain yourselves over here."

Ecmund glanced at Jesco, grinned. "If you say so, Perica."

"When Eirlin comes in, you grab her quick. I want to make this work."

He could see she was serious, so he hid his smile and nodded. Jesco muttered something about 'politics,' and received a wink in return. Then Perica swept away across the room.

Ecmund stood, his eyes following her, his hand on Kitten's hilt.

Are we listening?

"What a sneaky idea."

Good. She expanded her senses.

"Gavia, how are you?" Perica glanced at the others, nodded politely. "Hello, Piluca, Mausi."

"Oh, hello, Perica. I heard you were back from exile. How is life out in the woods?"

"Definitely more exciting than I expected, I'll say that."

Gavia looked her up and down. "I hear all sorts of stories. Apparently you've been making some interesting friends." She glanced pointedly across the room. "What is he? A woodcutter? A mercenary?"

"You're getting them mixed together. The dark one is Jesco. He's the swordsman. He's also the heir to their family Blood, but don't get interested."

"Why not? It might be a little fun. He looks..." she glanced again at her friends, "...dark and mysterious."

Pericia shook her head. "I'm sorry, Gavia. I did not say that to pique your interest. He is a dangerous man, and believe me, you don't want anything to do with him. Ecmund, on the other hand..."

"The tall one? He's too blond for me."

"That's good, because he's mine."

"You're serious?"

"Very."

"As in...?"

"As in betrothed. So keep your greedy little claws in, unless you want them snipped off, in which case you have my permission to try Jesco. Would you like to meet them now?"

Gavia glanced across the room, then back at Perica. "If I dare."

Perica smiled and led the three young women across the room.

"Ecmund, Jesco, I'd like you to meet an old acquaintance of mine, Gavia of the family Vega. Also Piluca Quentar, and Mausi Cauchina. Ladies, my betrothed, Ecmund Liutswin Falkenric, and his cousin, Jesco Coenfri Falkenric, heir to the Name."

They are so impressed. They shine! They want you to like them.

Of course. She set them up for it.

Of course I did. Perica had taken her usual position at Ecmund's left arm, allowing her contact with Kitten. *This is important.*

Certainly. Kitten sent a wash of open friendliness and cooperation towards the three women.

"Gavia, can you do a favour for me?"

"And what is that?"

"I want word to get around that I'm not in competition, and that Ecmund is off limits. I knew if you spread that, people would believe you."

"Really? That's all?"

Touch her.

Perica laid a hand on the other girl's arm, and Kitten fed her a trickle of warmth.

"It isn't that simple, Gavia. I have come back to court with higher status and a possibility of increased power. Now the girls who never saw me as competition will start to get worried. Then when Ecmund becomes known, there will be another lot who set their eyes on him. Then the men will start to see him as an adversary. Think of all the trouble it will save, when everybody knows we're truly out of the game!"

"Then why don't you just tell everybody?"

Perica sighed. "You know that doesn't work, Gavia. Everyone would consider it another ploy of some sort."

The taller girl grinned. "There's nothing so persuasive as a juicy bit of gossip. Especially when it's romantic, with a touch of the forbidden."

"Exactly. Will you set it going for me?"

Gavia glanced at her two friends. "This ought to be an easy one. It's so obviously true. Look at the two of them. If they weren't so cute, it would be sickening."

Perica shifted her grip to Ecmund's arm protectively, and the others laughed.

"I'm glad that's settled. Now. What about the rest of your party? I have already been warned against the dark and dangerous Jesco." Gavia winked at him and he frowned and blushed to his hairline. "I hear you have a sister, Ecmund. A Healer, rumour has it, of great talent."

"Yes. Eirlin Bryghtwyn. I'm not so concerned about her. She already has a place with the Healers, and she doesn't play your party games."

The girl glanced across the floor. "In that case, I hope that's not her over there."

They all turned. Eirlin, standing near the entrance, was watching the approach of a beautiful young woman, almost as tall as Eirlin herself, as dark as the Healer was blonde. Her dress was simple but artfully fitted, emerald green, and she moved with a predatory grace.

"Uh-oh. Let's go, girls. Rescue party needed."

Ecmund raised a hand. "Don't bother yourselves."

"What? You don't want your sister talking to that shark, Cuquita da Launca. The moment she smells blood she comes cruising around. Why do you think she just sauntered over?"

"This ought to be interesting, then."

With doubtful expressions, they formed a semi-circle so they could watch without seeming to.

"Can you hear them?"

Ecmund nodded. "If you keep very quiet."

Kitten focused her attention on the Healer's conversation.

"Good afternoon."

Eirlin turned to face the other woman squarely. "Good afternoon. This is a lovely party, isn't it?"

The dark girl looked around, as if in surprise. "Oh, I suppose it's all right, but it could use some livening up. You must be Lord Ostersund's little friend?"

Eirlin smiled in an amiable way and moved half a step closer, so the other had to look up into her eyes. "Lord Ostersund's little Healer. I am Eirlin Bryhtwyn Falkenric," she waited just long enough to give the other a chance, "...and you are...?"

"I am Cuquita da Launca."

"I am pleased to meet you, Lady da Launca. It is kind of you to come over and welcome a complete stranger."

"Ecmund! The others are closing in! What is she saying?"

"She's just told the other girl how kind she is to come and speak to a lonely stranger."

"She what?"

"Shhh!"

Cuquita made a flowing gesture with her hand. "It was the least I could do."

"If you don't mind, then, could you tell me who everyone is? I hardly know a soul. Oh," she placed her hand on the other's arm, "unless you're not up to it today."

The dark girl's eyes slid quickly to the three other young women who had sidled in. "Why wouldn't I...?"

"Oh. I'm sorry. I won't say anything about it."

"What do you mean? There's nothing wrong with me!"

Gavia grabbed Ecmund's other arm. "What's she doing? Why did she touch her?"

"She's expressing concern for Cuquita's health, I believe. That's what she does when she's reading a patient."

"But that's not..." This time three people shushed her, and they all listened avidly.

Eirlin smiled. "That's the spirit!" She patted the other woman's arm, then turned to look at the crowd. "So tell me. Who is everyone?" Suddenly, she turned back. "But first you must tell me who you are. When you introduced yourself, it was obvious that I was supposed to know, but I don't. I'm so unfamiliar with everything. What should I know about your family?"

Ecmund made a placating motion to calm the girls' questions. "Eirlin just said she was obviously supposed to know who the other girl's family is, but she doesn't, so please tell her. The girl is now rhyming off her family background, but she doesn't seem so happy about it."

"She did what...? All right. I'll be quiet."

"Now the dark girl is telling her about the other people around the room. She certainly knows them all. Hmm. Some of the things she is saying are quite shocking."

"Tell us!"

"Not on your life. I think she's trying to upset Eirlin. Good luck, lady. Oops. They're looking our way."

Everyone tried to look somewhere else, and the two women strolled towards them.

As they neared, the whole group caught the end of their conversation. "...sometimes it helps to just talk, you know?"

The dark woman had no time to speak, only shook her head, somewhat bemused. Then the groups joined and Perica, careful to be proper with everyone's full title, introduced Cuquita to the two men.

Don't touch me!

Surprised, Ecmund lifted his hand off Kitten's hilt as he greeted the woman. Her fingers seemed cool and stiff. He bowed formally and looked up into her eyes as he straightened. They regarded him with a flat lack of curiosity that he found slightly unnerving.

When she turned to Jesco, he could feel her demeanour change. She softened, somehow, and her smile became more genuine.

What was that about?

I did not want her to feel me. Kitten sent her tightest message. *I did not want to feel her. She is wrong.*

Wrong? How is she wrong?

Like Jesco was, but worse. Much, much worse. And I did not want her to feel me.

She can?

She is Sensitive like Perica. Maybe even stronger. Maybe not... I can't tell. She is wrong.

They regarded the woman with interest as she made small talk then excused herself, obviously uncomfortable. As soon as she left, Eirlin turned to Jesco.

"You will have nothing to do with her, Jesco. You hear me? Nothing!"

The swordsman frowned, off balance for once. "What do you mean?"

"I know you, Jesco, and I saw that look. It would be a terrible thing; don't do it."

He raised his hands in defence. "If you say so, Linna, but I usually like to know what I've done before I'm tried and convicted."

Eirlin sighed. "I am a Healer, Jesco, and there are things I may not reveal. Can you accept that she is drawn to you as a moth to flame, and the results for her would be as devastating?"

"You're serious?"

"Never more. We can talk about it later. This is not the place."

"No, that's fine, Eirlin. I don't want to take advantage of anyone."

"Thank you, Jesco. I knew I could count on you."

She looked around, smiled. "But now I can meet everyone else."

Perica stepped in to make less formal introductions. When all the pleasantries had been completed the party relaxed, but Perica frowned. "Well, Linna, I hope you realize what a hurdle you just jumped. I couldn't believe it when Ecmund wouldn't let us rescue you."

He just grinned. "I said she didn't play your games. I didn't say she was helpless."

Gavia regarded the taller woman curiously. "Obviously not. Did you know what she was after, Eirlin?"

The Healer smiled. "Someone who dresses and moves like that doesn't usually slide over and start conversation with a country girl. Not just to be nice."

"But how did you...?"

"I just wouldn't play."

"You wouldn't play?"

"That's right. It's a game, right? Like swordplay, but using gossip and wit. You slash and parry, bind and twist, and the better fighter wounds the enemy and drives her from the field in disgrace."

Gavia glanced at Perica "And she's a Healer?"

Eirlin smiled wryly. "I spend my time with the wrong sort of people, I guess."

"But how did that help you with her?"

"Jesco explained it to me once. If you were up against a boxer, what would be the worst thing you could do? Stand back and trade punches with him. That allows him to work at his strength, and he wins."

"Right. You close in and grapple. Then he can't get a good swing at you."

"That's it, Ecmund. So when that girl wanted to overawe me with her family, her manners, and her knowledge of society, I jumped right in and started asking all about them."

"You pretended not to know."

"I didn't know. I pretended to care."

"But she'd catch on to that."

"She did. But after that I had an unfair advantage, and all I had to do was make her aware of it, and she had to reassess."

"What advantage?"

Now Eirlin looked uncomfortable. "I'd rather not say."

Perica nodded. "It's the Healer thing, isn't it? We've all known for years that there's something wrong with her, but nobody's had the nerve to tell her straight out. She'd kill them, like as not."

Gavia looked straight at Eirlin. "Do you know what it is?"

"No, and I couldn't tell you if I did. I just let her know that I was aware of it, and sympathetic."

"Sympathetic!"

"I'm a Healer, Perica. I am sorry for people who need my services. She has done nothing to make me feel any other way. It worked, didn't it? She was very nice to me."

Perica laughed. "She tried to overawe you, she tried to upset you with crude stories, and she tried to embarrass you. That's nothing?"

"Perica, if a child wants something that is bad for her, and she hits you and yells at you because you won't give it, do you get angry?"

The smaller girl threw up her hands. "See why he wouldn't let us charge in, Gavia?"

The others traded looks. "I don't think I want you angry at me, Eirlin."

"Why would I be angry at you, Gavia?"

The girl raised her hands defensively. "Now you've done it to me anyway!"

"What?"

"You've just made me feel like a little child in the presence of adults. Please don't frown at me and send me away!"

Eirlin laughed. "I'm so sorry. I had no intention of making you feel upset. I'll tell you what. Tomorrow, why don't you take me around to the ladies' shops, and you can advise me on what to buy. This is the only dress Perica could come up with on short notice."

"I can? I can take you around and help you shop?"

"If you want to."

"Oh, I'd love it."

"Right. Then you can feel very superior, and I'll act like a naïve little country girl."

"Oh, thanks. Now you've spoiled it all. All the time I'll know that you're just humouring me!"

The others hid their smiles, unsure how serious Gavia was. Eirlin had no such reservations.

"Gavia, if you're worried about that sort of thing, I think I'll be dealing with you as a Healer, not as a friend."

"Is that a threat, or an offer of friendship?"

"Isn't it nice that I gave you the choice?"

"I've just been put in my place again. Perica, how do you cope with her?"

"I make sure I don't start anything."

"And she has a hostage."

They looked puzzled until they noticed Perica's grip on Ecmund's arm. That, plus the forlorn look on his face, broke them all down.

You are making a scene. Many people are watching.

Perica allowed herself one more giggle. "We are out of line, gentlefolk. These receptions aren't supposed to be quite this much fun."

They laughed again, but suddenly Eirlin sobered. "Gavia, you're good at gossip, aren't you?"

The dark girl threw up her hands. "It seems everyone is of that opinion."

"Fine. Can you do me a favour?"

"Of course. What dastardly tale do you want me to spread?"

"Just that I met Cuquita da Launca, and we parted friends."

"Parted friends! You confounded her completely!"

"And if she hears rumours to that effect, she will hate me forever. I don't want that."

Gavia shuddered. "You don't want that. Of course I can help. If I get the chance, I'll make it sound right for both of you."

"Thank you. Now," she looked around, "all this adventure, and I haven't even had a drink yet. Is there a bar? No? Then somebody please find a server."

Gavia nudged Jesco. "What's she like when she's drunk?"

He looked down at her, straight-faced. "Worse. Two glasses of wine and she gets sarcastic."

"The Powers preserve us!"

9. Gavia Reports

Two days later, Ecmund came into the sitting room where Eirlin was working with Excisor, teaching him to identify a selection of medicines she had laid out on the table beside her chair.

"Eirlin, I have to go out. There is some sawmill equipment I want to look over, and Jesco knows where it is."

"Fair enough. Have a good time."

"I'm going to leave Kitten with you."

That got her attention. "Why?"

"If I see the equipment I want, I might be bargaining for it."

Bargaining? I could help you bargain.

"Exactly. I've been trying to tell you, Kitten. We don't use your skills to take advantage of people."

Unless we have to.

"Yes, in an emergency or a fight. Not in the market. It wouldn't be fair."

The Hand has spoken. I will stay and play pattycake with the baby.

Ecmund shook his head. "The idea of you two playing pattycake is beyond my imagination." He undid his belt and laid the scabbard beside his sister. "Have an interesting time with the children."

"Well, that's a certainty."

Ecmund bent to give Perica a peck on the cheek. She grabbed him and pulled him closer. When he had kissed her properly, she released him. "Don't spend all our money, now. I might need a dress or two more."

"Whatever you say, my dear." He winked at Eirlin.

Eirlin's eyebrows went up. "My, isn't he getting polite."

Perica snorted. "If you define 'polite' as saying what people want to hear whether you mean it or not, then yes, he has made some progress."

Ecmund departed, and Perica strolled around the sitting room. "This must have been a very nice home, once."

"What do you mean, once?"

"All the beautiful furniture getting ragged around the edges. How long has Tyrbrand lived here alone?"

"His father died a few years ago, but it was just the two of them for many years, I believe."

"Mother died?"

"He doesn't talk about it. I suspect when he was a boy."

"Well, the rooms look like it. All of them." Perica strolled to the window and peered down. "Carriage pulling up. It's Gavia. Alone. Looks in a hurry."

"I hope everything is all right."

"We'll soon know." Perica stuck her head out the door and called down to Eowin to send the visitor up right away.

Gavia stumbled slightly as she entered. Small tendrils of hair had escaped from the sides of her bonnet and her face was flushed. "Eirlin Falconric, I have to speak with you!"

Eirlin turned her surprised frown into a smile. "Of course, Gavia. Please sit down. What's the problem?"

"Cuquita da Launca." Gavia perched at the front of a brocade-trimmed chair and edged it closer to Eirlin. Perica moved away and leaned against the window ledge, listening.

Eirlin nodded. "I can't say I'm surprised. What has she done?"

Gavia opened her mouth, gulped, started again. "I saw her at Lady Chimenea's today."

"Yes?"

"She was talking about you!"

Eirlin forced a smile. "I hope it was all good."

"Well...I guess it was, actually."

Eirlin raised her eyebrows, waiting.

"Well, she was talking to Lady Chimenea and some other women when I came in. You wouldn't know them, but they're important."

"And...?"

"As I joined them, Lady Chimenea was saying, 'I hear you've met this new Healer,' and Cuquita said, 'Yes, I met her.' Then she just looked at the other woman, like she does sometimes."

"What does that mean?"

"You have to understand Cuquita. On any given day, she might be perfectly polite. Distant, but polite. Then suddenly it's as if she doesn't care any more. She might say anything, do anything. She's a very bright person, Eirlin, and if she decides to hurt you, she can cut to the bone with a word."

"I see."

"So after a moment, Cuquita nodded and said, 'I hear we got along rather well,' and then she gave a very cold smile. Lady Chimenea was squirming, let me tell you, but there wasn't much she could say."

"And what happened then?"

"Well, Lady Chimenea was really stuck, and I could see that Cuquita knew it, and wasn't about to do anything to help. So finally, Lady Chimenea said, 'So you're friends, then?'

"And then Cuquita said the strangest thing. She said, 'I don't think Eirlin Falconric makes enemies.'

"She looked around and must have realized that we didn't know what she meant. She got this fake patient look that she gets just before she cuts someone to pieces. 'An enemy is someone you are afraid of. Someone you think might hurt you.' As if that explained anything."

The girl looked up at Eirlin. "What did she mean by that?"

Eirlin shrugged. "It could be taken either way, I suppose."

Perica giggled. "Yes. Either you don't threaten anyone, or nobody can threaten you. Which do you think Cuquita meant?"

Gavia shrugged. "With her, it's hard to tell. She's probably happy that it could be either."

Eiriln held her palm up. "And that was it? That's what has you so upset?"

"No, no. It was what happened after." She took a deep breath. "Then she turned away from them and laid a hand on my arm. I almost jumped out of my skin. She said, 'Now Gavia and I need to have a chat. I'm sure you'll excuse us.' The others were quite happy to escape, believe me.

"We were strolling along, her hand still on my arm, and she said, 'Why are you spreading rumours about me, Gavia?'

"She waited just long enough for it to sink in, and then she stopped walking and faced me. I was trying to think what to say, but she just looked at me.

"I have to admit, I stuttered a bit. Finally I got out something witty like, 'What do you mean?' but she didn't even answer, just stood there looking at me. It's scary, Eirlin. It's like she doesn't need to explain. She just stands there and looks at you, like she's doing you the honour of letting you figure it out for yourself. And you better not let her down!"

Eirlin laid a calming hand on the shorter girl's shoulder. "So what did you tell her?"

Gavia looked up at her, and she could see fear in the girl's eyes. "I told her the truth, Eirlin. I would lie for you if you asked me, but not to her. Please, not to her."

Eirlin took a deep breath. "I certainly don't want you to lie for me, Gavia."

She is very upset, Eirlin. Look at her hands.

Eirlin looked down. Gavia's fingers were knotted around her reticule handle, her knuckles white. "What did you tell her?"

"I told her that you asked me to."

"Fair enough. I did."

"And she said, 'That was very kind of her, but I'm not completely fragile. Tell your friend she doesn't have to be quite so careful.' What do you think she meant by that?"

Eirlin smiled. "I guess that means we aren't enemies."

"Oh. That's good." Gavia took a deep breath, let it out. "Then she just walked away. It was as if I wasn't there anymore. Like I didn't exist. Why does she do that, Eirlin?"

Eirlin spoke without thinking. "Pain does that to you."

"Pardon? What pain?"

Eirlin brought herself up short. "Nothing, Gavia. I think Cuquita must be in pain sometimes, and that causes her to act the way she does."

"Pain? Real, physical pain? What's wrong with her?"

Perica casually leaned over to fondle Kitten's hilt where she lay propped against the back of the settee. *And how does the Healer handle this one?*

Kitten increased the Power of that message so it reached Eirlin, who met her friend's glance. *You're right, Perica. I'm going to have to do something about this.*

"Gavia, as a Healer, there are some things I am not allowed to reveal. And if you're going to be my friend, you have to realize that sometimes I may say things that you cannot reveal. Do you understand that?"

Perica moved to Eirlin's shoulder, looking down at the other Maridon woman, who edged back in her chair. "In other words, if word goes round that Cuquita is in pain, then Eirlin will know where it came from. So will Cuquita. Get the idea?"

Gavia shuddered. "I think I wouldn't like that very much. One of them after me would be bad enough."

Then she looked anxiously up at Eirlin. "So you think I did the right thing?"

"Of course. You did what I asked you, and it seems to have worked. Then you told the truth, which doesn't seem to have done any harm either."

The other girl relaxed visibly. "Thank you, Eirlin. I feel much better, now."

"No, I should be thanking you."

Gavia's usual quirky grin returned. "In that case, you're welcome."

They passed smiles all around, and there was a brief silence.

"Well, having settled that, I have to go now."

With an amused glance at Perica, Eirlin nodded. "Away you go then."

Gavia stood and moved to the door, but Perica winked at Eirlin.

"Gavia?"

The girl turned back.

"Who are you going to rush off to tell?"

A comical shock slowly grew on Gavia's face. Then she frowned. "No one!" With a disgusted shake of her head, she stomped out, leaving the other two in gales of laughter.

10.   Tyrbrand at Court

"Eirlin, whatever are you doing?"

The Healer stopped, turned to face her friend. "What do you mean?"

Perica grinned up from the settee, laid her embroidery aside. "You've only been pacing up and down the room like a mad woman. If I didn't know you were talking to Kitten, I'd say you were muttering to yourself. What's wrong?"

Eirlin flopped onto the nearest chair with an unusual lack of grace. It was the only spindly, Maridon-style chair in the room, and it creaked alarmingly. "It's Tyrbrand. He went to see the king today."

"Why is that a problem?"

"It's the first time he's been to court since we got here, since he was so ill."

"I see. Don't you think he's strong enough?"

"He says he's fine, but I know better."

Perica shrugged. "He's a grown man, Eirlin. He's going to do what he thinks he has to. About all you can do is stand by and put him back together if he fails."

"And this good advice is from my almost-married friend? Whose future husband always does what she asks?"

Perica shot her friend a sharp glance. "Not half as often as you think, and not nearly as much as I'd like."

Eirlin had to smile. "Sounds about normal, then."

"I think so."

I just love girl talk. It is so refreshing. I really hate to end it.

"Then don't."

Not me. Him. The Magician returns.

Eirlin's gaze flew to the window.

Perica stood. "I think a polite withdrawal is in order. Call if you need me." She patted Eirlin's shoulder and left the room.

The Healer didn't seem to notice, her mind a whirl of anxiety. She sat, but the moment she heard his foot on the stairs she jumped up.

He entered with a sombre look on his face, and walked past her to his usual chair, where he sat heavily, a sigh escaping his lips.

"Tyrbrand! Was it that bad? How are you?" The Healer's mind reached out, but was met by an impenetrable wall. She retreated in confusion, which he ignored.

He dredged up a smile for her. "Your concern is misplaced, my dear. My problem today is at court, not in my body."

"What is it? What did the king say?"

"It's not what the king did or did not say. Is Jesco here?"

"I believe so."

"He needs to be part of this. Ecmund and Perica as well." He stood and placed an arm around her shoulders. "Come and sit down and we can talk."

She stiffened, then belatedly tried to accept his guidance, but he had already dropped his arm.

Why did you do that? Don't you want him to put his arm around you?

I wasn't expecting it. Be useful instead of intruding where you aren't wanted. Call the rest.

Whatever you say, my Lady.

Kitten sent a summons to the other three, ignoring Eirlin's confusion as she decided how close to sit to the Magician on the settee.

Too far away.

Mind your business, Sword.

You are my business, Healer.

Jesco must have been waiting because he appeared immediately, the other two close behind him. "What is the situation, my Lord?"

Tyrbrand looked at each in turn. "Fuentes da Baneza is back in the Capital."

They glanced at each other, then back to him, expectantly.

"He was there, today. In court. I heard him speak."

"Did you speak to him yourself?" Eirlin frowned and moved closer to the Magician.

"It was not the time or place. From the way he talked, the moment I rise to face him it will be a confrontation."

"What makes you say that?"

The Magician shrugged. "I'm not sure. I have known him for years, of course. We have crossed both words and swords a few times, but never for serious stakes. Now...there's something different. He's always had a lot of bluster, but it used to sound hollow to me. You know how bullies are: there's always a bit of uncertainty, down deep. He feels different to me now. More confident, more sure of himself."

Jesco shrugged. "If what I saw at that meeting at d'Angelo's manor is any indication, he's just spent the last two months bolstering his courage with the emotions of a lot of supporters."

Tyrbrand nodded. "That may be true, Jesco, but it still doesn't seem right. I am almost sure there is something more."

"I never want to see an opponent gain sudden confidence. It usually means he's picked up an advantage, and sooner or later I'm going to find out about it. Usually too late."

"That's what I'm afraid of. We are going to have to watch him carefully." The Magician paused, frowning. "Another thing. Cuquita da Launca was there."

"Cuquita?" Perica shook her head. "She never attends court. What is she up to?"

"That's exactly it. I hardly know who she is, and suddenly she makes an appearance. You know her better, Perica. What do you think?"

"I have no idea, but whatever it is, I can't think it will be good. Did she say anything? Who was she with?"

"She said nothing, and she spoke to no one. I noticed Lord Vanemar tried to make conversation with her, but she cut him dead. Now that I think about it, that makes sense."

"Why?"

"Her family has always been of the moderate sort. Vanemar is a great supporter of da Baneza, and I wouldn't expect her to have anything to do with the rabid Maridon fringe. At least her father has been moderate. As I say, I don't know a thing about her."

"Well, she's worth watching." Perica shrugged. "Although I can't help but think that anything she does won't be good for anybody but herself. And maybe not even that."

"From what I gather, she's equal trouble to everyone." Ostersund's face lightened. "Maybe she'll throw trouble at the Maridons."

Perica grinned. "Maybe she'll join them. They deserve some bad luck, too."

11.   Conclave of Peers

The Magician finished his breakfast and laid his napkin aside. "Eirlin, how would you like an interesting outing this afternoon?"

She wiped her own fingers and regarded the Magician a moment. "I am suspicious of what you might term 'interesting,' my Lord."

He grinned. "Politics. The Conclave of Peers meets today, and I think it would do you good to get a grasp of what's going on."

She shrugged. "I'm not that interested, but if you think it would help…"

"Don't overwhelm me with your enthusiasm, my Lady."

When you two start with the 'my Lord, my Lady' business, I want to run and hide in a corner. If Swords could run.

"Did you catch that?"

His grin reappeared. "Of course, and I couldn't agree more."

"So now you two are ganging up on me."

"Probably. It's our only chance of winning."

She nodded, as if seriously considering. "And what are we trying to win?"

"Nothing important. Merely the control of this kingdom."

A small frown appeared on her brow. "You're serious, aren't you?"

"Deadly, I'm afraid. Eirlin, you are, whether you like it or not, one of the powers in the coming struggle. Knowledge is strength, and especially for you, the knowledge of our opponents will be of great use."

"I suppose…"

"And today in the Conclave I believe you will get an opportunity to see our enemy in action. As well as some of our less useful friends."

"That's a strange way to put it."

"I put it so to pique your interest. I have reserved a place for you in the visitors' gallery. I think you should be there."

"Well, you have succeeded. I confess to being curious about da Baneza. Who are these 'less useful friends'?"

"If I tell you, will you promise to go?"

She reached out to where the Sword leaned against the buffet cabinet and hefted her experimentally. "Kitten, if I throw you very hard, will you promise to hit him in the head, no matter how bad my aim is?"

Violence is my métier, my Lady.

"I will consider that an answer in the positive." Tyrbrand glanced at the water-clock in the corner. "We will leave right after lunch. Ecmund, I suppose you'll want to go, since Perica will be taking her family's traditional seat."

Ecmund grinned and pushed back his trencher. "I'd love to see my betrothed in all her pomp and glory."

Perica frowned. "Sitting down there with that bunch of yahoos throwing their self-importance around is not my idea of glory."

"That's fine. I think Kitten should be there. What about Excisor?"

"What do you say, Excisor? Do you want to see the king?"

King? See king? Talk to king?

"No, dear. Today we just watch. Other men are talking to the king, and we must be very quiet. Very, very quiet. Do you understand?"

Like this?

There was a sudden blankness, as if a constant noise had stopped.

Eirlin actually looked around the room. "Excisor? Excisor, where are you?"

He is still in your hand, Eirlin.

"No he isn't." She looked down. "Oh, yes, I suppose he is. But he isn't there. Not really."

Yes he is. He's just doing my 'wind in the trees' trick. But he's very good at it. He disappears completely.

"Tyrbrand, you don't look surprised."

"I'm not. I found it interesting that Kitten had developed the skill, because it isn't one that a Sword often needs. I felt that Excisor, as a small and delicate tool, might have more need to hide. It was one of the basic elements I built into his creation."

"Well, it works beautifully. You do that when we see the king, dear one. There might be some bad men there, and we don't want them to know about you."

Hide from bad men?

"That's right, dear. You hide from the bad men, and you can come and watch the king."

Their carriage dropped them off in the circle in front of the imposing main gate of the castle. They stated their mission to the sentries and passed up the low, dark tunnel that guarded the space between the outer and inner walls.

Eirlin shivered as she looked up at the holes in the ceiling. "I know what those are for."

Jesco nodded cheerfully. "Burning oil, arrows, rocks and boiling water, usually."

As they entered the main courtyard and left the shade her tension eased. "I just hate that sort of thing."

Each to her own pleasures, Healer.

The Magician sent her the image of a large hand aiming a cuff at her ear. *Behave yourself, Cat.*

Yes, O mighty Magician. I cower and obey.

Don't set a bad example.

Eirlin looked around. *Be serious you two.* "Tyrbrand, is there anybody here I should know here?"

"No one at the moment. Don't worry. Once you see the main Hall, it will be perfectly clear."

The Conclave Chamber was close to the gate, up a wide sweep of stone stairway that led to an atrium the width of the hall. Ecmund peered up at the expanse of glass, calculating the number of panes, the loads and beam lengths.

"This is where we part. You three go that way," Ostersund indicated a smaller door. "I must join the king's party."

"I go that way, too." Perica took decorus leave of her betrothed and strolled towards the towering main portico. The Magician bowed formally to Eirlin and Ecmund, nodded to Jesco and strode away, his posture exuding strength and confidence.

The cousins exchanged smiles at this show and headed along the indicated route. They climbed a short stair, then followed a long, plain corridor down what seemed to be one side of the chamber. Half way along, an open doorway broke the left-hand wall, and a guard in a splendid uniform ushered them through. He glanced at their weapons but made no comment.

As they entered the Conclave Hall, Kitten only had time for a vague impression of grandeur before she was blasted by the strongest and tightest message she had ever received from the Magician.

Kitten. Excisor. Disappear!

Argument was not an option. Excisor flicked to nothingness, and Kitten blended with the shuffling of feet on the floor.

She opened her senses slowly as the party found their seats, easing her range to just beyond Ecmund's reach. They were in a balcony, raised above the centre of the room along the west wall. Several others sat nearby, but Kitten did not dare to touch them. That blast had been snt for a reason. The Magician would let her know.

Then she found it. Not a search, just a faint tendril of feeling. There was another magic Sword in the room! Her initial interest was choked by the memory of the Magician's warning. Even more cautious now, she blended her thoughts with the excitement of those around her and slipped out.

He was easy to find. His presence cut through muddled human minds like a scythe through wheat. Once she had it, she could reduce her own scrutiny further, yet still be aware of him.

Again a tight thought from the Magician. *Easy, Little One.*

She sent the merest whisper of acquiescence.

She got the impression of age and strength. And boredom. And a lofty disregard for anyone around him.

Magician, he isn't scanning.

No.

He isn't searching.

He is not.

He isn't doing anything.

I believe you are correct. Keep your presence very low, but collect everything you can. This makes your task more difficult, but it must be done.

Yes, Magician.

I must concentrate, now.

Good hunting, Magician.

Silent hunting, Cloud Cat.

She suppressed a burst of pleasure at the Magician's use of her Name, and concentrated.

Ecmund? Eirlin?

Yes, Kitten. What was that about?

Another magic Sword.

Where?

A moment...over to the left. You must be very quiet, Eirlin.

"We can speak aloud to each other and none will remark." She turned to her escorts. "There seems to be one like Kitten in the room. Possibly over to the left. Fortunately not as active as our friend. Not active at all, in fact."

Ecmund glanced around. "Not good. Too many dark heads over there."

Kitten picked up an image of the north end of the chamber: a horseshoe of seats focused on a central group of dark-haired, dark-skinned nobles in rich attire. Opposite the visitors' balcony a central dais faced them, containing a throne and several ornate padded chairs, empty at the moment. To the right, the horseshoe was mirrored, except the occupants were mostly blond and in less elaborate garb.

Who has a sword, Ecmund?

"They're all wearing swords, so that doesn't help us much."

Jesco shrugged. "The Hand will be a leader. When he stands to speak, his Weapon will react."

The swordsman speaks true.

Then trumpets sounded and everyone rose. The king and his advisors, led by pages and flanked by his honour guard, paced into the room and took their places. Lord Ostersund was at the far right end of the dais, standing behind one of the chairs.

Jesco leaned closer. "Doesn't look like a position of influence."

Eirlin smiled back. "He doesn't work that way." Then she looked farther to the left. "There's Perica. She's quite close to the centre."

"Delfontes is one of the original families." Ecmund didn't try to keep the pride out of his voice.

The king bade everyone sit, and then began a speech of welcome. Kitten listened for a while.

There is no substance to this. It is empty.

There is purpose. Listen.

Kitten allowed her attention to return to her real target: the emotions of those around her. *When we entered, there was much tension, especially in the centre groups, left and right. Now it is fading. I understand now.*

Jesco touched her hilt. *Ritual eases tension.*

Not over there.

Where?

She sent him the image. Over to the right, in the ranks of the Inderjornese, two or three individuals showed anxiety approaching rage. To the left there was less anxiety, only a unified tension among those in the centre seats. The other Sword was somewhere in there as well, supremely indifferent to the emotional chaos around him.

The king finished his speech. Candles were lit, scrolls were opened, and the rigamarole droned on. Ecmund felt it safe to speak.

"How is our little friend taking this?"

Eirlin grinned. "He loved the king's speech. I am teaching him to listen without being heard. He is being very good."

I hope so. This could be dangerous. That Sword is very powerful. Old, strong, supremely confident.

"A swordsman or Sword who faces few worthy opponents can get too confident."

True, Jesco, but that doesn't matter until he finds a worthy opponent.

"And if he does? How will that affect a battle with magic Swords?"

Then the outcome leans more on the skill of the Hands involved.

Jesco flexed his right hand. "That might be interesting."

Eirlin flicked his knee with the tips of her fingers. "Don't get any ideas."

"I don't get ideas. I prepare for emergencies."

"Well, just stay prepared. The actual Conclave is starting."

The tension in the room began to build as the opening rites wound down. Speakers were lining up behind the podium below their balcony. It looked like members from each party would speak alternately.

Ecmund took it all in. "The leaders do not begin."

Jesco shook his head. "It is like a swordsmen's competition. These are the warm-up matches with lesser names. The true contest will come later."

Eirlin glanced at her brother. "Tyrbrand says to watch for the discussion about schools. That's where the trouble will start."

"Schools? Why would they be the flash point?"

"They are less important in themselves, but a point where the Maridon and Inderornese divide sharply. Listen and you'll see."

"That will be interesting."

Various debates started, continued, stopped or were sidetracked into other complaints. Watching the king manage the melée, Eirlin couldn't help but think of a teacher trying to shepherd a group of six-year-olds through a fitness lesson. Jesco's images leaned more towards a general trying to control a battle.

Finally, without anyone seeming to notice, the issue of schools drifted into the field of discussion.

"That was very clever." Eirlin nodded and glanced at Ecmund.

"What was?"

"The way he followed his compatriot's reference, and suddenly it became an issue of schooling. That had to have been planned ahead."

Ecmund shrugged. "I imagine a lot of this was planned ahead, in spite of how it looks."

Human minds are so messy.

Her Hand grinned. "And messiness can hide a lot of careful planning."

Good point. Get it? Point? Ha?

Not now, Kitten.

I know. Not a joking matter.

"This is important. You can tell by the way everyone else is listening. They know."

Ecmund, intent on the dark faces to the left, only nodded.

"...and I demand the right to train my sons in any way I see fit, at any school I choose to send them to!" Smiling, the Maridon returned to his seat, to the loud applause of his cohorts.

A blond man with a supercilious smile replaced him at the podium.

"I would like to thank the preceding speaker for making his desires so plain. He has demonstrated clearly that the question before us, your Majesty, is whether any one of us has the right to rear his child, male or female, in ignorance and hatred."

An uproar stormed from the Maridon seats. Fists waved, and a babble of insults flowed around the chamber. Inderjornese members rose as well, and the din intensified.

The king sat through this in stony silence. Finally, he raised a hand, and a blare of trumpets cut through the babel. There was instant silence, through which the voice of one unfortunate laggard came clearly, "...see some blond heads stuck on my battlements..." then winding down as he realized his mistake.

"Remove him."

Guards closed in, and the cowed Maridon noble was hustled without ceremony from the meeting.

The king fixed his attention on the lord who had spoken. "Lord Haragund. Your comments were the cause of much unrest. Can you give reason why you should not be removed as well?"

"Your Majesty, I meant no insult to any individual. I mentioned no specifics, and I named no subject of this realm. I was merely disagreeing with a general principle and giving an example of how it might go wrong. If any chose to pull that garment over his own head, it was through no intention of mine. I apologize to your Majesty and to this assembly for any misunderstanding."

The king kept the Conclave in suspense for a long while. Finally, he stood. "I must accept your apology, because the words you spoke do indeed read as you suggest. However, I question the motive behind such manipulation, and thus warn all of you against causing unseemly uproar in this house." He pinned the unfortunate noble with a glare clearly forceful, even from across the wide hall. "You have been the indirect cause of one of our number being ejected from this gathering. Well I know how this conflict will play out. He will blame you, and thus we have created a new pair of enemies. This is not my will, nor the will of my people."

He mused a moment. "You have seven days. At the end of that time, the two of you will present yourselves to me with evidence that you have met at least three times. You will show me demonstrable proof that you have settled any and all differences."

A general murmur ran through the assembly.

They like that.

Ecmund nodded. "He is a wise man, our king."

The king's voice rose. "And at any time in the next three years, if there is any conflict between your two houses at any level down to to scullery maids, no matter who is at fault, I will remove both your names from the Lists of this Meeting."

He chopped his hand downwards, and again the trumpets blared, drowning the rise of reaction. The king sat, and motioned to the next Maridon in line.

"Our sovereign takes a strong stance." Jesco tipped his head in admiration.

Eirlin shook hers. "And a challenge to the leaders of both sides. If their followers get in trouble they are duty bound to support them, all the way down the line. A drunken fight between two kitchen drudges in a tavern could lead to civil war."

He shrugged. "If such triviality starts it, then it was coming anyway."

"I can't argue with that."

They returned to listening, but the king's actions had taken effect, and the next speakers toned down their rhetoric considerably.

Another private message hit Kitten. *Watch this one.*

Eirlin, Ecmund.

Yes?

The Magician warns us to note this speaker.

"Jesco, do you know this man? He is apparently important."

"Lord Vanemar. A loudmouth and a firebrand. And I'm being polite in case someone overhears me." He tilted his head. "There was something about him being an excellent swordsman, I recall."

Lord Vanemar strutted to the podium. He was fortyish, dark-haired, tall and capable-looking.

Do you think he's handsome, Eirlin?

In an arrogant way, yes.

Good answer.

The speaker's words shut off any further response.

"Your Majesty, I stand before you in awe of the blindness demonstrated by this august body. Here we stand, the strongest, the wisest, the most important men of this land. All look to us for guidance and support. All depend on the success of our enterprises for their daily bread. And what do we do? We argue over trifles. We antagonize each other over minor matters. And we leave the most important issue to loom over us.

"And what is that issue, you may ask? Well, your Majesty, it is simply the matter of who should rule this realm. Who has the ability, the strength, the courage to get things done. To handle the problems of our country as they should be handled. Not those has-beens who cling to their power by their demands for long-forgotten privileges. Not the hangers-on who suck at the teat of the king's largesse. The people who should rule are those who deserve to rule. Those who have worked to make something of themselves, and of this realm."

Lord Vanemar paused, stared a moment at the seats opposite him. "Perhaps it is time for those who hold their places on sufferance from those in true power to be made aware of their delicate position."

A low growl rose from the Inderjornese ranks, but no voice called out. Kitten could feel the tension oozing from both directions, building from the left as the old Sword tied his followers together. Vanemar held his pugnacious stance a moment longer, then turned his back to his enemies and strolled to his seat. The tension fell as the Sword released the Maridons from its thrall.

The king waited until silence returned. He turned to the next Inderjornese speaker, but the man deferred to a lord who strode from the centre of their bloc. He was a stocky Inderjornese of indeterminate age, clean-shaven, but with a touch of grey at his temples.

"Any idea, Jesco?"

"Lord Skonric. Another intolerant one."

Lord Skonric was dressed in black, and his queue of blond hair tumbled over his shoulders.

"Even his hair style throws dirt in Maridon faces."

"Trust a woman to notice." Jesco shared a grim smile with Ecmund.

His head high, the lord began to speak.

"Your Majesty, Lord Vanemar speaks of sufferance, although he is too diplomatic to indicate the specific people that he means. At least this demonstrates his continued acquiescence to the power of our king and his rule. May that situation continue.

"I draw the assembly's attention to the fact that those – and I speak in general terms here, wishing to cause no offense to any individual – that those who question the right of their peers to their positions soon progress to questioning the right of those who rule them."

The king's hand rose, and the growing mutter among the Meridon ranks subsided. He turned the hand into an admonishing finger pointed at Skonric, but said nothing.

The lord nodded in tacit agreement. "At your Majesty's pleasure, I will take that line no further. But let it be known to all within the range of my voice that I support your Majesty's reign, I acknowledge the positions and traditional rights of all who do their part in the ruling of this great realm, and any man who would undermine that hierarchy for his own personal gain will receive his just deserts at my hand, and at the hands and arms of those loyal to the realm who think like me."

A roar of applause erupted from the Inderjornese faction, rolling on as Skonric returned to his seat. Finally, he rose and made a calming motion, and his supporters subsided. He nodded in a polite and formal gesture to the king.

Eirlin's mouth twisted as if she had eaten something sour. "Jingoism. Pure rabble-rousing."

"But very clever." Ecmund covered her hand, tensed on the railing in front of her. "How can the king chastise one who so strongly supports his reign?"

"And one so likely to bring it down in warfare and strife."

"I have to agree with you there, Eirlin."

The Healer and the Hand agree. It is certain.

Ecmund laid his hand on her hilt. "How did your friend react, Kitten?"

He is no friend of mine. That much is certain. Both he and his Hand treated that speech with massive indifference. In fact, the Hand seemed pleased, rather than otherwise.

Jesco nodded. "Bringing the enemy and his minions into the open is a good tactic. The feeling of satisfaction means that he wants this conflict."

Eirlin shook her head. "I wish I didn't agree with you on that as well."

After this exchange, the rest was anti-climax. Tensions abated, and the enemy Sword moved from regarding the human actions with indifference to the point of not regarding them at all. Kitten was too careful to take advantage of this, and Excisor, for once, obeyed without question. When the closing ritual droned its way into silence, the room felt almost as if no conflict had existed. Almost.

They rose from their seats and went to meet Perica and Tyrbrand in the atrium. The Magician took some time in leaving the king's party and when he arrived the hall was almost empty. He joined them with a look that precluded comment, and they went silently to their carriage.

Once they had left the official precincts, the Magician relaxed. "Well, Sword, what do you think of that?"

An interesting development, my Lord Magician.

"It is. What did you think of him?"

My experience with other Swords is small, and far in the past. He certainly is nothing like me. What are you laughing at?

Eirlin patted her hilt. "Not at you, my dear. I think it was mostly a release of tension. No, he is most certainly not like you. Even I could tell that from what little echoed through your senses. I have never met a more unconcerned individual in my life."

That seems true. He is completely uninterested in humans. He accomplishes the service his Hand requires and disappears into indifference.

The Magician ran a hand through his hair. "Well, that may work in our favour."

Do not underestimate him, my Lord. Part of his lack of concern comes from lack of fear. He is very powerful. I feel he is old, and has experienced many battles, taken many lives.

"He has taken many souls, then?"

I am unclear on that matter, Eirlin. When a Sword kills, the soul of the victim is forfeit. I know that. Whether the Sword has a choice in the disposal of the soul, I am uncertain. I recall the men I have killed in battle in the past. I had no interest in such souls, and I did not touch them. Where they went, I have no idea.

"But that was in battle. A duel might be different."

A good point that only a swordsman would bring up. With an individual in close combat there is a much more intimate relationship, and that may mean the Sword has less choice. It is worth considering.

"But nothing that helps us at present." The Magician slumped back against the cushions.

"Tyrbrand, you have overtired yourself. You must rest. No more chatter."

He smiled wanly. "I hardly consider this conversation chatter, my dear. But I agree, I need rest. Let us think on these things and speak again this evening after supper, when our minds are rested and clear."

He sank back again, and Eirlin pillowed his head on her shoulder. Kitten sent a wry grin to Ecmund, and received the image of a wink in return.

It was a solemn group that gathered in Ostersund's sitting room that evening.

"Kitten, you are sure that the owner of the Sword is Fuentes da Baneza?"

I can't see anyone else in that hall having the power.

"Eirlin?"

"From my limited knowledge, I agree."

"Well, that explains his attitude. He thinks he has the key to power in the kingdom."

Perica frowned. "But Kitten said that it is forbidden for a Sword to become Joined to an Overlord."

"He is a Maridon. He wouldn't know that."

The Sword would know. If he cared.

"A good point, my Lady Kitten. He did not seem concerned."

"But how could a Sword ignore such an important principle?"

Ostersund shook his head. "He is very old. Perhaps the training was not so strict in his younger days. Also, there is a foreign touch to his mind. Perhaps the rules are different in other realms. In any case, he is here. We must deal with him and the Hand who wields him."

"Lord da Baneza thus has a great advantage. How well he can use his Sword's talents is another question. Jesco, have you heard anything?"

"He is known as a competent swordsman. Not exceptional."

"And what of the Sword's other talents?"

Except for manipulating the emotions of the group, I saw no evidence of any talents.

"Which is not to say they don't exist."

True.

"So all da Baneza really has at the moment is a way to amplify the talent for rabble-rousing he already possesses." The Magician looked at each, received a nod.

"Then let us look at his disadvantages: he doesn't know that Lord da Falken is on the opposing side. He doesn't know that the king is Sensitive like himself. I doubt if he even understands his own powers. Like the king, he has always been that way and probably just considers it his superior intellect. He doesn't understand the whole situation with the Sword, but it works, so he does it. What have I missed?"

...that if he isn't careful with manipulating people's emotions, he could throw this realm into chaos.

"Kitten, surely you're exaggerating. How could one Sword do that?"

Well, let me think. She drew up a picture of a long line of men, all tied together with a single rope, all standing along the edge of a cliff.

The Magician's thoughts had a grim tinge. "I see. Just one little push on one man..."

Correct.

"Is there anything we can do about that?"

Nothing.

"Then I suggest we go on to something we can deal with. Any other weaknesses?"

"He most certainly can't tell his followers about the Sword." Eirlin opened her hands. "They don't believe in things like that."

"Probably right. Although a charismatic leader, especially backed by the Power of a Sword, can make his followers believe surprising things."

He doesn't know Excisor and I exist. We were very careful.

"Yes, you two did very well today."

Listened to the king.

"You did, and you disappeared beautifully."

Hide from biiiiig horse.

"Horse?"

The Magician shrugged. "A Sword must have a soul. I used old Bugler for Excisor. Obviously, Hanflaed used a cat of some sort for Kitten. This old fellow must have been a horse once. I wonder if that will make any difference to how he acts?"

Jesco laughed. "Charge straight ahead into battle, ignore everyone the rest of the time."

"Kitten, do you agree?"

He certainly wasn't helping his Hand like he should.

"Oh, I disagree. He was definitely manipulating the emotions of his supporters."

The Magician knows better than that. There are all sorts of other ways a Hand needs help.

The Magican's forehead clouded. "There are other worries."

"Yes." Eirlin's brow furrowed too. "Why didn't da Baneza speak?"

"That is even more disturbing. Letting a demagogue like Vanemar take all the glory. I wonder what he's up to?"

"Maybe he's acting like Eirlin."

"Jesco! Whatever do you mean?"

Careful, Swordsman. You offend Eirlin the Terrible at your own risk.

Jesco's grin had that old wry twist. "You know exactly what I mean, Eirlin; Ecmund is the Hand, I am the swordsman, Lord Ostersund uses his magic, and you sit and seem to do nothing."

The Healer's brow darkened. "And...?"

"...and we all look to you for approval."

"Now that is the most utter nonsense I have ever heard! Who looks to me for approval?"

He shrugged. "I can only speak for myself. You know I always have looked to you. I always will, and neither of us would want to change that even if we could. And we can't."

"And that makes it all easy for you, and harder for me."

Again the grin. "That's right. It's much easier to get killed than to send someone out to be killed."

"Jesco, that's a horrible responsibility to put on anyone!"

"Any officer in the army would agree. Fact of life. Get used to it."

"I'm not in the Army. I'm a Healer!"

Magician...

"Thank you, Kitten, I agree. Jesco, this conversation is off our topic and you're upsetting Eirlin. What has this to do with our enemy?"

"A whole lot, and it affects how we deal with him. It's very hard to beat an enemy who never appears in person. You can destroy his minions, but he will stay hidden, to attack again where you least expect it. We need to draw him out, bring him into the battle, so that we can accomplish a lasting defeat."

"And have you any other wisdom in this direction?"

"Yes. If we carry the comparison to Eirlin further, we find another question to ask. We know that, even if we are beaten, Eirlin carries the support of the people, and thus will be able to continue the battle, no matter how many of us fall. What kind of support will da Baneza have, once Vanemar and his army of thugs are defeated? All the Maridons? Just the nobles? Just the rogue Sensitives?"

"Much though I protest being cast as the secret general in this campaign, I must allow the truth in the rest of your thinking, Jesco. If he uses his powers wisely, I think he can drive such a wedge through this realm that every dark face will support him fully, for fear of what will happen if he loses."

"And how do we deal with this?"

"Our lore teaches that we can win over this type of foe by living our lives in peace and demonstrating the strength of cooperation for the common good."

The Magician shook his head. "That takes time, Eirlin, and time we don't have."

She looked up at him and her eyes narrowed. "Then speaking as your 'general,' we must decimate his armies, then entice him into the open and personally destroy him. And I can't believe that a Healer just said such a thing." She buried her face in her hands.

Tyrbrand was at her side instantly. "Easy, there, Eirlin. You only spoke the truth. It's not your responsibility. It's up to the king."

"Well, I hope you all remember that. You're making it sound like I'm going to be running a war. I'm a Healer." She stood and faced them. "Do you all understand that? I'm a Healer, and I don't kill. I Heal!"

The Magician rose as well. "Yes, my dear. You Heal people and the realm. Never forget that."

"I don't see how I could, with all of you here to remind me all the time."

"Eirlin, I never..."

But she was gone from the room, leaving the rest of them staring at their empty hands.

Those of us who have hands.

To their relief, Eirlin was her usual cheerful self at supper, and no mention was made of her outburst.

As the evening progressed, however, the conversation became more strained, and finally Eirlin put the Scalpel down on her worktable and looked around at the others. "All right. I apologize."

"For what, my dear?" The Magician did not look up from his reading.

"You know very well. I acted like a petulant child, and I'm sorry."

That's fine, Eirlin. It's part of growing up.

"Don't push it, Sword. I'm not apologizing to you. You don't need it."

You don't think I have feelings to be hurt?

Eirlin's hand clamped down on Kitten's sheath. "I don't think your feelings were hurt at all. In fact, I think this is all going exactly the way you want it to."

Whatever do you mean?

"I mean that ever since I have known you I have noted how you manipulate people. When Ecmund first brought you home, it was one of your worst habits."

I have since learned other methods to achieve my objectives.

"Which neatly ducks my point. I know what you're doing, and since you make no apologies for it, then I fail to see the need to make any."

That sounds fair.

"Now, why does this sudden agreement not make me feel any better?"

I don't know, Eirlin. I thought that was part of your ethos. Getting people to agree. You should be ecstatic.

"Well, I'm not, but that's neither here nor there. Tyrbrand, what is our next plan?"

"Plan?"

"Put down that scroll and stop acting innocent. What are we going to do now?"

"There is another Reception scheduled. We might attend."

"We should. For any specific reason?"

"Just to keep aware of what is happening and who is making it happen. Who is meeting with whom, that sort of thing."

She shrugged, smiled. "I suppose I could wear that new dress Gavia picked out for me."

12.   A Lesson for Two

Trouble, Eirlin.

The Healer glanced back along the deserted street. The tall stone facades of the Maridon quarter offered little hope of sanctuary "Danger?"

No. Trouble. Ahead. Someone is arguing just around the corner.

As Eirlin strode forward, Kitten helped the words become clearer to her, the emotions stronger.

"Mind your betters, barbarian scum!"

"Listen, you Maridon snot! You keep your hands off her."

"I never touched her. Why would I want to?"

"Then why is she crying? Just the look of your ugly black face, I suppose."

A man's voice broke in. "All right. What's going on here?"

There was a sudden silence. "Nothing, sir."

"That's not what I heard. Charche, are these young ruffians giving you trouble?"

"Um...no, sir. I can handle them."

"Well, I hope so. We can't have blond barbarians roaming the streets, roughing up decent people."

"What do you mean, roughing up? He was the one who..."

The man's voice rose. "Listen, you little gutter snipe. If you had any upbringing, you would know that you don't speak to your betters with that tone."

"Betters? Who gives you the right to speak of betters?"

"What? You dare to argue with me? I'll have the proctors on you! What's your name?"

"One you should know, so you could..."

At this moment Eirlin rounded the corner, her left hand firmly clasped over Kitten's hilt, her mouth a straight line. She forced her voice to be calm.

"Good afternoon, gentlemen. Is there a problem?"

A Maridon man, arrested in the act of reaching for the throat of the young blond boy in front of him, turned his sneer to Eirlin. "Nothing that a good thrashing wouldn't cure."

She stood, regarding him with interest but saying nothing. He was a short, dark man, dressed as a tradesman. The Inderjornese lad in front of him was about twelve years old, obviously of better class, although his clothing was not as clean as it should be. Several other boys stood around in various poses of aggression, and a little girl

100

pressed against the wall of the nearest building, her mouth agape, her tears forgotten.

Fear. Can you feel it?

Yes. What is he afraid of?

The boy. You.

Me?

You are taller. He hates looking up to colourless faces.

My face is not...

Concentrate, Eirlin.

The man's belligerent pose wavered. "This boy and his friends were attacking people in the street."

"Attacking? Were you, yourself, in danger?"

"No, not me. These good lads here."

The two boys in the front of the Maridon group had the grace to look guilty.

"I see. Perhaps I can be of some assistance." She turned to the leader of the Inderjornese. "What happened?"

"Charche and Rodri were teasing Goodrund, here, and we went to help her."

"I see. And how did you approach them?"

"What do you mean? I just told them to stop."

"There are ways of telling people to stop that say all sorts of things. How did you tell them?"

The boy's sandal scuffed the pavement. "I suppose I might have been a bit...quarrelsome."

"Right. And I suppose he answered the same way?" She held up her hand to forestall the Maridon boy's protest. "And then you started teasing each other. Very mature."

Both boys hung their heads.

She focused on the blond boy. "What should you have done when he started teasing you?"

"I don't know."

"Yes, you do."

He glanced up at her, and the rest of the defiance left his stance. "Said to myself, 'He's having a bad day,' and laughed and walked away?"

"What kind of laugh?"

"What do you mean?"

"What kind of laugh?" The Healer's eyes pinned the lad.

"I guess a laugh that says, 'I'm not bothered.' But he always teases us, and it does bother me!"

"And what do you do when he teases you the second time?"

The boy moved his head from side to side. "I'm supposed to say to myself, 'He's having a bad week,' and laugh and walk away."

"And if he teases you a third time?"

This time the boy was sure of the lesson. "Then I say to myself, 'He's having a bad life,' and I tell someone, so they can help him."

"That's right. And how do you deal with people like that, who have a bad life?"

"The only way to deal with those people is to show them by example the proper way to behave."

"Correct. You have learned your lessons well."

"Thank you, my Lady."

"But you have yet to apply them to your own life."

The boy's smile faded. "Yes, my Lady."

"Work on it, and I think you will succeed. It's just the next step, and you are ready for it."

As she turned away, the Maridon man stepped forward. "Um...if these boys were truly at fault...I will...um...punish them, my Lady."

"You may do what you think you must, sir, but I did not punish this lad. I hope I gave him a lesson that means something."

The dark man thought a moment. "It certainly seemed to make a difference."

She smiled. "I hope so. I bid you a good day, sir."

The man bowed his head slightly. "And you, my Lady."

As she turned away, there was a pattering of footsteps and the blond boy jogged up beside her. "My Lady, may I walk with you?"

"I'm going to the Ostersund ceasterhof. Where are you going?"

"I'm going to walk with you, my Lady."

"As you wish. What is your name?"

"Rhysun."

"It is a pleasure to make your acquaintance, Rhysun."

They walked down the street, and she could see that he was making up his mind.

"I saw what you did, my Lady."

"Did you?"

"Yes. That Maridon man wanted to fight."

"In a way."

"And you told us that we were not to fight. That we were to show by example. So, instead of fighting, you showed him how he should have dealt with us. And he believed you."

She smiled. "And you helped me."

"Did I?"

"You made it work. If you had run away screaming abuse at me it wouldn't have been such a good example, would it?"

He grinned. "I suppose not."

They strolled in companionable silence for a while. Again, the boy seemed to be getting up his nerve.

"I know who you are, my Lady."

"Do you?"

"Of course. Everyone knows about the Healer who wears the Sword. Everyone knows the story."

"What story is that?"

"About how your brother saved you from bandits by attacking twenty of them by himself and killing ten with his magic Sword." His eyes glistened with fervor.

"So you know about the magic Sword, do you?"

"Aye. Everyone knows about the Cat with Many Claws."

That is a Name!

"The Cat with Many Claws. Do you know what that means?"

"Of course. It means she has huge talons to rip and tear her enemies." He made enthusiastic slashing motions with clawed hands.

"But a Sword only has one point."

The boy looked puzzled.

"If a Sword only has one point, yet they call her the 'Cat with Many Claws,' it must mean something different."

The boy frowned, thinking furiously. "I see. I suppose it does. What does it mean?"

"You'll have to think on that, won't you? But I will tell you something that might help. You have the story a little bit wrong. There were only fifteen bandits. My cousin, Jesco, who is a very good swordsman, killed six of them before he fell. My brother faced the others, but he only made one swing with his Sword. He struck the leader's sword and broke it. Then all the bandits ran."

"He only broke a sword?"

"That's right. She can tell when there is a flaw in the steel, and she strikes true."

"So he won the fight without really fighting?"

"Exactly. My brother has never fought with the Sword. They have always found another way to solve their problems. Does this help you understand her Name?"

"Oh. I see...I think."

"Good. I hope that helps you understand."

"Oh, it does, my Lady, it does. Thank you so much."

"And now I have reached my destination. Thank you, Rhysun, for your escort. It was a pleasure speaking with you."

The boy made a presentable bow. "The pleasure was all mine, my Lady." With a final grin, he turned and sprinted back up the street.

Eirlin turned into the doorway, shaking her head and smiling.

I have a Name!

"It seems you do. Do you like it?"

The Cat with Many Claws. What do you think it means?

"As I said to young Rhysun, you're going to have to think about that."

I suppose I am. The Cat with Many Claws. I like it. It has a ring to it.

Later that evening, while Eirlin was poring over some texts she had found at the Infirmary, there was a commotion down at the front door. Soon a rather red-faced Eowin came to her.

"There is a gentleman to see you, my Lady."

"Oh. Well, show him up."

"But my Lady...It is Lord Skonric."

"Hmm. I wonder why he would wish to see me? We don't exactly move in the same circles. I have never even met him."

"Should I get Lord Ostersund, my Lady?"

"I'm not sure. How did Lord Skonric seem?"

"He seemed quite calm, my Lady, and very polite."

"Then bring him to the small reception room downstairs and inform Lord Ostersund."

"Yes, my Lady."

Don't worry, Eirlin. We can handle him.

"I'm not worried. Just interested."

When Eirlin was properly ensconced in the prime chair in the formal room, the servant opened the door, and Lord Skonric strode in. Eirlin remembered his stance from the Conclave the week before. There was no discourtesy in his demeanour now. Up close, he looked younger, less sure of himself.

"My Lady, I apologize for disturbing you at home."

"Not at all, my Lord." She rose. "I am honoured by such distinguished company. What brings you to visit me?"

"My son. I am here to ascertain the extent of his error."

"Your son?"

"Yes, Rhysun. I understand he was the cause of some difficulty today."

"Oh, Rhysun! Of course. I didn't ask his family name. It wasn't a formal sort of situation. More of a chat."

"A chat, you say? I am given to understand that he caused you a great deal of trouble with one of our Maridon friends."

"Trouble? Not at all, my Lord. In fact, I took the opportunity to make a clear point, which was received very well."

"But he said he helped you beat a Maridon in an argument."

Eirlin thought a moment. "I suspect there is a misunderstanding. I wish that Rhysun himself were here, since he is the topic of the discussion."

"He is here, but I left him in the anteroom while I determined the level of his guilt."

"Well, by all means, let us have him in to aid in the discussion."

Eowin is outside. Listening.

She rose, opened the door and nodded to the servant, who disappeared immediately, returning with the boy in tow.

"Rhysun, well met once again. I did not know you were of such a distinguished family. Would you and your father like to sit?"

The father and Eirlin did so, but the boy hung his head and remained standing. "I did not wish to bring dishonour to my family after I had acted in such a childish way."

"Ah, but we solved that, didn't we? Now, what is this your father tells me about you helping me to beat the Maridon man?"

"Not beat, my Lady, best. We didn't beat him at all, did we? We followed our training and showed him the proper behaviour, and he saw it and learned. He said so."

Lord Skonric looked to his son, then to Eirlin. "You think my son acted wisely?"

She smiled. "Not at first. He made an error, which was a learning experience in itself. Then, when I demonstrated the proper behaviour, he followed my lead perfectly. The Maridon man was forced to consider my actions, and I think he learned from the experience. Rhysun and I had a good chat about it while he escorted me home. I think he had a good learning experience himself."

"Is that how you see it, son?"

"Oh, yes, Father. Lady Eirlin told me many things that I must think about. Learning lessons for the sake of learning may be useful, but I have not demonstrated complete mastery of a lesson until I can apply it to my own life."

Lord Skonric shook his head. "Which I have been trying to beat into him for years."

Eirlin gestured with open palm. "Often a stranger can put something in a different way, and communicate what has already been told, but perhaps not yet heard."

"Well, I'm glad to hear he comported himself well. What was the original problem? The usual teasing, I gather?"

"It is to be expected. When adults are acting badly, their children can't help but learn the wrong lessons."

Now we attack!

The lord's brow clouded. "I fail to see how that applies."

"Lord Skonric, I heard how you spoke in the Conclave. You took that attitude into your home last week, your son brought the same feelings into the street today, and I have the same response to both of you. Our people have been taught better, and I look to them to apply their learning to their lives."

Skonric's mouth opened, and he took a deep breath.

"No, my Lord. It is not me you need to argue with. If you do not agree with the ethos of our people, fair enough; it is your choice. However, if you truly understand the lore of our ancestors, which has allowed us to control the Powers with which we are blessed, then you must follow the teachings of that lore. Not because anyone forces you to, but because they work."

The man expelled his breath and sat a moment, bemused. Finally, he spoke. "It would be unseemly to argue this point in front of my son, who has obviously learned the lesson better than I have."

He rose. "Come, Rhysun. We have used up enough of this good lady's time. You and I have some lessons to talk about," he shot a glance at Eirlin, "and perhaps I will learn something from you."

The Magician comes.

"Perhaps you would like to speak with Lord Ostersund."

"Briefly, before we depart. It would only be polite. Oh, there you are, Ostersund. I believe you know my son, Rhysun. I was just having a chat with your Healer friend here about the health of the realm. It seems we all have some learning to do."

He bowed formally, motioned to his son to do likewise, and departed.

The Magician regarded Eirlin a moment. "Surprise after surprise. What plots are you making now?"

"I'm not exactly sure, Tyrbrand. I helped his son out with a little problem with some Maridon boys this afternoon, and the father came around to make sure Rhysun hadn't offended me."

"And was he reassured?"

She grinned. "You know me. Couldn't resist the opportunity for a lesson."

"A lesson? What do you have to teach Lord Skonric?"

"Nothing but the same lessons he learned when he was a child. Sometimes we just need the obvious pointed out to us, you know?"

"Well, that's as polite as he's spoken to me for several years, so you must have made some progress."

"I think I did."

"Well done, Eirlin. If we could just reach a few more of them..." He ran a hand over his face, and she could see his shoulders droop.

A rush of pity flooded through her and she stepped closer to him. "Come, Tyrbrand. Up to the sitting room, and let me get you a hot drink."

His smile lacked its usual confidence. "I have servants for that."

"Not this hot drink. Created and served by my own hands. Come."

You take unfair advantage. He has no energy to argue.

Exactly.

Eirlin helped him upstairs to the sitting room and bustled out, leaving Kitten with the Magician.

You must listen to her more, my Lord Magician.

"You take unfair advantage, Kitten. I have no energy to argue."

That was a private conversation!

"Then don't shout."

I heard something today.

"Did you? Something about a Name, perhaps?"

How did you know?

"As I may have mentioned, you have difficulty keeping your inner voice down. Perhaps you should work on 'Silent Stalker,' or some such Name."

Phht.

"And so you have a Name. A real one, created by the people."

It seems so. The Cat with Many Claws. Eirlin says it means something.

"A Name always has meaning."

But she says it has more than one meaning. I don't understand.

"Perhaps the fact that your Name has many meanings might help you understand how a Sword can have many claws."

What?

"Think on it, my young friend. Perhaps it will come to you."

You always do that.

"Yes, I do, don't I? A good habit, I think."

A good habit, I don't think.

"Exactly. And I'm trying to get you to."

What...? Oh. You are a very frustrating Magican.

"Known a few, have you?"

No. You would be frustrating if you were a pig farmer, I'm sure.

"I once had a good friend who was a pig farmer."

What happened? Did he finally get tired of you and throw you out?

Eirlin swished the door open, followed by Eowin, each carrying a tray. "Kitten, are you insulting our host?"

Me? Insulting him?

"No, my dear. We were just passing the time with idle chat."

Kitten sent a tight thought. *You're blushing again, Eirlin.*

He looked at the servant, the trays. "I thought you went for a hot drink."

"This hot drink goes better with food."

"I wonder if I have the energy for a meal this size."

"If you don't, just relax and I will feed it to you."

"Is that a threat?"

"Yes."

"What do you think, Kitten? She talks grandly about lessons, but once the bets have been laid, she's as bossy as the rest of them."

She is not! If Eirlin wanted to be bad, she would be much worse than the rest of them. Who are the rest of them?

"I'd like to hear the answer to that one, as well, Tyrbrand."

"Sorry, ladies, I don't have the energy to eat, drink, and argue. Pick two."

You eat and drink; I'll argue. It's the only one I can do, anyway.

"There you go. A very sensible cat, don't you think? In spite of her many claws."

13.   The Wild Wolf of the West

I am Black Star, Wild Wolf of the North.

Eirlin put one hand to her forehead, dropping the thread she had been using to teach Excisor to stitch. "Not this again."

Ostersund laughed. "Sorry that happened. I had no idea…"

What is this 'Black Star' about? Kitten regarded the little Scalpel's dancing mind.

"It was that ballad singer Tyrbrand took us to hear the other day. He sang a song about a wolf. Our little friend seems to have found it compelling."

Black Star, Wild Wolf of the North. Scourge of the Tundra. What is Scourge, Healer Eirlin? What is Tundra?

Don't worry, Eirlin. I can handle this. Hey, Little Tooth?

Yes, Big Cat?

I'm sorry, little guy, but you cannot be Black Star, Wild Wolf of the North.

Black Star, Feared by…not?

Not.

Why?

Because there already is one.

Is one?

Of course. The one they wrote the song about. You can't be him, because he already is.

Want to.

Well, you can't.

Can so.

No, you can't.

Can so.

Look, why don't you be Fang, Wild Wolf of the West instead? You'd be the only one of those, I'm sure.

Fang?

Yes. You know, a fang is a big, sharp tooth. Very appropriate, in your case.

Fang, Wild Wolf of the West!

That's it.

Eirlin, I am Fang!

Eirlin, why are you laughing?

"Because you just gave little Excisor a Name."

No!

"Oh, yes you did. Listen to him."

Fang, Wild Wolf of the West. Fang the Feared, Fang the Ferocious.
Where does he find these words?

"Tyrbrand has educated him very well."

The Magician looked up from the scroll he was reading. "Hah! It was one useful way to keep him occupied."

I will not call him Fang.

"You don't have to. It's too late."

Fang the Fabulous. Fing Fang fong. Sing a song.
Why did you have to teach him to sing?

"Because it was better than listening to him yowl."

He is a very small Tooth with a very big mouth.

Tyrbrand snorted again. "A very sharp tooth. He nipped me yesterday."

Eirlin jumped to her feet. "He did what?"

"Took a nip at me. He hadn't been listening to the lesson, and I picked him up to get his attention. I felt a definite pang in my hand, as if it had been bitten."

"Why didn't you tell me?" Eirlin picked up the Scalpel. "Excisor...!"

"No, no, it's fine. I dealt with it."

She lowered her hand slowly. "What did you do?"

"I threw him across the room."

"You did what?"

"I threw him. Don't worry, he wasn't hurt. I just needed to give him an instant reaction that he wouldn't forget. There's a big wooden table in my workshop, and I tossed him, end-over-end like a throwing dagger, and stuck him into the leg. Deep. Then I walked out and left him there for a good, long think. He was very polite when I came back. Weren't you, Little Tooth?"

Fang is always polite.

"And what did...Fang learn from this?"

No biting.

"That's right. Biting hurts people, and Fang does not hurt people. Right?"

Yes, Magician. Fang never, never, hurts people.

The Magician glanced at Eirlin, his eyebrows raised. She nodded solemnly.

Kitten sent her a tight message. *A difficult lesson that must be learned. The Magician did well.*

"Yes, Tyrbrand, I think that was properly done. My experience is that any reaction to a fault must be immediate if it is to have effect."

"That is what I thought. Immediate and appropriate."

She sighed. "Sometimes I wish I could do that with adults."

"Throw them across the room? Has your brother been teasing you again?"

The Magician is feeling better today.

"No Tyrbrand. I have no need to toss Ecmund around. I was speaking politically."

He winced. "I was trying to avoid that. However, now that you have brought up the subject, I think it's time we went and talked to the king."

Her hand jumped to his arm. "Oh, no, Tyrbrand. I didn't mean that you should..."

His hand covered hers. "Not at all. With you and Kitten here to help with Fang, and Perica to keep an ear to the ground politically, we have done well. I think we can arrange your audience soon."

"What audience?"

"It is time we laid our cards out. Having all of you there will help me make this situation real to the king. Up till now he hasn't known what to believe, in spite of what has been staring him in the face all his life. I've been thinking over what Jesco and Kitten told me about that mob scene da Baneza created. That information may be even more important than you think."

"Well, whatever you think is best, Tyrbrand. I know you're not going to listen to me anyway."

"Now you're sounding like my mother did. 'You leave your helmet at home if you like, Tyrbrand, and if you come back with your head broken, I won't say a word, not one word...' I always went back and got my helmet, because she was always right."

"I'm sure that was a compliment, but I never met your mother."

"It was a two-edged compliment, if you must know. Mother and I...let's just say we were a lot alike."

"I'll remember that." She pretended to write. "Comparison to mother: means he wants a fight."

"I did not say that!"

"You didn't have to." She smoothed her dress. "So, we are going to meet the king?"

"I think it wise, before Perica and Ecmund return to Falkenby. Once he has gone but Kitten remains here, things get...problematic."

"Yes, I can't very well wander around the city wearing a Sword, can I?"

I can be very inconspicuous.

"Yes, that's a point. Most people won't notice you."

Eirlin shook her head. "Most people won't, but those who are inclined to violence will be more likely to see her. Swordsmen and the like."

"We'll have to be discreet, that's all." He stood. "Now, I have a letter to write."

"So do I buy another dress?"

"Definitely not." He turned in the doorway. "This isn't a frilly occasion. This is business."

"I'm sure Perica will disagree. Please let us know as soon as you can."

"I bow to the dictates of female propriety." He suited his action to the words and left.

Kitten could feel a definite bounce to his step. *He is better.*

"Not better enough, but there's no holding him back. I know that." She hefted the Scalpel. "The best we can do is take as much of his other burdens as we can. You, my young friend..."

Fang knows. No biting.

"That's right, and don't you forget it. Why don't you go into your sheath and think about that."

Fang is good. Tries hard.

"Yes, well, if you try really hard and are very good, maybe I'll take you when I go to see the king."

Fang see the king?

Oops. Not a good idea, Eirlin.

Fang go to palace, see king. Talk to king. Tell king that Fang is good, help the king.

"No, dear, I don't think you'll get to talk to the king. Just see him."

Fang talk to king. Tell him Fang is a good Scalpel.

"That will be up to the king. We'll have to see."

Fang talk to king.

"Right now, Fang needs to prove that he is a good Scalpel, and go into his sheath and be quiet for a while."

Yes, Healer. Fang will be good. Talk to king. Fang likes...

The sound was cut off as the sheath closed over him. Kitten chuckled. *I think you started something, Eirlin.*

"I know. He is so stubborn. I don't know if I dare take him, now."

I don't think you dare not take him.

"Kitten, we can't have him dictating what is going to happen. He already has an exaggerated idea of his own importance. If he won't cooperate, I'll just have to stay home as well."

Hmm. Maybe not so exaggerated.

14. King Vetrorrillo da Marida

Ecmund gazed up at the wall that towered over them. "Is this a big castle, Lord Ostersund?"

"Compared to what?"

Ecmund shrugged. "I don't know. To those in the rest of the world?"

Ostersund laughed. "It's the biggest castle in Inderjorne. I have heard that the king in Marida has a larger palace, but it's not quite so much of a fortification." He waved his hand at the tiers of stone stepping up the hillside in front of them, turrets ablaze with banners, sentries at every corner.

"Fair enough. Where do we go in?"

The Magician nodded to a small street that led off to the left. "That way. Those of us who know can access the throne room without running the gauntlet of all the courtiers and hangers-on in the public galleries."

Ostersund led the way with the ease of familiarity, obviously well known to the guards and officials who populated the many rooms and corridors between the street and the centre of power of the realm.

He touched his forehead with a finger in response to the salute of a well-armed sentry and ushered them through an ornate teak door with brass trim. "This is the king's conference room. We get polite from here on."

The party from Falkenby followed him respectfuly.

The room was as large as the Great Hall at Falkengard. It was lit by clerestory windows above tapestried walls, but the lower corners were dim. The king sat waiting for them, a look of pleasant interest on his face. He was a handsome man of medium size, dark of hair and skin, probably in his middle thirties. There was no ceremony, but they approached with measured pace nonetheless.

Danger. Hide!

Why...?

Do not argue. Hide!

Yes, Big Cat. I am gone.

The little knife disappeared like a spark hitting water.

Kitten sent a fine trickle of thought through Ecmund's palm.

Danger, Ecmund. He is Sensitive.

The king? How much?

Like you. Little Tooth has hidden. I am not here.

Ecmund sent his sister a glance. How much she had caught of the interchange was difficult to say, but the look she sent back revealed that she was warned.

"So, Lord Ostersund. Finally I get to meet your prodigies from the wilds."

It was a rich voice, overlaid with confidence and a certain extra tone that ranged into their minds. The king sat on...not really a throne, as this was his informal meeting room, but on a chair ornate enough to show his importance. The group from Falkenby knelt in front of him, each carefully dressed: not too formal, not too casual. Perica had made it very clear.

"Yes, Sire. This is Eirlin Bryghtwyn Falconric, and her brother, Ecmund Liutswin. Perica Delfontes da Falken has been presented to you."

They made appropriate bows, and the king motioned them to rise. "Ah, yes. Perica who wishes to be designated heir to the demesne of Falken."

"Yes, your Majesty. My father has sent the documents for your approval."

The king merely nodded and turned to the others. "So, Lady Eirlin, they tell me you are a Healer."

"An inexperienced one, your Majesty."

"But effective, nonetheless."

"I have studied hard, and I have had some success."

The smooth brow furrowed. "It does me no good to speak in empty polite phrases. Lord Ostersund has led me to believe you are much more than a simple country Healer."

Ecmund stroked Kitten's hilt.

Easy, girl. She can handle this.

She had better. If he is mean to her, he will be very sorry.

Very sorry. Grrr.

Go back and hide, Little Tooth. You will know if I need you.

Yes, Big Cat.

Again, there was complete emptiness.

This exchange had taken only a heartbeat, but something seemed to be bothering the king.

"Please, Lady Eirlin, I do not mean to be rude. I truly wish to know about your abilities. The problem is that I feel I am a good judge of character, and I am not getting the good feelings about you that I was led to expect."

His eyes turned to Tyrbrand.

The lord grimaced slightly. "Then I suspect a certain degree of frankness is required on all sides, Sire."

The king frowned. "By which you mean?"

"I mean that you and I have discussed my abilities at great length, your Majesty, and I have alluded to yours, but I never found it the proper time to discuss them in detail. Perhaps now, in this company, is the time.

"My abilities."

"Yes, Sire. You being such a fine 'judge of character,' as you put it."

"Do you suggest I am not?"

"Quite the contrary. I suggest you are more than that."

"Are you speaking of Powers like your own?"

Why do they beat around and around? Is this some strange duel?

Hush, Kitten. Let Tyrbrand do it his way.

Phht.

"I am getting uneasy feelings again, Lord Ostersund. Do I have reason to lose my confidence in you?"

"Quite the contrary, your Majesty. You are about to receive sure confirmation of all I have told you."

"Am I? Then show me."

Tyrbrand looked at the two other Blood. "How shall we do this?"

Ecmund frowned. "You mean he doesn't know?"

"Not really. He's been like this all his life; he thinks it's natural."

"Is he of the Blood?"

"I sincerely doubt it. I think he is like Perica."

"Then I suppose we should introduce him to Kitten. That seems to work."

"When you have ceased your discussion, perhaps you would find it amusing to let your sovereign know the result."

Why does he talk like that?

Perhaps he thinks it good manners.

Manners. Pfft.

"A certain amount of ceremony would be appropriate, your Majesty."

"Which ceremony is that?"

"I will guide you through it, Sire."

"Very well. Proceed." The king sat straighter on his throne.

He likes this.

I have no idea why some people love ceremony so much.

It makes him feel important.

"Ecmund, kneel and present your Sword."

The Hand did so, holding his Sword by the blade just below the quillions. "I, Ecmund Liutswin Falconric of the Blood of Falken, do hereby present my Sword to my rightful king, and swear to use it and all my powers in every way possible to aid in the proper ruling of this realm."

The king frowned slightly, thinking over the meaning of that oath.

"Now you, Sire."

"What is the form?"

"I, King Vetrorrillo da Marida of Inderjorne do accept your fealty..."

"I, King Vetrorrillo da Marida of Inderjorne do accept your fealty..."

"And do swear to use your Sword and your powers only for the good of this realm."

"And do swear to use your Sword and your powers..." The king shot Ostersund a frowning glance. The lord nodded forcefully, and gestured to continue.

"...only for the good of this realm."

"Now touch the hilt, your Majesty."

The king placed his hand firmly on Kitten's pommel. Without her volition, words came to her. *I, Ailur, Cloud Cat of the Leute, Cat with Many Claws, do swear my fealty to King Vetrorrillo da Inderjorne, and swear to use my powers in every way possible to aid in the proper ruling of this realm.*

The king's hand leapt away as if burned. "What was that?"

Lord Ostersund leaned forward urgently. "I, King Vetrorrillo da Marida of Inderjorne do accept your fealty..."

"Ostersund, what was that?"

"I, King Vetrorrillo da Marida..."

The king shook his head, gingerly placed his hand back. "I, King Vetrorrillo da Marida of Inderjorne do accept your fealty..."

"And do swear to use your powers only for the good of this realm."

"And do swear to use your powers...only for the good of this realm." The king raised his eyebrows towards Ostersund, who nodded gravely. The king removed his hand, slowly, frowning at his palm.

He watched as Ecmund was about to sheathe Kitten, then raised a hand. Ecmund stopped, and everyone looked at Kitten's blade. There, emblazoned in red, were the words of the Name she had spoken. She could feel the heat from them, and her whole length reddened slightly in response.

"She is a bit of a show-off, your Majesty."

I am not a show-off. It is part of the ritual.

"I apologize, Kitten. You are correct. It is an auspicious occasion, and you have every right."

Thank you, Lord Ostersund. Ecmund, you may sheathe me, now. The king has questions.

"How do you know?"

She considered. *I'm not sure. When I pledged, I could feel the Power in him. Now I feel a bond of some sort. Like the one with Eirlin, but not so strong.*

Ecmund looked up at the king. "That is interesting, your Majesty. She says she feels a bond to you. She knows what you are feeling."

"Like the Magician, here?"

"I believe so, but probably not as strongly."

The king turned to Tyrbrand. "Well, I suppose that was entertaining for you."

"Why, Sire?"

"After all my doubts and cavils, you can finally throw that," he tossed a hand towards Kitten, "in my face, and what can I say?"

The Magician suppressed a smile. "Thank you?"

The king frowned. "I do not find this an occasion for flippancy, my Lord."

"Nor do I, your Majesty. I have been trying for five years to get you to understand what is going on in this kingdom. I know that the reason you listen to me is because you have questions about your own nature, and I am the only one who comes close to answers for you. Now, I bring you surety, and when you think of the advantage this will give you in the coming struggle, I believe you will feel gratitude." The Magician shrugged. "At the moment, I'm sure astonishment is pushing other thoughts out of your head, Sire."

The king passed a hand over his brow. "I think that would be safe to say."

Then he rose. "I do not find this an appropriate venue for this discussion." He turned to Ostersund. "May I assume the ceremonial part of my lesson is over?"

"It is, your Majesty."

"Then let us retire to my personal sitting room. We will have more privacy there. I feel the need for privacy."

He strode towards a door in the end wall of the throne room, his steps becoming firmer as he walked. The door opened silently as he approached, and he turned his head back to raise a meaningful eyebrow at Ostersund.

There are many listening.

Ecmund looked with renewed interest at the shadows edging the tapestries.

He knows. It protects him as well.

We will protect him, now.

Yes, I suppose we must. Ecmund patted her hilt.

As long as he works for the good of the realm.

And if he doesn't?

The Magician's forceful thought came. *We shall have to persuade him.*

When they were all seated in the small, ornately furnished sitting room in the king's personal quarters, he looked around at them. "Now, with much less likelihood of flapping ears, just what is going on here?"

Tyrbrand glanced at the others for permission to speak. "I think you might like to touch Kitten's hilt while I tell you. That will explain more than words." He gestured to the Sword on Ecmund's left hip, just by the king's hand.

"All right." The king smiled. "Kitten. Does she scratch?"

Only when it is deserved, your Majesty.

"I heard that! She spoke to me."

Ecmund grinned. "She obviously has respect, your Majesty. Usually she answers that question with a demonstration."

"Kitten, you would never scratch your monarch, would you?"

Probably not, Sire.

"Probably not. That sounds ominous."

Ecmund nodded. "She has an independent spirit, Sire. She will obey her oath to the letter and beyond, but she will reserve the right to interpret your participation."

"You mean she is judging me?"

"We are trying to train her to have good judgment, Sire."

"You see a need to train her."

"She is young, as Swords go. Just over a hundred and fifty years. She has lived a strange life, and there is much for her to learn. Some to unlearn."

"Well, I hope you are doing a good job of it. I see possibilities. Perhaps Tyrbrand would continue his explanation, so I can see how they fit."

"As I have been telling you, your Majesty, the role of the Blood has a far greater effect on the functioning of this realm than it is possible to perceive. Not to seem disrespectful, but your reign here is to some extent on sufferance. Has been since King Alcudo."

"I know, I know. These are the tales that everyone pays lip service to. King Alcudo could not subdue the realm, but the leaders of the Blood felt that their defence would destroy everyone, so they agreed to his ascension of the throne."

"It is regarding that lip service where you are wrong, Sire. Those of the Blood who remain have not forgotten their duties, nor their sense of responsibility for their people."

"You mean, the Blood still think they rule?"

"No, your Majesty. They still think it best that you rule. They support you. Usually, they agree that your assigned lords rule the various demesnes."

"That is gratifying."

"But sometimes they don't."

"And then what happens?"

Tyrbrand shrugged. "Hard to say. It doesn't happen often. Usually, even the thickest noble gets the picture after a while and changes his ways. Once he is properly trained, they leave him to rule."

"And if he doesn't learn?"

"He dies."

"Assassination? Are you telling me there is a secret cabal of old-time rulers controlling this realm, and if I don't rule properly, they will remove me?"

"That would be a very fearful way of putting it, your Majesty. Rather think that you have a secret group of supporters who throw their weight behind your best policies and ease their implementation."

"And where does this magic Sword fit in?"

A good question, Sire.

"She is a new element. No one knows how she managed to get out to Falkenby. There doesn't seem to be a reason or plan. She just showed up. The circumstances since have been wildly unusual, but all for the good, it seems."

"What makes them unusual?"

"A magic Sword usually speaks only to her Hand, and only to a Hand who deserves and needs her aid. By luck, Kitten found it necessary to speak to Eirlin first. Then she discovered that Perica, against all chance, was Sensitive to her as well. Finally, because Eirlin learned how to perform Healing using Kitten's powers, and because extra strength was needed desperately to save her cousin's life, she pulled me into the circle. Now she has added you, the only other who would normally interact with her. The count is six. Unless you have added others, Kitten?"

Kitten sent a tight message to him. *Fang?*

Not yet.

"So there you have it, your Majesty. Just at the moment when you have dissension in your realm, when you have a political sect with the intention of destroying those of the Blood who are left to support you, along come two elements. First, that you yourself and others of the Maridon ruling race have developed Sensitivity, and second, the Sword who can respond to you. Almost makes you wonder, doesn't it?"

The king sat for a moment, frowning and nodding slowly. "It does."

He turned to Eirlin, who had remained silent through all this. "And now I am told that you, my Lady, are one of those who support our reign. That you are one of the leaders."

She smiled, shook her head. "It was not something I sought, your Majesty, but nonetheless, it seems to be."

"And Tyrbrand tells me you have a special connection to your demesne."

"Again, that seems to be the simplest explanation."

"So here we have the crux of the matter. We have my reign, balanced on the support of my Maridon nobles and your leaders of the Blood. We have a group who seek to upset that balance. It would seem that one of my best solutions might be closer alliance with your side. I gather you are unmarried?"

Danger! Warning! Danger!

Cut! Cut!

No, love. Control yourself! Never cut in anger!

Control yourself, Little Tooth.

He must not!

He will not. Trust me, love.

Yes, Eirlin. Big Cat, he must not touch her!

Do not worry.

The king had drawn his hand away as if stung, and grasped his own sword hilt, head swiveling. "I feel danger here! What is going on?"

Tyrbrand stared at his liege until the king calmed, looking in bewilderment at the stony faces around him. "You were in danger, your Majesty. You have come very close to negating your contract with Kitten, and worse."

"How?"

Ostersund frowned, opened his mouth, closed it again, shook his head. "I...I'm not sure."

"You're not sure?"

"A lot of this is new to me as well, your Majesty. I have never observed the oath of fealty between a magic Sword and a ruler. The only wisdom I can bring to the situation is that it will not be a hard-and-fast set of rules. Kitten has preceding loyalties and ideas which must be taken into account."

"And one of these preceding loyalties has something to do with Lady Eirlin's marriage?"

Tyrbrand looked helplessly to Eirlin. She shrugged, glancing to her brother.

"I suppose the best thing is to ask the Sword herself. Kitten?"

Kitten sent her message to Ecmund alone. *Eirlin is betrothed to the Magician. She can wed no other.*

Ecmund frowned. *No, she isn't.*

Ask her.

I can't do that.

I will ask her.

Not with everyone listening.

Why not? Do you not want the truth?

I just can't.

Humans!

Ecmund looked around the circle. "I don't think she really has it straight herself. In her opinion, somehow Eirlin's marriage has already been decided. She will not allow any other."

"She will not allow? What kind of fealty do I get from one who will not allow me to do as I wish?"

Have him touch me.

Wordlessly, he held out the Sword. The king again laid his hand on the pommel.

It is my duty to keep you from making a mistake, Sire. What you want has little to do with it.

"How could it be a mistake? A mistake of the kind that would negate your fealty?"

'For the good of the realm,' your Majesty.

"In your opinion, my marrying Eirlin would not be for the good of the realm?"

Yes, your Majesty. Also for your own good.

"How for my own good?"

You are not much good to the realm if you are dead.

"Is that a threat?"

It is a fact.

"How would I die?"

I cannot say.

"You cannot say." The king turned to Ostersund. "She threatens me with death, and cannot say by what means. Of great use, this magic Sword."

It was Eirlin who responded. "He has to know some time, Tyrbrand."

"Then tell him."

She turned back to the king. "Do you know what Tyrbrand's task has been, for the past year?"

"I have given him several tasks."

"Not those. His real task."

"No, I don't demand to know what he does with his time."

"He has been learning to be a smith."

"What?"

"He learned to be a smith. Then he used his new skills, combined with his magic powers, as the Smith-Magicians of old."

"You have made a new magic Sword? You said that took a great deal more time and skill than can be gained in one year."

"Not a Sword, your Majesty." He motioned to Eirlin and she opened her pouch. She held out her hand, and Fang lay across her fingers.

Calmly, love. If you are good, you may speak to the king.

May I? May I, Eirlin? I will be polite.

I'm sure you will. Be calm, now.

"Is that a knife? It is so small."

I am not...

Calmly, Little Tooth.

Yes, Big Cat. I am calm. I will speak to the king.

"It is a Scalpel, your Majesty. It is to be used by a Healer, as a Hand uses his Sword, but for Healing only."

"I see."

"This Scalpel is brand new. Very young, you might say."

"I see. Another personality to deal with."

"Yes, but think of him as a little child. He has great skills and much Power, but there are many things he does not understand. I will be years in training him. All my life, and the lives of my children after me."

"And how does this youngster view my proposal, theoretical as it may have been, that I marry you?"

Eirlin looked around helplessly. "I don't know. I was a bit taken aback, myself."

You were completely shocked. Every fibre of your body shouted against it.

Oh, come on, Kitten. Against the king?

Every fibre cried for the Magician.

Oh. And Fang?

He felt the same. How could he feel otherwise?

She returned her gaze to the king. "I understand now, your Majesty. It seems that in some way these two have made up their minds that I am to wed another. In the case of Kitten, that means she will advise you, and do all in her power to persuade you, not to make the mistake of forcing a union. With my little Scalpel, it is a different matter. He is not as mature. If I am in some way prevented from controlling him, he might make a mistake. Tyrbrand and I had expected that in normal circumstances I would have to be in contact with the patient before I could use the Powers of the Scalpel. We even hoped that it might not be necessary to physically cut into the patient to heal.

"These are not normal circumstances, because this experiment has never been tried before. We suspect now that my Scalpel can cut from a distance, with no need of contacting the patient at all. He could cut deep within the patient's body and leave no wound on the surface."

"What you are saying is that you could kill me from across the room and there would not be a mark on my body."

"I believe that to be the case and it concerns us, because he is so young and has such little self-control. No being should be given more power than he can control himself. We will have to find some way to experiment with this in the coming months, and train him at the same time. We will inform you."

The king leaned back in his chair, regarding Eirlin for a long time. "That is a very dangerous weapon you hold, my Lady."

There didn't seem to be an appropriate answer.

"Your Majesty, I believe I could contribute to your understanding of this situation."

Everyone turned to Perica. Until now, she had not been her usual bubbly self. In fact, once she had made her obeisance, she had retreated into the background. Now, she sat straighter, determination on her face.

"What wisdom do you bring, Perica Delfontes?"

"I have been through the same situation, your Majesty. I, too, have some of the powers of the Blood, and no one knows why. I, too, was shocked to discover a magical Object which had a personality, which could communicate with me to help or hinder me in my desires."

"I see. And how do you advise me, now?"

She smiled, with a trace of the usual impish twist. "It's this way, your Majesty. When I first met Eirlin, she was quiet and unassuming, and kind and helpful, and I thought everyone loved her. Then I got to know her."

"And...?"

"And she is quiet, unassuming, kind, and helpful, and everyone loves her. And nobody gets in her way. Ever. As soon as my father understood this small detail, his takeover of the Falken demesne became smooth. The Magic Sword became an asset as well."

"And there is a message in this for me?"

She shrugged, turning the gesture into a seated curtsey.

He laughed. "So what happened in your demesne is happening here, and your advice is to sit back and let it happen, because there is nothing I can do about it anyway."

"Everyone here has the good of the realm in mind, your Majesty."

"And at the moment, the good of the realm involves me being king, so I should be happy."

She inclined her head gracefully.

She is so sophisticated.

Isn't she wonderful? Why would a woman like that be interested in me?

Because you are wonderful.

Thanks. You are biased.

Of course. What does biased mean?

It means you love me.

Well, there we are, then.

The king nodded. "And one of my talents, apparently, is the ability to bow to the inevitable."

"That is called diplomacy, your Majesty."

"Thank you for your approval, Lord Ostersund. Obviously I must look elsewhere." He smiled meaningfully at Perica. "Perhaps one of more obvious Maridon ancestry, but with first-hand knowledge of these matters?"

A wash of emotion pushed him back against his chair. It took a moment for everyone to take control of themselves, for Ecmund to calm Kitten, for Eirlin to control Fang.

After a while, silence descended on the room. The king wiped sweat from his brow, glanced around the circle, gave a hesitant smile. "Spoken for already, I gather?"

"Yes, your Majesty. Ecmund and I are officially betrothed."

"I don't recall you asking your king's permission."

"I don't recall you appointing me official heir, your Majesty."

"I see. And once I appoint you official heir to the demesne of Falken, I can then direct your marriage."

"I am sorry, your Majesty, but that would set in train a very complicated set of events…"

"Which would bring in the Powers I have just recently felt arrayed against me."

Talk to king. Eirlin said.

The Magician's powerful thought answered. *Yes, time for a change of subject, Eirlin.*

"Speaking of the Powers, your Majesty, we have a favour to ask."

"Of course. What do you wish?"

"My Scalpel is too young to understand swearing fealty, but he really would like to speak to you. Would you oblige him?"

"I don't know. Does he bite or anything?"

"He will be on his best behaviour. He really is anxious to meet you."

"What do I have to do, then?"

"Just hold out your hand, please."

He did as she requested, and she placed the Scalpel on his palm.

"Hello little one. What is your name?"

Fang. I am Fang, the Healer's sharp tooth. I cut. I am very sharp. I cut very well.

"Hold on a moment there, youngster. I can't follow. You say your name is…Fang?"

Eirlin smiled. "His name is Excisor, your Majesty, but he finds that too complex."

I am Fang. I cut. Cut to heal.

"I see. You are Fang, and the Healer uses you to cut the bad things away from people."

King is very smart. Yes. Cut bad things.

"Well, I am very glad that you are helping Eirlin. She is a very important person to me. You will be very important to me as well, if you help her."

Help Eirlin. Important. Help king. Cut bad things.

"That's right. You do whatever Eirlin says, and learn to cut bad things."

He handed the Scalpel back to Eirlin, suppressing a smile. "He is very enthusiastic."

"Enthusiastic. Yes, your Majesty, he is that."

"I am glad I met him. I understand your problems a bit better."

Problems?

"Not you dear. Training you. We must do a lot of work so that you can help me to help the king."

Work. I work. I learn. Help Eirlin. Important to king.

Eirlin patted his handle, and replaced him in his sheath. "Thank you, your Majesty. He understood more of that than I expected. I think you made a friend."

"I need all the friends I can get."

The king sat straighter, regarded each of his visitors individually. "I thank you for coming. You have given me a lot to think about. Lord Ostersund, I believe that your actions have been committed in true fealty. I will consider all your suggestions, and the ideas you have expressed at other times, with that point in mind."

The formal statement closed the interview, and they all rose, bowing and curtseying as required. Since this was an informal meeting, they all left together.

Eirlin stopped in the doorway and regarded the king for a moment, sitting alone in his ornate chair in the richly crowded room. Then she walked back. "Your Majesty, I think it would be good to remind you that every one of us is completely committed to the good of this kingdom, and all of us have freely sworn fealty to you. You would have to accomplish a complete inanity to lose our support."

The king only shook his head. "I'm sure most would not take it so, Eirlin Bryghtwyn, but that actually makes me feel better."

"Good. That was my intention." She smiled at him, then turned and joined her friends at the door.

That was very nice, Eirlin.

"He was sad, Kitten. Sad and worried. He has a difficult job to do."

We will help him. He cannot fail.

Yes. Help. Big Cat and little Fang will help.

Eirlin laughed. "Yes, love, you can help, too."

15.   A Maridon Healer?

"Say, it's that Healer again."

Eirlin turned. A group of Maridon children was scattered along the street and she recognized a few from the earlier meeting.

"Hello, boys."

One of the older ones glanced at his companions. "Good day, my Lady."

"And what are you about today?"

Again he checked his friends for their reaction. "Just looking around, my Lady."

"And have you decided that I am to be your entertainment?"

He grinned. "I suppose so."

Eirlin.

Yes, Kitten. I can feel him. Which one is it?

I can't tell. They keep moving around.

Keep looking.

"And how can I entertain you today?"

"I don't know, my Lady, but we have hopes. The last time we met, you were quite amazing."

"In what way?"

"You managed to get us out of a beating we probably deserved."

"Would it have done any good? I could still arrange one, if you prefer."

"No, my Lady. That has been tried before, and it only made me mad. I would have been more careful not to get caught next time."

I can startle him. You watch out for the one that jumps.

Be gentle, Kitten. Try something funny.

Funny? I think I can do that.

She sent out an image of the Maridon man from the previous encounter with his pants falling down. A smaller boy, hanging back from the group, giggled, then put his hand over his mouth as all eyes turned to him.

"Don't worry about him, my Lady. That's Bejarin da Tiena. He's a bit strange, but he's all right."

Eirlin smiled at Bejarin, then turned along the street. "Well, I don't mind being entertaining, but I have a meeting to attend at the infirmary by the West Gate. Would you like to walk along with me?"

"With pleasure, my Lady."

Once they were moving and the rest of the lads were strung out behind, Eirlin could speak more privately. "What is so strange about Bejarin?"

"Oh, I don't know. He just seems to know things he shouldn't. But his father is important, so we let him tag along. He's the best lookout you could ask for. Always spots the proctors before anyone else."

"Not quite the best." A second boy had pushed up on her other side.

"What do you mean?"

The boy shrugged. "He's a good lookout if he wants to be, but if he doesn't like what we're doing, he's no good at all."

The other lad laughed. "He's worse than no good. Ask Rodri."

Eirlin looked from one to the other. "Is there a story here?"

"Oh, yes. Rodri – he's not here now – he's sometimes pretty mean. He's the one who took Goody's book the other day and started the whole mess. A while ago he found a kitten and was tossing it up in the air. Bejarin told him to stop. He said, 'of course,' and threw the kitten into the fountain."

The second boy took up the tale with enthusiasm. "Bejarin went completely strange. Started yelling at Rodri and hitting him. You know, he's just a little guy, but he's strong. When he hits you, it hurts!"

"If he stood up to a larger boy for hurting a kitten, I'm impressed."

Both boys laughed. "Rodri was impressed, that's for sure."

"So when Bejarin is with you, you're not mean to any person or animal."

"No. It isn't worth it. As I said, his father is important."

"And he hits really hard!"

Eirlin laughed. "Whatever the reason, I think he's a good influence. You keep him around."

"Yes, my Lady. Whatever you say."

"He is the best lookout we've got."

"I'm not going to ask what you need a lookout for. I know boys your age too well."

"You're very wise, my Lady."

She dipped him a curtsey. "Thank you, kind sir."

They were approaching the infirmary, and she paused at the gate. "And now I must go to my boring meeting, so you will have to find something else to entertain yourselves with. Something appropriate, I hope."

They all bowed, called out their laughing agreement, and scattered away down the street. As she watched them go, the first boy suddenly stopped and sprinted back.

"My Lady?"

"Yes?"

"You really are a Healer, aren't you?"

"Of course I am. What a strange question."

"No, I mean you can do that 'Jornese Healing stuff?"

She smiled. "I wouldn't quite call it that, but yes, I do have the Power of the Blood of Inderjorne, and I use it for Healing. Why do you ask?"

"Can I come and call on you? It's important."

"Certainly. Come by Lord Ostersund's home late in the afternoon, any day."

The boy glanced over his shoulder to where his friends had gathered, looking back. "Thank you, my Lady. I have to go."

"I'll see you soon, then."

He nodded and dashed towards his group, scattering them as he ran through.

Eirlin stood watching them all scamper away. "I wonder what that was all about?"

Someone is sick.

"Of course, but who? The Maridons have their own doctors, competent enough. Why hasn't this person been to see them?

I don't know.

"I didn't think you would."

Then why did you ask me?

"Just thinking out loud."

You don't have to think aloud. I can hear your thoughts perfectly well.

"Can you, now? What a surprise."

Yes. It must be all the practice I get.

"Hmm."

16.   Parting

"Are you sure you're going to be all right?" Perica's horse, sensing her emotions, circled on the cobblestones.

Eirlin laughed up at her. "Don't fuss. Everything is going to be fine here." She glanced back at Tyrbrand, upright now, less gaunt of cheek and hollow of eye than he had been a month earlier. She lifted Kitten's scabbard. "We have all the help we need."

Ecmund circled his horse as well.

"Yes, Kitten, you take care of my sister, now. And the baby."

I will take care of Eirlin. Little Tooth I am not so sure about."

"Well, just do what she says, and don't worry about it."

Since when did I not do as the Healer says?

Eirlin laughed again. "All the time, as I remember. Have a safe trip home, you two."

"Aye." Jesco's barking laugh had a softer touch, now. "Have a pleasant trip, and a slow one this time. All those cosy inns you can appreciate far better when you have the leisure to use them properly."

Perica's face reddened. "Jesco, whatever do you mean?"

He chuckled. "Nothing at all, my Lady."

She leveled him a stare. "Any messages to take back? Words for anyone special?"

It was his turn to blush. "You know. We already talked."

"Fine. I have your greetings to Wynna. Let's leave it at that."

Jesco should know better.

Eirlin stroked her hilt. *I think it's wonderful that he even tried. A year ago...*

Good point. Love seems to have a beneficial effect on humans. I shall ponder this.

"Our escort is mounted, Perica, and the wagons with the machinery left at dawn."

She straightened in the saddle. "Yes. We have duties to attend to elsewhere." Her gaze swept the little group on the ground. "Good luck to us all. By the next time we see you, we can hope everything will be more settled."

Their faces became somber, and everyone nodded. Perica touched her riding crop to her hat brim and wheeled her horse away. Ecmund saluted less formally and followed, the five soldiers jingling in carefree disorder behind them.

Jesco, Eirlin, and Tyrbrand stood while the quiet descended. After a moment they roused themselves without a word and moved towards the front door.

In the hallway, Jesco excused himself. "I have some business to attend to."

Eirlin raised an eyebrow, but did not comment.

He shrugged. "I don't have those soldiers to look after. Now I have time to check out some rumours I picked up recently."

Tyrbrand's head came around. "What sort?"

"Oh, you know..." Jesco's head wagged left, then right. "Nothing specific. If we weren't suspicious already we'd probably ignore them. But there's an unsettled hum. People are antsy. More fights in the bars, more weapons on the street. That sort of thing."

"I'm going to see the king this afternoon. Can you give me more than that?"

Jesco shook his head. "He'll be getting the same from his people, don't worry. There's something going on, and I'm afraid we'll be finding out more very soon."

"Yes, just the moment after we need to know it."

Jesco shrugged, nodded to Eirlin, and turned towards the back of the house.

17. Poison

"Oh, Eirlin. You look positively stunning."

Eirlin turned. "Why, Gavia, what a nice thing to say."

The other grinned and reached out to adjust one of the ribbons adorning Eirlin's gown. "Well, since I chose the dress, I suppose the compliment was a bit self-serving."

A good thing she isn't carrying me, don't you think?

Jesco's laugh inside his head was just as sharp as outside, but his hand on Kitten's hilt was warm. *A real fashion statement, you are. Hardly appropriate for a reception like this.*

"How have you been, Gavia? I haven't seen you lately."

Gavia shook out her fan, then closed it with a snap and scanned the crowd for a moment. "Oh, I thought I'd take a rest from being the football in that game between you and Cuquita. I found it rather bruising, if you want to know."

"Gavia, I never intended..."

"Of course you didn't, and I never backed away." Her eyes strayed off to the left again, and her chin came up. "In fact, here she comes now, and I'm staying."

Eirlin grinned. "Well, just stand aside then and watch for the feet."

"Good advice."

The two women turned as Cuquita approached. Jesco took a half-step closer to Eirlin, his hand on Kitten's hilt.

No Bad Lady today.

Thank you, Fang. Be very quiet, now.

Yes, Eirlin. The small presence snapped out.

"So, I see Lady Vega has been advising you on your fashions."

Eirlin raised her eyebrows, looked down at her dress, then at Gavia's. "Is her signature so obvious?"

The dark woman slanted her head. "She does have a penchant for bows. Plus you made such a hullaballoo in the Street of the Tailors that everyone was talking about it for a week."

Eirlin grinned. "I thought we had a rather good time."

The cold dark eyes appraised her. "Well, I suppose it didn't do any harm. You certainly tarnished your reputation as a serious bookworm."

Eirlin shrugged. "Glad to hear I was successful."

"But you didn't fool me."

"Oh, well. You can't expect to fool everyone."

Warning. Enemy.

Eirlin's eyes narrowed, and she glanced around. A familiar figure was approaching from behind Cuquita's shoulder: tall, haughty, dark.

Following the Healer's glance, the Maridon woman turned. Kitten could feel her mind close.

"Good afternoon Lady da Launca. I had hoped to find you here at the Civic Reception."

"You have found me, Lord Vanemar."

He glanced at the others. "I find you in strange company."

There was a pause, and the dark eyes bored into him. "Do you presume to critique the company I keep, my Lord?"

He shrugged. "Only if I think it could do you harm."

She laughed, but there was no humour in it. "Your concern touches me, my Lord, but I beg leave to live my own life."

She took a half step towards him and gazed up into his eyes. "And that includes speaking with whom I choose and leaving when I choose."

With a nod to Eirlin she spun and strode away. There was a moment as they all watched her go. Then Eirlin turned to the Maridon lord.

"We have not been introduced, my Lord. I am…"

"I am quite aware who you are, and I do not make the same errors as others." He spun on his heel and followed Cuquita, leaving Eirlin with hand outstretched.

Plain steel.

Eirlin was startled into open speech. "What?"

His sword is plain steel. No Magic. Good weapon, though.

"What was that about, Eirlin?" Gavia's forehead wrinkled. "He was so rude!"

"I suppose you could call it that. He is Lord Vanemar, is he not? Can you think why he would be so abrupt?"

"Yes, that's who he is." The Maridon girl giggled, caught herself. "And I've just made another error, I'm afraid. I've been seen talking to you. There is a certain group that will shun me now, I suppose."

"You don't look too upset."

Gavia looked around, then turned to Eirlin and dropped her voice. "I know many people think that gossiping is a waste of time for empty heads, but it also makes me aware of what is going on. Perica knew that. You do too, I think. So I have some idea of who you are, and what you are doing, and what others like him," she gestured with her fan over her shoulder, "are doing as well. There are a lot of us Maridons who are being placed in a very difficult situation. Many just put their heads down and hope it will all blow away, as it has done many times in the past.

"Those of us who for various reasons have been seen as committed, one way or the other, are just going to have to brave it out."

Eirlin grinned. "No football this time?"

"That's right." The other girl's head came up. "I didn't really make my choice on purpose, but I think I made the right one, and I'm sticking to it."

Her voice dropped again. "If there's any way I can help, just let me know."

Eirlin laughed. "Well, I suppose you could stay and talk to me if you dare. I would hate to enhance my reputation as a serious wallflower."

The other girl took her arm. "Right. In that case, let me introduce you to some people who will completely destroy any reputation for seriousness you might have." She glanced over her shoulder. "Come along, Jesco. You're really going to love this."

Smile, Jesco. It's called diplomacy.

Do you know what we're going to have to listen to, now?

I can't even guess, but maybe we'll learn something.

I can't think what.

It was nearing the end of the Reception and numbers were thinning. Gavia looked up from her conversation, then leaned over to Eirlin.

"I think old spoilsport is on his way."

Eirlin did not look around. "I can't have you calling my host names, Gavia."

"Well, he's not much fun, is he?"

"Oh, he's very nice, once you get to know him better. Do you want the opportunity?"

Gavia seemed to consider. "Not today. He looks too serious." She looked around. "And I think the party is over. It looks so bad to be one of the last to leave."

She swung around to reach out a hand to Tyrbrand. "Good afternoon, Lord Ostersund. I have done my best to counter the good influence you have on your guest, and I think I have succeeded admirably."

He took her hand and bowed. "Well met, then, my Lady. I will now do my best to repair the damage."

She laughed. "Perfect. And between the bending and the rebending, soon she will be strong enough to withstand any stress."

"Or so brittle that she snaps."

Gavia shrugged. "In that case, she wasn't good enough steel to start with. Good luck, my Lord. Good bye, Eirlin." She slipped in for a formal kiss on the Healer's cheek and a whisper in her ear. "Don't forget. Whatever you need."

Then she winked at Jesco, laughed gaily and flounced away.

Ostersund watched her go. "What was that all about?"

Eirlin watched as well. "I think there are depths to that girl."

"We need all the allies we can make, and the stronger the better."

Eirlin frowned. "Couldn't I just consider her a friend?"

There are no friends in this business, Eirlin.

"Swords don't need friends. People do, Kitten."

"Shall we depart? I'd hate to be one of the last to leave."

Not quite yet, Magician. 'Ware behind you.

Bad Lady, Eirlin. Bad, Bad.

Thank you, Fang. Hide now.

Ostersund turned to see Cuquita stalking towards them.

Eirlin regarded the woman. *She looks different, doesn't she?*

Positively feral.

He took a pace forward and waited until she stopped. "Lady da Launca." He gave her the correct bow.

She made no gesture. "Lord Ostersund."

"Are you enjoying the Reception?"

Her shoulders dropped, and her head tilted to one side, an expression of weariness on her face. "Don't waste my time with inanity, Ostersund."

Then she straightened and leaned forward. "And don't waste your little Healer's time, either. You have a task that only she can do, and she isn't doing it. What's wrong with you?"

"What task?"

A sneer of disgust wrinkled her lip. "A man is dying. You have a Healer who can be trusted. Do I need to add one and one for you?"

With a snort, she spun on her heel and walked off, head high.

Bad Lady.

Eirlin turned to Tyrbrand. "What was that all about?"

"I'll tell you in the carriage." He took her arm and steered her out the door. "I don't know why she's mixed up in it, though."

When they were settled in the carriage, Eirlin turned to him. "So?"

Tyrbrand shook his head. "It's a difficult situation. The best of the Inderjornese leaders, Lord Coelric, has been ill for almost a month. He is one of the moderates, perhaps the man with the best chance of brokering peace between the two factions. He has been in the infirmary for some time now, but he does not get any better."

"You think he has been poisoned?"

"Yes, and suspicion falls on his doctor, Lord Carrones, who just happens to be Maridon, seeming non-political, but a known friend of Lord Vanemar. However, no one has any evidence that he was poisoned, and there is nothing to be done."

"A month? I cannot think of a poison that would kill that slowly. I suspect he is being dosed regularly."

"I'm glad to hear a Healer agree."

"Why not remove him from the care of Lord Carrones?"

"There is no cause, and it would be just one more reason for antagonism. Carrones is, as I said, known to be non-political. At least on the surface."

"So a man must die in order to keep the peace."

"It is possible."

"May I see this patient?"

"I doubt it. Carrones is restricting all contact in order to reduce the possibility of poisoning."

"Convenient, if he is the one administering the poison."

"Carrones is a well-respected doctor, but not a well-liked man. Being of noble Maridon blood and a doctor has not done much for his modesty."

"But being unlikeable is no grounds for a charge of murder."

Ostersund spread his hands. "The king is seen as a fair man, and must maintain that reputation. He has taken what steps he can, but without further evidence, he will not act. "

Kitten could feel a now-familiar emotion rising. The Healer was starting to draw Power from some deep well, which the Sword was beginning to recognize. She felt the chill of an old memory.

Calm down, Healer Lady. He doesn't deserve it.

"Thank you, Kitten. It's not me, Eirlin. I'm on your side, remember?"

The Healer made an effort to calm herself. "I'm sorry. I find it so frustrating when people can't see the truth when it's staring them in the face."

"That's the problem. The king is very suspicious about what is going on, but he can't act without bringing the whole battle out into the open."

"I think his Majesty needs a talking to."

The Magician grinned. "Like a recalcitrant schoolboy who hasn't done his work?" Then he sobered. "Think about it, Eirlin. I find an excuse to get you an audience with the king, and he asks you what evidence you have, and you say, 'I just know I'm right.' Do you think that's going to persuade him? I have to use my influence very carefully, and I can't waste it. It wouldn't be very wise for me to help you barge in and shout at the king any time you like."

"So we're going to sit and do nothing? Worse, we're going to let the king sit and do nothing? That is just not acceptable, Tyrbrand."

"No, we are going to do some planning before you go and talk to the king."

"Then you are going to let me speak to him?"

He shrugged. "It isn't a matter of letting you, Eirlin. It's more like deciding not to try to keep you away. However, I don't think it's good enough to go there just to try to influence him with your opinion. You need real evidence to justify a meeting."

"Having no real evidence doesn't make me wrong."

"That's true, and so I will try. Just don't expect miracles."

"So where does Cuquita fit in?"

"I think Coelric might have a connection to Lord da Launca, Cuquita's father. That would explain her interest."

"But does it explain Lord Vanemar's interest in Cuquita?"

"What? Lord Vanemar?"

"Yes. Earlier in the afternoon he came up to her specifically, and warned her off being seen talking to me. When she left, he snubbed me and followed her."

The Magician frowned, shook his head. "I don't see any connection."

"He couldn't be...interested...in her, could he?"

"We can't completely discount it. How did she react to him?"

"Like someone who had just put her hand on a large, squishy insect."

He laughed. "That's to be expected. Well, anything that looks like a setback for his plans can't help but be good for us. I'll do some more thinking on that. Vanemar and Da Launca. Hmm..."

The Magician visited the king the next day, but when he returned it was evident from his face that he was not satisfied with the result. When the Healer tried to probe his condition, she was gently turned away by that same frustrating wall of...nothingness.

Eirlin made no comment, but sat him down with a cup of herbal tea and some biscuits, then quietly watched him eat, Kitten across her lap.

I just had a thought.

"What thought is that, Kitten?"

If the Magican would speak into your head as I always do, he could talk and eat at the same time without sounding rude.

Tyrbrand put this suggestion to the test with a splutter of laughter that turned into cough.

"Tyrbrand! Are you all right?"

He coughed again, wiped streaming eyes. "Yes, just a crumb went wrong. Sorry to be so rude, Kitten."

It was only an idea.

The Magician set aside his plate, took one last gulp of tea, then sat back. "There. That feels better. Thank you, Eirlin. I don't like keeping you in suspense like this, but I was feeling a bit shaky."

"I know. That's why I didn't ask."

But we can ask now. What did the king say?

Ostersund tilted his hand one way, then the other. "He certainly agrees that Lord Coelric's ill health is a problem. We have discussed that at great length already."

"But..."

"I'm sorry, Eirlin, but he made me see that it wouldn't be a good idea for you to go and talk to him about it. I can visit him without causing comment. You, on the other hand, must have a very good reason or..." he held up his hand to forestall her outburst. "...or it will draw unwanted attention to you. That was the king's point, and I couldn't argue. I know you don't want to be seen as a secret general in this conflict, and we certainly don't want anyone else thinking the same."

"So what can I do?"

He grinned. "You can do what you just did."

A puzzled frown. "Which was?"

Send the Magician as your page.

Tyrbrand laughed again. "Exactly, Kitten. The king also made that comment."

The king is an astute man.

"No argument there. So the upshot of the meeting was this. The king still cannot take action. He cannot meet with you on the subject unless there is more certain evidence of wrongdoing. However, he did call in Panos Genil – his Guard Captain – and make him aware of the situation, and my part in it."

"I suppose that will help."

"More than you think. If a situation does arise, it means Captain Genil can take action immediately, without waiting for the nod from his sovereign."

And it also means that the Magician can ask the Captain to act.

"Precisely."

And Eirlin?

"Once again, we do not wish her to be at the front of any conflict. However, Panos is aware of her involvement, and will be able to make up his own mind in any situation."

"I suppose we must be satisfied with that?"

He shrugged. "It's not everything we wanted, but I think it's the best we could do."

She nodded. "I suppose you're right."

As long as Lord Coelric doesn't die in the meantime.

"That is too truthful to be pleasant."

18. Charche's Sister

"Lady Eirlin?"

"Yes, Eowin?" The Healer looked up from her work.

"Someone to see you, my Lady."

"Who is it?"

"...um...one of the street boys, my Lady. Maridon. I wasn't sure..."

"...you weren't sure you should let the little ruffian in?"

"Yes, my Lady."

"Eowin, you are showing the prejudices we are fighting against. Those boys may have dark faces, but some of them are the children of important people. Show him up, please, and also show him due deference. I don't know who his parents are, but it shouldn't matter."

"Yes, my Lady."

When Charche entered, Eirlin could see why the servant had been unsure. He was not exactly dressed for a visit. His cloak was dirty, his shoes were scuffed, and he was sporting a dark bruise on his cheek.

"Well! It is pleasant to receive your visit, but you seem to have forgotten to dress for the occasion."

He grinned, scuffed a toe on the carpet. "I couldn't dress up, my Lady; somebody might have asked why."

She smiled. "I see. This is a secret meeting, then. And what happened to your face?"

He touched his cheek gingerly, but with a bit of pride. "Oh, that's nothing, my Lady. We were playing ball against the 'Jornese boys, and Rhysun tackled me."

"Ah. May I?"

He nodded and she reached out with her hand and her mind. *Fang? See what I am doing now?*

Yes, Healer. I see. Clean out blood.

There. All done. "Does that feel better?"

He touched his cheek. "Yes. What did you do?"

"Just some 'Jornese healing stuff. Now. What are we meeting about?"

He looked around, as if expecting to find eavesdroppers. "It's my sister, my Lady..."

"Yes? I gather she is ill?"

"Not ill, my Lady." The boy seemed to be gathering his courage. "Injured."

"I see." She waited a moment. "Go on. What sort of injury?"

"Um...Do you remember that riot down in the Street of the Goldmiths last fall?"

"No, I wasn't in Koningsholm last fall. What happened?"

"Well, it was...your people, my Lady. A bunch of them started a big fight. It began in a tavern, but then it got into the street. There was a mob of them, running around attacking everyone."

"I see. How did your sister get hurt?"

"We don't really know. The men were running along the street, breaking shop windows, stealing stuff, that sort of thing. She was out shopping with my older sister, and the mob just ran over them. My sister must have fallen on some broken glass." His finger traced down the side of his face. "She was cut. Very badly."

"But this was last fall. Did it heal?"

"Yes, but it's the scar."

"I see." There wasn't anything more to say.

"She was so beautiful, my Lady. So happy."

"And now?"

He blinked back tears. "She's still beautiful...inside. But it hurts so much, my Lady."

"Her wound still hurts her?"

"No, it hurts me, my Lady."

"I see. And your doctors?"

"They have done their best. She fell in the street and the wound wasn't clean. There was blighting. Now that it has healed, there is nothing more they can do."

"And you think I can do something?"

"I don't know, my Lady, but Bejarin says that you do wonderful things. He's the one sent me here."

"Bejarin sent you?"

"Aye. He knows things." He glanced at Kitten, propped against Eirlin's chair. "You and that Sword, he told me."

"You know about the Sword, do you?"

"Everyone does. The Tyrant's Claw, they call it."

What?

"The Tyrant's Claw is a ridiculous name. You tell your friends that she has several more appropriate names they can use."

"What should we call it then, my Lady?"

"Why don't you ask Bejarin? He knows."

"If he knows, I'll ask him. They say it can tell what you're thinking."

Eirlin laughed. "She can't really know what you're thinking unless you want her to, Charche. She reads emotions. And it's easy to see

141

that you love your sister very much, and are anxious to do whatever you can to help her."

He glanced once more at Kitten. "Oh. And can you help her?"

"I don't know. I'd have to see her. Where is she?"

"Well...that's a problem. She's at home."

"And why is home a problem?"

"It's my father, my Lady."

"Ah. Let me guess. He was never very fond of 'my people,' as you term them. Then, when he thinks they hurt your sister, he got worse. Now he hates them."

"You really can tell what I'm thinking!"

"No, lad, I don't need the help of my Sword to figure that out. It's too common to be pleasant. So what can we do about it?"

"I don't know, my Lady. She doesn't go out of the house any more, so I can't bring her to you."

"That's a problem." She indicated his clothing. "And she probably wouldn't want to dress like that."

A sudden light dawned on the boy's face. "Wait a minute. That's a good idea!"

"It is?"

"Yes. She might. She has a great imagination. If I make a game of it, and tell her we're on a pilgrimage, and we have to dress up in cloaks..."

Eirlin shook her head. "No, Charche. I am not going to be part of some harum-scarum plot which will get you in trouble with your father and possibly cause a political uproar if it becomes known."

"All right, my Lady. I'll have to think of something else."

"Have you thought of telling your father and having him bring her? Or your mother?"

He just shook his head.

"I see. Well, you think on it. I'm here most mornings and evenings, but I'm usually away in the afternoons."

His face brightened. "I'll think of something, my Lady. Thank you."

"Fine." She called for the servant, who arrived so quickly that Eirlin wondered if she was standing outside the door.

She was.

"Eowin, you may see this lad out. And you'll recognize him another time?"

"Oh, yes, my Lady. However he is dressed."

"Very good. Good-bye, Charche, and my love to your sister."

"Thank you, my Lady." With an impish grin at the servant's courtly gesture, he paraded out, head high

"What do you think, Kitten?"

It would be a good test of Fang's abilities.

"I thought so. We'll have to practice that fine stitching we were working on."

If she ever comes.

"When a father's politics comes in the way of his daughter's health and happiness...well, I don't know, but if I have to, I'll go and talk to this man."

If it is not politically unwise.

"That's a very astute comment, Kitten, unpleasant though it may be. When a Healer can't tend her patients due to the political situation...well, that's even worse."

19.   Declaration of War

Kitten surveyed the sitting room. The Magician sat in his usual chair, his mind engrossed in the scroll he held. Eirlin was murmuring to Fang. Jesco was toying with a glass of wine, an unusually pleasant look on his face. It was much too peaceful.

My Lord Magician?

"Yes, my Lady Kitten?"

She expanded her voice so all could hear clearly. *I believe there are words that need to be said.*

The humans exchanged glances.

"You sound serious."

I am. You understand, I have been in this situation several times in the past.

The Magician's puzzlement grew. "What situation is that, Kitten?"

Exactly. Your response is precisely what I would have predicted. This is what happens every time. Sometimes you humans are far too predictable. I find myself wishing to be surprised, just once.

Eirlin laid her hand on Kitten's hilt. "If you were trying to get our attention by insulting us, I hope you have good reason."

Another predictable reaction, although in this case you are way ahead of the usual timeline. You are already killing the messenger when the message has not even been delivered.

Kitten caught a whiff of humour passing between the Healer and the Magician. "All right, Kitten. You have our undivided attention. What is happening that we have missed?"

It is ever thus with peaceful and well-meaning people. Because of your nature, you cannot fathom the essence of your enemy. As a result, you make a huge tactical blunder, which gives that enemy a great advantage over you.

Now the Magician's mind began to work. "And what is that advantage, Kitten?"

I think you already see, Magician.

"I think I do."

Eirlin frowned. "I don't."

It was Jesco who answered. "Ask a swordsman. What is Kitten beating us over the head with? We are at war."

"What a strange thing to say!"

Ostersund shook his head. "I'm afraid not, Eirlin. Kitten's analysis is too accurate, painful though it might be. We are so concerned with behaving in an appropriate manner that we disregard the actions of the enemy. We are thus always one step behind, always reacting instead of attacking."

"But we must not be seen as attacking! It would destroy our whole approach to the problem."

The Magician shook his head slowly. "What you say is true. However, it does not help us in this situation."

Jesco smiled without humour. "The moral high ground is not much use in a battle."

"But what do we do?" Eirlin's mind was whirling. "You are not suggesting we attack anyone, are you?"

"I don't know. Kitten, you started this. What were you going to suggest?"

Nothing. I have achieved my purpose.

"You have?"

Of course. Once you start this conversation, you have cleared the first and most serious obstacle. The war has now begun.

Eirlin looked to Tyrbrand, then Jesco. "How can that be? We can't just decide there is a war, and suddenly there is one. Can we?"

"Take it from a swordsman, Eirlin, war isn't exactly what you might have thought. War is a state of mind, and now that we are thinking about it we cannot help but act accordingly."

"But how can a Healer think about war?"

"I don't know, Eirlin. If you thought there was going to be a big battle tomorrow, what would you do?"

Again her mind was whirling, but this time with purpose. "Well, there are all sorts of things that need to be done. We need bandages, and supplies and wagons, and we need to start preparing our Healers and surgeons..."

Well done. Now it starts.

"...what do you mean?"

I mean that now you are using your talents in the right direction. Don't worry, Eirlin, you haven't started a war just by thinking about one. You are only making yourself and your people mentally and physically prepared for the inevitable.

The Healer suddenly froze, her eyes on the Magician. "Tyrbrand, is this necessary?"

"Most definitely. I must talk to the king. Resources must be made available to smooth your work. Who needs to be involved? There must be surgeons and Healers in the realm who are already experienced in this sort of thing."

Now Eirlin's face brightened. "This might be good. This might be the one idea that both Inderjornese Healers and Maridon doctors can agree on. The health of all."

"Very good, Eirlin. When I speak to the king, I will emphasise that point. Now you must give me a list. What will you need? Who are the most likely ones…"

The humans moved off, intent on their purposes, leaving Kitten alone in the sitting room humming softly to herself.

That's more like it.

20. Jesco's Mission

The pace of life in the Ostersund home quickened. Messengers came and went. A storage room was emptied for the medical equipment and supplies they would gather. Jesco no longer mooned around but kept unusual hours, leaving and returning at any time, day or night.

Eirlin and Tyrbrand had been spending a rare evening at home together when she raised her head from her work with Fang. "What do you know about Cuquita da Launca?"

"I know that she's poison in a thin glass jar. Not much more. Her father is a reasonable man. Was, I should say."

"Is he dead?"

"No, he was injured in a joust and never fully recovered. He can't walk and I gather he's in pain a lot. He's pretty well confined to his bed. Under his guidance, Cuquita has been managing their estates and their politics ever since."

"That must be interesting."

"Yes, it's a weird combination. They're doing fine with the estates, but the politics are another matter. They still have a lot of moderate allies, friends of her father. But I don't know how she herself thinks of the Inderjornese. Seems to blow hot and cold."

"That sounds like Cuquita."

"Her mother was a nasty piece of goods, from all accounts. Died years ago. Probably suicide, but they hushed it up. I never met her, but I gather nobody is really surprised how Cuquita turned out. Too bad."

"Anything else?"

"Now that I think about it, she might be one of our rogue Sensitives. I have never tested her, but there is always something in the background...I'd have to take a closer look. Why do you need to know?"

"She might become a patient."

"Hmm. I wish you good luck with that one. The more stable she is, the better for all of us."

"You mean, politically?"

"Yes. Her family still has influence with the moderate Maridons, if she doesn't throw it all away or swing it towards our enemies in a fit of pique."

"Are they a big enough group to make a difference?"

He shrugged. "Things are pretty delicate at court right now. There are a lot of moderate thinkers who are uncommitted. There's always the fear that any group making a move could be enough to start a landslide."

Eirlin frowned. "You are worrying too much, Tyrbrand."

"There is much to worry about."

"I've been meaning to talk to you about it."

"About what?"

"I don't think you're healing fast enough."

He grinned. "I didn't know that. I'm sorry. I'll try harder."

"This isn't a joke. I'm doing all I can to Heal you, but it isn't working. I think there is more damage at a deeper level that I haven't found. It's like treating a wound, but there's a fractured bone underneath and it keeps breaking open again."

"You're doing all you can, Eirlin. No one could do better."

"That's just it. I could do better." She took a deep breath. "But you won't let me."

"What do you mean?"

"I mean that you won't show me all the damage. You're hiding something."

He frowned, thinking. "I'm not hiding anything on purpose, Eirlin. I'm not that foolish."

"Maybe you're not, but you won't let me look. You can't expect me to help you if you hide your injuries from me."

"I don't expect you to do more than you can, Eirlin. I am very grateful for what you have done."

She sat, looking at him in silence.

"What? What did I say that was wrong?"

"Nothing. You didn't say anything wrong."

"Oh. Good." With a further anxious glance, he went back to the scroll he was reading.

That went rather well.

Eirlin laid a hand on Kitten so they could talk more privately. *That went terribly. Why won't he let me Heal him?*

I don't think he's doing it on purpose, Eirlin.

Then why won't he let me see what's wrong?

He's a Magician.

What does that have to do with it?

Can you imagine what that must be like? Being open to the emotions of everyone around him, all the time? He must have learned to control the onslaught from a very young age. He isn't going to open up just because a pretty girl asks him to.

Don't be smart. You mean he can't?

Probably not. It is a key part of his training

148

Then what do I do?

Not my realm of duty. Use your woman's wiles, I suppose.

My what?

Your clever womanly skills. You know the ones. Worm your way into his affections and get what you want.

Kitten, you are being very obnoxious.

I thought you wanted advice.

Advice, not insults.

You just don't like the advice.

Well, it is very frustrating.

I know. And it isn't just Tyrbrand, is it?

No, it isn't. I just feel like I'm not doing anything.

Once again, you're talking to the wrong person.

I am?

Of course. If you want to help politically, talk to the politician.

Eirlin patted Kitten's hilt. *Finally, some good advice.*

Just doing my best to help. Go ahead. Ask him.

She looked over at Tyrbrand

"This is just so frustrating."

The Magician looked up from the scroll. "What is frustrating, my dear?"

You are just so funny.

Why am I funny?

Every time he calls you 'my dear,' your heart does a complete flip. I think he does it on purpose.

Don't be ridiculous.

"I hate to pry, but I thought you were starting a conversation."

"Oh, I'm sorry, Tyrbrand. I was just venting my frustration, and then Kitten said something completely inane. I was complaining that I can't do anything to help."

"You're doing everything to help. I couldn't do this without you."

"I don't mean helping you with Excisor. I mean helping the king. The realm. Everyone is doing his or her part and I'm sitting here, selfishly working on my own project. The new medical cadre could be useful, of course, but that's just a reaction. It's like giving up and preparing for the battle we don't want. We should be stopping this war before it starts."

"If it makes you feel any better, you're not alone."

"I'm not?"

"No. The king mentioned it yesterday. We have a basic problem. Out in the countryside where the enemy is just starting his campaign, we can slip people like Lord da Falken into his camp. Here in the

Capital, the lines have been drawn for so long that everyone knows us. Lord da Baneza is running a secret battle, and we have no highly-placed spies to counter him."

"It would seem that we need to bring in someone new."

"That's the problem. To get information at the higher level, we need someone of rank. Here, everyone of rank is known."

"Then we need to send someone in at a lower rank, and have him work his way up."

"I don't know if we have time for that."

"I'm no good at spying, Tyrbrand. I'm just taking the logical path."

"Unfortunately, your logic is correct."

"Then what do we do?"

He smiled. "Well, we don't ask our favourite Healer. We won't like the answers she gives."

"Exactly. We have all been taught the same lessons. 'Live your life properly, and prove them wrong by example.' That's my solution."

"Again, I think we need a little more time for that approach. Probably about another hundred years."

"I did have one small triumph in that area recently."

"What was that?"

"I've discovered another Maridon Sensitive. One of the boys who play along the street, here. He has Healer qualities, I'm sure of it."

"That's good."

"His last name is da Tiena. Do you know the family?"

"That could be even better. Can we use the boy to approach the father?"

"I don't want to use him, Tyrbrand. What a thought!"

"That's because you're a Healer and I'm a politician. If you can help the boy to use his Power, and we can impress his father, or at least throw doubt into his bigotry because of the boy, then everyone will benefit. Fair enough?"

"Unless we help the boy become what his father hates, and cause a rift between them."

"Eirlin, do you honestly see this boy denying his Power and living any kind of happy, useful life, if you don't help him become a Healer? Can you imagine the result if he starts to use his Power against people?"

"How could he do that?"

"A Healer's ability to manipulate people's bodies means that he can cause pain as well as stop it. I can see all sorts of possibilities, few of them pleasant."

"Are you talking about a rogue Healer, using his Power for evil?"

Ostersund shrugged. "I know it sounds far-fetched, but if we have all sorts of Maridons like Cuquita and da Baneza growing up with untrained Powers something like that is bound to happen. That could send the realm down a very nasty path."

Eirlin's mind was racing. "But we have to stop this! We have to test all the children immediately and identify those with Power. We have to put all the Maridon children, not just the Sensitives, into the same schools so they can all learn how to deal with this situation, just like the Inderjornese children have always learned. It's the only way to control the Power."

"Eirlin, these sound like good ideas, but I think you've missed one small step."

"What is that?"

"We have to win this battle first. If the king tried anything like you're suggesting he'd have open rebellion. I told you to listen to the debate on schools at the Conclave."

"I see. So I guess we'd better concentrate on winning. Which brings me back to the original problem. It's just so frustrating, not being able to help. What can I do? They know me. How can I help penetrate their cadre?"

A third voice broke into their conversation. "I just might be able to help you there."

They both looked up in surprise as Jesco strolled into the room. "Jesco! You don't listen around corners!"

"Yes, I do. Quite often. It's a useful technique, and your voices weren't exactly soft. Besides, I was just coming to look for you. I've found a very interesting tavern."

They looked at him in silence for a moment. "I'm working on this, Cousin, but I can't quite picture how our problem is going to be solved by going to a nice tavern."

"I didn't say a nice tavern. In fact, it's a very nasty tavern. Filled with the vilest sort of Maridon lackeys. You wouldn't like it at all, Eirlin."

"And why do you like it?"

"Because I have met some people there, and they have given me an invitation."

At this the Magician leaned into the conversation. "An invitation to what?"

"To a meeting. The way I picture it, the Maridons have the same trouble you do. All their ranking people in the Capital are well-known. So they're recruiting at the lower echelons."

"And you've been recruited."

"Not yet, but I've been invited."

"You're willing to become our spy in their ranks?"

"Jesco, that's too dangerous!"

He shrugged. "I thought it might be fun. I was getting bored, sitting around with nothing to do, no way to help." He shot her a quick glance. "Sound familiar?"

It is his duty, Eirlin. He is pleased to help. Like you would be.

"All right." She raised her hands in defeat. "It's not my business. Go to the meeting or whatever. You can take Kitten to protect you."

"I can't do that."

"Why not?"

"She's too dangerous and too valuable."

"What do you mean?"

"Too many people know her." He grinned. "I believe she is 'The Cat with Many Claws' these days. I'm not going in there to fight. I'm going in to spy. If I get in a battle I spoil my chances. If I get into a battle and lose, then she could be captured."

We would never lose!

"Can you defend against an arrow? Several arrows from different directions at once?" He stared straight at her. "How did you get separated from your original Hand, all those years ago?"

It's all quite hazy. I was very young. We were in a battle. We were winning, of course. Then, he was just...gone. I don't know what happened after that.

"He was just dead. Somebody got him with an arrow, or a thrown stool or something else you couldn't deal with. No, you've been captured once, and it could happen again. I'm going into this alone. That's the way it has to be."

Ostersund nodded. "That's the way it usually goes, Eirlin. It is the solution to our problem. Jesco has only been in the Capital for a few days. Chances are, nobody knows him."

"But he went to that reception with us."

"I'm not exactly working at that level of society. Not at the moment, anyway. Besides, I was with Perica, and they think her father is one of them."

He is enjoying this.

Eirlin tossed her braids back over her shoulders. "All right. I give up. This is not my field of duty, and I know when to back down gracefully. I won't even tell you to be careful, Jesco, because I know you will. I just don't want to know the details." She rose.

"Eirlin, what's wrong?" He stood as well. "Are you...?"

"Yes, I'm crying. It just shows how unsuited I am for this sort of thing. You go and do what you have to, Jesco, and you can come to me to be patched up when you're done. That way we'll both know the world is going the way it's supposed to. Right?"

Jesco's hands wavered helplessly. "I'm no good at this sort of thing, Ostersund. Can you...I don't know...give her a hug or something?"

He would be delighted.

The Magician complied and Eirlin stood, her head pressed close against his, until she could control herself. Then, slowly, she drew erect, and his arms dropped.

"All right. I'm over it, thank you both. Jesco, Tyrbrand, you have plans to make, and I have work I could be doing." She created a smile for them, then slipped Kitten into her scabbard and left the room with dignity.

That was very brave of you.

"I was a complete blathering idiot. Jesco is about to go off and do something dangerous, and there I am distracting him with my weakness. I'm ashamed of myself."

Your little scene had its desired effect.

"What effect? I didn't desire anything, except perhaps to regain my dignity."

Jesco is even more determined to succeed. The Magician is more determined to help him. They will make a good team.

"Kitten! Are you suggesting I did that on purpose, to twist them around to do what I wanted?"

No, Eirlin. Nobody thinks that. Of course, that's what made it so effective.

Eirlin's fingers fumbled with the buckle. She threw the Sword across the room and stormed out without a word. Kitten lay on the floor in the corner humming to herself, going over the preceding events in her mind.

I couldn't have planned it better myself.

21.   Rider in the Night

Tired. So tired.

Eirlin stirred in her sleep.

Kitten roused. Was the Healer dreaming? She listened, and the faint thread came again.

Keep going. Stay awake.

That wasn't the Healer. It came from far away.

Eirlin. Wake up.

"What? What's wrong, Kitten?"

Join with me. I think it's Ecmund.

"Ecmund? Where...?" The Healer fumbled to get her hand on Kitten's hilt.

Tired...keep going. Come on, horse...gallop.

Can you hear him? That's Ecmund, I'm sure.

"Yes, but I can't really get anything except fatigue. Where is he?"

A long way away. He must be on his way here.

"Can we reach him?"

We can try. Kitten reached out. *My Lord Magician, may I disturb your sleep?*

The reply came immediately, clear and alert. *You already have. I'll be there in a moment.*

With the three of them, Ecmund's thoughts came clearer.

Come on, horse. Don't give up...might fall...

Hands on my hilt, you two. Concentrate. ECMUND!

What? That you, Kitten?

She felt satisfaction, fatigue. No fear or sorrow. But he was too weak, too far away. He gathered his forces and sent one clear thought. *Sunrise.*

Then it was all washed out by the fatigue. She let the connection drop.

"What's happening, Kitten? Why is he coming? Send again."

No, Eirlin. It is too far. It takes energy for him to speak at this distance, and he is very tired. He will try again at dawn.

"But what if there's a problem? What if he's hurt? Or Perica...?"

I didn't get the feeling of anything like that. Exercise patience, Healer. Wait for dawn.

As the rays of the sun peered in through the windows of the Ostersund ceasterhof, a tense group sat in the drawing room. They had recruited Jesco, and all the Power they could muster was arrayed against an invisible foe.

All right, everyone, touch my hilt. Let's see if my Hand has made enough progress. She gathered their disparate minds together and moulded the Power into a searching beam. *Ecmund?*

Keep going, horse. Let's not quit now.

Ecmund! Wake up!

...not asleep. Kitten. Is that you? I dreamed I talked to you.

You did talk to me. Stop the horse and talk again.

Have to keep going...

Why? What's wrong? Eirlin's concern blasted out in force.

Eirlin? That you?

Yes, Ecmund. What's wrong? Where are you?

Somewhere on the road. Got a message. Tell the king.

What do we need to tell the king?

It's started. Vanemar showed up, gave Lord da Falken his orders. Hassle the 'Jornese lords. Move stock onto their land. Take over wells and watercourses. The usual.

The Magician's calm strength took over. *Anything else? Any attacks?*

No attacks. Just hound and harry. React later.

I understand. I will tell the king. Well done, Ecmund.

Good. Going home, now.

Eirlin's concern washed over them. *But aren't you coming here? Don't you need Kitten?*

No killing...need her more...tired.

Ecmund, you're fading out. Kitten, what's wrong?

Kitten threw her whole being into maintaining the connection between the disparate human minds.

Going home, Eirlin. They need me, you...

Kitten, keep him...

Kitten forced herself until her whole being shook.

Bye, Eirlin. Bye...

She was failing. He was gone. She sought further, digging deep for more energy, to give her all to help her Hand when he needed her...

"Kitten. Kitten, where are you?"

Huh...? What?

"Kitten, what happened?"

Don't know. What happened? Where is Ecmund?

"You tried to reach him. Then he was gone. Then you were gone. Where were you?"

Oh...right. He's gone. Gone home.

The Magician's calm thoughts intruded. *I think she overdid it.*

Overdid it. You might say that.

"Oh Kitten, I'm so sorry. I didn't realize..."

Neither did I, Eirlin. I've never tried to do that before. I guess I overdid it.

Eirlin laid a Healing hand on the Sword, her head turned to the Magician. "I don't think I understand, but you said that you did. What's happening?"

Tyrbrand shook his head. "Vanemar has decided on his strategy. It's nothing new. They pick on some Inderjornese lord and hound him. They put their cattle to graze on his cropland. They keep his stock away from water, steal a few, set upon his retainers. Sooner or later someone responds with violence, and they have an excuse for a real attack. Then they kill him and his heirs."

"But they can't just take over someone's land like that?"

"They won't. They just break his power, destroy his family and ride away. Then they'll move on and do the same to someone else. They're out to destroy the Inderjornese power, one noble at a time."

"That's horrible. What can we do?"

He smiled grimly. "We don't do anything. That's the king's job. I'll be seeing him first thing this morning."

"Is there anything I can do to help?"

"No, my dear, much though I know you want to. The king is quite capable of handling this sort of tactic."

"But what about Lord Delfontes? What will he do? They expect him to attack someone."

"He's quite resourceful. He'll find a way to make it look bad, but not do anyone any real damage." He suddenly smiled. "And there's no way anyone could have got this information all the way to the Capital this fast. Ecmund was probably two days ride away when he turned back. So they'll be suspecting a traitor here, not out there."

He rubbed his hands together with satisfaction. "Yes, I think this is going to work out just fine."

22.   A New Patient

It became obvious to Kitten that something was wrong. Eirlin had closed the door behind her and was now shaking the rain off her cloak. If they were innocent passers-by, they would have had time to continue along the street. They did not.

We may have a problem, Eirlin.

"What kind of a problem, Kitten?"

Someone is following you.

"Right now?"

Not right now, Eirlin. How can someone follow you when you are at home?

"My point exactly."

You need to concentrate, Eirlin.

"I'm sorry, Kitten. I'm listening. What is going on?"

Someone followed us home. At least two of them Maybe three. They are too far away to recognize, but probably Maridon. I thought they would go away, but they did not.

"Where are they now?"

In the park at the end of the block.

"How many did you say?"

Kitten scanned the area carefully. *Two, no three. Very interesting.*

"Yes?"

Two are Maridon. The other is an open mind, but hard to read.

"Someone with experience, then. A Magician?"

No, nowhere near that. Young. I think they are children.

"What are they feeling?"

Give me a moment. One is very nervous. The other is more anxious than nervous. The third...I can't tell, because he keeps hiding.

"Do you feel any danger?"

Not to us.

"Then let us go out and meet our visitors."

Is that wise?

"I don't know, Kitten. I am depending on you to tell me if there is a problem. Sometimes people are reluctant for various reasons to visit a Healer."

I detect no antagonism.

"Then let us go." She tossed her cloak back on and stepped outside. The street was bare.

Turn left. They are that way. Keep going. Ah! We know him. The street boy. Hah! They see you. One wants to run. She is afraid of you. The older one wants her to stay. The third...oops, there he goes.

"What do you mean? Is he running away?"

No, he's just gone. Like the wind in the trees.

"So he can hide himself, just like you do."

It would seem so. Move ahead. Be cautious. They are to the left, now. There. Behind those bushes.

Eirlin stopped just short of the park and waited. There was a rustling in the shrubbery, and hasty whispers. Finally, the leaves parted and Charche stepped out, looking rather abashed.

"Good day, Charche."

"Good day, my Lady."

"May I assume your sister has come to see me? Who is your friend?"

The boy turned back. "See? You might as well come out. I told you she'd find us."

He reached back into the bushes, then slowly withdrew his hand. A small figure, head covered by a hooded cloak, stepped hesitantly out. "My Lady Eirlin, this is my sister, Taresita."

"I am pleased to meet you, Taresita. Would you like to come inside?"

The hood nodded.

What about the other one?

"And your friend?"

Charche faced the bushes impatiently. "Come on, Bejarin. She knows you're there. I told you the Cat would find you."

There was no response.

"Well, we're not standing around out here in the open. Taresita will be much happier indoors."

There was immediate movement and the bushes parted. The youngster they had noted before appeared, looking fearfully around.

"Lady Eirlin, this is Bejarin."

The boy's attention snapped to her, and he made a proper bow. "I am pleased to make your acquaintance, Healer Eirlin."

"I am always pleased to meet another Healer."

"What?" The boy's head came up, and his face was visible for the first time.

"Another Healer. Surely you have that figured out by now."

"Well...I..."

Eirlin turned, holding out her hand to the girl. "As Charche said, let's not stand around out in the weather. I have a nice, dry room to sit in, with comfortable chairs, and I would be surprised if Mistress Waldwine couldn't find us something very tasty to nibble on while we talk."

Kitten bolstered the Healer's calm air and the two boys fell in line behind. Once they were inside, Eirlin turned to her new patient. "Now, Taresita, I think it is much too warm in here for such a heavy cloak. Please allow Eowin to take yours."

There was a moment's hesitation, and then the girl shrugged off her cloak, her head turned away. She was about six years old, and looked perfectly healthy until she turned to face them. A ragged, angry red scar ran down her left cheek, just missing the eye, pulling the side of her mouth up in a horrible permanent grin. The servant, under Eirlin's firm eye, took the cloak without comment.

"So this is my new patient. I'm pleased to meet you, Taresita. Come into the reception room, and let us sit. I'm sure the boys will be pleased with what Eowin brings back."

Eirlin filled in with pleasant chatter as she got them all seated around a low table, which the servant soon filled with plates of various goodies. Once everyone had a chance to sample the cook's wares, she sat back and looked straight at Taresita.

"That's quite a scar you have there."

"Yes, my Lady."

"May I touch it?"

"...yes, my Lady."

Kitten, you know what to do.

Yes, my Lady.

Don't be smart. She is very nervous.

Of course she is. We will work to make her calm.

Thank you. Excisor, are you ready?

Readyreadyready, Healer. What do we do?

There is nothing for you to do, dear. Just watch. We must see how to fix it.

Readyreadyready.

Sliding the Scapel out of his sheath, Eirlin reached out with her other hand to run a tender finger down the rough mark. As she did, Kitten expanded her senses beneath the skin, building up a picture of the damage.

This is very bad.

Yes. There is damage deep inside, and the scar is very twisted.

Can we fix it?

We can certainly help. Look at those muscles.

Yes. Shall I make them relax? Yes. There. Did that help?

159

Cutcutcut?

No, dear, not yet. We have to see all around first. Then we must ask permission. Then, maybe, we will cut.

Not cut?

No, Fang. We will cut later, when everything is prepared.

Not cut?

Kitten sent an image of a huge grey paw, claws extended. *No cutting today. Don't argue with the Healer.*

There was a rebellious moment, then the resistance faded. *Yes, Big Cat. No cutting today.*

Eirlin lowered her hand, and smiled at her patient. "That wasn't so bad, was it?"

"You have soft hands."

"To deal gently with soft faces."

She turned to Bejarin "Could you tell what we were doing?"

His face held a puzzled frown. "You were talking in your head."

"That's right. I was talking to my Sword, who helps me see inside the patient. I was talking to my Scalpel, who needs to see so that when I operate, he knows what to do."

"Operate?"

The little girl's eyes flew to her brother's face. He took her hand and she clutched his fearfully.

"Not today, Taresita. Today was just for looking. Now that I know what your problem looks like, I have to get your father's permission. Then my Scalpel and I will do the operation."

"Can you fix her?" The brother's head pushed forward anxiously. "The other doctors tried. It hurt a lot and didn't help."

"We can certainly make it better. We have already."

The girl's hand flew to her face. "It does feel different!"

"We just relaxed some muscles. If you learn to keep your face feeling like that, it will look more normal, and it won't ache so much." She turned to the smaller boy. "Do you understand that, Bejarin?"

He nodded enthusiastically. "You can make people relax by rubbing the stiff spots."

"That's right. We just do it from the inside. Then she has to work on it herself."

"I see."

"You know you are a Healer, don't you?"

"Yes, my Lady. I guess so. But I don't know what a Healer does."

She gestured around the room. "Just this. People come to see me, or I go to them. I Heal them with my Powers and with potions and remedies I have learned."

"Where did you learn to be a Healer?"

"It was different for me, because I lived out in Falkenby, and I learned from other Healers in my village. Here in Koningsholm, Healers learn at the infirmary."

"How do I do that?"

She shrugged. "Same as anyone. Study hard and learn your lessons. When your schooling is over, go to the infirmary and ask for a position."

He looked at her skeptically. "I don't think it's that easy, my Lady. I'm Maridon. Our doctors don't work this way."

She sighed. "No, I suppose they don't. But they should. You have talent. You have Power. You should be able to train in your Calling."

"I am going to talk to my father."

Eirlin turned at the sudden vigour in Charche's voice. "You are?"

"Yes. I hear you two talking about how Bejarin can just go to the 'Jornese and get trained, and I say to myself, 'Why not? What's so different, that Taresita can't just go to them and be Healed?' And I'm going to tell my father the same thing."

"He may not be quite as comfortable with the idea as you are."

The boy's grin held a touch of snarl. "I'm going to take Taresita with me when I go. I'm going to plant her in front of him and make him look at her face. Then I'm going to tell him about you. I think he'll listen."

Eirlin shook her head. "He's your father, and you know him best. I wouldn't presume to tell you what to do."

He grinned. "I know. Just like the other day in the street. You didn't tell anybody what to do, but look what happened."

"What happened, Charche?"

"Everyone did exactly what they were supposed to. I was very impressed."

"And it takes a lot to impress you, does it?"

He fingered the fading bruise on his cheek. "I guess you could say that." Then he turned to his sister. "You'll help me, won't you, Taresita?"

Her eyes widened. "What if he shouts?"

The boy winked at Eirlin. "Then you cry. That always works."

Her face softened. "It used to. Now he doesn't want to look at me."

"Well, we're going to make him, all right?"

The little girl looked up at her brother. "If you say so."

He put a hand on her shoulder and steered her towards the door. "Oh, I say so. Don't worry, Healer Eirlin is going to fix you right up. Aren't you, my Lady?"

Eirlin smiled. "I can certainly make it better." She turned to Bejarin. "And don't you worry. There's no rush. If your family will allow you, come and visit me again. But tell them where you are going."

"Yes, my Lady."

"Good-bye for now, you three." She ushered them out the door, but the little girl turned back.

"My Lady?"

"Yes, Taresita?"

"May I touch the Cat? Just once?"

Eirlin swung her left hip forward. "Of course. Right on the hilt is best."

The little girl held out one hesitant finger, as if to caress an uncertain animal. When she made contact, Kitten sent her a wave of warmth. Her eyes opened wider and she grinned up at Eirlin, then touched her wounded cheek with the same finger. "It feels better already!"

Eirlin merely smiled with the same warmth, and then the three small figures bundled away down the street, each boy with one arm around the girl.

I think that was well done, Eirlin.

"Yes, I do too. I really hope we can help her."

Of course we can.

Help, help. Pretty face. Soft face.

"Yes, we'll just have to put that pretty, soft face back together, won't we?"

23.   Another Forge-Cursed Magician

Eirlin glanced at the Magician's face when he returned from court at noon the next day. "You're looking happy."

"I certainly am. The Maridon lords near Falkenby will be more surprised than pleased to find three companies of the King's Lancers on 'training exercises' in their area for the next few weeks."

"That sounds like a good solution. For the moment, anyway."

"Oh, yes, and we will be having a visitor this afternoon."

She looked up from the intricate pattern she was drawing with Excisor on a piece of leather. "An important one, I gather?"

"My old mentor, Rathread."

"A Magician. I've never met another Magician. I was beginning to wonder if there were any."

He never mentions them. I wonder why?

"I never mention them because they have nothing to do with what we are trying to accomplish."

Eirlin cocked her head to the side. "They have nothing to do with us, or they will have nothing to do with us?"

Tyrbrand's smile was partially a wince. "More the latter, I'm afraid."

"Dare I guess why?"

He shrugged. "I am a bit of a wild card. I skirt the borders of propriety."

"Politics?"

"At the beginning, yes. But now..." he gestured towards Excisor who, while Eirlin was distracted, had continued to cut away at the leather.

She looked down at the mess. "Oh, Fang. Look what you've done."

Nibble, nibble nibble. Tasty. Cows. Ashes. Tannin... don't know others...

Eirlin laid him down in the midst of his work. "That's very good, love. The others will be the dye and the oil used to soften the leather."

Dye, oil. Yes, Healer. I will remember.

She looked up at Tyrbrand and they exchanged smiles.

"Are they going to be a problem?"

He waggled a hand. "Yes and no. Rathread is very proud of me, of course. The rest of them are a pretty stuffy bunch and don't approve of improvising."

"The rest of them. Are they all coming?"

"No, just Rathread. Depending on what he decides, I will then receive an invitation."

"Invitation or summons?"

He smiled. "A little of both. Depends on your point of view." He sat beside her, his elbows on his knees. "They could be a great deal of help. Both with Excisor and with the political situation, but I don't think they will involve themselves."

"Why couldn't someone help you when you were having such trouble with Excisor?"

His smile became grim. "First, because they didn't want to. There is always a certain amount of professional jealousy, as you might expect. There was a certain feeling that I should be allowed to stew in my own juices. Also, I didn't ask them. You know how Kitten says that a group of human minds together make such a mess?"

"Too many hands spicing the sauce."

"Exactly."

"So, what do we want from this meeting?"

He held out empty hands. "Politically, I want either their help or their neutrality. For Excisor, it doesn't make any difference. He is what he is, and he's yours. So it all depends on what Rathread wants."

"Well, I suppose we're going to find out."

He is coming.

"You can tell?"

Very powerful mind. Not as powerful as my Lord Ostersund, but stronger than any other I have met in a hundred years.

"You have met other Magicians?"

Of course. A Magician made me, remember.

"Oh. Yes. What else do you read?"

Not much, Eirlin. He is happy and excited and a bit worried. He is now very close. I must be careful.

"Fang, you must hide. You may speak to this Magician when he is ready."

Yes, Eirlin. Powerful Magician. I will hide. Fang disappeared.

Kitten closed down her senses to the barest trickle, depending on her link with Eirlin for most of her perception.

"Shall we greet him in the reception room downstairs?"

"He is an old friend. Here would be better." He nodded to Eowin and she went to bring their guest up.

The man who entered the room was younger than Eirlin had expected, with a trim salt-and-pepper beard and an unremarkable figure. If it hadn't been for the aura which preceded him, she could have passed him on the street.

"So, this is the famous Healer of Falkenby. I am pleased to make your acquaintance, Eirlin Brightwyn."

She made him what she hoped was an appropriate courtesy. "I cannot claim so much knowledge of you, my Lord, but as you are mentor to my mentor, I must show due respect."

His smile seemed genuine, although not warm. Kitten had no way to penetrate past it. It reminded her of someone else she knew. Mentioning no names.

"You make me feel old. A grand-mentor, I suppose we should call me."

"I hope I might learn equally tempered wisdom from you, then, my Lord."

He made a cutting gesture with his hand. "Grand words, my Lady. Grand words and empty, which serve only to smooth beginnings. Now, shall we speak our true thoughts?"

She shot a glance at Tyrbrand, who only smiled.

"Rathread never had much use for social amenities." He indicated three chairs in front of a table set with plates and cups. "Perhaps we could sit?"

"Good idea. Let us sit and allow Lady Eirlin to pretend she is merely a hostess, and pour tea and serve sweets, and waste some more of our time."

Eirlin seated herself with exaggerated grace and reached for the urn. "I don't know, my Lord. You have only been in the room for a dozen sentences, and already I begin to catch your measure."

He shot her a sharp glance. "Good. Then we can speak of business."

"You have requested the meeting. It is for you to direct the conversation."

"I will. Tyrbrand, Lady Eirlin, I have come to apprise myself of developments in this situation. As a long-time associate of Tyrbrand – his mentor, if you will – I feel some responsibility for what we charitably call his creativity. I encouraged it when he was young and was repaid more than I ever expected. Or wanted, for that matter."

"This is not news to me, Rathread."

"Not up until this point. The problem is whether your independent behaviour has become a problem for our people and our realm."

Eirlin cocked her head. "And for your fellowship?"

He nodded to her. "A fair question, and a fair term. We are not an organized society or club. We exert no power over members. There are no fees, no initiation rites, no entrance examinations. One is a Magician or one is not. One who holds the Power takes as much training as he or she wishes. Because of the Power some of us have and the damage we are capable of inflicting, we have always followed the precepts of our people. We train, we urge and we encourage, but we do not force ourselves upon our members or upon the rest of Inderjorne."

"To a fault, some would say."

The elder Magician flicked his hand at Tyrbrand. "Of course you would say that. You, who have embroiled yourself in the political affairs of the kingdom."

Tyrbrand shrugged. "This is an old argument, useful only in appraising Lady Eirlin of the situation. Since we are being forthright to the point of bluntness, why are you here, Rathread? What do you want from Eirlin and myself?"

Rathread raised placating hands. "My own techniques used against me." He smiled at Eirlin. "I have taught him well, have I not?"

He plays a game.

Eirlin sat taller. "I think my Lord fails to follow his own precepts. Once again the conversation circles back on itself."

There was a brief silence, as he regarded her. "Do I detect an echo in this room?"

I am the hiss of the coals in the fire.

"My Lord?"

He smiled knowingly. "Is the lady of two minds? At least she seems to be agreeing with herself."

Ostersund slapped a hand on the table. "Oh, come on, Rathread. If you have a question, ask it. We are not children to be frightened, or touchy Maridon lords to take offense. If you wish to meet the Magic Sword, just say so."

"In that case, I would like to meet the famous Cat with Many Claws."

Eirlin exchanged glances with Tyrbrand, then lifted Kitten from the settee.

"So this is the Weapon that is causing so much stir, so many stories on the street?"

I greet you, my Lord Magician, and afford you the due of your rank and abilities.

"And I greet you, Sword. What have you to say for yourself?"

I am who I am. I need not defend my existence with words.

166

Rathread turned to Tyrbrand. "I was led to expect more. No offence to it, but this seems an ordinary Magic Sword. I have seen its like before. Loyal to a fault to its Hand, but otherwise uninterested in the affairs of men."

He seemed surprised when Tyrbrand laughed. "You have received what you expected."

"I have?" He regarded Kitten more seriously, and she could feel the Powerful mind probing. She gave him nothing. She could learn from Magicians.

The elder Magician turned his attention back to the humans. "All I feel is total indifference." His eyes slid to Eirlin, then back to Tyrbrand. "I am missing something?"

Eirlin took pity on him. "Are you familiar with cats, my Lord?"

"Cats? What...? Oh." He regarded Kitten a third time. "So that's it."

"It is. When she feels it is the right time she will speak to you. Not before."

"And who decides the right time?"

Eirlin rocked a hand back and forth. "She does take the opinions of Tyrbrand and myself into account."

"I am beginning to get the picture."

"If you wish to learn the situation here, I hope that is the case. You came in here with circumlocution, false formality, and equally false brusqueness. She has given exactly as much as you have earned."

There was another silence, during which Kitten could detect Eirlin squashing a slight tremor of guilt, and Tyrbrand likewise suppressing surprise, an equal amount of worry, and, yes, definitely admiration. She did not try to read the other Magician.

If we are finished with the human preliminaries, perhaps we can now get to the substance of this meeting?

"A fine idea, Kitten. Rathread, once again I am offering you the opportunity to ask and be answered. What do you wish to know?"

The older man nodded. "Mainly, what I have already learned. I came with concern about your experiments and the dangerous company you were keeping. I came prepared to discover that you had strayed into strange paths with stranger companions. Instead, I find a mature and tightly-knit unit of Power, against which I am quite helpless, both socially and Magically." He turned to Eirlin. "My Lady Healer, you obviously deserve the reputation you are gaining. My only worry now is whether your close association with such a Powerful entity as your Sword, combined with your connection with the most potent Magician in the realm, does not constitute a danger to all of us."

"I hasten to reassure you, sir, that Kitten is not my Sword. She is Joined to my brother, and takes no orders from me."

"Where is this brother, then?" The Magician's body stiffened. "Who is controlling this formidable Weapon?"

"I can give you no answer besides the one you gave me."

"I gave you?"

"Yes. Think of how a Magician wishes to be treated."

"A Magician?"

"Magicians, Swords and magical Beings of any sort all pose the same problems, and require the same solutions. This has been the lore of our people for untold generations, and I see no reason to believe otherwise now."

For the first time in a long while, Rathread smiled. "Well, that ought to settle the fuddy-duddies who complain about Tyrbrand's 'modern' ways." He sobered. "However, the Healer and the Sword were not all I came to enquire about. How is your other project coming along?" He regarded Tyrbrand critically. "I would say it has taken a lot out of you. Much more than is good for your health, although your guarding is as strong as ever, so I can't get any kind of a picture..."

Kitten could feel Ostersund's wall strengthen. "Fortunately, I have a Healer to take care of my physical well-being, so you need have no concerns on my behalf. However, if you came to meet Excisor, I suppose you must. Eirlin?"

Eirlin laid Fang's scabbard on the table. With a gesture that was part ceremony, she slid him out and laid him on the table. A slight shake of her head stopped Rathread's reaching hand. "This is Excisor. He is very young, and we have carefully limited his connection with humans. Outside our small circle, he has spoken only to the king."

"The king? What did the king think of that?"

"He was quite impressed, I believe. They got along well."

"If he has interacted with the king, he can't be that dangerous."

"Where did you get the idea he was dangerous?"

The Magician shrugged. "It was a possibility to be considered. We just had this discussion about another Entity, I believe."

Eirlin nodded. "Quite true. And we are applying the same remedies. Do you wish to speak with him?"

The Magician frowned. "Speak with him? I get no indication of...well, of anything. Does he speak?"

"He is merely on his best behaviour. Excisor?"

Yes, Healer?

168

"This is the Magician we told you about. He was teacher to the Smith. You may speak to him."

Oh.

"Go ahead."

...can't.

"What do you mean, you can't?"

Can't say anything.

"Of course you can, dear. Go ahead and speak to him."

There was an uncertain pause, then Fang disappeared. His presence snapped out of their thoughts and his visible self was gone from the table.

Eirlin burst out laughing. "He's being shy. He's heard too much about your power, and he's afraid of you."

The older Magician smiled. "I see. Well, if he's that timid, I suppose he can't be much harm, can he?"

Tyrbrand spoke quickly, overriding Eirlin's response. "We are working with him every day, and he has made great progress. Eirlin is training him in all the uses he might be put to as a Healer's tool. It is of great importance that he learns concentration and obedience, due to the delicate and dangerous work he will do."

"Yes, of course. So there is no need for him to have any connection with the political problems we are having."

Eirlin took the hint and slipped Fang back into his sheath. She tried to make it a smooth motion, despite the fact that she had only a hazy idea of where he lay on the table. She replaced the sheath on her belt and turned her attention to the two Magicians, who had slipped into discussing the political situation.

"There are too many brushfires sparking up all over the realm. I have to admit that the Maridon technique is working."

The older Magician frowned. "Surely the king's soldiers can keep the peace!"

"The king's men are being spread thinner and thinner. Most of his forces consist of levies from his nobles. He's trying to stop Maridons from attacking Inderjornese; sending levies from either side to stop the fighting would be like trying to quench a fire by adding fuel. All he can use are his foreign mercenaries."

The older Magician nodded. "I see."

"And things are going to get a whole lot worse before they get better, Rathread. Don't the rest of the Magicians realize that?"

"Of course they do, but I know you understand. We have always been a reclusive lot, trying to keep from seeming too powerful.

Having you messing about with the king's policies scares the life out of them."

"Well, if the Maridons increase their control, and more rogue Sensitives start showing up without proper training, this realm is headed for disaster. You take that idea back to them, and see if they aren't more frightened of that."

"Yes, yes, I'll tell them. And don't worry. No one in the group will get in your way. Their nature works to your advantage in that sense."

"Well, it still frustrates me that they can see danger approaching, and still sit on their hands and do nothing."

"That's the way they have always been, Tyrbrand..."

Kitten could feel the frustration building in Eirlin, and finally it burst through.

"Gentlemen!"

The force of her voice chopped into their conversation like an axe.

"Rathread, I understand your problem and the problems of the other Magicians. However, there is one element that none of you are considering. Your Magicians have lost themselves in their narrow concern for their Powers and their own dealings. They have perhaps forgotten that there is a greater imperative: the need of the people of Inderjorne." She turned the full force of her gaze on the older Magician. "You tell your fellowship that there may come a time, and it may come soon, when their aid is required for the good of the people of Inderjorne. Do you understand what I am talking about?"

"I...I think so."

Kitten could feel her drawing Power and gave freely.

"I hope you do, and I hope you can explain it to them." She took a deep breath and focused her mind on his. "Because if the time comes when the people need the Magicians, their help will be requested. And they will give it. Freely and without stinting. Because that is the way of Inderjorne."

The older Magician sat in silence for a moment, regarding first Eirlin, then Tyrbrand. Finally he spoke. "Yes, Healer. Now I do understand."

Suddenly, he rose. "Well, I believe I have received what I came for. That and more. I came for facts, and I leave with understanding.

"Much though it would be nice to sit and chat, Tyrbrand, and relive old times and old acquaintances, I believe this is not the occasion."

Ostersund stood as well. "I hope that time will come soon. However, at the moment I agree with you."

Rathread bowed to Eirlin, deeper than he had when he entered. "It has been an honour to meet you, my Lady Healer. And your Sword and Scalpel as well. I hope that your feet will always follow the path of the good of Inderjorne," a quick smile flitted across his lips, "at least those of you who have feet."

The younger Magician preceded him to the door and saw him out. Eirlin and Kitten exchanged a wordless communication which include relief, concern, and not a little bit of exultation.

When Tyrbrand entered the room, he was shaking his head.

"What? What's wrong? Was I rude?"

He smiled. "No, no, you did nothing wrong. In fact, I think you did just right. I was too caught up in thinking that my political manipulations would save the kingdom. I, too, had forgotten the imperative of the people. You have given us both a timely reminder."

He laughed, "And you flattened poor Rathread. I doubt if he's ever had the Power turned on him so forcefully."

"Power? I used no Power."

Tyrbrand shook his head again. "Eirlin, you pulled Power from Kitten, Power from Fang, and I think Power from the stones of this house and the ground it is planted on. You'd have pulled it from me if I hadn't caught on. You completely overwhelmed him."

"But I just wanted him to realize..."

"Oh, he did, he did."

Yes, Eirlin, it is good that you can draw on this Power, but it bothers me that you don't know you are doing it.

"I'm drawing Power from people, and I don't even know it?"

"Yes, Eirlin. You have done this several times recently."

"But...what can I do?"

You have to be very careful, Eirlin. Do you realize that you could march a whole village of people to the bank of a river and make them jump in?

"Don't be stupid, Kitten. Why would I do a thing like that?"

Kitten felt a snarl curl the lips she no longer owned. *How about marching a whole tribe of people into a battle where they all would get killed?*

"But I don't think..."

That's right. You're not thinking. And you're not listening. You have a terrible Power and if you misuse it, your little 'I can't kill' problem is going to look like children playing stick-ball.

"Kitten, I have never heard you speak like this."

Because you have never needed it.

The Healer took a moment to digest this. "All right. You have made your point. Obviously you know something about this that I don't, and I have to trust you. What do you want me to do?"

Recognize when you are drawing that Power, and only use it when it is absolutely necessary, keeping in mind the dangers.

"I will do that, Kitten. At least I will try, since I don't know what the dangers are. Will you help me?"

I can tell you any time you start drawing Power.

"That's all I ask. Anything else?"

Learn. It will come, in time.

The Magician chuckled. "Sage words from the youngster." He sobered and came and sat beside her. "But now we must discuss what effect this meeting will have. What he came for, and what he went away with."

"Can we take him at face value?"

"For the most part, yes. He and the rest of them are concerned about your use of Kitten. I think we reassured him on that matter. He was also concerned about Fang: his power and his potential to cause trouble."

"...and you lied to him about that."

"I didn't exactly lie, but I let him believe what he wanted to believe."

"And you think he didn't notice you changing the topic?"

"He may think of that later, but it can't be helped."

"What about the last part? Will he pass my message along truthfully?"

Tyrbrand grinned again. "You know, I believe he will. The Magicians are, as you have heard me complain, traditional to a fault. You just reached back into time and pulled up a tradition that is absolutely basic to our realm and our people, and slapped him across the face with it. He'll be only too happy to pass it along."

"So when we need them, they will be there?"

"I don't exactly know what form that need will take, and I'm sure that some will be more willing than others, but yes, I think they will."

"That's good, then."

"I believe so. At least..."

"What?"

He shrugged. "I'm not sure, but I think it's going to have to be you who asks them."

24. Guardians

"Now, Fang, we're going to cut this thong." She laid it on the table by her chair, the table that bore the nicks and scars of the Scalpel's lessons.

Yes, Healer. Cut.

"But I want you to cut it very carefully."

Always cut carefully. Fang is always careful.

"I know you are, love. This time is special. Do you see this other piece of thong?"

Cut that, too?

"No. I want to cut this piece exactly as long as that piece."

There was a long pause.

Tanin. Tanin and dye and leather oil.

"No, dear, we aren't smelling, now. We're cutting."

Fang cut leather.

"Yes, dear. And I want this one the same as that one. Exactly the same. Do you understand?"

Cut the same.

"That's right. Are you ready?"

Cut the leather.

"All right. Here we go..."

Goat. Not cow. Goat leather.

Eirlin sighed and put the Scalpel down.

You know, Eirlin, I'm glad I'm not in your shoes.

"Why is that, Kitten?"

Because I'd have scratched his soft little nose about three times by now, and I know that wouldn't help, because he really doesn't know what you want.

"That's true. But don't you get just the slightest impression sometimes that he doesn't really care?"

Four scratches.

"Mm hmm."

Magician comes.

Tyrbrand strolled into the sitting room, a bemused expression on his face. "Was that a dark face I saw going out the door a moment ago?"

"Was Charche still here? I suppose he was chatting with MistressWaldwine."

"And since when do we have Maridon lads coming to pay court to my cook?"

She laughed. "I sent him for a snack as a reward."

"A reward for...?"

"Do you really want to know all about this? It's not very important."

"Indulge me. In the present political situation, you never know what is going to spring out of the bushes. A Maridon boy in my home could be a problem if his father doesn't know about it."

"I see. Well, it's not just him. It's the whole group of them. The children who hang out on the street. They have decided that I need an escort. Actually, I think they're bored. There isn't enough schooling for them, you know."

"We agree on that. So how does it work?"

"You know, I'm sure, that this area is mostly Inderjornese homes."

He nodded.

"So the Inderjornese boys, and sometimes some of the girls, come around just after noon to see if I'm going to the infirmary. Then they escort me as far as that park with the playing field. That's neutral territory. They play games there against each other. Rather rough, I gather. From the field it's Maridon territory, and the Maridon boys take me the rest of the way."

"I see."

"It's the same on the way home, but it's rather ad hoc. Today there was no one at the field to take over, so Charche brought me all the way."

"At some risk to himself?"

"Not really. I don't think they would tangle with him. Besides, all he would need to do is tell them he had been with me, and there would be no problem."

"I must say, Eirlin, you never cease to surprise me. That is positively subversive."

"What do you mean?"

He grinned. "While the fathers are getting ready to do battle against each other, you are secretly giving their offspring duties together."

"But I didn't start it. It was their idea!"

"Which makes it even better." His face sobered. "Besides, with the unrest, I'm not that happy about you traveling the streets alone. Yes, this is a good idea. I like it a lot."

She is not quite alone.

"No, Kitten, you are always there. However, you and I know Eirlin. She would risk a great deal of trouble before she would actually take steps to defend herself."

That is too true to be comfortable.

The Magician sat beside her on the settee, leaned back and stretched his hands over his head. "Yes, I think this is all going rather well. There have been very few incidents in the countryside, and the unrest in the capital has been confined to the poorer areas. Jesco is getting us better information than the king's own people can, and his Majesty is making the right moves. Maybe this whole thing will blow over."

"Do you really think so?"

"No, I don't, but I think we have reason for optimism."

He's going to hug you. Don't jump this time. Very good!

His arm dropped around her shoulders and he gave her a quick squeeze. "Not in a small part due to you and Kitten, I have to say." He released her before she had time to react, then jumped to his feet. "And now I have some work to do, to make even more sure of success."

Kitten saw his energetic stride as he left the room, and Eirlin's proud smile as she watched him go. Should she tell the Healer that it was a show for her benefit?

No. Let them have their hour. They deserve it. Soon there will be no time for moments like this.

25. Pain!

PAIN! FEAR! ANGER!

"Wha...?" Eirlin dropped the scroll she was reading, grabbing for Kitten's hilt.

Jesco! Something is very wrong!

Blazing pain, overlaid with searing anger, burned their senses.

"What is it? What's wrong?"

It's Jesco. He's in trouble. He's in pain, and he's angry about it. Meeowwee! That hurt!

"What can we do?"

I don't know, Eirlin. He's too upset to get any information. I don't know where he is, or what's happening. We can't help him, we can't send help. What do we do?

"Send him reassurance. Dull his pain. I don't know, Kitten!"

I cannot do either of those things at this distance, Eirlin.

"Then think of something!"

Another wash of pain, this time tinged with indignation.

"What is happening? Why is he feeling like this?"

I am sorry to tell you, Eirlin, but I think I know. I have felt these emotions before.

"Well...what? Tell me."

He is being tortured.

"Oh, no! Are you sure?"

I have seen men tortured. The emotions are familiar.

"What can we do to stop it?"

There is nothing, Eirlin. With your help I can tell which direction he is in, but...

"Then why are we sitting here? Let's go!"

Eirlin...

"How far? In the city? Do we need horses?"

At that moment they were blasted by a withering wash of pain, which brought Eirlin to her knees. She was just staggering erect again when Tyrbrand stumbled into the room.

"What is going on, Eirlin? Someone is in awful pain, and you're broadcasting it over the whole city!"

"Me?"

"Yes. Who is it?"

"It's Jesco. He's being tortured somewhere. We have to find him!"

"All right. Where is he?"

Power and emotion swirled through the room. Kitten reached out to the other two minds and gathered their talent together. *He is that way, Lord Magician.*

"Very good, Kitten. I didn't know you could do that. How far?

There.

"Yes. Not far." The Magician spun out the door, calling for horses.

As they rounded out of the stable, Ostersund began to spread his awareness ahead through the early evening darkness, and Kitten did the same, showing them where to go. A quick clatter through the empty streets and they were pulling up in front of a ragged warehouse.

"Draw the Sword, Eirlin. You might need her."

"Tyrbrand, I don't think..."

"Only to defend yourself, my dear. I can handle this." He strode into the building, brushing the rotting door aside.

He can handle it, Eirlin. This is going to be fun!

"Jesco is hurt."

Of course, Eirlin. That is not fun. He is not hurting so much now. They have stopped. They are afraid. The Magician is sending fear ahead of him like a huge wave. I am driving it into their minds. They run, Eirlin! They are screaming in terror. Help me reassure Jesco. He doesn't know what's going on.

The Healer joined in, calming the frightened swordsman, while yells arose from the bowels of the warehouse. Then there was a clattering of hooves; three horses burst out of a side door and galloped away. Only two of them had riders. Then the Magician appeared in the doorway, a bent figure beside him.

"Jesco!"

"I can walk." Fierce determination washed over them, and the swordsman straightened. "You deal with that one."

Tyrbrand met Eirlin's eyes, nodded, and returned into the building.

Eirlin slid from her horse and ran forward. "Jesco, what did they do to you?"

"Nothing that could make me talk." He stumbled as he walked.

"What is Tyrbrand doing?"

"One of them didn't get away. They had my arms tied, but they forgot I still had my feet." He wiggled his right foot and winced. "That was very satisfying. Now the Magician will continue the job."

It is his hand. There is blood.

"What happened to your hand, Jesco? Let me see it."

"I haven't actually looked at it myself, Eirlin, but it won't be pretty. Best you leave it."

She reached into her bag, pulling out a roll of cloth. "I'm going to look at it sooner or later. You'd better let me bind it to stop the bleeding, whatever is wrong."

He glared defiance at her as she took his hand. Kitten expanded her senses so that she could twist a quick, firm bandage around the tattered flesh. "There. That will do until we get home."

Eirlin laid a hand on Kitten's hilt. *Tyrbrand?*

Go home, my dear. I have work here, and Jesco needs healing.

Are you sure?

It is rather a long walk. Send Nadorst with another horse. Take Jesco and go, Eirlin. He needs you now.

They mounted, Jesco suppressing a groan as he managed with one hand. Kitten refrained from remarking on the blood on his face as well.

"Be careful, Tyrbrand. Do not over..."

The Magician's answer was a wash of anger which required no words. She winced and tugged her horse's head around, reaching for the reins of Jesco's horse and she passed.

Watch him, Kitten. Let me know if he weakens.

His anger is keeping him strong at the moment.

I am worried what will happen when it fades.

I've never heard you express that concern before.

Don't think of making anything of it.

I wouldn't dream of it. He is fine, Eirlin. You are here, and you will Heal him.

Of that, you may be sure.

26.   Jesco Half-Hand

When they reached home, she had the servants support Jesco to his bed while she gathered her medical equipment.

She sat beside him, Kitten lying along his body, Fang in her fingers, and leaned in to touch his chest.

"Here we are again."

You seem to need patching up quite often, Swordsman.

"A drawback to my trade, Sword. Makes me appreciate your skills so much more."

Erlin straightened. "Well, you have a lot of bruises, but no broken ribs. We will deal with those first. It will be good practice for Fang, before we get to the serious part."

Which we are avoiding at the moment.

Don't be nasty, Kitten. This isn't fun.

Sorry, Healer. It is only my way.

She continued with her work. "So, Jesco, how did you get into this condition?"

"Huh. Bad luck. Remember Tajar?"

"After he abducted me? I could hardly forget. I thought I made some progress with him, actually."

"Well, not enough to keep him out of the service of Vanemar."

"Oh, no."

"Yes. We were sitting there at a meeting and he walked in. Stared at me a moment and said, 'What are you doing here?' When they asked him what he meant, he said, 'Do you know who this is?' and that was the end of it for me.

"Do him credit, he didn't take part in the rest of it. Not that he needed to. He left pretty quickly, I think. I had other things on my mind."

What kind of questions were they asking? What do they know?

"Good point. They started to thump on me at first, just because of who I was. Then they wanted to know who Eirlin really was, what you were up to. Then they got onto the usual troop strengths and movements, and who the leaders were. Especially what Lord Delfontes was doing."

"I hope you told them!"

"I hope I did not. They got serious about it then, but that just made me mad. After a while, they gave up on the beating because they realized it wasn't going to work. Then one genius got the idea that a swordsman would be afraid to lose his hand. That's when they started on...this." He indicated his bandaged hand.

"Jesco, why didn't you just tell them? You couldn't have given them any information really useful to them."

"Pardon my saying so, Healer Eirlin, but you're getting out of your field of duty again. I could most certainly have told them any number of things that would have given them military advantage. But I didn't." He grinned crookedly. "They got me mad, remember?"

Eirlin sighed. "I have to believe you know best, Jesco. Now let's see if it was worth it."

His good hand stayed her. "One thing, Eirlin."

"Yes?"

"You're not going to put me to sleep like last time, so I wake up when it's all over. There may be some decisions to make, and I'm going to be there, every moment."

"It might hurt some."

He barked out a laugh. "To get to watch the great Healer working on me? I'd pay that pain any day."

She began to remove bandages. When the remains of his hand were revealed, Kitten could feel the pain in the Healer's heart.

"Jesco, this is very bad. I can't fix this."

"I didn't think you could. Just do your best."

She shook her head. "All right." She removed the Sword from her sheath. "Rest your right hand on this table. Put your other hand on Kitten's blade."

"Very appropriate."

"Now, Kitten, just like last time. We don't have Tyrbrand here, but Fang will add his help. You keep track of him, because I may be concentrating on other things."

Of course, Eirlin. We will save Jesco's hand.

No, we won't, Kitten. We will make it as useful as we can. That is all.

Whatever you say, Healer. You heard her, Little Tooth. We must give Erlin what she needs, and not distract her.

There was a wash of dismay.

Healer is sad.

Yes, she is sad. He is family.

Fang will help. Fang will be very good.

That's great.

"Kitten, I want you to take care of Jesco. You know how to deaden the signals from the hand to the brain, to dull the pain."

Yes, Eirlin.

"That feels better. What did you do?"

"That's Kitten. She can keep you from feeling most of the pain."

"Useful Sword, this one. I like her."

Thank you, Swordsman. I like you, too.

"Say, she's talking to me again. What does that mean?"

"Probably that she's trying to distract you while I work. Keep it up."

"What do you say to a Sword?"

"I don't know, Jesco. You're the swordsman. I'm the Healer. Talk silently and let me do my duty."

Well, there we go, Kitten. I've been told off properly. No sympathy from the Healer.

No sympathy from the Sword either. Don't distract her. This isn't fun for any of us.

You've said a truth there, Cat.

There was a sober silence while Eirlin worked, using her extended senses and sometimes the point of her Scalpel to assess the damage. Finally she straightened up, stretching her back.

"Well, Healer? What's the verdict?"

She winced, shook her head. "I can save the two outer fingers, but the two middle ones, well...there are...bits...missing. I can't Heal what isn't there, Jesco."

"How's the thumb?"

"Better. It's only broken in two places."

"Oh, nothing to it, then."

"No, that's the easy bit."

He looked into her eyes. "You're serious, aren't you?"

"Oh, yes. I could fix your thumb without any help at all. It's the places where the sinews are cut that I'm worried about."

"The middle fingers?"

"There is no way for you to control them any more. If I leave them there, they will be worse than useless."

"If you have to take them off, take them off."

"I think I have to."

"Well don't sit there blathering, woman. Do what you have to do!"

Sword-man is rude to Healer.

"No, that's normal, dear. This is very difficult for him. He has to be angry at someone."

Don't worry, Little Tooth. He loves her.

"So, as the man says, let's get started. Kitten, keep up what you're doing. Fang, concentrate hard, love. Jesco, don't move; this is very delicate work."

As Eirlin began her difficult task, Kitten noticed that little Fang was not making his usual chatter as he worked. She sent him a glow of quiet approval, gentle enough not to distract him. Then she went about her task, tracing the fine white lines that ran from Jesco's arm to his brain, squeezing them just enough to keep the signals from flowing.

As the operation progressed, Kitten began to get a sick, familiar feeling. She moved deeper into the swordsman's mind, noting absently that the darker corners had lightened since the last time, but that one twisted corridor was worse. With a sinking heart, she aimed her attention at the troubled spot. Once again, what she saw appalled her. The scar from her earlier efforts to help him was warped and cracked, and she could feel pressure building behind it.

Keeping part of her awareness on Eirlin's task, she bolstered the weakening tissue as well as she could, then withdrew. Hopefully, that would hold until a better time. When she returned her full attention to Eirlin, the Healer was stitching a flap of skin over the gap where Jesco's two middle knuckles had been.

"Neat work, Healer."

"Women's work, Jesco."

"No complaints."

"Thank you. We like our customers to be satisfied. Good job, Fang, dear. You made beautiful cuts."

Fang bites well. Nibble, nibble. Tiny, tiny bites.

Finally, Eirlin bandaged the maimed hand and fashioned a sling. "Well, there you are, Jesco. The best I could do, I'm afraid. It won't be much use to you for a month or so, but you should get full mobility in the fingers you have left. Kitten, can you leave a bit of numbness...Kitten?"

Kitten? What's wrong?

Trouble, Eirlin. You have to see this.

I can't do that without his permission, Kitten.

Then ask him.

You're certain?

Ask him.

The Healer laid her hand on her patient's arm. "Jesco, Kitten says she has found another problem, but it will require me to probe deeper. Is that all right?"

He looked at his cousin, then simply returned his good left hand to the Sword blade. She nodded.

All right, Kitten. Show me...oh.

There was a long pause while the Healer viewed the damage. Finally, she pulled herself away.

"What's wrong? What did you find?"

She sighed. "Jesco, remember when you were injured before, and we Healed you?"

"I'm not likely to forget that little experience."

"Do you remember that we Healed more than your body? That you felt much better about everything after that?"

He frowned. "I have a very muddled idea of you and that Magician stomping around in my head. I didn't like it, but I did feel better after you were gone."

"There is no easy way to put this. That old problem is back, and it's worse. The rage and the desire to hurt, to kill, and even to die is there. Stronger than before."

"And we are surprised?"

"No, there is no surprise. What those men did to you brought back all the old memories, brought them back fresh and strong. Jesco, I know what you want to do."

"Again, no surprise."

"But you can't."

"Why not? For once, it will be the right thing to do. Those men are criminals in the eyes of the king, as well. I'll be doing the realm a favour."

"And you'll be doing yourself great damage. If you give in to your anger now it will destroy the person you have become. You will become worse than your father. Your anger will rule you, and I might not be able to help you. You might not want me to."

"I don't want you to help me now. Not if it means letting those vermin get away with what they did to me. It's not good enough for them to be put in prison by the king's guard." His voice rose and his good hand shook. "What they did to me is personal, and it demands my personal attention. They made me angry, and I am going to stay angry until I have dealt with them."

"That is your anger speaking, Jesco."

"I'm sure it is. I have every right."

Eirlin sighed. "Well, I can't help you if you don't want me to." She turned to face him squarely. "Actually, I don't have to help you. It would be much better if you helped yourself."

"Oh, I'm going to help myself, all right."

"No, I don't think so. Come, Kitten, we're going to take Jesco on a little journey."

"Where are you taking me?"

"Into your head."

"What?"

"I want to show you what Kitten found in your mind. I want to show you the scars where we Healed you, the scars which are about to break open again."

"You're going to show me inside my own head?"

"I don't see why it should be a problem. You were complaining about Tyrbrand and me 'stomping around' in there. This time you can come and see for yourself."

"I don't know..."

"What, the courageous Jesco Falconric afraid of what's inside his own head?"

"Most people are. Most people should be."

"Time to stop arguing, Jesco. Do this just once, for me. After that I won't bother you, not matter what you decide to do."

"Is that a promise?"

"I just said it."

He threw up his good hand. "All right, Eirlin. You're the Healer and I trust you. What do I have to do?"

"Nothing, really. Just follow me as I move inside your mind. Kitten, help us."

Close your eyes and look around you. See that red? That's your nervousness about this new experience. Think about something that makes you afraid. Yes, afraid. Think about it, and watch the colour change.

It's redder.

Now think about something that makes you happy. Come on, Jesco, there are things that make you happy. There. It's getting paler. More orange. Oh! What was that bright green? Such a pretty colour, but you hid it away again. No, I won't pry.

I have a good idea what that was.

So do I, and we don't pry.

Yes, Healer.

All right. Does that give you an idea of what we're going to do? This isn't real. It's just a way of picturing what is happening in your mind. If we wanted to, we could go to any place you like. We could go to where you think about Ecmund, for example, and we would see how you regard him.

Not necessary. You know how I regard him.

You understand how this works?

I suppose.

184

All right. We're going deeper now, into the places where your strongest and oldest emotions lie.

What are all those dark places?

The ones you won't be telling other people about.

Hmm. There seem to be a lot of them.

It's your life. You should know. Now, come and look at this.

There was a long moment of stillness. Finally, Jesco made a growling sound. *That's an ugly wound. Who patched it up?*

Kitten and I did, but we were in a bit of hurry. We thought it would do. It would have, if you hadn't had your recent experience.

What's going on behind it?

That is your anger, Jesco.

You asked me to think of something that scared me. That scares me. What if it breaks loose?

It's going to rip a hole in your heart. Your soul is going to spill out on the ground and you will never rise, a true man who can stand on his own feet and say he is equal to other men.

What do you mean?

I mean that once that anger breaks through and you lose control of it, then you will have crossed the line into madness. You will never recover. Oh, you might seem normal for days at a time, but you will never be able to trust it. Sooner or later, you will always return to this. You will hurt and you will kill, and some day, whether by your own hand or another's, you will kill yourself.

Oh.

You hear the truth in what I say, don't you?

Aye. It is all so much clearer when I can see it like this.

I'm going to bring you back now, Jesco. Take your hand off Kitten's blade.

There was the familiar cold wrench of loneliness, and their senses came back to reality.

The swordsman ran his good hand across his brow. "Well, that's not an experience I'd like every day."

"Very few people require it any day at all. I thought you needed to see it."

"I always had some kind of idea, you know."

"So what are you going to do about it?"

"What can I do?"

"Kitten and I can fix it just like last time, but it isn't strong enough, it seems. It would be better if you controlled it yourself. That is the most difficult and the most effective solution. Kitten and I can help you with the pain. We won't make you forget it, but we will make it not matter so much. The problem is that we can't strengthen you against another event, which might bring back the problem all over again."

"I know, I know. I have to do it myself if I want to make progress."

"That's right. Of course, your friends will give you all the support they can, but it's really up to you."

"And how do I deal with my feelings towards those vermin who tortured me?"

"Jesco, how were you taught to deal with people like that?"

He sighed. "I remember this from my training. The only way to win against those types is to live my life and succeed. Nothing I can do to them will ever help me."

"That's right. They had power over your body once. By planning revenge on them, a revenge you know is wrong, you give them power over your mind and your life. For all of your life."

"It sounded much easier in the training class."

"Of course. This is life, not training. It seems ironic to be saying this to you."

"I suppose."

She regarded him a moment longer, but she could tell his mind was no longer with her. He had already begun to tread a long and difficult path. She turned and left him to his battle.

27.   Cuquita's Claws

As Eirlin started out to the West Gate Infirmary the following day, a figure glided up beside her, blonde braid falling over a slim shoulder.

"Why so quiet?"

The girl grinned. "I didn't want to disturb you, my Lady."

"I'm not disturbed. Startled, perhaps. What can I do for you?"

"Nothing, my Lady. It's my turn to walk with you."

"Fine. Let's walk, then." They strolled down the street. "So, how did you get the duty today?"

To her surprise, the girl reddened.

"I gather there is a story there. I have time."

The girl glanced up. "Well, my Lady, the boys didn't really want me to come."

"I'm not surprised. How did you persuade them?"

The slim shoulders shrugged. "I asked them who was supposed to come. They told me it was Sigeric Nesse. So I threw him down and sat on him until he let me take his place."

"Hmm. A rather direct way of making your wishes known."

"Yes, my Lady."

"Let me see. You are Godflaed, and your father is Lord Ljusdal."

"Yes, my Lady."

"Then you outrank me by two places. So I suppose I should be calling you 'my Lady' as well. My Lady."

"I suppose so, my Lady. My mother says we should always be polite." The girl's eyes shot up the street. "There's someone waiting up there."

Cuquita.

Eirlin peered ahead. "I think it's Lady da Launca."

"Ooh. That's not good."

"Don't worry. She is an acquaintance. Hello, Lady da Launca. Do you know Godflaed?"

No Bad Lady today

The Maridon woman's eyes raked the girl, who stood steadfast. "Oh, one of the Ljusdal brood. Your father's a good man. Don't disappoint him like your brother did."

"My brother did not disappoint Father. We are all very proud of what he did. My Lady."

Cuquita raised her eyebrows. "So, you've got spunk, too. Glad I'm not your mother."

"So am I, my Lady."

Cuquita's brows gathered. "I think this is exactly the right time for you to run along and play, little girl. I want to talk to Lady Eirlin."

Godflaed's eyes shot to the Healer.

"You can do your duty from a distance."

The girl nodded and stepped back, and Eirlin motioned Cuquita to join her as she continued up the street.

Kitten sent Godflaed a tight message. *Well spoken, little one.*

The girl started, stared at the retreating backs, then smiled broadly.

"As I said, I wouldn't want to be a parent to that bunch."

"What did the brother do?"

"I have neither the time nor inclination to gossip. I wish to talk to you."

"You made that abundantly clear to Godflaed."

"That's right. And I want to make it abundantly clear to you that it is only in your capacity as a Healer that I speak to you. I will not gossip, I will not be your friend, I will not join your political conspiracy."

Eirlin calmed herself. "Those are the usual conditions under which I treat my patients, so of course, I agree. With the exception of conspiracies, to none of which I belong."

"In other words, keep my politics to myself. Fair enough. Except for one personal matter. Have you dealt with the poisoning?"

"The king is aware of my concern, but it is not enough to force him to act. He has set up procedures that we can use the moment we have more information. Until I can get in to see the patient, we are stymied. I'm sorry, Cuquita, but at the moment..."

"Wonderful. Not that I expected much. My father will..." She faded into thought.

They walked in silence for a moment.

"And what would you like to speak to me about?"

"About what you already know is wrong with me."

Eirlin nodded. "I think you overstate my abilities. I know you are ill. I have some idea of the nature of that illness. I would be very hesitant at this moment to state any diagnosis."

"Gobbledigook and politicality. You know exactly what's wrong with me, because everyone will have told you. I have terrible mood swings, and when I'm in a bad mood, I say anything or do anything that occurs to me, and hurt a lot of people in the process. People who usually deserve the hurt, if you want my opinion."

"Usually, but not always."

"Hence my problem. If I only destroyed those who deserved it, I would be a hero."

"Do you have a problem knowing who deserves it and who doesn't?"

"Not at all. In fact, I have a feeling I'm much better at that than most people. The rest of them believe such horrible pap. Can't they see how stupid they are?"

Eirlin smiled. "Most people can't, and they certainly don't take it as a favour to have it pointed out to them."

Cuquita sighed. "Well, there we are, then. Maybe I don't have a problem after all. Maybe it's all their problem."

"And maybe it isn't."

"Who says?"

"I do and so do you. Your problem isn't other people's stupidity. It's your own lack of control."

"What?"

"Control. Everyone has the desire to say something they shouldn't once in a while. Most people control it. You obviously don't. I think the question is whether you can't, or won't."

Careful, Eirlin.

I know.

"So it's that again, is it?"

"What again?"

"I've been hearing this all my life. 'Cuquita, you must control your temper. Cuquita, you can't just say things like that. Cuquita, what would your father think?' I'm tired of it. I expected better from you."

Eirlin stopped walking and looked straight into the other's face. "And what makes you think they are all wrong, and you are right?"

Cuquita smiled. "And what makes you think that I'm wrong and you're right?"

Eirling began walking again. "Both of us have to assume that, because I'm the Healer, and you're...perhaps...going to be the patient. There has to be a certain amount of trust."

"Trust? What gives you the idea I might want to trust you?"

"I don't know. Perhaps the possibility that I'm the only one you might trust. I don't have any reason to want to do you harm. Quite the opposite."

"No reason? You're 'Jornese, and I'm one of the Invaders. That's enough reason in my mind."

"I fail to see how someone whose family has been here for nine generations could be considered an invader."

Cuquita stopped dead in the street. "How did you know that?"

"What do you mean?"

"How did you know how long my family has been here?"

"I didn't. I just made a guess, based on the average Maridon family."

"I don't think so. I think you've been checking up on me. And then I have to ask myself, 'Why is the little 'Jornese Healer so interested in me that she wants to know all about my family?' And now I know."

"I assure you, Cuquita, it was only..."

"Of course. Only a guess. A suspiciously accurate one. That wasn't a guess, Eirlin the Not-So-Smart. That was a slip of the tongue, and I've caught you."

"Cuquita..."

"That would be 'Lady Cuquita' to you, you 'Jornese slime. I can't imagine why I thought you might be of any use to me. I can't even imagine why I'm standing here talking to someone as inconsequential as you are." A painted fingernail jabbed at Eirlin's chest. "You just keep your snooping blonde head out of my affairs, or you'll soon find out what I'm capable of."

The dark woman turned and strode away up the street, her boot heels striking sparks from the paving stones.

Oh, my.

"Oh, no."

That one is definitely not on an even balance.

"Why did I say that?"

Why did you say what?

"Why did I make that comment about her family? I should have known better."

I fail to see why. She's obviously unbalanced, and there's no telling what will set her off.

"But I'm the Healer. I'm supposed to know what will set her off."

That is complete nonsense. There's no way of knowing what will spark her anger.

"And I'm the Healer. What she said was true. If she's going to trust me, I have to earn the trust. Today I threw it completely away, and it was so important! I have failed Tyrbrand, and I have failed my Calling."

Pffth!

"It's easy for you. You're a Sword. You don't have to understand these things."

I understand when I hear someone talking complete drivel.

"Well, thank you so much, Kitten. You are supposed to be helping, not calling names."

Great. First Cuquita and now you. Why don't we all get angry and storm off in different directions? Of course, I can't really storm off, and I doubt it would be wise to leave me lying in the street. I'll tell you what. Why don't you restrain yourself until we get to the infirmary, and then you can throw me into a corner. That will make you feel so much better.

"Kitten, I think I have had just about enough of this. Why don't you shut up and let me think about how to solve it?"

Shut...? All right, Eirlin. Whatever you say.

Kitten decided to shut up. *Sometimes there is no dealing with these silly humans.*

She sent a caution to Godflaed, and the girl completed her escort duty at a respectful distance.

28.   Battle Is Joined

Her mind in a turmoil, Eirlin was not prepared for the summons that arrived at the infirmary in the hands of a very polite page later that the afternoon.

"My Lady Eirlin, his Majesty requests your presence."

"He does? Me? Why? When?"

"I don't know why, my Lady, but he asked, 'at your earliest convenience.' He and Lord Ostersund and Surgeon Calicasas have been discussing something for quite a while now."

Eirlin, wake up. You know what 'earliest convenience' means when a king says it.

"Yes, yes of course." She stood up, straightened her apron, and tossed her braids back.

"I have a coach waiting, my Lady."

"Oh? A coach? Is it that important?"

"No, my Lady," the boy's face creased in a grin, "but I gather you are."

She shot him a firm glance, to which he responded with innocent sobriety. She took off her apron and followed him.

They got down in the main courtyard in front of the palace, and the boy led her by a familiar route to the king's reception room. However, when they approached the door, the guard stepped forward, a frown on his face and a finger to his lips.

The page stopped, glancing at Eirlin in confusion. Raised voices could be heard from behind the door. The guard stepped back to his proper post, a worried look on his face.

His Majesty is not happy.

Can you tell why?

Listen.

Kitten expanded the Healer's senses, and the words became clear.

"Your Majesty, we have heard all this before. We all know that our Maridon ways are the best. Those who want anything else are trying to go back to the old ways, the time of darkness before we came to this benighted realm and brought them learning and discipline."

I know that voice.

Da Baneza.

Eirlin's eyes widened.

Do not worry. He does not have his Sword with him. Listen. The Magician speaks.

"Your Majesty, the discipline he talks about is enforced from the outside by the power of proctors and soldiers. It only works when they are there to enforce it. It will never replace the self-discipline of one who has been taught all his life what is right and what is wrong."

Da Baneza gave a scornful snort. "Oh, certainly. 'We'll discipline ourselves, as long as you let us do what we want.' Your Majesty, how can you rule this realm if half of your subjects won't do what you tell them?"

"I can't help but think, your Majesty, that there is a certain amount of 'what I tell them' in Lord da Baneza's theories."

"And why should what you think have any importance? Your Majesty, this is the perfect example of what I am talking about. This petty noble of a declining family has no place in making the decisions that affect this realm. Why is he even here?"

For the first time the king spoke, and his voice was even and cold. "Lord Ostersund has proven his ability and worth to the realm many times over. However, that is beside the point. It is my prerogative to choose whomever I wish to advise me, and since you are so concerned with prerogatives, you are well aware that it is not your place or any man's to interfere. You were allowed to attend this meeting at your own request, and through no desire of mine. If you have said what you came to say, perhaps you would be wiser to retire."

"Of course, your Majesty. I thank you for the honour you do me by allowing me to attend you."

They are coming out. Turn away.

The door opened and Eirlin turned her back just in time before da Baneza strode out, his head high, the Power of his presence preceding him, a satisfied smirk on his face. He looked neither left nor right, but swept on his way, two Maridon nobles flanking him, their cloaks swirling as their feet hit the stone floor, paces and minds in unison.

They are so childishly proud of themselves.

The Healer shuddered. *Dangerous children.*

I will inform the king that we are here.

Kitten narrowed in on the king's mind. *Your Majesty, you have requested that we attend you?*

There was a moment's confusion, and then the king's voice came through the open door. "Of course, of course. Please come in ... ah... my Lady Healer."

The guard stepped aside, and Eirlin entered. The king sat rigid on his throne, Lord Ostersund and a dark-haired man in a Surgeon's cloak standing one on either side.

The king gestured her in. "Be welcome, my Lady. I apologize for disturbing your labours. However, we have made more progress in setting up our medical cadre. Have you met Head Surgeon Calicasas? He has agreed to join you in the planning."

"Only briefly, your Majesty. I am honoured, Head Surgeon. It will make a great deal of difference to have someone of your experience with us."

The Maridon nodded, but it was the king who spoke. "However, as I'm sure you noticed, our meeting was interrupted by affairs that need my immediate attention. Head Surgeon Calicasas, I believe we have laid the ground for this task. Perhaps you and Lady Eirlin will meet and continue with the details."

"Of course, your Majesty." He met Eirlin's eyes. "I will contact Healer Eirlin tomorrow and arrange a conference." He bowed to the king, nodded to Ostersund, and left the room.

There was a brief silence as the king caught the Magician's eye and shook his head. "I suppose that tells us something."

Ostersund pressed his lips together. "We have heard his demands before."

He is lying. He only wants power for himself.

"I don't need my Magic to know that, Kitten. I have heard all this so many times. The problem is, people believe it. And what can I say? All I can do is start an 'I am not, Yes you are,' shouting match."

Kitten clamped down on her dismay. Even in his illness, she had never seen the Magician feel helpless to the point of anger.

The king glanced at Eirlin, his brow wrinkled. "People outside heard all that?"

"All that was audible outside was raised voices, but no meaning. Kitten can enhance my senses so that I can hear. It is especially easy when those involved are Sensitive, as all of you are."

"Including Lord da Baneza?"

"Yes, your Majesty. The other two as well."

Once again the troubled glance between king and Magician.

"And that tells us even more, your Majesty."

"If I am permitted to ask, what did he want?"

"He requested urgent audience with me, and basically pushed his way in without proper invitation. My guards are unused to improper behaviour from one of such high regard in the realm." The king's voice became harsh. "Their experience will be corrected."

194

"What did he wish to speak of so urgently, your Majesty? If I may ask."

"Of course you may. It was the same demands that Vanemar has been making all along. He blames the Inderjornese for the violence. In his view, they have been clinging to power to which they have no right, and now that their position is challenged, they are resorting to more desperate measures to maintain their unearned place."

Ostersund shook his head. "Which, if you do not know the truth, sounds probable."

The king rested an elbow on one arm of the chair, his chin on his fist. "Yes, it is very clever. I have never been faced with such a subtle challenge. We are going to have to move very carefully. He really had nothing new to say to me. It was a ploy to demonstrate his power to his followers. Hence the forcing in without permission."

He seemed to recall himself and sat straighter. "Well, thank you for your support. I will think on this, and make conference with my usual advisors." His lip twisted. "Before anyone gets the idea that the petty scion of a declining house has undue influence. The gods alone know what he would think of Lady Eirlin's presence."

Ostersund bowed. "And it is best that he never knows."

"I agree there. I will contact you both once I have thought further. If that helps any." The king shook his head, and they left him deep in thought.

They shared a worried glance, bowed and left the conference room.

"What are your plans?"

Eirlin looked about. "I suppose that since it's not late, I should go back to the infirmary. If I can concentrate on whatever I'm doing there."

"Right. I will see you at home, then. We can talk more of this tonight. Maybe we can come up with something."

"Maybe..."

29.   The Healer Needs Healing

Eirlin was still out of sorts when she returned that evening from the infirmary, and Kitten felt it better to say nothing. The Healer went immediately to Jesco's room, where he was sleeping restlessly.

His hand is hurting. Put me close to him.

She placed the Sword against his arm, then stood there and regarded him, lying there so still and grey. Her heart sank. She sat on the chair by the bed, her eyes filling.

Kitten, snuggled close beside him, gradually eased the pain, allowed him to wake naturally.

Slowly, his eyes opened. "Oh. Hello, Linna." His voice was low, without life.

"Oh, Jesco, I am so sorry."

His eyes opened wider. "Something wrong?"

"Of course something's wrong. Look at you. Look what I've done to you."

He slowly lifted the bandaged hand, regarded it with awakening interest. "Yes, I guess you did."

The tears spilled over. "What can I say, Jesco? What can I do?"

"I sort of thought you'd done enough, Eirlin."

"You have a right to say that."

"Kitten, what is going on?"

She's having a 'poor little Eirlin' moment.

"Ah. That explains a lot."

Yes. It seems nothing is going right.

"Well, nothing is. I can't heal Tyrbrand. I try, but he just won't let me get close enough. Then this happens to you. Now I've just messed up dealing with Cuquita, and that affects the political situation everybody says I'm supposed to be taking care of..."

One side of his mouth pulled up. "What do you think, Kitten? There's got to be some advantage to being one of her patients. You think maybe she'll listen to me?"

I doubt it. Listening is not one of her strong points. Telling, now...

"Kitten! That's not a very nice thing to say. I listen..."

"Aye, there she goes again. Telling instead of listening."

Yes, and I'm sure that if she listened, she might hear something good about herself.

"That's very true, Kitten. You see, I was about to tell her what she had done for me. You'd think she'd want to hear that."

You'd think so, wouldn't you?

"She doesn't realize that when she and her precious Magician stomped around in my head and Healed me last summer, she took away the thing that might have made me the best swordsman in the realm."

Or more likely given you a chance to get yourself killed young.

"You get the point. I don't think Eirlin does."

That would take listening.

"Which we have just decided she doesn't do very well."

The Healer's voice rose, and Kitten could feel her emotions swirling. "I don't know what you two are doing, but will you stop talking about me as if I wasn't here?"

Jesco laid his good hand on Kitten's hilt. "What do you think? Are we getting through?"

I don't think so. She's still giving orders.

"It's a real problem, you know. People who give orders, I mean."

Why is it a problem, Jesco?

"Well, when someone gives an order and expects everybody to obey without question, then that person takes all the responsibility for the consequences."

That's very perspicacious of you, Jesco.

"Yes. I'm a very perspic-whatever sort of person."

So how does that apply to you and Eirlin?

"WILL YOU TWO STOP THIS?"

"Well, it's this way, Kitten. Let's say, for example, that this spying task was all Eirlin's idea and I was just following orders."

Ah. And then it all went wrong.

"Right. Then whose fault is it?"

Eirlin's.

"Right again. What a smart Cat you are. So how do I feel about Eirlin and this?" He raised his bandaged hand.

I would have to guess you'd be all bitter and upset, and hate her forever.

Jesco nodded slowly. "Yes, I think that would be appropriate."

Well, now, I think that would be a real shame, her being your favourite cousin and all.

"Exactly. A real shame, Kitten."

So how can we solve this?

Jesco put on a judicious frown, shooting a quick glance at Eirlin. She was sitting, dead still, listening. "I think we have to attack this from a different angle."

Sound military thinking.

"I thought so. Instead of just doing what I was told, what if I agreed with Eirlin, and went on the spying mission because I thought it was the right thing to do?"

I see. Then when it all went wrong, there was nobody to blame, it was just bad luck.

"Exactly. I just went into a fight for a good cause and I lost. Big deal. It doesn't mean the cause is any worse, or the people fighting it are any worse."

Of course not. It just means you cut your losses...oops. Bad metaphor, sorry.

"No problem. You cut your losses and move on, find a better way to win."

Exactly. You're going to have to find a new way to kill yourself, now.

Eirlin leaned forward. "But Jesco, you can still be a swordsman. Ecmund always said you could beat him with your left hand."

"Will you listen to the woman? It's not enough that I lose my right hand for her, now she wants my left!"

"Oh...I'm sorry, Jesco. I didn't mean it that way. I just wanted..."

"You were just being a Healer, wanting me to feel better. Don't worry, I already thought of the left-hand thing. I won't be helpless. I just won't be at the front of the battles, now. I'll have to find other ways to amuse myself and keep you on your toes."

She snorted. "I hope you don't think you're amusing me at the moment. You two and your street-corner comedy routine."

He shrugged. "I know about anger. I was just using yours. Seems to have worked."

At least she's stopped giving orders.

Her shoulders slumped, and she sighed.

"What was that for?"

"I was just thinking what a pass I have come to. I'm being lectured on my profession by someone from the opposite side of the argument. My patient is being kept from proper rest to heal me. I've come a long way in the past few months, and it hasn't been a good way."

Jesco covered her hand with his good one. "Linna, do you remember how I used to say that as long as you kept being you, the world was in its proper place?"

"I used to like that. Now I think it's a horrible responsibility to put on anyone."

"No, it isn't. I didn't mean you had to be perfect. Just that you had to keep trying. I never expected you to succeed all the time."

"I did."

"I know. That's part of being you, but it isn't the important part. Just keep trying. As long as you're trying, I'm happy. Then I can go and make my bumbling way through life, knowing that even if things don't turn out perfectly it's not because we didn't try."

He lay back on the bed, patting her hand again. "Take your own medicine, Healer. Work with your strength, reduce the damage, keep your spirits up, and the body will heal itself. Now, I've lost a bit of blood, and it'll take a week of rest to get over that, so maybe you'll take your little problems away. Cry on the breast of your handsome Magician for a while. He'll appreciate it more, I'm sure."

She half-rose, sat back down.

"No, go ahead. Kitten will put me back to sleep, and sleep's what I need. You go out and do Eirlin-things, and let me heal." He lay back and closed his eyes. Then he opened one. "Go on with you."

"Yes, Jesco."

"I just love a woman who does what she's told. Ready, Kitten?" His body wiggled deeper into the mattress.

Excuse us, Eirlin. We have Healing to do. Yes, Healing. Me, the Cloud Cat, Fearless in Battle. Healing. Think about that one, if you're going to count up your accomplishments.

Eirlin tossed her head and rose. "I will allow myself to be lectured by my cousin. I will not tolerate an uppity Sword."

If that means you'll leave us in peace, it's fine with me.

The lift returned to her step as she left the room.

What do you think, Jesco?

"She needed that. They always do."

True. If you don't push them how can they develop a good fighting attitude?

"I think she's shaping up nicely, don't you?"

She needs to. Things aren't getting any better in the realm.

His attention dwelt on his maimed hand. "I'd have to agree with that."

Right. She'll be in fighting trim when she's needed. You'll be of more use when you're needed if you get a lot of sleep right now.

"I'd have to agree with that, as well." Then she could feel his eyes open again. "Kitten, are you planning all this?"

Wish I was. I'm improvising, just like the rest of you.

"Too bad. It would be nice to think somebody has it under control."

That's the king's job. We're just loyal underlings. She started to ease him into sleep.

He grinned. "I believe that. 'Night, Kitten."

Have a good rest, Swordsman. You were a hero just now.

"Again? I don't think I want to make a habit of this."

We'll see what we can do. She closed his mind down, and he drifted away.

She sent him a soft purr, and allowed it to soothe herself as well.

30.   A New Arrival

"What's wrong, Eirlin?"

She held out a tattered piece of paper to the Magician. "This."

He eyed it. "Cutting practice again?"

"Yes. Look at this corner. Perfect arcs, and so tiny you can hardly see them. But then look at this. They're all square!"

"Is that a problem?"

"I was trying to work on arcs, and he remembered something you taught him about geometric shapes. So away he went. The work is too fine for me to force him. That's the point. He has to be able to do them himself, but he just won't listen."

"I see. Is there anything you'd like me to do?"

"I don't think so. I just need to work on his concentration. He's bored and he doesn't realize how important this is."

She glanced up at Tyrbrand and smiled. "But don't let me bother you with these minor worries. How are things in the rest of the realm?"

He glanced down at the papers in his hand, and she could feel his worry.

Her smile faded. "What is it?"

He shrugged, an unusual gesture for him. "It's not good, Eirlin. I just got these dispatches. The first three especially. I had wanted you to look at them, but perhaps..."

She reached out. "Of course I will."

He sat and watched while she read the top letters on the pile, her mood becoming grimmer. Finally she looked up. "What is this 'state of siege' business?"

He shook his head. "It's obviously a ploy. A couple of Maridon lords out east of Hartgast have worked da Baneza's trick perfectly. They have provoked their neighbors into defensive actions, which they say are attacks, and now they have declared that they are in a state of siege and have closed their borders."

"To everyone?"

"Exactly. Which leaves them independent of the king's powers. They won't let traders through and they've cut off the Post carriages. They're choking the whole eastern end of the realm."

"What can we do?"

"Nothing at the moment. He can hardly send in his troops, can he?"

"Not unless he says they are coming to help."

"Hmm. That might be a plan. Thank you Eirlin. I'll suggest that to his Majesty this afternoon." He stood. "Will you look over the rest of them? I'd like your opinion on some minor problems as well."

"If you think I can help in any way..."

He touched her cheek with one finger. "You help a lot, and I'm very aware of how hard it is for you."

They shared a smile and then he departed, leaving her poring over the dispatches.

How interesting.

Eirlin glanced up absently. "What's interesting, Kitten? I'm rather busy."

You'll see. I think you're about to get distracted.

"If that was meant to attract my attention, you have succeeded. What is so interesting?"

You'll see when she gets here.

"When who gets here?"

It would be better if you went down to the door. She is a bit upset.

Eirlin rose. "Who is upset? Kitten, will you stop playing games and tell me what is going on?"

She is at the door, and she will tell you herself, I'm sure.

With a disgusted snort, Eirlin strode from the room. Kitten lay contentedly, listening to the voices down in the entrance hall.

"Wynna! What are you doing here?"

"Take me to him, Eirlin. He needs me."

"Who?"

Eirlin, she isn't here to make you a dress. Figure it out, but take her to him while you do. She has come a long way in a hurry.

"Yes, please take me to him, Eirlin."

The Healer regarded the girl more closely. Her clothing was wrinkled and travel-stained and her face had a drawn look. There was no denying the fierce resolve that radiated from her.

"Of course, Wynna. His room is this way."

Kitten could feel the girl's determination drive her up the stairs and along the hall in spite of her fatigue. Once at the swordsman's doorway, however, she paused. "May I enter, Jesco?"

He had been sitting on his bed, staring into space. Seeing her, he tossed the corner of the blanket over his injured hand. "Wynna!"

"May I assume that is an invitation?" She strode into the room, but Kitten could feel her body trembling.

Taking her curiosity firmly in hand, Eirlin reached around and pulled the door shut behind her.

That was very polite. Do you want to eavesdrop?

202

"Kitten! Of course I do not." She returned to the sitting room. "But if you are finished having your fun, you can tell me what you know."

I know very little.

"Right now, Kitten."

I told you. She Listens.

"Yes. I understand that, now."

Her Power is like that of others. It works best when touching, and least when farthest away.

"I see."

Do you remember when we called to the Magician?

"Yes. The Power of many minds communicates farther." Eirlin froze. "You mean, when Jesco was being tortured...?"

There were many Powerful minds involved in very strong emotions.

"Oh, the poor thing! She had to listen to it all!"

It was very difficult for her, because she could only feel the emotions, not understand what was happening. I imagine she thought Jesco was in a battle, and that he was being killed.

"So she immediately got on the Mail coach and came."

She will tell us when she is finished.

It was a long time before Wynna left Jesco's room. When she came out to the sitting room, her face was tear-stained, but there was a triumphant glow to her whole being.

"He is asleep, now."

Eirlin smiled up at her. "Then please come in and rest. You must be very tired. When did you last eat?"

"Oh...a while ago."

Eirlin indicated a crowded side table. "I thought so. I have had something laid out for you."

"All this for me? But...it isn't dinner time yet."

"Then save some room for dinner if you like." She gestured for the other girl to go ahead. "But please, you must tell me what is going on."

"Kitten already did." She stepped forward, and Kitten could feel her effort to restrain herself from stuffing the delicate pastries in her mouth.

You are very hungry. Don't stop to talk. I have told Eirlin what I knew, and you heard me. You always Hear me, don't you?

The girl nodded, crumbs flying. "Yes. You speak so clearly."

Thank you.

"So was it as Kitten said? You felt everything?"

The smile faltered and Wynna set down her food. "Yes. It was terrifying. I thought someone was killing him. I knew when you Healed him, though. There was Power in that as well. So that made me feel better. And I came. It felt like the right thing to do."

"I'm sure it was. He needs you more than you think."

Perhaps not, Eirlin.

"I know what he needs, Eirlin."

"Of course. Pardon me. I keep forgetting." She frowned at the younger girl. "There is a great deal that you never let on. Why?"

"I don't know how to explain it to you, but I find people to be...noisy. Especially large groups of them. I prefer to be by myself most of the time."

Eirlin cocked her head to one side. "You don't just mean noise, do you? You mean the noise in your head."

"You understand."

"Didn't someone teach you how to block other people's thoughts? When you were a child, that must have been part of your training."

"Yes, Father was a Listener as well, and he was teaching me. When he got sick, he couldn't any more. Then, when I...grew up, you know...?"

"Sometimes the Powers increase greatly when you become a woman."

"Yes. I could Hear people so much stronger, but I didn't know how to block them out completely."

"You can talk to Tyrbrand about that. Magicians must have the same trouble." She glanced at the girl. "Surely you find Jesco difficult to be around, then. His mind is so noisy."

The girl smiled, shook her head. "Not at all. Ever since that day...you know the one, last year, when you rescued me from those soldiers who were teasing me, and then had to keep Jesco from fighting them?"

"Yes. What happened then?"

"Well, I was upset, and he was upset, and you sent him to calm me down."

"You heard that, did you?"

"I Hear everything you send, Eirlin. You send very clearly."

"I see." Eirlin's face reddened.

The girl shook her head. "No, no. You are very discreet."

A relieved laugh. "Well, that's nice to know. Tell me about Jesco."

"He came over to me, and he was so...so protective. He didn't know he was doing it, I'm sure, but he threw up a wall around me. Suddenly, everything went absolutely still. It was the first time I had been able to relax in years. It was like sitting in a sheltered garden, knowing the wind was howling outside, but inside it was completely calm."

"Jesco did that?"

The girl shrugged, and one side of her mouth quirked. "You told him to calm me down. He always does what you tell him. He calmed me."

"I see. But he hasn't stopped being angry sometimes..."

"Oh, no. When he's angry I can hear him clear across the village and sometimes all the way out to the farm. That's not calm!" She smiled again. "But the moment he realizes I'm around, he controls his anger and uses the strength of his emotion to put up my wall for me."

"So he's always calm in your presence."

Wynna giggled. "That day I went into the tavern? He wasn't calm, then. He was so worried! I was torn in half. Part of me wanted to cry, because I was so scared, and the other half wanted to laugh, because Jesco was so worried."

"That wasn't very nice, Wynna."

She shrugged. "I had to do something. A girl doesn't want to be shut up in a garden all her life. I just had to wake him up."

"You did that, all right." Eirlin laid her hand on the other girl's. "You're good for him."

"He's good for me. We'll make a fine couple."

"Are you in love with him?"

"I don't know. Not yet. I just love being around him." She looked left, then right, and leaned in closer. "I also love being able to control him. He's a big, powerful man, and I can get him to do just about anything I want." She straightened suddenly, frowning. "Does that sound awful, Eirlin?"

Eirlin burst out laughing. "No, Wynna, it sounds pretty normal to me. Most women don't have a lot of power, and one good way to get it is to borrow it from a man. You've latched onto one of the more difficult ones, though."

Wynna shrugged. "I didn't really choose him. It just happened, and I realized that it was good."

Eirlin leaned back with a satisfied smile. "Well, you say he's good for you, and you certainly have a good effect on him."

"So you approve?"

"Why should it matter what I think? If you want him, have at it."

Wynna tilted her head, frowning. "Of course it matters. You can't lie to me, you know."

"I wasn't lying!"

The corner of the smaller girl's mouth quirked. "You never actually lie, Eirlin."

"Why don't I like the sound of that?"

"I think you select the truth you want. Then you make it happen. There's nothing wrong with that, I don't think."

"I'm not a liar, I'm just selective about the truth. Hmph." She shot the younger woman a glance. "You're not as soft as everyone thinks, are you? All the time we thought you were shy, but you aren't. You let us believe it because it meant we left you alone."

"It was quieter that way."

Eirlin grinned. "And when Tyrbrand teaches you how to dampen the noise, then we find out what you're really like?"

"Maybe I'm raucous. I've always wondered what it would be like to be raucous."

"I think that takes practice."

"I'll have to work on it, then"

I could help. I have seen many raucous people.

"I wouldn't take her up on that, Wynna. She probably means many drunk people."

The Magician comes.

Eirlin turned as Ostersund entered. "We have another guest, Tyrbrand."

"So I gather. I am pleased to meet you, Friedewynn. It explains so much of what I see in Jesco."

Wynna blushed, and Eirlin put a protective arm around her shoulders. "That's not fair and not polite, Tyrbrand."

He grinned and brushed her objection aside with a sweep of his hand. "Friedewynn is used to dealing with the truth behind the words."

"I suppose I am, my Lord."

"I hope you don't mind, but I have an idea of your conversation. I am not as used to living with noisy minds as you are."

Eirlin raised her nose a bit. "And did you hear anything interesting?"

"No, I wasn't close enough to hear the actual words until just a moment ago. I gather Friedewynn needs some training."

Yes, in the art of being raucous.

"Oh, I can handle that, too. In return she can do something for me."

"Certainly, my Lord. Anything."

He sat in his usual chair. "In the first place, you can drop the 'my Lord' all the time. We're all friends here. I don't expect you'll get used to using my first name until we've had a few training sessions, but you can relax."

"Thank you."

"What you can do for me is tell me about your journey here. You came by the Post, I assume?"

"Yes, except for Lord d'Angelo's demesne. I had to ride through in a farm cart and walk part way."

"I was afraid of that. Did you get stopped anywhere else? At other than the normal Post Houses?"

"Oh, yes. Several times."

"By whom?"

"Usually a troop of mounted men. Once it was footsoldiers. Always in full livery, and always led by an officer. A Maridon officer."

"Hmm. And what did they do?"

"They questioned everyone. Twice they took someone off the coach and wouldn't let him back on."

"Arrested him?"

"I don't think so. Both people were Inderjornese, and both times I didn't get much fear from them, just anger and frustration. I think they were simply turned away, and not allowed to cross into that Lord's demesne."

Wynna, can you read Maridons?

"I get a general feel for their emotions, but I can't read anything specific. Never words. Why, Kitten?"

Could you read any of those who stopped the Coach?

"Oh. Yes, now that you mention it. Those who stopped the coaches were all Maridons, of course, but I could read quite a bit from three of the officers. Not as much as from most of us, but a surprising amount."

Ostersund rose and began to pace. "So the Maridon lords are pushing harder. They're restricting passage for certain Inderjornese, and some of the perpetrators are rogue Sensitives."

"That's what it seemed like to me, Lord Ostersund."

"Thank you, Friedewynn. I know some people who will be very interested."

"Anything I can do to help."

He turned a smile on her. "You help the most by being here for Jesco. He has endured a great deal for our cause, and whatever you can do to help him will be appreciated by everyone. Including the king."

"Oh. Well...thank you...but..."

My Lord Magician?

Yes, Kitten.

I don't think she really wants that.

"Oh. Of course. You would rather not be involved in all that noise?"

"If you don't mind."

"Certainly. Whatever you wish. We won't be spreading this story around in any case."

We don't really want to admit that our spy got caught.

"True, and we don't want to spread excuses for anger on either side. So you can rest easy, Friedewynn. Only those who really need to know will even be aware you're in the Capital."

"Thank you, my Lord."

"Better for everyone. Eirlin, how is your patient?"

"Sleeping. Healing."

"Good."

There was a short pause. "Why do you call her 'Friedewynn,' Tyrbrand?"

"Probably because that is her name."

"What do you mean?"

"Eirlin, once in a while Jesco calls you 'Linna,' right?"

"Yes. It's my nickname from when Ecmund was small and couldn't say my full name."

"It is similar with Wynna. She used that name because it made her seem smaller."

"Because she was hiding her Power, which might cause people to be afraid of her."

"Is that right, Friedewynn?"

"Yes, Lord Ostersund."

"I see." Eirlin glanced at the younger girl, then away." We'll call you 'Friedewyn' then. It's the least we can do to make up for how we treated you."

The girl shook her head. "No, Eirlin. You treated me the way I wanted you to. You have nothing to atone for. It was my choice."

Eirlin's mouth turned down. "I suppose. But a choice made by a young child may not be a good one."

Sounds to me like you're doing it again. Treating her like a child.

Wynna reached out and put a palm on Kitten's hilt. "Eirlin has had a tiring day. She doesn't need trouble from a naughty Cat."

I was just trying to help.

"What makes you think I need it?"

Ah. The Lady With Many Swords has bested the Cat with Many Claws.

208

"Perhaps that is for the better, don't you think?"

I have decided to call you Wynna. You need that.

"Thank you, Kitten. I'll know I can count on you to keep my feet on the ground."

I was created to serve.

31. Bad Lady

Trouble, Eirlin.

"What is it this time?

Cuquita. She just stormed in and...

Eowin, obviously rattled, opened the door. "My Lady..."

"That's all right, Eowin. I'll take care of it." She picked up her Scalpel. "Come on, boy, let's go see what she wants."

No, Eirlin.

"Why not, baby?"

Bad Lady, Eirlin. Bad, bad.

"You said that before. What do you mean?"

Today Bad Lady. Cuquita gone today.

"Today Cuquita isn't there, but she's a bad lady?"

Bad, bad.

Eirlin sighed. "All right, little one. I suppose I'll figure that out some day."

Not go?

"We are going to see what she wants, bad lady or no. You can hide if you want."

The tiny shudder that ran through him before he disappeared gave her pause, and she determined to be on her guard. Young as he was, there was no telling what form the magic Tyrbrand had imbued in him would take if he was frightened.

Take me with you.

Without comment, she belted the Sword on.

Not that you'd have the sense to draw me, even if you needed to. At least I can help with Fang.

In the lower reception room Cuquita was sitting in a rigid pose, her flat stare unwelcoming. She did not stand as Eirlin entered.

Eirlin sat opposite her, trying to send feelings of hospitality. Friendship seemed out of place.

Cut.

What?

Cut. There. See?

No, Fang. We do not just go cutting in people. We don't even go that far into their minds unless we have their permission, or they are very ill.

Bad Lady very ill. Cut Bad Lady. Cuquita well.

No, love, we don't do that.

"I don't suppose you have the manners to speak to me politely."

"I'm sorry, Cuquita, I was just thinking."

The other woman smiled sweetly. "That's what I meant by bad manners, dear. You don't ignore your guests just because something you think is important occurred to you."

Eirlin took a moment to register the other's words, then another moment to calm herself. "I do apologize, Cuquita. It comes from being by myself a lot. I guess I'm not used to other people being around all the time."

"Even back in the woods where you come from, they don't find you good company?"

"Oh, no. I just find myself reasonable company, so I don't go looking for others. I suppose you might see that as selfish."

"A good technique. Give yourself a flaw so that others won't be able to comment on it."

Eirlin smiled. "I like it."

"Only if others are stupid enough to fall for it."

Cut.

Quiet.

"I take it this isn't a good day for discussion."

"Oh? Are you indisposed? Poor dear." The sweet smile returned. "Is the complicated life of the city too much for you?"

"No, Cuquita. It's you I am concerned about."

"Concerned? Who are you to be concerned about me? You start that patronizing tone and you'll soon find out what you should be concerned about."

Cut. Bad Lady.

"A Healer showing concern for a patient is hardly patronizing."

"Patient? I have come here to make very sure that you have no illusions in that respect. If the day rolls by that I need the clumsy ministrations of an untrained hick from the provinces, I'll roll over and offer my throat to the nearest wolf." The woman rose and slid forward, her hands like claws. "If you know what's good for you..."

Eirlin clamped a firm hold on the squirming Fang, and rose to face the other woman, keeping her demeanour as calm as possible.

"Cuquita, it is now time for you to leave. You may return when you feel up to talking to me."

"I will leave when I choose, and I will return when I choose. You will get used to that."

"That is true. You may leave when you choose. So may I. I bid you a better day tomorrow. Please come back then."

Watch her, Kitten. She turned and walked to the door.

She stays. She hates. You expected different?

211

Fine. I thought she might jump at me.
I cut Bad Lady.

Eirlin glanced back as she closed the door softly but firmly. The other woman was standing in the middle of the room, her hands still clawed, a series of emotions running across her face.

"No, you don't, love. I told you."

Why?

"Because we don't know enough. We could hurt her worse."

She hurts now. Big hurt.

"I know, love. I know."

32.   The Taste of Blood

Eirlin paced over to the window and looked out. Then she turned and went over to her usual chair, the comfortable one with the table beside it for her work. She sat for a moment, toying with the ties that held Fang's sheath to her belt. Then she rose again.

Eirlin.

"Don't bother me, Kitten. I'm thinking."

I know what you're thinking.

"Then you know I don't want to be bothered."

I know you are thinking the same thing you have been thinking over and over, around and around, for about three weeks. It is getting quite boring.

"Then don't listen."

Have you thought of just speaking to him?

"About what?"

Phht.

She sat down again. "It's not something you just talk about."

Phht.

"Well, it isn't."

You know, a few lucky humans have this marvelous skill that allows them to say everything two different ways. In their heads and with their mouths. Those lucky ones sometimes forget how useful the mouth way can be. It makes things very clear and important.

The Healer sat straighter. "It does? I thought it would be the opposite."

Oh, no. It is very easy to think something. The pictures and emotions and ideas come together naturally. To speak it aloud requires you to construct it more carefully, to shape it into words. It carries more impact. Sometimes, much though I hate to admit it, that can be an advantage.

"I understand."

Good for you, because he is coming. Talk, woman. Use your vaunted skills.

"And what are you supposed to talk to me about, Eirlin?" Tyrbrand entered, touching her shoulder as he strolled past her. "Kitten sounded exceptionally earnest. It's not often I hear that serious note in her thoughts."

"Well..."

He sat in his own chair, the one that held him in exactly the right pose for thinking. "Is it personal?"

"No...Yes. Well, it is and it isn't."

"I see. Well, of course I don't see, but I do see that it's complicated." He sat and smiled at her. Kitten could tell he was trying to radiate the exact combination of concern and lack of concern that would allow her to confide in him.

It must be difficult. All you know, and you still don't know exactly how to influence her just enough, but not enough to drive her away.

And I will do it much better without feline assistance.

I can take a hint.

"Eirlin, I agree with Kitten."

"You do?"

"Yes. When it comes to humans and difficult ideas, sometimes sitting face to face and speaking words is the best way to communicate."

"Which is a polite way to tell me to speak up or give up."

"I would never be so impolite. What is bothering you, Eirlin? Why can you not tell me?" In spite of his comments, the Magician was adding emotion to his words.

She sighed. "I have tried to say it before, and I have not got through to you."

"Then try again. This time I am listening."

She turned so that she was facing him directly and leaned forward. "Tyrbrand, you know I am trying to heal you. I have been very successful in healing the wounds that I can find, the ones I can reach."

"And I thank you for that with all my heart."

"But you are not healing."

"Perhaps you have done all you can. Though I am reluctant to admit the fact, possibly this is the price I have to pay for the choices I have made."

"But what if it is not? I am sure there are other wounds, injuries to a deeper part of your being. If you would allow me to search for them, it is entirely possible that I could Heal them as well. With any other patient, your permission would be all I would need. But no matter what you say, when I reach a certain level of your mind, I reach a wall that is completely impenetrable. I can see nothing, do nothing."

"You have already made me aware of this. I'm afraid that wall has been created over the whole of my life, and for very good reason."

"I understand this. Since Wynna came, I understand it even better. But if you know about it and you really want me to help, can't you tell me how to get around it?"

214

He leaned his elbows on his knees. "Well, if I were to look at myself as a patient, I would say that you need to be subtle and devious. My wall is no longer voluntary. It is so much a habit that it is out of my control. Contrary to what you may think, I have made an honest attempt to let it down, but I am unable to. You will have to find me at a time when my defenses are down, or when I am distracted by some strong emotion, and then use a certain amount of force."

He glanced at her. "An action that contains its own perils, you understand."

All she has to do is outwit and overpower a mere Magician? No problem.

A faint smile touched his lips. "And now that I have made the suggestion, you realize that I will be doubly on my guard, so you will have to be doubly devious."

She regarded him suspiciously. "So what can we do about that?"

He shrugged. "As I say, I have no idea." His glance was longer this time. "And I do have something else I want to talk to you about."

"This is what happens every time. You evade the question, and move on to other matters."

He returned her stare. "I am not evading you. I have heard what you have said, and I will take it into consideration. I will try to find a way to let you look deeper into my being for whatever injuries you might find there. I am not optimistic, but I will try. Is that what you want to hear?"

She sighed. "Yes, Tyrbrand. But remember, it is not what I want to hear that is the problem. It is what you need."

He shook his head. "I must agree with you, because it would be self-destructive not to. I just don't feel very optimistic."

He hitched himself into a more formal pose. "So, without being charged with evasion, may I make my suggestion for Excisor's next stage of training?"

She smiled. "I suppose."

"Good. This is what I want to do. Your Scalpel needs to learn about blood. In case you didn't know, different diseases affect the blood in different ways. I have imbued the proper magic in the steel so that he can sense the differences. Since his mind is canine in nature, this sense is very acute. However, you and he have to learn how to interpret these differences."

The Honourable Magician uses too many big words.

"I caught that, Kitten. I'll give you an example. There is a condition called anemia. We think it is caused by weak blood."

Not enough iron.

"What do you mean?"

There is iron in blood. I know that from the taste. I like the taste of iron. If there is no iron, the person is weak.

"I understand. So there must be enough iron in a person's blood. If there is not enough iron, the patient becomes lethargic and weak?" The Magician smiled. "We have learned something already. Eirlin and the Scalpel must learn the taste of anemic blood, so they can recognize it if they find it."

Eirlin frowned. "So we have to go and cut a whole lot of patients in the infirmary?"

"Right. And another thing. I think you should go over to the Royal Infirmary on the other side of the city, where Calicasas is Head Surgeon. He has sent an invitation to you to speak again about the field hospitals, and this way we can accomplish both."

She nodded. "I would be pleased to help. Just a small cut will do?"

"That's right. Just the tiniest prick to get his metal into the blood. Then I want Kitten to help the Scalpel learn how to communicate these tastes to you."

Eirlin shrugged. "It sounds logical. How he will deal with it is another matter."

"That's true. I have given him a great deal of knowledge, but until you work with him, I have no way of knowing how he will use it."

He will use it wonderfully, Magician. Eirlin and I will teach him.

The Magician shook his head. "I wish I had your optimism, Kitten."

Eirlin reached out, laid a soft hand on his wrist, painfully aware of how the bones showed through the skin. "You have done what you needed, Tyrbrand. Now it is our turn."

The Royal Infirmary was a strange place. It had once been a manor house, so it had large, high-ceilinged rooms that echoed with every footfall. Curtains separated wards where patients lay on pallets, heads to the wall.

I don't like infirmaries, Eirlin. There is so much pain, of so many different types.

"Well, don't let your feelings escape." She motioned to the Scalpel, riding his sheath at her waist.

Of course not.

The Head Surgeon bustled out, welcoming but officious. Eirlin realized that although she had met with the man several times recently, it had never been in a medical situation. He seemed different, somehow. More competent, but more concerned with his position. He seemed especially uncertain of how to deal with Kitten, riding at Eirlin's hip.

He is Maridon. It is harder to convince him that I am really not here.

Ostersund greeted him with due deference. "If you would assign someone to introduce us to each ward, Surgeon Calicasas, we will perform our tasks and return for the meeting. If you would like to join us, there may be interesting information for you."

"What sort of information? I thought you were going to observe..."

"...Lady Eirlin is here to observe your patients. It is possible that she will discover symptoms unknown to you."

The Surgeon frowned, glanced sidelong at Eirlin, then nodded. "I will accompany you myself. I am interested in any information that will help my patients."

He is an old fussbudget.

He is a respected surgeon, Kitten, and you will treat him as such. We are going to be working closely together.

Do not fear, Eirlin. I will demonstrate my good manners.

Now, why does that not reassure me?

Eirlin shared a glance with the Magician. His fleeting grin showed that he had caught the whole conversation.

Calicasas gestured. "The wounds and broken bones are over here. Illness on the upper floor. Which would you prefer?"

Eirlin frowned. "Perhaps the wounds and breaks would be best. There is less likely to be anything unusual."

The Surgeon seemed unsure how to interpret this comment, so he led the way into the ward. An apprentice stood beside the first patient, a worker with his leg in splints. "Broken leg, last week, my Lord, Lady. No complications."

The Surgeon nodded approval. "How are you feeling, Tarn?"

"Much better today, Doctor. Startin' to get itchy, though."

The Surgeon smiled. "Better than how you felt when you came in last week."

"I'll thank you for that, Doctor."

"Would you mind, then, if this lady looks you over? She is a Healer as well."

The man shrugged. "Sure 'nuff, Doctor. If it'll help."

Eirlin knelt, Scalpel almost hidden in her hand. "All I'm going to do is make a tiny cut in your arm, to draw some blood. You'll hardly feel it. All right?"

The man glanced at the shiny blade tip, protruding between her finger and thumb. "Whatever you say, my Lady."

She nodded, laid her hand on his arm, and pressed. The point slipped easily through the skin.

What do you taste, Little Tooth?

Blood.

That's all?

Blood.

Kitten?

That's all I'm getting from him. He knows what blood tastes like, and that's blood. I could have told you more than that.

Such as?

Such as that he has strong blood, with lots of iron, and that he has had alcohol.

"Alcohol?" She looked at the man. "Have you had something to drink, today?"

"I had wine with my lunch, my Lady. How did you know?"

She smiled, withdrew her hand, and nodded to the apprentice, who efficiently twisted a bandage around the man's arm. "Nothing wrong that I can see."

At her gesture, the Surgeon led to the next patient. Since all the men in the room had observed the first testing, there was little need for explanation and next three went quickly. Each time the Scalpel reported normal blood, but now he recognized the alcohol that had accompanied their meal.

Then came the fifth patient. He was a large man, poorly-dressed and not recently shaven. As the Scalpel entered the blood, Eirlin's hand jumped.

Ewww!

Eirlin snatched back her hand and the apprentice, with a puzzled frown, applied the usual bandage.

"What is this man's problem?"

"Head injury. Brought in this morning. He's sort of fuddled, so we don't really know what happened."

"He's fuddled because he still has enough alcohol in his blood to knock a normal person senseless." She turned to the patient. "How much wine did you have with your meal?"

"I dunno. A glass like everyone else, I guess."

He's lying.

I don't need help to know that!

Chuckles broke out from the other men. "He had more than that, my Lady. When the attendant wasn't lookin', he took a coupla big slugs from her bottle."

"Is that so?"

The man's head shrunk into his shoulders. "Mebby a little. M' head was hurtin', like, and I thought the wine would help."

"Your head is hurting because you have an immense hangover, and there's no way the Surgeon can tell if there's really anything wrong with you until you're sober."

She rose, glancing at Calicasas, who nodded. "Thank you for that information, my Lady." He frowned at the unfortunate patient, then turned away.

The next man was in worse condition. He lay back, his eyes half-closed, his head moving restlessly on the pillow.

Eirlin knelt quickly. "What's wrong with his thigh?"

"He's a carpenter, and he fell off a wall onto a jagged piece of wood. Took forty stitches and more to pull the wound back together. He seemed to be recovering well, but this morning he began to complain again. I'm thinking it might have become blighted."

Eirlin applied her Scalpel to the leg above the wound, and the man did not react.

Yeuck! Out. Out. Want out!

Be quiet, Little Tooth. This is our work. Do you taste that?

Taste bad. Out!

Eirlin nodded, looked up at the Surgeon. "Definitely blighted. Can we see it?"

Calicasas motioned, and the apprentice began unwrapping the wound. After a few layers, blood began to show through the cloth. Once exposed, the wound looked ugly: red and puffy at the edges, the swelling especially bad near the knee.

Eirlin winced. "What is your usual procedure here, Doctor?"

The Surgeon probed gently with sure fingers. The man on the bed moaned. "First I would open the lower part, there where it's swollen, to see if draining helped. If there was no improvement, I would have to open the wound, try to clean it again. Sometimes I even cut away any diseased flesh. It's not a pleasant job, and very hard on the patient. Better than the alternative, though."

"Do you think it's general blight, or an actual piece of dirt left in the wound?

"That's what I don't know."

"Perhaps we can help you, there. Tyrbrand, will you?"

"Should we...?"

She sheathed her Scalpel. "I doubt he's ready for that sort of thing." She laid her hand on Kitten's hilt, and the Magician laid his hand on hers.

All right, Kitten. We have done this before.

Perhaps the little one could watch.

"Perhaps." Eirlin looked at her hands, both occupied. "Tyrbrand, could you hold him?"

The Magician reached over and drew the Scalpel.

You will watch. Just watch.

Watch.

Eirlin focused inward.

All right, Kitten. Let us look at this man's leg.

Yes, Eirlin. Come with me. Come Magician, we need your help. Little Tooth, you may come, but you must only watch. This is very difficult and it might be dangerous to the patient.

All right, Kitten, enough lecture.

Yes, Eirlin. There is the wound. It looks very bad at that end, doesn't it? See that?

Yes. It looks like a piece of wood. The Surgeon will have to take it out.

Does he have to?

What do you mean?

Why don't we take it out?

Can we?

Remember with Jesco? We used the muscles. We can make the muscles push it out.

All right. Be careful. Every move hurts him.

Less than the alternative.

True. Go ahead. Start with the muscles below it. Careful, those are torn. Move away, to the whole ones. Tighten those. Loosen the ones above. There, it's moving. Relax the ones higher up. Good. There it goes...Hah! Well done.

Eirlin reached down and pulled out a jagged sliver now protruding from the wound.

The Surgeon took it from her fingers. "Is there any more?"

"We'll continue to check."

There is no more, Eirlin. What about the diseased flesh around that area?

I don't know what we can do about that. It should be cut away...

Cut! I cut!

You will only watch and listen! I told you!

Gently, Kitten. It is what he is meant to do. Not this time, Little Tooth. Some day we will cut. For now, I think we will give this man some energy, then we are done.

All right. Watch, now, Little Tooth. This is how it is done. Not too much, not too fast. He will now have strength to defend against the blight. There. It is finished.

Eirlin took her hand from the patient, and the connection was broken.

The Surgeon looked critically at his patient. "His breathing is easier, and his colour is better."

"Yes, we gave him some energy. It will help him fight the disease. There is nothing left in the wound, but there is still a lot of inflammation."

The Surgeon's hands opened helplessly. "It is always thus. He fights it off or we amputate. What other choice is there?"

Eirlin shook her head. "I wish there was another choice. I can see the blight, but I have no way to stop it."

The Surgeon smiled. "Well, my Lady, I have never seen a sliver come out of a wound on its own accord before, and the patient seems to be doing better. Whatever you did, it certainly has helped."

There was open curiosity in his eyes. She looked to Tyrbrand for guidance.

"These are new techniques, Calicasas. When we know how to use them ourselves, then will be time to explain them to others."

The Surgeon nodded. "I understand, Lord Ostersund. Let me show you the upper ward."

As they mounted the stairway, Eirlin paused. On the landing beside them stood two armed soldiers, their backs to a door.

Something wrong, Eirlin.

I feel it, too.

Kitten extended the Healer's senses. *What's wrong with him?*

Something evil. I can feel it.

"What's the matter, my Lady?"

Eirlin looked around. "What's behind that door?"

"Oh, you need not concern yourself with that patient, my Lady."

Eirlin regarded the soldiers, who ignored her with the stoic faces of those on guard. "There is a patient behind a guarded door, a patient with something terribly wrong, and I am not to be concerned?"

"That's right, my Lady. That is a patient of Lord Carrones. We have very strict orders..."

"What seems to be the problem, Surgeon?"

They turned to see another soldier, this one better dressed and armed than his fellows, striding up the stairs towards them.

Eirlin met him before he could reach the top, stood over him. "Your problem, soldier, is to find the man who has given these orders of yours, and to bring him here just as fast as he can move. Do you understand?"

Move!

"Yes, yes my Lady. Right away. I'll get Lord Carrones. Right away, my Lady." The man almost stumbled turning on the stairs, and he disappeared even more quickly than he had come.

Eirlin turned to the two at the door. "You," she pointed at the darker of the two, "will go immediately to the Palace to find Guard Captain Genil, and bring him here. At a run. Got it?"

The second soldier followed his officer's lead and was soon gone. The third soldier, tall and blond, regarded her impassively. "And I, my Lady, will accompany you to see that my Lord is not harmed."

She smiled. "That is exactly what I had in mind. You may open the door." She glanced at Ostersund, who nodded.

This is the one.

The room was lavishly furnished, but that probably made little difference to the man who lay on the bed. He was tall and may have once been robust, but now his hands were little more than claws, his long fingers lying inert on the sheets. As they entered, the eyes opened slowly, the head moved wearily towards them.

"Who have you brought me now, Theobald? Another doctor?"

The soldier glanced back at Eirlin. "I'm not sure my Lord, but she is of the Blood and a very forceful lady. She seems to have a Magician in tow."

"The lady will find she scarcely needs to be forceful with one in my condition, and I suspect I would need a different kind of magic to do me any good. The doctors have certainly been unsuccessful."

Eirlin seated herself on the bed, one hand raising the patient's lower arm, the other reaching for her Scalpel. "Hush, my Lord, and rest. I am only here to assess your condition, nothing more."

When his mouth opened to speak, a look and a shake of her head silenced him. Carefully, she pressed the blade into his skin.

YEUCK! DANGER! DANGER!

What? What danger?

EWWW! AWFUL, AWFUL! AWAY! TAKE AWAY!

The patient struggled to rise. "What? What is wrong? What have I done?"

Small Tooth! You will be silent! Eirlin, you must take him out of this blood. There is something wrong with it. It reeks. Even I can taste that.

Eirlin removed the Scalpel, cradling him in her hand.

There, there, dear. It's all right, baby. You did very well. That was a horrible experience, but it's over now and I won't make you do it again.

Not a baby.

No, dear, you're not a baby. You're a very brave boy. You settle down, now, and I will help the patient. She slid the Scalpel into his sheath and turned to the man on the bed.

"I'm sorry about that, my Lord. It is a new method, and it got away on me a bit. The severity of your condition was a bit of a surprise."

The skeletal head moved weakly. "Surprise? When I look like this?"

Eirlin rubbed a finger across her lips, as if wiping something away from her mouth. "We have not been introduced, my Lord. May I assume you are someone important?"

"I used to be, I suppose."

"Any enemies? Anyone who would benefit from your death?"

"Enemies? As every man does. Why?"

"I'm trying to figure out who would want to poison you."

"Poison!"

She gently restrained him from rising. "That's right. There is a great deal of some very noxious substance floating around in your body. I don't know what kind of poison, and I don't know how it is being administered, but I think you would be better out of this place and somewhere safe."

She turned to the guard. "Will you see to that, please?"

He nodded, once, slowly. "Yes my Lady. As soon as someone comes to relieve me."

Lord Ostersund laughed. "The perfect guard. Completely unshakeable. Don't worry, Theobald, I'll see to it myself." He strode towards the door, but was prevented from leaving by a large, dark-haired man who stormed in, a heavily armed soldier behind him.

"Who has disobeyed my orders? Who has disturbed my patient? Who...?"

He stopped in confusion as Eirlin rose to her feet. "I am the one who asked to see you, my Lord. I wanted to see the man who was allowing this patient to be poisoned."

"Poisoned? Ridiculous! Who are you to be throwing such accusations around?"

He is lying.

"I am one who can tell that you are lying."

The man's hand went to his sword hilt. "No one calls me a liar!"

Kitten jumped into Eirlin's hand even as the Healer reached for her, and her point was at the man's throat before he could draw.

"You will remove your hand from your sword, and place it flat against the wall behind you. Your soldier will carefully remove your sword from its scabbard and place it on the floor." Her eyes did not leave the lord's face, but Kitten's senses fed her a view of the whole room.

"Do it now, soldier, and be very careful. One slip, and he dies."

Eirlin, you are such a terrible liar!

Don't bother me, Kitten. Do your duty.

Of course, Eirlin. Your wrist is rock-steady. I am feeding fear into his every joint. He cannot move.

What's the soldier doing?

Standing behind you, deciding whether to strike you or not.

"Don't let the thought cross your mind, soldier. Take the sword. Place it on the floor, as I told you."

His face blanching, the man did so.

"Thank you. That was a wise choice. Now go and stand by the other soldier."

He is very concerned about the pouch at his belt.

She resheathed her Sword. "Lord Ostersund, will you take charge of this criminal?"

"With pleasure, my Lady."

"It might be instructive to see what the pouch at his belt contains."

Ostersund reached in, came up with a small, dark vial. "Come, Lord Carrones, it seems as if you have finally overstepped yourself. It will be a pleasure to see you to your new quarters."

Many men. Running.

With a final pat to Kitten's hilt, Eirlin stepped back. "I think that may not be necessary, my Lord. Help will be arriving."

Steel-shod boots echoed up the stairs. Genil assessed the room as he entered and snapped out orders. Once his men were in place, he turned to the Magician. "What have we here, Lord Ostersund?"

"We have a situation which the king has discussed with you. Could you put Lord Carrones under arrest, please, on the charge of poisoning Lord Coelric?"

"Yes, my Lord. With pleasure."

The dark man frowned, drew himself up. "What? You are going to take this lordling's word against mine? I demand that you..."

His speech was interrupted by a forceful hand on his shoulder, propelling him into the arms of the two Guardsmen inside the door. "As Lord Ostersund says, the king has already prepared me for this situation, and as far as I can see, it has come out exactly the way the king expected. Take him away." The Captain nodded to Lord Ostersund, and marched off behind his prisoner.

"Now, my Lord, what are we going to do about you?"

The face on the pillow tried to smile. "Seeing that last little drama has cheered me up immensely. Not that it's likely to do any good. Still..."

"I'm glad you are cheered up, my Lord. Now let's get a little energy into you, so that we can move you without danger."

"Energy. I could use energy. But I haven't been able to eat properly for weeks."

"We have our ways." She sat on the bed.

Kitten?

Ready.

Help.

What? You want to help?

Help man.

You want to help him? After you scared him so badly?

Sorry, Big Cat. Sorry, Man. I help.

What do you think, Eirlin?

I think it would be appropriate. He certainly has enough energy. Keep a close eye, will you, Kitten?

Certainly. Now you be very careful, Little Tooth. When Eirlin and Lord Ostersund connect with us, then you can give him energy. That's right. Not too much!

More!

No.

Needs more!

No, Little Tooth. The man is very weak. Too much energy would kill him.

Very weak. Little puppy weak.

That's right. He is weak like a little puppy. There. That is enough. You did very well.

"Did I? Did I do well, Big Cat? Did I do well, Eirlin? See, Smith. I did well!"

Yes, you did very well. Now calm down. We have things to arrange.

Eirlin broke their connection, cutting off another spate of emotion from the little Scalpel.

She turned to the blond soldier. "Do you trust these two?"

"This one, yes. That one is new, so I don't know."

"Fine. Send that one to his barracks, tell him to stay there until the king investigates." With a quick glance at the Surgeon for

225

permmission, she turned to the apprentice. "I'm sure you can find a stretcher somewhere around here."

The young man smiled and disappeared.

"So, where do we take him?"

Tyrbrand shrugged. "You're the one going to nurse him. Where better than my house?"

She glanced at the soldier, eyebrows raised.

"Don't ask me, ask Lord Coelric."

"Yes, that would probably be polite."

She smiled at the patient. "I'm sorry, my Lord, but last time I checked you, I didn't think you were up to much."

"Neither did I. What happened to me? I have this strange impression that my face has been thoroughly licked by a small puppy, and now I feel much better. Was that a dream?"

"Not quite, my Lord, but a close enough explanation for the moment. Do you feel up to a short journey?"

"Better than the long one I have been contemplating."

"Fine." She turned to Calicasas. "I think this takes precedence over the field hospitals. I will return another time, with your permission."

The Surgeon nodded, almost a bow. "Of course, my Lady. Any time you wish. How about tomorrow?"

"At your pleasure, Calicasas."

33.   Cuquita's Speech

"No, Fang. Don't do that!"

Cut, cut, cut. Pretty circles.

"Yes, those are very neat, but you're cutting too deep. Look at the board."

Wood. Cedar. Yum!

"No, Fang, you don't cut the wood. Just the cloth."

Cloth is yucky. Wood is nice.

"I know you like the cedar, Fang, but you have to learn…"

Ostersund walked in. "I'm sorry to spoil your fun, Eirlin, but I have something you might be interested in."

"What could be more important than this one's discipline?"

The Magician frowned. "Excisor?"

Yes, Magician?

"Are you being a good little Scalpel?"

Um…sort of. I cut. I cut lots!

"I know what that means. Now, do you want to go out?"

Out? Out? Yes. Let's go out!

"I don't know. This is very important. If we take you, you have to be very good."

Important. Fang can be good.

"Yes. We are going to watch the king again. Just watch."

Talk?

"What do you think? Do little Scalpels who don't mind their Healer get to talk to the king?"

…Fang minds the Healer.

"Does he? It didn't sound like it. We are going to the Conclave again, and we won't be able to talk to the king. We just have to watch."

Yes, Smith. We can watch the king.

Eirlin shook her head. "Do I assume that some time you're going to tell me what this is all about?"

"Yes. It seems your friend Cuquita is scheduled to address the Conclave this afternoon."

"Oh." Eirlin rubbed her forehead. "What does that mean?"

"I don't know. As I told you last week, it could be good, could be bad. I thought it would be best if you were there. You might pick up something nobody else does."

"Of course. When do we leave?"

"After lunch is fine."

As Eirlin seated herself in the gallery, Kitten allowed her senses to expand cautiously, as if tracking edgy game. It took a long, agonizing stalk, but finally she was sure.

He is not here.

The Sword?

No, the man who sells pastries outside in the street. Who do you think?

Calm down, Kitten.

Phtt.

What's got into you? Were you hoping he would be here?

No... Sort of... Maybe.

Kitten, do you ever get lonely?

With all you noisy minds around? Not likely.

That's good.

Now that you mention it, I think I used to get lonely. Especially in that swamp. Not any more.

Here comes the king.

Right. No more chat.

The king and his ministers made their ceremonial entry and the opening ritual droned on, identical in every way to the one before it. And probably every one before that for the last hundred years or so.

You didn't ask me if I ever get bored.

No, and I'm not going to. This is necessary.

Yes, O Eirlin the Wise.

Don't you forget it. Pay attention, Kitten. Cuquita is standing.

This should be interesting, at least.

Probably more interesting than anyone wants.

Cuquita had stepped to the podium below them, and the king gestured towards her.

"And now we have the rare pleasure of hearing the inaugural speech of a new member of our assembly. Marchal da Launca has no expectation in the near future of returning to us. It is therefore his wish that his daughter, Cuquita da Launca, be installed in his place, with all the rights and privileges that the position entails. It is our purpose that the wishes of our faithful liegeman be honoured in this matter.

"Does any man among you have reason to gainsay our will?"

There was shuffling in the hall. Obviously quite a few had reservations, but none wished or dared to voice them.

Someone might stand up and shout, 'She is completely insane.' Would that suffice?

Shut up, Kitten. This is a sombre moment.

Somber to the point of tragic...I'll shut up.

Good idea.

"Having heard no legitimate impediment to my intent, I declare Cuquita da Launca to be a full member of this Assembly, with all the rights and privileges entailed. I would ask for a demonstration of both our appreciation for her father's generous contributions in the past, and a welcome to his daughter."

There was a greater round of applause than Eirlin had expected.

Her father must be well respected.

Or a lot of them don't know what she's really like.

Probably a bit of both.

Cuquita stood forward and looked around. Since the podium faced away from the balcony they could not see her face, but Kitten was able to get hints of her emotions, which were a roil of fear, pride, anger, and determination.

This is going to be interesting.

Cuquita took a deep breath, exhaled part of it, then spoke. "Your Majesty, Gentlemen, and all you others as well."

There was a muted rumble in the hall.

"That's right. Some of you are acting like true gentlemen of the realm, and others are not. I will leave it to you to decide which you are."

She paused and scanned the arch of seats to her left, then to her right.

"My father has asked me to speak to you. He has decided that he no longer has the energy to maintain his position in this assembly, and has asked me to take over.

"Having sat through the last three weeks of 'discussion,' I now understand what he means. I don't know how anyone has the energy to put up with you. You wrangle and bicker and posture to your friends, who applaud you but stick a dagger in your back when it suits them. Even worse, you constantly disrupt the proper working of this assembly for the selfish building of your own personal power."

The murmur grew, and she had to raise her voice to be heard.

"I do not find this assembly worth the effort of listening, but I have a duty to my family and my realm to put up with it, the gods know why."

There was open anger in the hall now, and voices began to carry over hers.

Suddenly the king slapped his hand on the table in front of him. "Let the woman speak. I find this refreshing."

229

Cuquita dropped the king a slight curtsey and a tilt of her head. The noise subsided.

Kitten, can you help her?

What?

Like the other Sword did. Pull them in with her.

Are you sure?

Please.

I don't like this, Eirlin, but I will try. Join with me.

As Cuquita spoke on, Kitten hesitantly reached out to the room, beginning the difficult process of joining the wild and twisted strands of consciousness to meld with her voice. She could feel them begin to join, begin to listen. It was a powerful feeling, but it carried with it the echo of a long-hidden memory, a thought that twisted in her mind.

"I have only one request. Leave me out of it. I am not interested in your petty quarrels, your stupid male rutting contests. In fact, I think this august body would function a whole lot better if about twenty of its members were to take themselves to the bottom of the deepest hole in the kingdom and perform their idiotic and destructive competitions there, where they can stop doing damage to the rest of us!"

She suddenly spun and pointed up into the gallery, straight at Eirlin. "And you! You, I will deal with now!" Then she turned without another word and marched out of the hall.

There was an amazed hush in the room. Then a buzz started. Eirlin was aware of the eyes turning her way.

Time for a strategic withdrawal, I believe.

I think so.

Her face burning, Eirlin rose and hurried out.

Well, I did warn you.

What do you mean?

I have grave reservations about the exercise of that skill. Cuquita does likewise, I gather.

How did she know?

I would have thought that was obvious.

Yes. And now she's angry at me. Eirlin's feelings fell.

Bad Lady angry.

Yes, Fang. I wasn't polite to the Bad Lady.

Angry with Healer?

Yes, Fang, I'm afraid she is.

Fang will protect Healer.

No! No, Excisor. That is not your task.

230

Don't worry Little Tooth. I will protect Eirlin. You just do as she says.

Not cut Bad Lady?

Fang, don't you dare! Kitten?

She had never felt the Healer so frightened. *Don't worry, Eirlin. I'll take care of him. You just get us out of here.*

I am doing that as fast as decorum will allow.

I think decorum had better... too late.

"You!"

Eirlin turned. Cuquita stormed across the atrium, her whole body radiating anger.

"What do you think you are doing?"

"I'm leaving, Cuquita."

"Oh, no, you're not. Not until I've finished with you."

"I don't think that this is a good time..."

The Maridon woman leaned closer, her face writhing in fury. Her voice dropped to a hoarse whisper. "You...Stay...Out...Of...My...HEAD!" She glanced around, as if afraid anyone had heard.

Cut!

No, Fang!

As the woman's attention turned back to Eirlin, Kitten could feel the rage building, and knew beyond a doubt that it was about to break out.

"Cuquita, please. I had no..."

"Oh, yes you did!"

Bad Lady will attack.

Eirlin's eyes took in the approaching foe, glanced around.

Cut Bad Lady.

"I am tired of your fumbling interference in my affairs. Now...

Kitten! I can't deal with her and Fang at the same time...

The madwoman's fingers hooked and she took a deep breath, leg muscles tensing, feet seeking purchase.

Eirlin froze, eyes darting left and right in terror...

And Kitten took action. *Fang, cut now!*

Cut?

CUT!

The Maridon woman's face froze in a look of astonishment, which gradually faded, leaving...nothing. The tension in her body relaxed, and there she stood, aimless, looking around as if puzzled as to why she was there.

Eirlin's eyes widened in horror.

Fang, what did you do?

Cut Bad Lady. Protect Eirlin.

Oh, Fang, no!

The little creature's voice shrank. *Bad Lady hurt Eirlin?*

No, dear, she didn't...

There was a sudden commotion as someone pushed through the crowd.

Vanemar. What does he want?

The Maridon rushed up beside Cuquita, siezing her hand. She glanced at him with mild curiosity.

"Lady da Launca, that was wonderful!"

"It was?"

"Oh, most certainly, my dear. I have never heard our position stated more clearly. You were fantastic." He glanced at Eirlin. "What are you doing, acknowledging this blonde trash? Come and speak to the people who really count in this realm."

He put his other arm around her waist and swept her away. She gave one helpless glance at Eirlin over her shoulder, and then his words flooded over her. "Did you hear the king? He agreed completely. Oh, you should have seen their faces, their stunned, pale, stupid..."

And Eirlin was alone, unmoving in the crowd of functionaries and minor nobility regarding her with curiousity as they passed by.

What am I going to do?

Kitten reeled back from the despair that washed over her. *Eirlin, what's wrong?*

What did I do, Kitten? I've ruined everything completely. Don't you understand?

I understand that you're being completely stupid, if that's what you mean. You didn't do anything at all, as far as I can see. I was the one that messed up with Cuquita, and Fang rescued you from getting your face clawed to ribbons. Did you see her talons!

You don't understand!

No, I don't. Will you please explain?

Not now, Kitten, I have to find Tyrbrand.

Don't worry. He knows.

A new pang of fear shot through the Healer. *He does?*

This little scene could hardly have passed the notice of...here he is. Lord Magician, will you please talk some sense into this woman?

Ostersund appeared at her side, taking her hand, an arm around her waist. *Not now, Cat.*

"We are leaving." Under the stares of the crowd, he hurried her unresisting body out the door. Once on the street, he glanced around.

Then he stepped out in front of a passing carriage, raising his voice to the driver.

"Lange, I need a favour."

"Yes, my Lord."

"The lady needs transport. Where are you going?"

"To pick up Lord Wulfmir at home, my Lord."

"Fine. We'll go along."

He was helping Eirlin into the carriage before the driver had a chance to nod his head, let alone get down to help the lady enter. Lacking anything else to do, the man flicked the reins and the horses moved off.

There was silence in the carriage as they jogged through the streets. Finally, Eirlin straightened, pushed herself upright.

"Are you all right?"

"Not really."

He regarded her. "I can assume that means you're at least better?"

She glanced at him. "Yes."

He watched her for a moment, noted her restless movements. "Do you want to walk?"

She glanced back as if to see if they were far enough away. "I think so."

He nodded and tapped on the wall. "We will alight, now, Lange. The lady is feeling better."

"Certainly, my Lord."

This time the coachman was able to get down and open the door in the approved manner, position the step, and help Eirlin to the street. Ostersund passed him a coin. "Tell Lord Wulfmir thanks for the ride. I'll drop by and explain later."

The coachman grinned at the size of the coin, made a silent bow that spoke volumes about his ability to be discreet, and drove away.

The two walked in silence for a while.

"Well, that was certainly interesting."

Eirlin merely glanced up at him.

Kitten's query slid off an opaque wall. It was as if the Healer did not exist. *That's interesting, too.*

Leave her be, Kitten. I understand.

That's good, because I don't.

"Cuquita's speech. It was interesting."

Eirlin frowned. "What do you think she meant?"

"What she said, I suppose. She stated it clearly enough. The king was impressed."

"So was Vanemar."

"What?" The Magician stopped and stared at her.

"Yes." She continued walking. "He obviously wasn't listening too closely. He came rushing up, told her he had never heard their side of the argument presented so clearly, and carted her away, praising her the whole time."

"You're joking! Their side of the argument!"

That's not the first time.

"Yes, I recall that he spoke to her at court."

The colour was beginning to come back to Eirlin's face. "That's right, and he came up to her at the reception last week and tried to make conversation. She cut him down to size, of course."

Suddenly she put her hands to her face. "But now..." She turned to Ostersund. "Tyrbrand, she just went with him. She had this awful vacant look on her face, and she looked at me as if she didn't understand what was happening. I've done something to her, and now he's got her, and I don't think she even knows what's going on."

He walked on for a moment, then reached out and gave her a quick hug around the shoulders. "I don't think you should be too worried about Cuquita. I got rather a jumble, but it felt to me like she was about to explode in rage, and you were the object. I think that whatever Fang did, she probably deserved it."

They had reached home, and their conversation paused as they entered and shed their cloaks.

They went up to the sitting room, and Tyrbrand, after another look at Eirlin's face, ordered tea. Then he sat her down on the settee, placed himself beside her, and turned to look directly into her face.

"Now, Eirlin, you have to tell me what's really wrong. Certainly, it's unpleasant to be the subject of that sort of attack, but you're stronger than that. What is it?"

She shook her head slowly and avoided his eyes. "I...I just made a complete mess of everything, Tyrbrand."

"No, you didn't. We've been trying to tell you..."

"That's not it. Do you know what I did to Cuquita? In the Assembly?"

"Yes. I could feel it. Very interesting. I thought it was risky, but worth the attempt. Both the king and I thought that what she said has been needed for a long time, but nobody has the nerve or the authority to say it. If we could use Kitten's powers like that..."

"NO!"

NO!

The denial burst from both of them with enough force to set the Magician back physically

234

There was a brief silence. "Not a good idea. I see."

"No, Tyrbrand. I don't ever want to do anything like that to anyone again. We don't have the right to interfere in people's heads without their permission. I knew it was wrong, but I thought...for the good of the realm..."

"But that's not what I'm talking about. I'm thinking about helping speakers, but <u>with</u> their permission. Like da Baneza's Sword helps him. In fact, I'm not sure that now is the time to be saying this, but there is one other person with the authority to tell that message. One who will command everyone's attention."

"No. Not me." Eirlin spread her hands out flat. "I will not do that."

"Why not?

I will not do it.

"But Kitten, that was not a good test of your abilities. If you practised with Eirlin..."

I will NOT do it! Why do you not understand simple words? NOT. NOT. I WILL NOT!

"All right, Kitten, all right. I'm sorry." The Magician paused and looked down at her thoughtfully. "That was a rather strong response. Is there something we don't know?"

Probably. People who refuse to listen often miss things.

"Nobody here refuses to listen, Kitten."

I have been trying to tell you ever since you all started in on this stupid idea that it is very dangerous. And you won't listen! You just go on as if you know all about it, and you don't. You act as if my experience has no meaning, and you want me to do something that could have terrible consequences!

The Healer laid a calm hand on her hilt. "Kitten, there is something you haven't told us, isn't there?"

...Yes.

"...and...?"

And I will not talk about it. She thought about the wall that Eirlin had put up. She thought about it harder. She took the "wind in the trees" idea and made it into a wall that no one could see through, hear through.

And she curled up and sat behind it.

For a long, long, time.

Then she got tired of sitting and she took the wall down. They were gone.

Fine. That's what I wanted anyway.

For the next few days, the Ostersund home was not a happy place. Eirlin paced through the rooms, settling at some task, only to rise again and pace some more.

Tyrbrand continued with his duties and tried to take more time with Fang, but he finally confided to Kitten that it wasn't working.

"This is getting serious, Kitten. I don't know what we're going to do with Fang."

I know.

"He is too young. He doesn't understand, and I can no longer help him."

You can't?

"No. I have turned him over to Eirlin. He is hers now."

Then she must deal with him.

"And she is not."

Then we must speak to her.

"I keep trying. It isn't working. It's like she has put up a wall."

What an interesting reversal.

"I do not need to be reminded of that irony."

Why won't you let her in?

"If she goes any deeper into my emotions, she might learn something that would put her in a difficult position. You see, the love that she feels might have been created by Magical means when we joined to Heal Jesco last year. It may not be real love at all. She must make up her own mind in that respect, with absolutely no more influence from me or my Magic."

Magician, you make everything too complicated. As far as I can see, you humans have a very limited number of emotions. Love, hate, fear, happiness, sadness. Oh, yes, and boredom, which is a lack of emotions. That's about it. Everything else is a variation of those. You can make up any ritual you choose to explain where the love came from: magic or mundane, lineage or lust, but once you love someone, it's just love.

Why don't you just tell her out loud in plain old mundane speech that you love her? Then she will have something to make up her mind about, and no Magic involved.

"I cannot do that. I will not pressure her."

I give up. I am a Sword. Why should I understand these soft emotions?

"That is a good decision, Cat. Now, how do we get her out of this problem?"

We gang up on her.

"Do you think that is wise?"

I'm only a Sword. I think in terms of power. You're the Magician. You're supposed to be the wise one.

"I suppose we gang up on her."

She is in the sitting room.

"No time like the present."

When Tyrbrand brought Kitten into the sitting room, Eirlin sat slumped in her usual chair staring at Fang, who lay on her worktable, trying to make himself seem as small as possible. "What are we going to do with you, my love?"

The Magician knelt in front of her. "Does something have to be done with him?"

She turned anxious eyes to him. "We have been concerned for months that he is too powerful and too willful. We worried that he would do something dangerous, and wondered whether he might need to be destroyed.

"When you gave him to me you broke the rules, Tyrbrand. No being should be given more Power than she can handle, and he is too Powerful. I can't handle him. I'm just not strong enough!"

Kitten could feel her hands shaking and the tears ready to break out.

"And now he has done what we feared. He cut Cuquita against my direct command. He has done her irreparable harm and played into the hands of the enemy. I've been waiting for you to come and tell me."

With her palms turned up, she reached out to Tyrbrand. "How can we avoid destroying him?"

The Magician, for once at a loss for words, could only clasp her hands.

Actually, that's not true.

Tyrbrand frowned. "What's not true?"

She has the story completely wrong. Fang didn't mess up. She did.

The Magician's brow furrowed. "Mind what you say, Cat."

Don't get upset. It wasn't her fault. Not much, anyway. She's a Healer, for the Smith's sake. How did you expect her to handle a head-on physical attack?

"A what?"

Cuquita was about one heartbeat from doing Eirlin serious injury. Eirlin hasn't the character or skill to handle something like that. I took over.

"You did?"

Yes. I am a Sword. Battle is my metier. Eirlin's mistake was in thinking she could control the situation. She could not.

The Healer was listening intently, but she shook her head. "Fang still shouldn't have cut. I told him not to."

Magician, we need your decision here. In the middle of a physical conflict, who makes the decision? The Healer or the Sword?

Tyrbrand gave a wry smile. "Now you're spreading the responsibility to me."

Of course. That will make us all feel better. Who?

"I can't speak for individual cases, but in general whoever has the most experience should make the decision."

So if Eirlin made a stupid decision in the heat of battle, I would be correct to countermand it.

"Kitten, what are you getting at? What really happened that afternoon?"

Simple. Eirlin had no idea of the danger she was in. By the time she figured it out, she would have been on the floor with serious injuries. Even if she thought of it, there was no chance of her drawing me in time to defend herself. So I was helpless and she was helpless in the face of immediate destruction. The other member of our party said he had an effective solution. I decided it was time to trust him. After all, you two have put a whole lot of time and effort into his training. I thought we should see if your work had paid off. I wouldn't call the result a complete success, but I still think it was the best we could do under the circumstances.

Eirlin's head came up. "You mean you…"

Now you are listening. I told Fang to cut. He did. It worked.

"But…"

Eirlin, there is no 'but' involved here. You got into a situation you couldn't handle because you haven't really got it straight in your head that there is a war going on, and all that entails. That's all right. You are making very good progress. But at this moment, I'd suggest your best course of action is to stop stomping around the house beating yourself over the head with your own ineptitude, and get out there and figure out what to do next.

The Magician laughed, and Kitten could hear the echoes of relief. "I think Footsoldier Eirlin has just had a dressing down from crusty old Sergeant Kitten, and will now be told off to do a five-league march in the hot sun in full weapons and armor."

And while you're at it, get back to training your Scalpel. This pouting isn't good for him either.

Eirlin sat back and scrubbed both hands down her face. "I just don't know what to think."

Tyrbrand took her hands again, shook them lightly. "I think Kitten has just solved all the guilt and fear that was keeping you from thinking and acting. A problem has arisen. Get out there and solve it."

Yes. You'll have plenty of time for thinking on the five-league march.

She took a deep breath. "All right. What are we going to do about Cuquita?"

"More important, how are you going to get anywhere near her to do it?"

"I didn't think of that."

"I did." The Magician brushed his hands together. "But there is no immediate danger. Let's keep our eyes open for the next few days."

Kitten slowly closed her eyes until the world was a blur. Not that she had eyes to close, but the image helped her think. *Eirlin can't get to Cuquita. Then Cuquita must come... Hmm...*

34. Back to...Normal?

"Lady Eirlin, you have visitors."

"Who is it?"

There was a hesitant smile on Eowin's face. "I believe it's Charche, my Lady. However..."

"Oh no. How is he dressed this time?"

The smile broke out. "I think you would prefer to come down and see for yourself, my Lady."

She certainly did. This was a Charche she had never seen before. Spotless tabard, seamless hose, his face shining as if it had been scrubbed with a brush. Someone had finally tamed the wave in his hair. He stood her inspection proudly.

She regarded him. "So why is such an upright young lordling associating with this rough lot?"

He glanced at Rhysun and Bejarin, dressed as usual in smocks and britches. "They need to look normal or it won't work."

"What won't work?"

"The plan, my Lady."

She sighed. "I suppose nothing else is going to happen until you sit down and tell me all about it. Come into the reception room."

Once in the formal atmosphere the other two settled, but Charche stayed on his feet.

"My Lady, we know about your problem. With Lady Cuquita."

I told Bejarin yesterday while we were walking to the infirmary.

I'll deal with you later, Cat with Too Much Mouth.

I discussed it with the Magician, and he said it was a good idea. I think you'll be pleased.

"All right, Charche. You have a plan."

"Yes. None of you people can go to her, because she is being watched by Vanemar's people."

"She is?"

He grinned. "You think he can have one of his men hanging around in the alley near her house all day and we won't notice? He's interested in her – I'm old enough to know what that means – and he knows something is wrong, but he can't just do what he likes, because she's politically important, right? The Cat told us that. And you can't go and call on her, because you just had a big public blowup with her, and you never know how she'll react. Or how Lord Vanemar will react."

240

He held his palms up. "It wasn't hard to figure out that part ourselves. The story's all over town."

"I'm afraid so."

"But I can go to her. Lord da Launca is a friend of my father. If I go and take an invitation to her, she'll come with me and nobody will think to say anything."

"What does your father say about this?"

"He said to do what I thought was right. Father and I have been having interesting discussions lately." He paused, then smiled. "I had help from Taresita. She cried beautifully. Father is going to let you look at her when this is all over."

"Oh. That's good." She took a moment to digest this information and what it meant. "And what if you are followed?"

He jabbed a thumb at his friends. "The rest of them can deal with that."

"I don't like it, Charche. I don't want to put you boys in that kind of danger."

"Danger? What danger? I take a message, I lead her here. If there's trouble, we do what we always do. Run."

Eirlin shook her head. "I don't know."

Charche moved directly in front of her and stood firmly, although Kitten could feel a quiver in his knees.

"Lady Eirlin, my father said I should do what I think is right."

"Yes, Charche. That is a good way to act."

"So I will be bringing Lady Cuquita here this afternoon, as soon after luncheon as I can manage. It will be up to you whether to accept her visit or not."

Whee!

Eirlin nodded. "I see."

The boy nodded formally. "Will that be convenient, Lady Eirlin?"

"If that is your schedule, I suppose it will have to be convenient."

"Thank you, my Lady. It has been a pleasure to see you, as usual." He exited with measured pace into the entrance hall and gestured to the servant, who saw the three of them out with due ceremony.

Whee!

There was a faint feeling of laughter, quickly stifled.

Tyrbrand! Were you listening?

There was no response, just a feeling of invitation. Eirlin slapped Kitten's hilt and mounted the stairs.

Tyrbrand was in the sitting room, his face slightly red. "My dear, I think you have just had one of your teachings rebound on you."

She frowned. "Do you think it's safe?"

He flicked his fingers. "Of course it is not. If it was all safe, none of this would be difficult. Do you realize what this means?"

"Oh, I get the implications. That's Skonrik's heir out there, with his father's tacit approval to help us. No risk for him, because if it goes wrong he can blame you and pretend to punish his son."

"Exactly. And if it goes right, he can have all the credit he wants. And Cuquita will be here this afternoon, and you can Heal her."

"I hope."

As he had promised, Charche showed up on the doorstep just past noon, a puzzled Cuquita in tow. Eirlin, waiting at the door, heard the last part of their exchange.

"...but this isn't the Rhysun cityhome, dear. It's Lord Ostersund's. I don't know if I'm supposed to be here."

"That's all right, Lady da Launca. This is where the message said you were to go. I'll just knock."

"Well, if you say so..."

Eirlin opened the door before there could be any problem. "Cuquita. Do come in. I was hoping you would visit." She turned to Charche. "Thank you for passing on my message. If Lady da Launca needs an escort home..."

"We'll be standing by, my Lady."

Eirlin waved him through to the kitchen, shut the door and turned to her guest. "Do come in and sit down. We have something to talk about."

"Do we?"

Eirlin seated her guest in the formal receiving room and then sat at a prudent distance. "Cuquita, I have a problem."

"What is it, dear?"

"I...I did something to you."

An expression that might have been a frown crossed the calm face. "You did?"

"Yes. Can you tell? Do you feel different?"

"I don't know. Yes, I do feel different, I guess. Sort of...hazy."

"Hazy?"

"Yes. I remember being sharper, caring more. Now it's not so bad."

"Caring was bad?"

"Sometimes. Do you know what has changed?"

"Sort of. I changed you. When you were...ill."

"Was I ill? I don't remember being ill."

"Not ill like sick in bed. Ill as in angry and screaming."

"Oh, that. I get like that sometimes. It goes away."

"I'm afraid it's gone away forever."

"Oh. I suppose that's good, then."

"It would be, if that was all."

The other's brow furrowed. "What more is there?"

"Well, you're not exactly better, are you? You say life is hazy. You don't care as much."

"Perhaps. I sort of like it. I didn't really like caring. Sometimes it hurt."

"But I'm worried that I did you some damage."

Cuquita gave a slow smile, so different from the old, sharp grin. "Don't worry, I don't mind."

"All right, Cuquita. I'm glad you don't mind. I think I have to speak to Lord Ostersund. Would you mind waiting here a moment? I will have tea sent."

"Certainly. I had nothing planned this afternoon." A frown wavered across her brow. "I don't think."

They walked slowly up the stairs, Eirlin thinking furiously.

Bad Lady gone. Healer happy?

"No, love, I'm not happy. Maybe the Bad Lady is gone, but a lot of Cuquita is gone, as well. We did something wrong, love. We tried to help her and we hurt her."

Bad cut? Fang bad?

"No, love, you aren't bad, but we made a big mistake. We shouldn't have cut when we didn't know enough about what we were cutting."

Uncut.

"Sorry, love, you can't uncut. Once you cut, that's it. No going back."

No?

"No." She stared out the window, her mind revolving on unpleasant possibilities.

Oh.

She stood in silence for a while, then got the impression of a careless shrug.

Healer heal.

"What?"

Heal cut.

"You think I could heal her? It isn't that simple, love."

Try.

Eirlin sighed. "I suppose I should. It won't be hard. She'll probably give me permission with no question. I just don't know…"

She took her courage into her hands and went to look for the Magician.

He is in his study waiting for you.

She was too distracted to thank Kitten.

Tyrbrand listened to Eirlin's explanation. "What, exactly, did you do to her?"

"I don't know. Not exactly. I was paying attention to other things at the time. Fang said there was a bad lady inside and he could cut her out. I wouldn't let him. It seemed that some days the bad lady was in charge, some days she wasn't. Some days Fang didn't want to be anywhere near her. She scared him."

"She scared the Ferocious Fang? She must have been pretty scary."

"Oh, she was." Eirlin was silent for a moment. "But Fang said he could cure her. He did it, all right. Too much. The bad lady is gone, but so is some essential part of Cuquita. She just has no spunk. I'm worried about what will happen to her when word gets around that she's helpless."

"I hadn't thought of that aspect."

"Yes. She has made a lot of enemies. What will they do to her?"

"No worse than she has already done to them, I'm sure."

"But she's defenseless. What are we going to do, Tyrbrand? I'm responsible for this."

"Not entirely, Eirlin. She was responsible for the enemies. But I do agree that you should help her. Especially if Vanemar is sniffing around. Do you think she would agree to Kitten and I helping you?"

"Tyrbrand, she would agree to anything I said. She has no ideas of her own."

He mused that over. "I can see that being a real problem. What if someone else gets hold of her?"

"Someone already has."

"Vanemar."

"It sounds like it."

The Magician nodded. "He wants to marry her to cement his power."

"But she can't!"

"Why not? She's a free woman. She can do what she likes. Has been all her life."

"But marry him? He'd end up killing her."

He shrugged. "Her choice, her lookout."

244

"Tyrbrand, she doesn't have the ability to make a choice any more." Eirlin's mind firmed. "We have to do something."

"What?"

"I don't know. If only I hadn't meddled."

Why so sad, Eirlin?

"It's Cuquita, love. We should never have killed the bad lady."

Kill? Not kill. Killing is bad. Bad, bad, bad.

"But, dear, we did. We killed her. I was there. You cut and she was gone."

Eirlin said never kill. Killing is bad.

"But we did, dear."

Did not.

"Yes, we did."

Did not.

"Fang, don't contradict me, love. I told you…"

Did not.

Eirlin…

"Kitten, this is important. Please don't interfere."

You aren't listening, Eirlin.

"What do you mean?"

He says he didn't kill.

"But he's wrong."

He says he didn't. Time to show trust, remember?

"I see. Fang, dear, I'm sorry. I wasn't really listening. What do you mean, you didn't kill the bad lady?"

Bad Lady says bad things, Cuquita does bad things. I cut. Bad Lady can't talk.

"You didn't kill her, you just cut her off."

You told me not kill. Healer must never kill. Bad, bad. You said.

"Yes, that's right, dear, I did. And you listened!"

Good Fang. Fang always listens.

"I wouldn't quite go that far, but let's get this straight. The bad lady is still in Cuquita's head, and you just cut her off so she couldn't speak to Cuquita, tell her to do all those bad things."

Tiny, tiny cut. Bad Lady gone from Cuquita. Good Cuquita.

"But it isn't that simple, dear. They aren't two separate people. We all have a bad side and a good side. We just control the bad side better. Cuquita needs her other side, Fang."

Bad Lady comes back, Cuquita is bad sometimes.

"We'll have to teach them to do better. If there was only a way to put her back together."

Tiny cut. Tiny, tiny cut. Healer heal.

"Do you think so?"

Eirlin heals tiny cuts. Easy.

"So all you have to do is show me where you made the cut, and I can Heal it, and then Cuquita will be whole again?"

Cuquita will be bad again.

"We'll have to deal with that. Right now, we have to heal Cuquita." She headed downstairs.

The Maridon woman was sitting where Eirlin had left her, a cup of tea forgotten in her hand. When Eirlin entered the room, she regained some semblance of life, took a sip of tea, put the cup down and regarded the Healer with polite enquiry.

Eirlin took her courage in her hands. "Cuquita, I think I can help you."

"That's good."

"Do you give me permission to Heal a small incision I made a few days ago?"

"Of course. Everyone says you are a marvelous Healer."

"Right. Just sit there, and we will have a look."

Where is it, Fang?

He sped unerringly to the spot. Eirlin tried to ignore the twisted, angry side of the mind she ranged through. The other side was no calm forest pool either, but it was fairly normal.

There. Little, little cut.

I see. Ready to Heal?

Ready, Healer.

Ready to retreat, Healer?

What do you mean, Kitten?

In case she decides to finish what she was doing when this started.

I will be ready. Here we go.

With careful precision, Eirlin joined the broken fibres together, and applied Healing Power until she could feel them twist in her hands and liven. Satisfied, she pulled back out into the calmness of the room.

Cuquita sat unmoving, eyes wide open.

With growing concern, Eirlin stood and moved back, regarding her patient intently.

Cuquita's calm face suddenly twisted in rage. She leaped up and forward, her fingers clawed, profanity spewing from her mouth.

And stopped just as suddenly, her eyes crossing as they regarded the Scalpel confronting her.

Bad Lady!

"You. Will. Stand. Still!"

The dark eyes narrowed. "Do you know what you did to me, you bitch? Do you know what I have suffered through, these past days? Do you know what she was going to do, the little fool? I am going to make you pay for this."

"I know exactly what I did, and for what it's worth, I'm sorry. But that isn't your problem right now. You need to get yourself out of this predicament as quickly as you can."

"I know exactly what I have to do. There is a list of people I have to cut to size, and you," she pointed a sharp fingernail at Eirlin's face, "are about the third one down."

"That's fine. First you deal with Vanemar and whoever else you must. Then you can come and talk to me. I'd like it if you would."

"Are you giving me orders? Who do you think you are, telling me what to do?"

Eirlin lowered Fang, placed him in his sheath. "I am two people, Cuquita. First, I am someone who is going to help you out of this mess. I owe you that, and it will be good for the kingdom as well. Second, once we have the time, I am probably the only one who can help you get some balance in your life."

She caressed Fang's hilt, just once. "Oh, yes, and third? I'm the one who cut your strings before, and I can do it again." She leaned forward, towering over the other woman. "With a thought, Cuquita. From across the room. Keep that in mind."

Then Eirlin smiled. "But we don't have to worry about that, do we? We're actually both on the same side in this. You go and do what you wanted to anyway, and when this little mess is settled, come and talk to me."

She raised her hands, palms forward. "Don't worry, I'm not going to do anything without your permission. I tried that once. Never again." Her eyes narrowed. "Unless you force me to. Now go. You're wasting time."

Cuquita's mouth opened, but no words came out. Her face white with anger, she strode from the room.

Bad Lady.

"Well, what did we expect? How would you like to be penned up, unable to speak, for days?"

No fun.

Eirlin sighed. "That's right, Fang. No fun at all."

35.   Atrocity

Eirlin was relaxing in the sitting room, using her own hand as a model to show Fang where all the bones and blood vessels were. Kitten was listening idly and relaxing as well, when she caught a disturbance.

Someone is coming, Healer.

"Who?"

Street boys. In a hurry.

That caught her attention. Without a word, she sheathed Fang and started for the stairs.

Good reaction. She is learning.

She opened the door, just as Charche lifted his hand to knock. He was red-faced and panting. Rhysun was two paces behind.

"My Lady! There's trouble!"

"Where? What's wrong?"

"We don't know, my Lady, but there's been a battle or something. A messenger came in, and his horse had cuts all over. He went to the palace. We thought you might be needed."

"How far do you think he came?"

"His horse wasn't even running, it was so tired."

"A long way, then. Thank you, boys. You have done your duty. Now I must get ready." She motioned them inside, and they collapsed on the bench inside the door. With a nod to Eowin to take care of them, she spun back up the stairs to her room.

It has started.

"I'm afraid so, Kitten. We must be ready to move. Can you contact Tyrbrand?"

No need. A messenger comes.

"Good." She slung a cloak and a small pack of clothing over her shoulder. "We can meet him in the foyer."

Once again she was at the door ahead of the visitor, a page from the castle. "Lord Ostersund says you are to come immediately with your equipment, my Lady. There has been a battle, and surgeons and Healers are needed."

She looked over her shoulder to where three servants stood ready. "My horse with three days' grain in one pannier, this pack in the other one. The big leather instrument case on top. You know the one." She glanced at the cook. "I'll need some food. Bread, cheese, dried fruits. A sack of wine, and one of water. Nadorst, Lord Ostersund has a pack in his room laid ready. Put two suits of extra clothing in it, suitable for travel or hard work, and bring it to the castle on his horse as soon as you can. Same supplies for him."

As they hurried away, she turned to the page. "When you get your breath back, can you go to the infirmary at the West Gate and make sure they have all been informed?"

"Yes, my Lady." The lad started off at a jog.

By the time her horse arrived she had all her personal effects arranged, and she swung up and trotted towards the castle.

Well done, Eirlin. You move quickly.

"Thanks to you, we are prepared. Tyrbrand will have sent to the Surgeon, and he will meet us at the castle. I wonder what happened?"

So did a lot of other people. There was a buzz in the air, and traffic was heavier than usual on the main thoroughfare, hampered by the large number of citizens gossiping in the street. Eirlin did not hesitate to use Kitten's Power to clear herself a path, and soon they were at the castle.

Tyrbrand was in the main courtyard and the Surgeon was just puffing up the street towards the gate behind her. The Magician took the two of them aside.

"It's going to be bad, if that messenger's report is true. There has been some kind of massacre. The village of Ringvagen in Lord Vanemar's domain has been ransacked. Many deaths, fire, destruction, everything bad you could think of. Surgeon, we're going to need the largest team you can put together."

"They are already assembling, my Lord. We can leave immediately."

"Eirlin and I will be travelling with the King's Light Cavalry. I'll ask for a place for your people in the convoy that follows the footsoldiers."

There was a sudden increase in the commotion of the courtyard, then a spreading silence. The king stalked to the centre, his dark red travel cloak swirling. He waved his hand in a "continue" gesture and the hubub resumed.

Ostersund strode over to him and the guard parted to let the Magician through.

"Lord Ostersund. Have you taken care of the medical cadre?"

"Yes, Sire. They are ready."

"They can tail in with the supply wagons."

"I thought so, your Majesty."

"We'll be at the head." He raised his eyes. "Lady Eirlin as well? Good."

"Are you going, Sire?"

"I have to, Ostersund. Yes, I know it's dangerous, but I have no choice. My people are dying, man!"

The Magician leaned closer. "Of course, this may be exactly what they want."

"It may, but if I don't go I look weak, and I miss the chance to find out exactly what is going on. We were complaining there was nothing we could do. Now our enemy has acted, and we are free to respond."

"What about the part of the message that identifies the attackers?"

The king frowned. "That is the other reason I must go. There is something wrong about this whole thing."

"I agree with you, Sire. Lady Eirlin and I are ready at your command."

Once again the king met Eirlin's eyes, and he nodded. "We have what we need." He raised his voice. "Let us depart."

A groom brought his horse and he vaulted into the saddle without aid. Eirlin mounted as well, and Tyrbrand grabbed the reins of his horse as Nadorst slid off. "All packed?"

"As Lady Eirlin ordered, my Lord."

He tossed her a grim smile. "I hope you put in my pipe and slippers and a good saga to read. This little holiday might get boring."

Even I know that is not funny.

It most certainly isn't, Cloud Cat. Are you ready?

As I have been for weeks, my Lord Magician.

Yes, you have, and I thank you.

He nodded to Eirlin and they slipped in behind the king as the cavalcade formed. As they passed out the gate, Eirlin spotted two small heads in the crowd, blond and dark. She gestured, and the boys trotted alongside a moment.

"Tell everyone not to believe what they hear. Do you understand that?"

Charche grinned up at her. "Yes, my Lady. Nothing is as it seems, as usual."

"Do what you can to keep it that way."

He tipped a finger at his forehead in salute and allowed her horse to carry her ahead of him. She saw him clap his friend on the shoulder and start shoving away through the crowd.

"What was that?"

She glanced over at Tyrbrand. "The boys have a finger on the pulse of the lower town. They can inject some scepticism into the more blatant rumours."

"That's going to be needed, I'm afraid. There is more to this attack than meets the eye."

"Exactly what I told them."

They rode in silence down the lane that the king's guard opened through the crowds. When they got outside the city gates the press faded, and the king signalled a trot.

"How far is it to Ringvagen?"

"About four hours' ride, I believe. A cavalcade like this might take longer. With so many people, there always seems to be something to slow us down."

"And the king could rush ahead, but he isn't that stupid."

The king glanced over his shoulder. "My Lady's praise is good to hear."

She went red. "I'm sorry, your Majesty..."

He barked a short laugh. "Blame it on your Sword. My hearing isn't usually that good."

She frowned down. "Kitten?"

We are at war. He is the king. I do all I can to support his reign.

She tightened her sending. *Even at the expense of embarrassing your friends?*

Embarrassment is good. It heightens the senses, prepares for quick response.

She glanced over at the Magician. "I've never seen her like this."

He nodded. "I'm afraid we are all about to see a lot of new things, and I doubt if we are going to like any of them."

"I'm not sure I like that."

In her mind, Kitten arched her back and her fur rose. She opened her mouth in a hiss. *Like? Like? This is War! You are of no use to your king or your people if you mewl and cavil about what you like and do not like. Look around you. Prepare to be attacked, physically, mentally and emotionally to the core of your soul!*

She dropped the strength of her sending, but left in a hint of snarl at the edge. *You can never prepare yourself completely for your first experience of the horror and stench of the battlefield, but try. After a few battles, it gets easier.*

The king glanced back. "A good lesson for all of us. Thank you, Cloud Cat."

The Magician, too glanced over, and did not narrow his sending. *I was unaware that you would help the king in this way. What are the limits? What can you do?*

Sorry, Magician. I have never helped a king before. It just seemed the best thing to do. I have no idea of the limits until I reach them.

251

The king gestured, and Eirlin and Tyrbrand rode up, one on either side of him. "This could be important. We have a few hours' ride. How can we test these limits?"

"We could drop back and allow you to ride ahead, Sire, and see what happens."

"Do so." He gave a grim smile. "If we do not have new thoughts to occupy our minds, there are many dark alleys they might stray down."

"Yes, your Majesty. Very dark."

They reined their horses out of the column and found a wider section of the road to wait in. "Do you know what you are to do, Kitten?"

Call the king. Not too loud.

"Your Majesty!" They watched up the line as the monarch's head came up. *Very good, your Majesty.*

Thank you, Cloud Cat. Why does Ostersund call you that?

It is the Name the Leute gave me, your Majesty. The Cloud Cat is a hunter of the Western mountains. Long haired, grey and white. It hunts in snow and shadow, and appears as if by magic. It is a fierce fighter and tireless hunter. I strive to live up to their honour.

I hear the Leute are a fierce and tireless people. Their honour is a treasure to cherish.

She sent the king a flattening of her ears. *Thank you, your Majesty, but there is no need for the honeyed phrases and inspiring speeches of the council chambers. This is war, and the Cat with Many Claws is always ready.*

I stand corrected, my Lady.

Actually, you are sitting, your Majesty. On a horse, I suspect.

I warn you, Cat. I can accept correction with far more tolerance than I can stomach bad humour.

I consider myself warned, Sire. I will have Lord Ostersund call again.

This time the Magician had to raise his voice considerably in order to be heard, but the king was still pleased.

That is a long way, Cloud Cat. What else can you do for me?

What do you need?

Can you tell what those around me are thinking?

No, Sire, but I can tell what they are feeling. Including your horse, who...probably has a stone in his left rear hoof. You will notice the limp soon.

There was a flurry of activity, and the whole column stopped while the horse was seen to.

Eirlin and Tyrbrand walked their horses back to their positions. "You see what I mean about the speed. The king must stop and dismount. The message must go to the advanced parties so they do not get too far ahead. Those behind always seem to pile on top of one another, because they are not paying close enough attention."

She smiled. "Sounds like any group of people anywhere. Only worse."

"Five hours, perhaps."

However, the problem was solved with dispatch, and soon they were moving. Once again the king called Healer and Magician to ride with him.

"That went smoothly."

It occurred to me when your Majesty was about to give the order that your ability to reach into the minds of your subjects could be amplified. So when you spoke, I had them already set to listen. Thus the orders to those ahead went faster, and those behind were alerted to the change, so they did not bunch up and have to sort themselves.

The king nodded to Ostersund. "This is a great advantage." He grinned. "Every general wishes his officers would listen better, react quicker."

They rode in silence for a while.

"What do we expect to find, Lord Ostersund?"

The Magician winced. "The messenger carried more fear than facts, Sire. For certain we will find a number of townsfolk dead and wounded, and serious destruction in their village. We will set our field infirmary in whatever building is available or in the tents the wagons carry. I will let the Surgeon and Eirlin take care of that.

"Also, the people will be frightened. They will want to see protection."

"We can arrange that." The king's hand indicated the long line of horse and foot that followed. "And then there are the perpetrators."

Ostersund shook his head. "They will be long gone."

"Of course. What I don't understand is why they did it. What could they possibly gain?"

"If they were Inderjornese, they were sending a message that they would not put up with the harassment."

"What do you mean, 'if?' The messenger was certain. 'Masked faces, blond hair,' he said."

"An interesting choice, don't you think?"

"Ah. I see. And if they were not?"

"Then we have true evil, your Majesty."

"Yes. Someone has killed his own people for political gain."

"I'm afraid so."

The king sat straighter. "So we have three tasks. The Healer will deal with the wounded. The king will see to the fears of his people." He looked over to Ostersund. "And the Magician will find the true killers."

"I will do what I can, your Majesty."

And the Cat will help however she can. This is not my usual task in war.

"It may not have been in the past. 'A strong hand in battle, a strong voice at the conference table,' as I believe I have heard you say." The Magician laughed. "The Cat develops even more claws."

I suppose I do.

It took them more than five hours, so it was mid-afternoon before they crossed into Vanemar's domain. As the cavalcade wound down out of the hills that formed the boundary, Kitten sent the king's senses up and down the road. He scowled, and called for Panos Genil.

"We have been riding a long time, Captain Genil. We look tired."

The Captain's back straightened even more than usual and his eyes, too, shot up and down the line. "Yes, your Majesty. That will be corrected."

At the king's nod he spurred his charger back along the line, his mere presence and sense of purpose firming the ranks.

That looks better, your Majesty.

"Yes. We must show all our strength. We do not have much."

Ostersund frowned. "That's a point we have not covered, your Majesty."

"The fact that this could be a physical trap, not a political one?"

"Correct."

"Our scouts are out. So far there is no sign of a larger force."

The Magician nodded, but his brow furrowed. "I'm still concerned."

"As am I. We must all be at our most cautious, roadweary or not."

Swords do not sleep or tire, your Majesty. I will be alert. Do you smell smoke?

"No, but I see it."

Several plumes of black smoke pillared up from below them, merging into a low-lying grey smear above the valley.

With grim faces, the column plunged downward.

As they approached the town, Kitten sent her senses all around, helping the king and Eirlin do the same.

"No people anywhere near the road."

"Afraid of us."

"Probably."

They rode farther. Now the smoke towered above, and a stench like burning garbage swept over them.

They came out of the trees and saw the village across the fields. Or what had been a village. Stone walls still stood, but many houses had no thatch left. Charred beams stuck up at all angles, and smoke rose from everywhere. As they rode closer, they could see figures poking aimlessly through the rubble or crouched over forms that lay on the ground. The sound of wailing wafted on the stinking breeze.

Now is the time to be strong, Eirlin.

"Yes, Kitten." She set her teeth and rode ahead.

"The same for all of us." The king's face hardened and he followed her.

Eirlin surveyed the scene. "It has been a full eight hours since the attack. Has no one organized any help?"

"It seems not."

The Magician pulled up beside them. "I wonder if it hasn't been left to us on purpose."

The king's frown deepened. "And Vanemar's castle is just around that bend in the valley."

The column stopped some distance from the wreckage and arrayed itself in good order. Kitten could see that there were sound military minds in the troop. The perimeter was secured, the king's standard placed on a small rise with good view and better defence.

The medical cadre had no such discipline. They rode straight to the town, the surgeons and their apprentices jumping from the wagons before they had stopped. Eirlin dismounted and strode into their midst, joining the Head Surgeon to make decisions as to disposition of resources and supplies and assignment of duties.

The locals had made some attempt to tend their wounded, but many were beyond the simple skills of their friends. They had set up a rude hospital in the inn, but the Surgeon deemed the smoke and smell unhealthy, so the tents were set up half a bowshot upwind of the village.

Soon the villagers caught on, and a flow of wounded began to wind into the infirmary area.

Once things were going well, Eirlin looked around. "Surely there are more injured than this."

The man she spoke to, leather-apronned and bloody, merely growled and spat on the ground near her feet.

She pinned him with a stare, and Kitten sent what she could into his closed Maridon mind. "We are trying to help. Where are the other wounded?"

He shrugged with his one good shoulder. "Over t' other side. There's less burning near t'crick."

That was logical. She sought out the Surgeon. "I've been told that there is another group of casualties on the west side of the town. There is less burning there, and perhaps another good site for the wounded if the wind keeps blowing the smoke away."

He nodded and turned back to the sword wound he was stitching up.

Eirlin tapped three apprentices. "With me, lads. There may be more wounded."

They grabbed their gear and followed.

She skirted the worst of the damage, coming back into the town from along the creek. There was less burning here. It seemed that the clutter of outhouses and gardens had impeded the attackers' horses, and the water in the creek had allowed the people to deal more easily with the fires. There were houses with only part of their thatch burned.

Many people. Up that alley.

She signalled her small crew and turned into the narrow street.

As she strode along, Kitten began to get an uneasy feeling.

Careful, Eirlin. They are very fearful.

"And we are here to help." But she slowed. As she came out of the buildings into a small square, several people turned to look at her. To her dismay, they ran back into a larger building that looked like a barn. There were frantic calls and a woman screamed.

Eirlin stopped, perplexed. Then men began to file out of the barn. Some were bandaged, some were limping, but all carried weapons or sharp farm tools. They moved slowly forward, frightened but determined.

"Who is in charge here?"

A man stepped forward. Better dressed than most, a bloody rag twisted around his head, his face ashen. "You. You did this!"

"We're here to help. We have an infirmary set up. Have you more wounded?"

He cracked out a laugh. "Have we wounded? You should know, you blond devils. Yes, we have wounded, and we aren't going to have any more." He raised the sickle in his hand and stepped forward. His followers did likewise.

Eirlin glanced back at her three companions and winced. Three blond heads.

She felt the hatred flowing at her, building past fear towards action. She had never experienced such an emotion, and it shook her to the core.

Kitten, what do I do...?

I don't think it is time to draw your Sword yet. But they are beyond reason. You must attack.

Attack?

Yes, Eirlin the Fierce. Now is the time of your glory. Defeat them. Put them all to work. It is one of your stronger skills.

Relief rushed through her, clearing her head and returning her confidence. She stepped forward. "Don't be an idiot. You're bleeding all down your face. What hit you?"

He faltered. "I...I don't know. I was running, and somebody came from the alley beside me, and..."

That's it. Keep moving. I will help.

By this time she was within reach, and she pushed the sickle aside, her hand going to his injured forehead. With her gentle physical contact, Kitten could feel the man's fragile will to fight crumble. "Odomir, see to this man. Check the bones underneath before you bind the wound. Get rid of that dirty rag." She turned to the two men closest. "You two. Find some buckets. We need clean water from the creek. Go!"

Go! Do as the Healer says.

They lowered their weapons and stumbled away, and she ranged further into the crowd, assigning tasks and prescribing treatments.

Soon she was inside and began to see women. At first they shrank from her, but soon they fell into line, obeying orders and tending their friends. Palpable relief spread through the room.

Soon Eirlin looked around in satisfaction. "That looks better."

Over there, Healer.

"What is it?"

That one is interesting.

A groan from a pallet on the floor cued her. The man was half-sitting against the wall, one hand beneath him, the other grasping his stomach near the right side. Blood seeped through his fingers.

Kitten, this is one for us. She pulled Fang from his sheath and knelt beside the patient. Gently prying his hands away, she cut the shirt free. Fresh blood oozed from a gash in his side just below the ribs.

Kitten, work on the pain. Fang, we must find the damage.

As Eirlin and Fang dove into the wound with their senses, Kitten moved into the man's head, calming him and deadening the pain. There she met a surprise. She could read the emotions easily. As she worked on his mind, she became accustomed to his thoughts. He was not quite conscious. Fear and pain circled in his head. She began to get pictures. No, the same picture, over and over.

Oh, by the Forge and the Smith, this is interesting.

Satisfied with his condition, she pulled herself out, back to where Eirlin and Fang were working.

Nibble, nibble nibble. No problem here, Eirlin. All done.

Yes, Fang, that is good. Any worms?

Nibble, nibble, nibble, no more worms. All clean. No more blood, all healed.

Can we sew him up?

Put him back together, Healer. All happy.

Eirlin opened her kit and pulled out a needle, already threaded with clean linen. It was not a large opening, and a few quick stitches were all it required.

Not as serious as it looked, Kitten. Once we stopped the bleeding, he was fine.

That's good Eirlin. This is better.

What?

Maybe he would be more comfortable if he lay on his other side.

The Healer frowned. *Yes, I suppose that could help...*

And then you could see what is lying under him.

Under him?

She eased the man into a more comfortable position, and as she did some straw showed in his hand. Then she looked more carefully.

"Wait. That's not straw."

I think not. It looks more like...

"Hair!" She pulled it out. A crude blond wig, crusted with blood, but no question of the original colour.

He pulled it off the man who stabbed him. The dark-haired man who stabbed him.

She held the wig out. "Did anyone see how this man got this?"

Several of the women gathered around. "That's a wig."

"Yes. A blond wig. Apparently this man pulled it off one of the raiders."

The women started to chatter. Finally one of them clapped her hands together. "That's it! Dark eyebrows. They all had blond hair and dark eybrows."

Eyes began to turn to Eirlin.

258

"So they weren't blond men at all."

"No, my Lady, I don't think they were."

"The king has to see this." By now all eyes were on her.

"Those of you who can, spread the word around. You three apprentices, stay here and tend everyone you can. You'll be safe, now. I'll send stretchers for the seriously wounded, but I think the rest are fine here. We'll send more bandages when we can. I have to see the king."

"Is the king really here?"

She turned to the man who spoke. It was the one who had threatened her. He had a neat bandage on his head, and his colour was better. "Of course he is. His people are hurting and he has brought his Healers and Surgeons to help."

The man nodded. She turned away and hurried towards the other side of the town, cutting straight through this time, skirting the fallen beams and ignoring the stench, the bodies, and the stinging in her eyes.

When she reached the pavilion erected for the king, he was not there. She grabbed the first Guardsman she saw. "Where is the king? Where is Lord Ostersund?"

"The king has gone to Lord Vanemar's castle, my Lady. Lord Ostersund has gone with the trackers."

"Lord Vanemar?"

The Guard pointed. "Yes. His castle is just around the corner of that rise, there. Lord Vanemar wanted to show the king where he proposes to put the wounded."

This doesn't sound good.

She stuffed the blond wig in the Guardsman's hand. "You find Captain Genil and you tell him this was pulled off the head of one of the raiders, who had dark hair underneath. Do you know what that means?"

"Yes, my Lady."

"Then he will, too."

"But he's up at the castle with the king."

"Oh. Well, tell whoever's in charge here, and Lord Ostersund as well. We're looking out for Maridon raiders. Have you got that?"

"Yes, my Lady."

"Where can I find a horse?"

Since she was already moving, he only had time to point. She rushed over to the picket line, chose a horse with a bridle in its mouth, and swung herself into the saddle. A soldier ran up, open-mouthed, and she waved a hand at him. "I'm going to find the king. If you see Lord Ostersund, tell him." She was gone before he had time to answer.

It was a short gallop to the castle, and the main gate was open. She slid off her horse in the bailey, where she was surprised to see the Guard Captain lined up with his men in neat formation.

"Where is the king?"

"He is inside with Lord Vanemar. He told us to wait here."

"I need to talk with him." She strode up the stairs.

"Wait, my Lady. Is there a problem?"

She turned back at the top. "There might be."

As she sprinted into the main hall, she could hear him snapping orders.

But it was too late. The big doors swung shut behind her and bars dropped into place. The two soldiers inside turned their backs against the door and stood their ground with unpleasant smiles.

She turned back into the hall, and was surprised to find the king standing alone.

"Eirlin. I'm glad you came. This is where we're going to bring..."

Danger, your Majesty.

His hand went to his sword hilt, his eyes to the closed door and the soldiers guarding it. "Treachery?"

"Yes, Sire. The raiders were dark men with blond wigs. Your Guard has been locked outside."

Kitten had to be impressed at the speed the king's mind worked.

"So this was a ruse to get me out here. Vanemar will call challenge on me to take over my rule. There are four other high-level Maridons here. The required witnesses. I should have been more suspicious."

I'm sorry, your Majesty. I should have been here to make you more suspicious.

"That's all right, Cloud Cat. You have done your duty, and you are here now."

"Your Majesty!"

They turned. Vanemar stood at the end of the musicians' gallery that ran around the hall above their heads. He put his hands on the railing and stared down at them, his face a picture of satisfaction.

"Your stupidity in falling into my trap is the last proof anyone needs of your inability to rule this realm. Don't go away. I'll be right down for the festivities." He gave one last, sardonic smile, then turned and went out.

36.   A Cat and a King

The king drew his sword. The ornate, plain steel sword with the flaw near the tip. "Well, Eirlin, I guess it's just the two of us."

She shook her head. "No, your Majesty. It's just you."

"What?"

"I'm sorry, your Majesty. I'm a Healer, not a fighter. I might be able to defend your back, but I cannot kill. Kitten and I have been through this before. I am allowed to wield the Sword, but only for Healing. As a fighter, I would have too much Power, and it is not allowed for those with too much Power to wield her."

Kitten sent a tight private message. *Eirlin, that is not true.*

Quiet, Kitten.

The king's sword wavered. "Then we have a problem. I'm a good swordsman, but there are more of them than I'd like, and Vanemar is reputed to be deadly."

Eirlin...

I know, Kitten, but it isn't allowed.

Are you sure?

The king looked at her quizzically. "You're talking to your Sword privately, aren't you? I can sort of hear you."

"Yes, your Majesty. We have a problem. By Kitten's rules, she is not allowed to take anyone as Hand who has any form of substantial power already: Magician, Overlord, King. Even me."

Eirlin the Liar! We have already fought together.

That wasn't true fighting.

Have it your way. But I am not taking a Hand. And I am sworn to do all in my power to help him rule.

The king put his hand on her hilt. "What is she saying?"

I am trying to work this out, your Majesty, so I will speak with you directly. You are not allowed to be my Hand, because it would make you too powerful. However, I am sworn to help you. If you fight with me, you will win. If that is for the good of the kingdom, then I must do it.

"So all you have to decide is whether my rule is good for the kingdom?"

I am being very careful here, your Majesty. One does not bend the rules one was born with unless one is sure there is good reason.

"Who gets to decide? I find it difficult to think that a magic Sword would be allowed to judge her king and the fate of his rule."

A good point. Fortunately, we have someone else.

261

"Eirlin?"

If she can't judge, who could?

Both turned their regard to the Healer. She raised her hands in defence. "You want me to decide?"

"It sounds logical to me, my Lady. I am beginning to believe that your role in this kingdom is more important than even you know yourself. I would be happy to allow you to judge."

"You really mean that? And what if I say that Kitten may not fight with you?"

"Then I will take my own sword and go and do my best. It is what I would have done, had you not been here."

Eirlin laughed softly. "You are a very clever man, your Majesty."

"I don't hear a great deal of admiration. What mental feat have I achieved now?"

"It was a good gamble. The very act of recognizing that I have the power to choose proves your fitness to rule."

"It does?"

"Are you telling me you didn't realize that?"

"I didn't. It does sound logical, now that you mention it."

Truth.

Eirlin shrugged and held Kitten out. "You win, your Majesty."

He took Kitten, carefully moulding his hand to her hilt, sighting down her blade. "Not quite yet. I believe I still have to accomplish another task, one perhaps more difficult."

She smiled. "I don't think so, your Majesty." She laid her hand on the blade. "Kitten, I see this enemy as a great threat to the realm. I believe it is necessary for you to aid King Vetrorillo to the fullest."

To the fullest, Healer?

"I'm not sure exactly what that means, but I think it is necessary. I count on your training and your strength of character to make the right decision, Kitten."

It means I may ask for help. There are six Sensitives within range of this place. Three are not powerful and they are Maridon, but they will help their sovereign. Two other Sensitives are not cooperative. Also the Healers, although the infirmary tent is quite far away. I will not need any help from you or Excisor, Healer. Your Majesty, may I prepare you for battle?

"I would be honoured."

She nestled into his hand and sent her strength flowing up his arm, and her mind into his thoughts. He stiffened at first, then relaxed and allowed her to intrude farther.

You have a very strong mind, your Majesty.

Thank you. A requirement of my position.

Running footsteps sounded above them. A troop of archers began to file out along the gallery on both sides.

Eirlin! I cannot defend against swords and arrows at the same time! What can I do?

Use the Fang.

Kitten, I cannot kill, and neither can he.

Then figure out something else.

Oh. Certainly. She pulled Excisor from his sheath. There was a blaze of energy, strong enough to halt everyone for a moment.

"Gently, little one."

Bad men. Hurt the king?

Control him, Eirlin. I cannot help you.

Fang, dear! Remember your training!

Bad men.

Yes, they are bad. Soon we will heal them. Now they need to rest.

Rest?

Yes. You know how. I will tell you which ones, and you will put them to sleep.

Sleep. Bad men sleep, then we heal them. No more bad men.

That's right, dear. Start with that one. See him?

Bye, bye, bad man.

The lead archer in the gallery, in the act of drawing his bow, got a stunned look on his face. Slowly, he released the tension. Then, like a child going to bed he laid his weapons on the floor and collapsed in a ball, a peaceful smile on his face.

Now that one. Then those two.

Bye, bye, bad man,

Time to go to slee-eep.

Bye, bye, bad man,

Time to go to sleep.

Oh. Bad men don't want to sleep?

The remaining archers, seeing their leaders fall, skidded to a stop and began, slowly at first, then more quickly, to back away. Soon their speed increased and became a full-fledged rout, leaving their first rank snoring quietly on the floor of the gallery. Eirlin turned to see the two soldiers at the door frozen, terror on their faces.

Unaware of this drama, five Maridon nobles and several more dark-haired retainers filed through the inner door and spread out along the end of the hall, Vanemar at their centre and a pace ahead.

The king stepped forward. "So, Vanemar. Your plot has not succeeded. Do you deny that your inability to believe what is staring you in the face demonstrates your unsuitability to rule?"

The darker man smiled slowly. "Your Majesty – and I will call you that for the last time – since you say I am unable to perceive whatever it is that is in front of me, you can't really expect it to have any effect on me, can you? Now, why don't you just step out here, away from your imaginary friends, and let me prove, for once and for ever, that I am the man to rule this kingdom?"

The Maridon noble drew his sword and swept his cloak to the floor behind him. "I, Javier da Vanemar, formally declare you, the former King Vetrorrillo da Marida, to be no longer competent to rule this kingdom. I challenge you by the ancient laws of Maridon to defend your right to rule."

Your Majesty, Eirlin can put him to sleep.

No, Kitten. I must fight him. It is the rule.

How fair must it be?

It must seem fair to everyone watching. They believe these rules. If I win by their standards they will obey.

Well, I enjoy a good match as much as the next Sword, I suppose.

Remember, he is an excellent fighter.

We shall have to see about that.

The two men raised their weapons in salute. Without further speech they flung themselves forward. There was a clash of steel on steel, and the watchers went silent, their eyes wide in hope and expectation.

All right, your Majesty. Let's see what he's made of. A fine sword. Very light and strong. No flaws at all. Oh, very good! Parry, parry, don't attack yet. Let him reveal himself. Look at that! I've never seen that attack done so well. Watch his footwork. See that half-step? Don't be fooled. Parry, parry again...

Kitten, what is wrong?

Is something wrong, your Majesty?

What has happened to Vanemar? He moves so slowly. I thought he was a master swordsman.

He is. His speed is really quite impressive. There! See that triple beat? Very few could match the tempo of that.

But...

Your Majesty, you are finally beginning to understand what is happening in this realm.

I am?

I hope so. In case you didn't know, you are holding off one of the best swordsmen in several kingdoms, you haven't even started to sweat, and at the same time you're having a conversation with me.

Oh.

You must understand, your Majesty, that he has as much chance against you as a domestic kitten against a Cloud Cat of the western mountains. When you took me in your hand with the blessing of the Healer, you took all the power of the realm of Inderjorne. You have access to every loyal Magician, Healer, and Sensitive within reach of my Power. There are only three here, but just Eirlin would be enough for this task. Would you like to attack a bit now? Careful, you don't want to kill him yet. See the fancy overhand attack? Let the point slide by your shoulder...so...then just nudge his forte with my quillion. Yes, like that. See how that put him off balance? Oh! A very quick recovery. Well done, Vanemar.

Who are you cheering for, Kitten?

Come, your Majesty, be generous. Do you realize the level of skill required for a single man, all alone, to fight as well as he does? Parry that one; it would have taken your arm off. That's right. Now, the question is, what do we want to do with him?

I'd like to take his head off.

We could do that. But it would be very messy, and Eirlin would be upset.

Well, we don't want to upset Eirlin, do we? What do you suggest?

It's really up to you, your Majesty. Do you truly want him dead? Oops! Remember the dagger.

What dagger?

I'm not telling. Find it yourself.

What do you...? Oh. That bulge in his left sleeve.

Very good, your Majesty. Actually, I was talking about the bigger one in his belt at the back. Stay out of a bind, because then he'd use it.

I hardly call that fair.

You'd be right, but you'd still be dead.

Let's not get into a bind, then.

Good choice, your Majesty. So. Dead or not?

Dead. He's too dangerous to leave walking around.

How soon? Have we played enough to satisfy your other subjects?

I think so. They sound enthused.

So let's give them a thrill, shall we? Let them think he's going to win, then simply run him through the heart. Nice and neat, not much blood, very definitive.

I suppose you could call a sword through the heart definitive. You sound like a very well-educated Sword.

I have good teachers. Here we go then. I've been slowing your responses to the left side for a while now. He thinks you have a weakness there. Watch this lunge. Straight in, and you parry left, but he's over...and around...and here comes his point, straight for your ribs. But we slip aside and there's my point...in...and out...just that quick. Look; he's still standing. He doesn't know he's dead yet. Listen to them. Some of them even think he got you. Look in his eyes. Make sure the last thing he knows is that he was beaten. There. Down he goes.

As the body slumped to the floor, the uproar subsided until there was silence. The king held his sword in the *guarde* position, pivoting slowly to face each one of them. None could meet his eye.

The king whipped Kitten through a formal salute before he spoke.

"I believe I have made my point. The challenge was given and answered in full by the rules of Marida, a realm in which we do not live, which does not want us, and which has no power over us."

He lowered the Sword, keeping the point towards them. "The challenge was also answered by the rules of Inderjorne, the realm which I rule and in which we live. I, King Vetrorrillo of Inderjorne, having reaffirmed my competence by the rites of two kingdoms, the past and the present, feel confident that I shall continue that rule. If there is any man who would deny my right to do so, I invite him to say so now. No one? Very wise.

"Oh, and if any of you were waiting for the archers? I think they found the proceedings rather boring."

The king strode three paces closer, and they swayed back, as from a strong wind. "And now, you will stand down your men and return to your manors. You are all confined to your own lands for the next two months while I investigate who caused the atrocity down in the village. At the end of that time I will call a Conclave of Peers, and we will all discuss freely the new directions the realm must travel. Your king has spoken. You may leave."

The beaten men turned as one and left without a murmur. The king watched them with satisfaction.

It is traditional to use his cloak to clean me.

The king did so, then looked around, his left hand toying idly with Kitten's upper quillion.

"Your Majesty, I think now would be a good time to return the Sword to me."

The king began to hold Kitten forward, then hesitated.

Eirlin shook her head, slowly. "You are thinking, 'What if I keep her? What kind of king could I be, if I kept the Sword and used her for the glory of Inderjorne?' You are in great danger, your Majesty."

"I am?" He regarded the Sword thoughtfully.

"You are thinking those thoughts because you were not trained to control the Power you hold in your hand at the moment."

"I was trained to handle the power of a realm."

"You were trained to seize any power you could lay your hand on. If you give in to your present desires, you will destroy yourself."

"How could I do that?"

"There is more than one way to lose your soul, your Majesty."

"Ah." Reluctantly, the king took his fingers from Kitten's hilt, handed her back to Eirlin.

She ran a gentle caress down the side of the blade, then placed the Sword in her scabbard. "Besides which, if you think it through, you couldn't have done it anyway."

"Why not?"

"What did I say when I gave you the Sword?"

"But...oh. By refusing to follow the rules, I would be denying my fitness to rule."

"Exactly. Remember the problem with my Scalpel."

"No being should have more power than he can control himself." The king frowned thoughtfully. "You know, I'm beginning to see how effective this system is."

"Think also; would Kitten have allowed you?"

"Since I have rarely come across a being so stubborn, I suppose not."

Your Majesty, that is a harsh judgement!

He shrugged. "Well, since I have done the right thing and returned the Sword, I assume that I have retained my right to rule. Therefore I get to make some judgements without fear of losing my throne. Now, please answer me one more question. That fight was a complete charade."

That is not a question, your Majesty, but I will answer. The end of the fight was, as you requested, for Vanemar's supporters. The rest of the fight was for you.

"For me?"

Yes. The Magician has been trying to tell you for years, but humans have very strange hearing.

"We do?"

Yes, you only hear what you want to. It was necessary for you to experience your Power, so you could understand your responsibility.

267

"And if I did not accept the responsibility, as we have discussed, you had ways of dealing with me."

I am known as the Cat with Many Claws. Among other things.

"Lesson learned, Kitten." The king's shoulders lost their erect carriage, and he plunked down on a nearby bench. "It is a shock to learn that for all these years I have been living a shallow dream, completely unaware of what is going on under my nose. Now I am expected to rule a kingdom I do not understand, having very little power with which to govern. I'm not sure I'm going to like this."

"There is much that I don't like about my new responsibilities to my people, your Majesty. I put up with them because I don't have a choice. I suspect your role is similar."

"From what I have been able to gather, I think your brother has proved himself a much more successful Hand than I have."

"Why is that?"

"Apparently, the less fighting you do, the better you are."

A strong hand in war, a strong voice in council.

"That. Yes."

Eirlin chuckled. "He is another one who said he never wanted the job."

The king shook his head. "I never said I didn't want to be king. I just complain a lot when I keep discovering it isn't as easy a duty as I had hoped."

Eirlin sighed. "Well, that was the easy part."

"What do you mean? I have re-established my control over the realm. Those Lords leaving now represent the most powerful of my possible enemies."

"On a secular level, you are right. However, these were only the pawns. There is one more faction to be dealt with. The real leaders. The Maridons of Power."

The king was shaking his head, as if to dislodge an idea that was stuck there. "What are you saying?"

"I'm reminding you that the challenge to your authority as king was only the face of the plot. The real power faction remained hidden, working from the shadows. Don't you wonder why Fuentes da Baneza wasn't here? Where are his soldiers? I'll tell you. He didn't come, and he didn't send any soldiers. He has no need of them. His Power is in his mind and his Sword, and we still have to counter it."

The king smiled. "I suppose I'll just have to borrow your Kitten again, and go and confront him."

"I wish it were that simple. He will not attend a confrontation. He will use his Power to keep one step ahead of you. You can't send anyone else against him because you are the only one with the Power to confront him. You can't spend all your time chasing him because you have to deal with the rest of the realm. You have dealt with the armed forces of his allies. He will be out rounding up support of another kind."

"I see." The king slammed his fist into his palm. "As usual, nothing is simple. What do you suggest?"

"I have no idea. You're talking to a Healer, remember?"

"Much as I hate to think of it, we may have to wait for him to make the next move."

"I suppose. I think you're going to have to depend on your spies, now."

"What spies?"

"The spies that any king worthy of the name sets up to keep track of what is going on in the realm."

"Oh. Those spies."

Eirlin's lip twitched. "Don't look so much like a child with his hand in the cookie jar, your Majesty. I'm sure your spies are very necessary and quite useful." Then her face fell into harsher lines. "And if they can find a way to bring this man to heel, they will do the kingdom a great favour. This atrocity must be paid for."

They returned to the village, and for the rest of the night Eirlin and the others did what they could for the people of Ringvagen. As the sun rose the next morning on the smoking ruins of the town, the Healer, the Surgeon, the Magician and the king surveyed the scene.

In spite of Eirlin's fatigue, a fire still burned in her.

"This is the most evil deed I have ever witnessed."

The king's face was lined and drawn. "The man who performed the act has paid."

"But the man responsible lives and thrives."

The king nodded.

A wave of lethargy submerged her anger. "We have done what we can. I must sleep."

"And you, your Majesty, must return to the Capital. You cannot afford to be away too long." Ostersund bowed to remove any disrespect from the statement.

"I agree. I will sleep for a few hours, then leave with my fastest riders."

"We will follow tomorrow. There is still work to be done here." He nodded to the line of bodies laid out, mourners hovering near.

The king nodded. "I appreciate your duty in this case. There must be a healing between the Maridons and Inderjornese in this demesne."

"As long as Vanemar's heir is not as rabid as his uncle, they have a chance."

"Don't worry. He and I will have serious words before I leave."

With that, the king turned away, and Tyrbrand took Eirlin's hand. "Can you wake up long enough to walk to a bed?"

I was going to let her sleep.

The Magician laughed. "And when she fell over?"

You misjudge my Powers, my dear Magician.

"I still think she'd be better off in bed."

"Will you two stop talking about me as if I'm not here, and find me a bed?"

"Yes, my Lady."

Yes, my Lady.

She turned. "But I am not forgetting. Something has to be done about Lord Fuentes da Baneza. He has committed an unforgivable atrocity on the people of this land. On his own people! When we get back to the Capital, that is our first priority."

Yes, my Lady.

37.   The Teacher with Many Claws

Kitten regarded the Magician, sitting comfortably in his usual chair. Then she regarded the Healer, who was definitely not comfortable.

Eirlin.

The Healer stopped her pacing and looked towards Kitten where she lay on the settee. "What?"

The servants are avoiding you.

"What a ridiculous thing to say!"

Hmm. Now it's me that's ridiculous.

"Are you trying to anger me?"

What, me? Anger Eirlin the Wonderful? It is not possible. She is too calm, too steady, too sweet.

"I know what you're on about, you know."

Good for you. That's something at least.

"I have a right to be angry. That was a horrible atrocity, and the man who designed it walks away. And now the king says there's nothing we can do about it, because we have no proof?"

Tyrbrand shrugged, his lips pressed together. "We know he did it. We just can't prove it. The man who actually ordered the attack is dead. The Maridons are now more frightened than they were. The king dare not make an unwise move against anyone without tipping the whole balance of the kingdom into war. I don't like it either, but those are the facts."

It is true, but it is not just.

"That it isn't. You're going to have to take matters in hand, Eirlin."

She turned at the new voice. "Jesco, are you spying on me again?"

The swordsman sauntered into the room and drew Kitten from her scabbard. She moulded herself to his left hand. "She's still going on, is she?"

Pretty much the same as before.

"Good. Sooner or later she's going to come around to it." He hefted her, feeling the difference.

Sooner rather than later. Lord Ostersund does not like to train new servants.

"Kitten, this has nothing to do with servants. It has to do with Fuentes da Baneza. It has to do with what are we going to do with him. We know he is secretly creating the death of our realm, and we are powerless!"

Jesco made a few slow passes, watching the line of Kitten's blade. She kept his hand steady. "But we do know what to do."

"No we don't. Nobody has any idea."

"I do."

She took another turn about the room, her hands spread wide. "Well, I don't. Tyrbrand, why aren't you saying anything?"

The Magician shook his head, gestured for Jesco to speak.

"He has to die, Eirlin," he pointed Kitten's blade at her, "and you're the only one who can do it."

"What?" She stopped cold in her pacing, and her rage froze as well. "I don't kill people. I can't."

"Well, I'm certainly not going to do it."

"No, Jesco, I never suggested you should."

"Who, then?"

"Much though I hate waiting, we let the king's justice do its duty. That's the way of our people, Jesco."

"Hmm. Remember the story of the Rogue Mage of Weillen?"

"What has that got to do with it? Da Baneza is no Magician."

"No, but with that Sword, he's more powerful than anybody we can field at the moment. We can't trust ordinary people that the king might send. Just like a renegade Magician, Fuentes da Baneza has the ability to confuse them, trick them and overpower them, even turn them against us. Lord Ostersund, don't bother to volunteer. You are not recovering from your ordeal quickly enough. Ecmund isn't a good enough swordsman, and I'm out of the story." He sheathed Kitten again, and dropped her back on the settee.

The Magician passed a hand over his brow. "No. My Power is returning, but my physical state is too uncertain." He smiled wryly. "It would be embarrassing to fall into a faint at a crucial moment."

"So there you have it, Eirlin. You and Fang, with a little help from Kitten, are the most potent force we can field."

"I know he deserves to die." She sat and twined her fingers together, twisting them until they whitened. "He needs to die."

For the good of the kingdom. It could be arranged.

"But Kitten, you know I can't kill. You know what it would do to me. Besides, I don't have the right. I just don't know what to do!"

I know you think that I am young and inexperienced and that you need to show a good example for me, to train me to be ethical.

"Yes, I do."

Eirlin, I am 167 years old. That may be young in the life of a Sword, but it also means I have a great deal of experience.

"How do you know how old you are?"

It was quite easy, actually. Perica and I sat down one day and calculated it, based on historical events I remember. Perica is such an interesting human. She is very well educated.

"I know. And I am not."

That is true. If I need information, I go to Perica. She is knowledgeable, but sometimes not wise. You, but for a few notable exceptions, are wise. If I need wisdom, I come to you.

"And this is one of those notable exceptions, I suppose."

You are also notably perceptive. It is so nice not to have to explain everything.

"So why are we going through this list of my sterling qualities? May I assume there is some purpose?"

Of course. By the time we are finished, you will be calmed down enough to listen to what I have to say.

Eirlin smiled very slightly and sat straighter, her hands in her lap like a schoolgirl. "I am prepared to listen, oh venerable Sword. Enlighten me with your wisdom."

Sarcasm little becomes the Healer.

"So stop the moralizing and get on with it."

Jesco moved restlessly. "What's going on, Eirlin? I can't follow what you and Kitten are talking about."

I apologize, Jesco. Put your hand on my hilt. I want you to hear this.

He grinned. "So there's going to be a lesson for me, as well?"

"Probably. Kitten seems to be in a very philosophical mood today."

I see that you have returned to your usual even demeanour, Eirlin. I was merely about to make the point that there are certain moments in the life of any being when decisions must be made.

"And this is one of mine."

Correct. You have been luckier than most. You never had to worry about your calling. The decision to become a Healer was born in you.

"I suppose that is true. I see no reason to change that decision."

However, you have now come to the point where you must realize that a decision is needed.

"What decision must I make?"

A decision that, once again, has already been made for you. Your only task is to make your peace with the results.

"You are beginning to lose me, Kitten. What is this decision that I don't get to make?"

Eirlin, when I first came to you, you were the Healer for the Demesne of the Falcon. Today, if you look forward in your life, can you honestly see yourself ever returning to that position?

273

"Of course. Once this difficulty is over…"

Eirlin…

"No, Kitten, I know what you are thinking, and you are wrong. When…"

Eirlin, wake up.

The Healer frowned. "What do you mean?"

Wake up from your backwards-looking dream. You are already a different person from who you were then. And that's not even taking Fang into account.

"I see."

I think you do.

"And what deep conclusion do you draw from this fact?"

What would have happened if you and Fang had not been there to deal with Jesco's hand?

"I can answer that one. If I got that kind of wound on the battlefield, the Surgeon would have amputated all the fingers, clean off at the knuckle. If he was an especially good Surgeon, he might have recognized the chance to save my thumb. Since the word, 'good' does not belong in the same sentence as, 'battlefield Surgeon,' I doubt my hand would be good for much, right now."

And if there was no Surgeon?

"Then he would have at least two fingers that were completely useless and often in the way. He would also be in pretty much constant pain."

So even the lowest battlefield butcher realizes that there is a time when it is better to cut.

"I can see where you are going with this argument, Kitten, but how does that apply to me and how I deal with this man?"

It has to do with how you think of yourself. When you were the Healer of Falkenby, the only cutting you might do was to fix something like Jesco's hand.

"How has anything changed?"

I am going to do you the courtesy of not responding to the stupidity of that statement.

"Kitten! You don't have to be rude."

And you don't have to be stupid. You tell me how your position has changed.

"All right. I admit I am dealing with a larger number of patients."

It is much more than that, Eirlin. We have all remarked on your other position in Falkenby.

"What other position?"

The Protector of the People of the Falcon.

"Protector? There is no such person."

There was in Falkenby, and it was you. Now you have moved to Koningsholm, and you are working with the king. You are now the true leader of the People of Inderjorne: the Protector of the Realm. Whether you like it or not.

"And who has the power to crown me with this fictitious honor?"

I do, it is not ficticious, and it is no great honour. It is simply the recognition of your ability to perform the duty.

"Where did you get this power?"

Eirlin, I was created by Hanflaed the Smith, 167 years ago. I was created for a purpose.

"What is this purpose?"

I have no idea. He could not predict the future, but he made a great sacrifice to create me, so he must have felt that at some time someone like me would be needed. Whether that time is now does not matter. The fact is that I was born and trained to deal with this sort of situation.

"Why did you hide this from us?"

A situation did not come up. There are many things I know which I have not told you.

Jesco laughed. "In other words, 'I didn't tell you because you didn't ask.' Good answer, Kitten." Then he shook his head. "Let's get back to the original point. According to Kitten, and I know from experience she is right, you have always had a special place within our people, first in Falkenby, and now in all of Inderjorne. I think it's up to you to accept it, so you can do the most effective work you can."

Eirlin sighed. "I suppose. And this new task means I have to kill people?"

Think of it like a Healer should, Eirlin. You are the Healer for the realm of Inderjorn. If there is a part of the realm that needs to be excised, you are the one to do it.

"No matter what effect it has on me?"

It may affect your abilities as a Healer of people, but it might be a great benefit in your duties as Healer of the realm. Actually...

"Yes?"

I don't wish to upset you, Eirlin, but that aversion to killing was developed in you at a very young age, when you were quite naïve...

Jesco chuckled. "I think you should stop right about there, Kitten. You're starting to talk like a Sword, not a diplomat."

Diplomacy is knowing when to shut up.

"Good advice. Up to that point, you were making sense. I will think on what you have said, Kitten, and if I am placed in such a situation, it might help. I still cannot see myself killing anyone and being the same person afterwards."

Kitten refrained from agreeing aloud. It seemed diplomatic.

Jesco glanced at the Magician. "So now all we have to do is find a way to place her in that situation."

Ostersund nodded. "He's a difficult man to get close to, well guarded by his men and his Powers. And Eirlin is well known."

"And we don't even know where he is."

Once again, the Magician agreed. "The king's people have heard nothing. There have been no more raids, no further battles. Nothing. We don't know if he's in the Capital or out in the countryside somewhere. He just disappeared."

"So what do we do?"

"We wait."

38. Kidnap

Eirlin entered the garden and stood a while, watching Jesco and Kitten running through the practice patterns, Kitten's blade aflicker in the torchlight. Finally Jesco stopped in *guarde*, breathing heavily. He held the Sword in his left hand, and Kitten could feel his pride at the steadiness of the blade.

"How does it feel?"

He allowed Kitten's point to fall. "Not bad, actually. Of course, she's helping quite a bit. Aren't you, Kitten?"

Much less than before. Your strength is developing nicely.

"I didn't mean your swordplay. I meant your injuries."

He glanced at his bandaged hand. "Same answer, I think."

"Kitten?"

Same answer, Healer.

Eirlin nodded. "Well, since you sound so spunky today, can I ask you for a favour?"

Jesco sheathed the Sword. "I'm getting a bit restless, since you mention it. Not that Kitten isn't good company, but I could do with a real task."

She led the way in through the back of the house. "I'm not happy with that errand the king has sent Tyrbrand on."

He grinned. "Who's in trouble? The Magician or the king?"

"Not that unhappy. I just have a bad feeling about it. We talked about it before he left. There doesn't seem to be any good reason for the people out in Baldersholm to need a Magician."

"Why not? Didn't they say they had some problems only a Magician could solve?"

She nodded. "And that's suspicious in itself. Tyrbrand says it sounds too perfect to be true. Maridons and Inderjornese getting together to ask for a Magician."

"I see. And he had to go because it could be legitimate, but it could also be a trap of some kind."

"Or a ploy get him out of the way while something happens here."

He indicated the door to the sitting room. "And here you are, wringing your hands and feeling helpless."

"Right. And you were out at the tavern last night."

He threw himself into a chair and looked up at her. "I think I just lost you in a thicket. Yes, I was in the tavern."

"Which you told me is run by..."

He jumped to his feet. "That former soldier from Baldersholm. Right. And you want me to go and sound him out, to see if he can tell me anything."

"It doesn't sound dangerous, Jesco. Just talk to him."

He grinned. "Don't worry about the danger, Eirlin." He waved his right hand, covered with a simple bandage, in her face. "I'm not your poor little patient any more. This is just what I need."

He unbelted Kitten and handed her over. "I'll need my plain sword for this."

It doesn't fit your left hand properly.

"Not as well as you do, Cat, but it's good enough. It's not as if I'm planning on using it."

If you were a swordsman you wouldn't speak like that.

"Aye, but I'm not a swordsman any more, am I? I'm starting to develop other skills."

Eirlin laughed. "Like diplomacy?"

"I hear that takes a while. At the moment, I'm satisfied with quick feet." He suited action to words, and strode out of the room.

He is coming along very well.

Eirlin watched her cousin leave. "Yes, in many ways."

Jesco was back in a moment, dressed in his old tabard, his sword on his right hip. "You'll be fine alone? You've got Kitten, Lord Coelric has his guard, and Nadorst is a decent hand with a club."

"I don't expect any trouble here, Jesco."

"Neither do I." He gave her a meaningful stare before he turned away. "But if someone has made an effort to get the Magician out of the city, then what is the obvious conclusion? That da Baneza must be in the city." Then he turned back. "Tell Wynna where I've gone, will you?"

"I will do nothing of the sort. You tell her yourself."

He grinned sheepishly. "I suppose so."

"You suppose right. Off you go."

Oh, how the mighty have fallen...

It was a boring evening. Eirlin and Fang were practicing some esoteric task, and Kitten was looking around for something to entertain herself. Then she realized the calm of the house was being disturbed by a growing feeling of agitation.

Visitor.

Eirlin stood to peer out the window. "There is someone coming down the street, but I can't tell who."

Bad Lady comes.

"Cuquita? She's coming here?"

She's in a hurry. I think she's in trouble. Get her inside quickly.

"In trouble...? All right, Kitten, I know better than to argue." She rushed down the stairs and opened the front door as the Maridon woman started up the steps.

"Come in quickly."

With a last glance over her shoulder, Cuquita slipped in, pulling her hood down. "Lady Eirlin, I..."

"I know. You're in trouble. Whatever it is, you're safe here. At least safer than you were on the street. Let Eowin take your cloak, and come upstairs."

Kitten enforced the order with a gentle push, and the other woman allowed herself to be escorted up to the sitting room and seated comfortably.

Eirlin sat in front of her, just the right distance away. "Now, what's this all about?"

The old haughty look crept back onto Cuquita's face. "I don't like being here, but I have no choice. You are responsible for this, and I think you are the only one who can fix it."

"But Vanemar is dead."

"If only he was the problem. I could deal with him."

Eirlin sat back. "Obviously there is a whole lot more I need to know."

The other woman's lip curled. "Typical Healer. Nose stuck so firmly in her own business she misses everything else that is going on."

Eirlin dredged up a faint smile. "I assume this is the prelude to giving me enough information that I can help you?"

The other woman's face crumpled. "I'm sorry, Eirlin. I just can't help it sometimes. I...I could always handle it before. I could make them all afraid of me and then I was safe. I'm not saying I always liked it, but I was safe, you understand? And now I'm not."

"Who threatens you now?"

"Fuentes da Baneza. I can't deal with him. Nothing I do has any effect. He seems to have something..."

"Hmm. Yes, I imagine he does."

"You know about it, don't you? I knew you would. What's going on? Why can't I just destroy him like I can all the others?"

Eirlin smiled. "Not quite all the others."

"No. I couldn't deal with you, either. What power do you have over me?"

"The same Power you have always known you have, but that you have always denied. We just have it stronger than you do."

"Stronger? But..."

Eirlin reached out slowly, as if to a nervous animal, and touched the other woman's face. "The Power of the Blood of Inderjorn. You have it, as do many others. But yours is not in control because you have not been taught to use it. In fact, I would guess you have been taught to hate it. To hate a part of yourself. It must be very difficult. Lord da Baneza also has it, and he is also untrained, so he uses it for evil."

"Oh. And you have it, too?"

"Oh, yes. The reason you cannot deal with me is that I have great advantages over you. I won't go into them right now, but you already know that as a Healer I can affect your body without touching you. I did it once, without your permission, and that was a huge mistake, which got you into your present quandary. I reversed the damage, but obviously that did not solve your problems."

The Maridon woman's lip curled again. "You're damn right it didn't, you b..." Then her hands doubled into fists and she pounded on her knees. "I can't stop it! I don't really want to say those things, but I can't stop."

"No, Cuquita. You want to say them. They come from fear, and so you have never trained yourself to control them because they stop the fear. The only way to control them is to learn not to fear."

"Hah! A fine time to be learning not to fear. Do you realize what that man wants to do to me?"

"No, I don't. If I had to guess, I'd say he wants to marry you, though I can't see why. I'm not completely sure of the political situation, but I can't see that you are powerful enough to warrant his attention that way."

Cuquita shook her head. "I'm not, but it all got caught up in my problem with Vanemar. They had a big argument over it. Vanemar decided he was going to marry me, and da Baneza got angry and told him he couldn't. Vanemar asked why. I knew it was just jealousy, but da Baneza couldn't tell him that, so he had to back down, but he didn't like it." Her sneer returned. "I watched them, arguing in front of me like I wasn't even there. I wanted to scratch their eyes out, but I couldn't." She turned slowly to Eirlin, her fingers curling.

Help her, Kitten. She is fighting for control.

Yes, Healer.

"And aren't you glad now you didn't? What happened then?"

280

Kitten sent a soothing purr. She could feel Cuquita grasp the feeling like a drowning woman. Kitten sent more Power, and the tormented mind reached out tentatively, finding a way to use the Sword's strength to get herself under control.

"When Vanemar died I thought I was free, but then da Baneza came to me. He offered to marry me. He said I have all the qualities to be a queen!"

"A queen. Now, that's interesting."

"Yes, he said some day soon he was going to be the King of Inderjorne, and he wanted a queen worthy of bearing his seed."

"Of course! Well, that makes things a whole lot easier."

"It does?"

"Certainly. He has it wrong. He knows you have the same Powers he has, and he thinks that you and he would have children with more of the Powers. We only recently discovered that this idea is wrong. We don't know how the Powers come, but it has little to do with heredity. So all we have to do is tell him that, and he will lose interest."

The Maridon woman tossed her hair back and laughed bitterly. "That sort don't lose interest so easily. Let me tell you, once he sets his mind on something he gets it, no matter what." She turned back to Eirlin, her voice dropping. "That's what makes me so afraid. I don't want to live in a realm where he is the king. Being the queen would only make me his favoured victim."

"Well, I don't know what we can do. Tyrbrand is away and Jesco is out gathering information. But you can stay here. There's a bedroom made up on the ground floor. I can't see anyone bothering you in Lord Ostersund's home, if they even know you're here."

Once again the frightened girl appeared on Cuquita's face. "Would that be all right, Eirlin? I don't know where else to go."

She ran a hand through her hair. "Don't say it. I know there is a very good reason for that."

Eirlin smiled. "I wasn't going to say it. The fact that you are aware of it is a very good sign. Now come on, I know it's early, but let's get you to bed. We can talk more in the morning."

Kitten took the cue and sent calm and relaxation to the agitated mind. It seemed to work. Some.

Eirlin. Alert.

Eirlin looked up from the book she was drowsing over. "What? What's going on, Kitten?"

There's someone at the door. The Healer boy.

"Bejarin? What's he doing here at this time of night?"

I don't know, but I think we'd better let him in. Outside on the street doesn't seem very safe tonight.

Eirlin tugged a robe over her dress and hurried downstairs to the door. When she opened it, three small figures slipped in, closing it silently behind themselves. When she reached to turn up the lamp, a hand clamped over her wrist.

"No more light, my Lady. They might be watching."

"Who? Bejarin, what is this all about?"

"Men up the street, my Lady. Coming here. I heard them say so. They left their carriage up at the park. There are sacks on the horse's hooves."

"What did they say?"

"They said, 'The third window on the right.' That's all I heard. 'The light came on in the third bedroom.' I don't know what it means, but I thought..."

Cuquita.

"Yes, of course. I know exactly what you mean." Eirlin's thoughts whirled. "Now, I don't want you three involved. I think you should go. Do you know where the Turrona tavern is?"

"Yes, my Lady."

"Jesco is there. Send him here, then go home.

"But, my Lady..."

"No arguments. Slip out the door and away you go. I can handle this."

"But my Lady...!"

"Go." She opened the door, used Kitten's senses to check the street. "There is someone coming along to the left. Go right. Quickly, now."

"Yes, my Lady."

"And thank you, boys. You were very brave."

Kitten could feel their emotions swell as they disappeared into the night.

All right, mighty strategist. What do we do now? One soldier in the house and kidnappers on the street outside.

Eirlin was hurrying down the west corridor. "We have to get Cuquita out of there. I can't see that they're going to make an all-out attack. We can barricade ourselves in Coelric's quarters until Jesco gets here."

Cuquita. Wake up. Emergency. Get dressed. Kitten sent the thought forcefully into the Maridon woman's receptive mind. *She is awake, Eirlin. Do you want Wynna?*

No. She's better to stay upstairs for the moment.

Cuquita was pulling on her dress as Eirlin entered the room. "They must have followed you here. They're coming for you. Quick, we're heading for Lord Coelric's rooms."

It won't work.

"What? We'll barricade ourselves in. Jesco is coming."

Eirlin, these are strong men. We don't know how long Jesco will take, or whether he can get to me so we can fight together. The only way you are going to keep them at bay is if you fight them yourself.

"I can't do that, Kitten."

These men are from Fuentes da Baneza. They will be the best, and they will be afraid to fail. They will not leave here alive unless they get what they came for. Will you refuse to fight, and let her be taken for a fate you know well, when you are the only one who can stop them?

"Kitten...I..."

Kitten felt a wash of disappointment. *I had hoped for more from you, Eirlin Falconric.*

Cuquita finished lacing up her dress. "Then I suppose they will have to take me. Don't worry, Eirlin. There are other solutions. I will never be the Queen of Inderjorne, I can guarantee you that."

Eirlin looked around the room in desperation. "No, Cuquita, I can't let you."

Kitten felt a glimmer of hope.

They are coming. You must fight, Eirlin. You and I can stay here, and Cuquita can hide with the servants. They will come in that window, and we can be waiting for them. They will not expect resistance.

"Yes! That's it. Thank you, Kitten. They will not go without what they came for. So we will wait for them." Eirlin looked around the room. "Eowin, give me the candle. That small one, over in the corner." She placed a chair, just so, in front of the writing desk. "Now, Cuquita, give me your cloak and go down the hallway with Eowin to the servants' quarters. Wake Mistress Waldwine and Nadorst. Eowin, tell Coelric's soldier to stay with his lord. Lock the doors and be very quiet."

Wynna has been Listening. She goes to tell the soldier.

"Are you sure, Eirlin?"

"Yes, Cuquita, I have it all figured out."

With a last suspicious glance, the Maridon woman followed the servant away along the hall.

Eirlin looked around again, slung the cloak over her shoulders. "Perfect. Just about my size." She seated herself at the writing desk, pulling the shadow of the hood around her face. "Now we wait."

But Eirlin, I'm under the cloak. You won't be able to draw quickly.

"I said wait, Kitten."

It didn't take long. A shadow crossed the light from the street, and there was the tinkle of breaking glass. A hand reached in to undo the latch, and a head appeared through the open window.

A man crept over the sill, stopping when he saw the figure sitting there.

"What...?"

Eirlin rose. "I am ready. Let us depart." She walked towards the window before he could touch her. "What are you waiting for?"

She stepped down into the street, and a large man in a military tabbard grabbed her by the arm. "This way. Quiet, now, or you'll be sorry."

She said nothing, but allowed herself to be bundled into the waiting carriage. The wheels and hooves made no sound as they rushed away down the street.

Muffled. Very suspicious.

A little late, Kitten.

Don't you think we should have been suspicious of the carriage we couldn't hear coming?

Kitten...

Diplomacy is knowing when...

Kitten could feel the men's tension relaxing as they bowled along.

"How did it go?"

The voice beside Eirlin answered. "Like a charm, sir. She was already dressed and waiting."

"She was what? What are you saying?"

"Like she knew we were coming. She had her cloak on, the blue one like they said, and just stepped out the window."

The big man laughed. "Well, that was an easy one, then."

The men became silent again.

I'll bet they were told not to talk to you.

Probably. That's fine with me.

A good plan, for the spur of the moment.

I thought it was.

This is getting very interesting.

I suppose you might think so.

Don't worry, Eirlin. We will protect you.

Yes. Protect Eirlin. Grr.

Fang! You will not cut unless I say so. Do you understand?

Yes Eirlin. Always what you say.

Good boy, Fang. Just relax, now. Kitten, keep track of where we are, in case we have to come back alone.

Kitten sent her senses out into the night, watching as the carriage rushed through the empty streets.

We just passed the playing field. We are in the Maridon quarter, now.

No surprise there.

It was not long before the carriage slowed, made several quick turns and stopped. A door squealed ahead of them, and they drew into an echoing space. The carriage door opened, and light streamed in.

"Got her?"

"No trouble, sir."

"Good. Bring her along."

Eirlin shrugged off their hands and stepped down. By the shine of polished tack and the number of vehicles lined along the walls, they were in the carriage house of a large manor.

"This way, my Lady."

Military. He's an officer.

Soldiers, not family retainers.

Right.

"Thank you." She followed the erect figure up through the house. As they progressed, the ceilings became higher and the carpets thicker. Finally, they entered what looked like a suite of rooms befitting a lady. The officer turned, motioned her ahead.

"Your rooms are there, my Lady. May I take your cloak?"

"I'll keep it, thank you."

He eyed her suspiciously. "No, somehow I think not. Take it off, please."

With a shrug, she did so.

"You have a sword!" He stepped back, a hand on his own weapon. "Take the belt off. Slowly. Don't touch the hilt."

She did as he asked.

The bench by the inner door.

Without waiting for further instruction, she laid Kitten on the bench, her hilt nearest the bedroom.

Perfect. Now I can listen to all of them.

"Thank you, my Lady. You may go in, now. I hope you find all to your liking."

She regarded him a moment. "Since I have just been kidnapped, I doubt I will find it completely to my liking, but I appreciate your thoughtfulness, Officer."

She turned and went into the room. Kitten could feel her moving around, making herself comfortable.

The officer likewise seemed to be settling down to wait. He adjusted the candles, seated himself, pulled up a sheet of paper and a pen and began to write.

There was silence in the room except for the scratch of the pen and the crackle of the fire in the grate.

Then Kitten became aware of approaching footsteps. Loud, fast footsteps, accompanied by a very agitated mind.

Eirlin? Are you awake?

Of course I am. You didn't think I would sleep at a time like this?

I was just being polite.

Why, it's nice you're learning some manners at least. Thank you for your concern; I am awake.

Good. Listen.

The door crashed open, and a uniformed figure appeared, storming at the officer and looming over him.

"You idiot!"

"Watch your tongue, soldier."

"I can't help it. Do you know what you've done?"

"Yes. I have followed orders. It was a very smooth raid. We have the young lady right here."

"That's the point, you fool. You stole the wrong woman!"

Why does that voice sound familiar?

Because we know him, Eirlin.

Of course we do. Tajar.

Listen.

"What do you mean? We followed the girl in the blue cloak to Ostersund's manor. Just after she went in, a light came on in the third bedroom left of the door. We found the girl there. She had the dark blue cloak on. We brought her here."

"Do you have any idea what Cuquita da Launca looks like?"

"I've never met her. She's important to the 'Jornese faction, so I suppose she is blonde and fairly tall."

"You suppose? Who gave you the right to suppose?"

"Now just a moment, soldier. I have taken just about as much of this as I have to. If you don't..."

"You wait just a moment, dunderhead. As it happens, I know what both of the ladies look like. Cuquita is as Maridon as you are. Dark. Beautiful. I saw who you brought in. This woman is Eirlin Falkenric, the king's pet Healer."

"So what? She'll do just as well, then."

The other man sighed. "You just don't get it, do you? She wasn't kidnapped. She inserted herself into your feeble plot in order to get here. If you know what's best for all of us, you'll let her go immediately."

"Let her go? I think not. I was acting on specific orders, and you are not the one who gave them."

"Is that your final decision?"

"I don't see why that might concern you."

"It concerns me a lot. If you insist on keeping Eirlin Falconric here, then I am leaving. But first, I'm going to talk to her."

"You will do no such thing!"

Tajar's sword appeared in his hand. "Oh, yes I am. I'm going in to talk to her. Then, if she refuses to leave, I will. I'm not going to be in the same building with her, and I'm not taking the opposite side from her in any trouble. Now, you can do what you like, but you will stay outside that door until I'm done. Take it from me, you don't want to be in there."

He stomped over and jerked the door open.

"Lady Eirlin. I thought so." He shut the door, shot the inner bolt.

"Good evening, Tajar. Mixed up in trouble again?"

To their surprise, the soldier sheathed his sword and dropped to his knees. "My Lady, will you Heal me?"

"Heal you?"

"Yes. The last time we met, when I...when you were...in my camp, you said you could heal my problem, but I had to agree. At that time, I wouldn't. Now I do."

"When you kidnapped me."

"...I did, my Lady. And you made me see how wrong that was. Will you do it? Will you Heal me?"

"Right now? Here?"

"I'll give you a choice, my Lady. Heal me or kill me."

"You seem very upset, Tajar. What's wrong?"

"I tried, Lady Eirlin. I tried to change, but I can't. I always end up like this." His hand swept around the room. "It just drives me. You need to Heal me, and then I can make some choices of my own."

"I can't Heal you that quickly. What does your commanding officer have to say about this?"

"He will probably try to kill me when I leave. It won't matter. Will you come with me?"

"No, I have a duty here."

"I figured you did. Well, I won't be here. I'm leaving."

"I'm sorry, Tajar. When this is over, come and see me. In the proper time and place, I will be pleased to Heal you."

He bowed over her hand. "Thank you, my Lady. I will look for you."

He drew his sword again and stepped towards the door. Then he turned back. "Is Jesco all right?"

"Not really. His hand was very badly injured."

He shook his head. "Please believe me, Lady Eirlin, if I had known what they were going to do, I never would have told them. Those are some very nasty men. You know, I once thought I could be a great bandit leader." He shuddered. "Never like that. Never." He turned again to leave.

"Wait a moment."

"Yes?"

She walked to the door and opened it. "Excuse me, sir?"

The officer, who had been facing the door with drawn sword, stepped back. "Yes?"

"That is, 'Yes, my Lady,' if you please."

"Yes, my Lady."

"Thank you. Now, Tajar will be leaving. I suggest you do not hinder him."

"Oh, no. That traitor will get what he deserves..."

"That is correct. He will get what he deserves, but I will be the judge of what he deserves, not you. Tajar?" She stepped towards the officer, and the soldier followed her. When the way was clear, he sprang to the exit and was gone.

When the officer was about to follow, Eirlin held up her hand. "I think you misunderstood. My suggestion was merely a way of being polite. Tajar will be leaving, and you will stay here with me."

"I will do no such thing! I don't know who you think you are, but you are my cap..."

Eirlin took two swift strides to the left and reached out. Kitten jumped to her hand and swept up. "At the moment, I am the person with a Sword at your throat, so I suggest you calm down."

The man stared in surprise at the Sword. His own weapon drooped, and his left hand half-rose in a helpless gesture.

"Good. Now, I am going to sheathe my Sword, to show you that you do not need to be afraid of me. You will do the same." She did so, strapping the belt around her waist, and the officer sheathed his own weapon, watching her every moment.

That feels better. Now we attack.

Bite the bad man.

In a moment, dears. Calmly, now.

"And just in case you are thinking of moving against me, think of this..."

Now, Fang. Just his hand. Right...there.

Nibble, nibble, nibble...

"Ow!" The man shook his hand. "How did you do that?"

"Don't worry about how. Just believe that I can do it, anywhere on your body. Are you willing to cooperate now?"

"Y-yes, my Lady."

"Good. I want to meet your commander. Where is he?"

"He isn't here right now."

A lie.

"When is he coming?"

"I don't know. Maybe tomorrow, maybe the next day."

Another lie.

I could tell that, Kitten. He's a very poor liar. Fang, his other hand.

Nibble, nibble, nibble, nip!

"OW! Why did you do that?"

"Where is Lord da Baneza?"

The man glowered at her, rubbing his hand. "He's here. Upstairs."

"That's better. Take me to him."

"Right now? He didn't give any orders..."

She smiled, but there was no friendliness in it. "You may have noticed that I am giving the orders, now." She swept up Cuquita's cloak from the chair and slung it on. "Ahead of me, please."

Once again, they made their way upwards through the mansion.

39. Ecuas, Sire of the Qued Mora Herd

As they climbed, Eirlin sent her senses out.

There are many men here, Kitten.

Yes. Mostly soldiers.

You know the trick with many people...

I don't see how I could use it here.

How about to make them sleep?

Sleep? Just make them all sleep? I don't know how to do that.

Fang does.

Let me think. It is late. This might not be difficult. Fang, do you see that man?

Yes, Big Cat.

Can you make him just a little sleepy?

Sleepy man, sleepy.

Not right to sleep. Just sleepy. Now that one. Good. Now those over there. Not too sleepy, just a bit.

Sleepy-bye bad men, go to sleepy soon. Sleepy little bad men sleep in your room.

That doesn't rhyme, Little Tooth.

I will try better.

No, it's all right. Just add all those men in the lower floors. Very light, now, Fang. As you add more and more, the feeling gets stronger. Let's go look for more.

Fang and Big Cat go hunting?

Sure, little guy. We'll hunt them all out and put them to sleep.

"Is this his door?"

"Yes, my Lady."

"I will know if you lie."

"Yes, my Lady. This is his suite. He is here. I don't know why the guards are sleeping."

"For the same reason you're going to."

Sleepy man...

The officer slumped, and Eirlin knocked on the door.

"Enter."

She opened the door and stepped in.

It was a luxurious apartment: spacious, panelled and carpeted. An ornate marble mantel enclosed glowing coals, and brass oil lamps provided soft, even light.

Da Baneza rose from the chair by the fire, a brandy snifter in his hand. "I did not give orders for you to join me, my Lady, but you are welcome in any case."

She tossed back her hood. "I doubt it, my Lord."

If he was fazed, he took it in stride. "Eirlin the Healer. What a pleasant surprise."

"I doubt if it's going to be that pleasant, Lord da Baneza. Kidnapping is a serious charge, even for one of your rank. Of course, not as serious as ordering the massacre of a village of innocent folk."

He shrugged and walked over to his writing desk. "I fail to see how you are going to make that a problem."

His Sword...

The lord reached down and pulled the old Sword from its sheath. The metal gleamed black in the candlelight. It was a long sword with a single, heavy cross-quillion.

Made for use with a mailed hand. Slash and batter.

Kitten could feel the stirring of a massive force.

"Well, my Lady? What are you going to do?"

She went to the nearest chair and sat. "Wait."

"For help?"

"Perhaps."

Hah! Help comes! Jesco is inside. Up the stairs.

"Would you like a drink?"

"I have had sufficient of your hospitality already, Lord da Baneza. I am considering what to do about you."

"And I am considering what to do about you."

"Are you?"

He took a sip. "I am, and there we have a problem."

The door blew open, slammed against the wall. "Well, maybe I have a solution to your problem, Lord da Baneza."

Both heads swivelled.

"Jesco! How did you get here so soon?"

He tossed a glance over his shoulder. "Bunch of kids came and got me. One of them seemed to know where you were."

"But how did you get in?"

Jesco looked slightly bemused. "I met Tajar at the door. He apologized."

"You didn't hurt him, did you?"

"Didn't have time. He let me in. He was on his way out."

Da Baneza smiled. "I'm glad to see you again, Jesco Falconric. I recognize you from the meeting at Angelo. It will be instructive to my followers to see what happens to a traitor. Your Lord will be next, unless he toes the line very quickly."

"I think that would require you to win this fight, my Lord."

"What fight? My men will be here in a moment."

Eirlin shook her head. "In fact, they won't."

"What makes you so sure? Your Sword has no power to reach outside these walls and kill; of that I am sure."

"No, that she does not. Yet your men will not come."

The man's eyes narrowed. "Be that as it may. Then I will fight your champion, and afterwards I will deal with you."

Jesco said nothing, only reached over and pulled Kitten from her sheath. She fitted herself into his left hand. She fed the strength to his arm, the confidence to his heart. She took a chance and dove deep for a quick look. The usual scars were there, but solid white, the old redness gone. After a glance she came back to the fight, her heart lifting.

Eirlin, now is the time.

As you wish, Kitten. Do whatever you need.

With Eirlin's permission she reached out, and there were four Magicians nearby, one of them quite Powerful. By combining their Power, she was able to reach three more. And that was all. She took a moment to curse Magicians and their antisocial nature. Of Ostersund, there was no sign.

"Your Magician is busy at the moment."

"I know."

Their opponent lifted his Sword as well, and Kitten got a good look.

He is longer and heavier than I am.

Da Baneza is bigger and stronger than I am.

You're a better swordsman.

With my right hand, I was.

We had better be light on our feet, Swordsman.

That we had, Sword.

This is not going to be like last time.

That time was fun. Now we get serious.

He'll try for the big slash at the first. Don't parry. Duck him completely. Watch...here it comes...Whee! Nice riposte, Jesco. That made him dance. As I suspected. Very fast, very hard. Don't try a direct counter. One of us could break, and it would be me.

Do we have a plan?

Not yet. Just keep dancing

The opponent stopped his heavy swings and stood at *guarde*, unsure of this strange defense. He was breathing lightly, obviously not exerted in spite of several strong swings with the heavy Sword.

"Are you afraid my Sword's touch will break your little twig?"

"You'll know after it's too late, my Lord."

Jesco led with a quick series of lunges, one side and the other, slipping each parry, again without contact.

His attention is distracted. Now he is thinking too much. Feint right, under, back right, now get him!

Ouch! That was some kind of parry. Almost had him fooled, though.

He is very fast, in spite of the weight.

That is a serious Sword, Jesco.

She felt, rather than heard, an amused snort.

And what have we here? A worthy opponent?

I hope to be, my Lord.

And a polite one. Well met, my Lady Cat.

What do I call you, my Lord? I am unsure of the protocol.

I am Ecuas, the Herd Master. The etiquette is simple. We meet, we fight. The stronger Sword wins.

And what of our Hands?

The Hand is of some value. Yours does not seem strong. I sense rightness, but he holds you in his left.

A minor injury. It will not inconvenience us.

Again vast, faint amusement. We will see. At least it will be entertaining for a while.

During the exchange, the two fighters had run a series of feints and responses, the usual testing of skills.

Kitten, have you finished with the formalities? We have a fight on our hands.

We do. He is old and wise, and I'm sure he has many tricks. Watch that overhand; it's not...Oh, well done! That stop-thrust was perfect. Go for a lower line, he's tall. There. That set him dancing. No! Don't follow him in, it's a... I told you. He knows tricks!

I was sure I had him.

Not a chance. Take care, Jesco. He is a wily opponent.

I have his measure, now. Let's see if...

Jesco began a series of disjointed attacks, changing angle and tempo constantly.

Nice work, Jesco, but it's not doing any good.

Damn, he's solid. I can't get him off his balance one bit.

Shall we draw him out?

Dangerous, but let's try.

Here he comes. He's very cautious. Watch out, he's picking up speed. Weeow! Where did that come from? Ouch! Keep your parries angled.

Damned left hand. I almost dropped you.

Don't do that. I wasn't designed to wrestle on the floor.

What's going on?

He's being careful. He isn't in a hurry, and he isn't the kind to take chances.

Not when he's winning.

Who says he's winning?

Don't lie to me, Cat. He's bigger and stronger, and I get the feeling that Sword is your match.

I won't lie, Swordsman. He's trouble.

Any chance of a flèche?

It could be suicide.

Nevertheless.

But I thought...?

Not that, Sword. I have no desire to die. But I couldn't call myself a swordsman if I didn't consider all the possibilities.

Kitten felt a wash of relief. *All right. We'll watch for a chance. Last resource.*

Last resource

...Watch it! He's picking up the tempo.

No time to talk. He can tell.

Right. Concentrate. Let's try a trip. Lead him in, make him think...That's it...Well done! We almost had him.

'Almost' isn't good enough.

Set him back, though.

Not enough. Here he comes again. Doesn't the man ever get tired?

Sorry. She fed more strength to his arm. *That better?*

I wasn't complaining. He won't tire, will he?

Neither will you. Until I run out of Power, and then we'll both fall down flat.

Thanks. I can't wait.

Kitten sent a desperate call to Eirlin.

We are going to lose this fight, Eirlin. He is too strong.

The man or the Sword?

Does it matter? Jesco is going to be dead, and I will be taken by the enemy. Do you want two Swords against you? Do something!

What?

Do your duty. Not matter what cost to yourself.

I don't want...

Ouch! Jesco just took a cut to the thigh while you were dithering. Now he cannot move as fast as before. He's already fighting with his left hand. How much more penalty does he need before you choose to act?

Kitten, you have no shame!

The whole realm is in danger. Shame does not enter into it. Act, woman!

Slowly, she drew Excisor from his sheath.

What about him? How will this affect his ability to heal?

If I am taken and Joined to a Maridon, they will know all about him, and you, and how to negate his powers. Now is the time, Eirlin, when you make the ultimate sacrifice.

What ultimate sacrifice?

That which you have treasured for so long. Your innocence. Kill, Eirlin, or all you live for will be lost.

I can't...

You said that the last time. I lied to you then. This time I won't. Kill, Eirlin. Kill now!

In spite of the intensity of the swordplay, Kitten risked a glance at the Healer. She sat, tears streaming down her face, her Scalpel held up as if in prayer.

A faint whimper came from Fang. *Killing is wrong, Eirlin, you said.*

A Healer must cut to cure, dear one. And now this man must die, that the realm may heal itself. Do you understand?

Yes Eirlin. I understand. Why are you sad?

Because it is such a shame to destroy a wonderful thing like a life, dear one. But we must.

All right. He is a bad man. He has hurt Jesco. Big Cat? Shall I do this?

Yes, Little Tooth. Do it now.

Yes, Big Cat.

The pain and simple trust in the little Creature's voice sent a wash of horror through Kitten's mind. Suddenly it all became clear.

NO! DO NOT KILL!

What? But you said...

There is always another way, little Fang...I have it! When I say the word, you cut his wrist. Just there, see?

I see, Big Cat!

Jesco, be ready for his point to drop to the left. Ready, Fang? Ready, Jesco?

Make it quick, Cat, I'm running out of tricks.

Here he comes...He's in for the kill. Lead him right, right, and NOW!

A shock of pain washed over da Baneza's face, and the old Sword's point slumped down and left.

Over, Jesco! Over, and...in!

She reached over the wavering Sword point, lunging for the unprotected breast and plunging deep. As the man fell, his Sword dropped with a clatter to the floor, its senses reeling. Without hesitating, she slid through the defences, driving into the confusion that reigned in the newly-separated soul.

And there, deep within, she was confronted by a magical Being. A huge black horse reared before her, gleaming hooves striking the air, teeth flashing, screaming a challenge. She crouched and inched forward, her claws digging for traction...

...and the horse dropped to all fours, his head down. Now she saw the many scars that whitened his hide, the sag of his backbone, the hollows above his eyes.

Who are you, little Cat?

The fur on her back prickled, and she rose to her full height. I am Ailur, Cloud Cat of the Leute. I am the Cat with Many Claws.

A faint wash of humour. *And you are also Kitten, who is friends with a puppy. And a Sword who rides the hip of a Healer. It is long and longer since I met anything new in this world. How fitting that it should be in my final moment.*

How did you...?

Oh, you were very careful, but I have met many Swords and I know our ways. I have been aware of you, but could never pin you down. Either of you. Your young friend is very powerful. A Scalpel and a Healer. She got the vision of the old horse snorting in laughter. *Who would have thought it?*

You know about me. Who are you, Sword?

I am Ecuas, Sire of the Qued Mora Herd, the Master of the Ghardala. I have roamed the world as I roamed the plains of my early life. I have Chosen my Hands as I Chose my riders. Men of strength, whose purpose is the weal of the Herd. I have trodden many paths and done many deeds and I tire, little Kitten. I tire of the corruption of men with no purpose other than to rule. I tire of the thoughtless negligence that lets evil men take command of the Powers that were meant to serve the Herd. The souls of men are weak and rusty and they drag me down. The burden is too much to bear, young Cat. Will you take it from me?

How...?

In the way of Cats and Horses...

An image came to her. The sprint, the leap, the plunging panic, the digging of claws into soft hide, and then the tearing bite. The pumping of hot blood through her teeth...

And he was gone. Like a moth in the flame, his soul shriveled before her eyes, shrank to nothing and disappeared. She was left alone in darkness, the thrill of the hunt draining from her.

Kitten?

Kitten! Are you all right?

Big Cat! Big Cat wake up! Please? Please? Yikeyikeyike. Please?

Oh, stop your whimpering. I can't stand it. What is wrong with you people?

"Kitten! What happened to you? We couldn't find you. It's like you weren't there. Like Fang when he disappears."

Eirlin walked over and looked down at da Baneza and the black Sword. "Did you take his soul, Kitten?" She turned and took the Sword from Jesco's hand. "That was it, wasn't it? You realized that if Fang killed him, he would have to deal with his soul."

Something like that.

She smiled. "So the Cat with Many Claws found another way."

I would have thought of it sooner, but I let the idea of another Sword distract me. I should have known I could outfox him.

Eirlin laughed. "Now, there's a scary thought. Can you imagine a Sword with the soul of a fox?"

Yes, actually I can. Clever souls, those foxes. Maybe a dagger. Are you putting in an order?

"The only order I'm putting in to Tyrbrand is for one healthy Magician. No more forges for him!"

She brushed an errant tear from her cheek. "You didn't save us, you know. Fang and I. You didn't keep us completely out of it."

I know. You were with me when the point went in. Fang abetted in the killing. It will be a learning experience for him and good for you, as well.

Good for me?

Yes, you needed this. You have spent too much time treading your own rosy little path, helping others who were mired in the mud at the edge, but never actually getting your feet dirty. Now you have a smudge. You will wake in the night with the feeling of the point driving through the heart. You will relive the moment over and over in horror, when the soul slipped into nothing. And that will be good for you.

"You are a horrible little Cat to say things like that to me!"

And you have been a complacent and self-indulgent Healer. But you'll get over it now.

"Kitten! How dare you speak to me like that!"

Aha! Now the real Eirlin comes through. Don't like to be crossed, do you? Not used to it. Well, you might want to listen to me, young Healer. I am at least six times your age, and I have met many people. Every Hand I am Joined to goes through great change, so I am a bit of an expert on that sort of thing.

"I...suppose you might be."

You suppose correctly. So when I tell you that you have had it too easy, you just might want to listen. It doesn't matter how wonderful you are, and how sympathetic you act. Winning too often is not good for you humans. You come to expect it to happen all the time, and when it suddenly doesn't, what do you do then? Do you crumble and quit? Do you get mad and blame everyone else? Do you cheat and lie and break faith in order to win? Or do you dig your claws in and fight some more?

She waited until the determination began to glow on the Healer's face.

Right. So now you have a whole realm out there with a big, gaping wound cutting clear across it. You have only stopped the bleeding. Now you have to get on with stitching it back together. Get to work, Healer. That's your task.

"You could start with me."

Eirlin turned to where Jesco sat, a bloody hand covering his thigh.

"Of course, Jesco. Let me see. Kitten, Fang, are you ready? We have work to do."

40.   There Are Always Speeches

Eirlin wiped a hand across her brow as she and the king left the Presentation Balcony and led the group into the castle, away from the sound of the crowd. "I know you enjoyed that, your Majesty, but I hope we aren't going to make a habit of it."

Tyrbrand grinned. "Goes against the grain, doesn't it? Showing off in public."

The king smiled as well. "There had to be blond heads on the balcony with me. Why not a Healer? Your skills are what the kingdom needs now."

You have proven a strong hand in battle. There was never a question of your skill during peacetime.

Eirlin threw up her hands. "Fine. Now can I get on with my duties?"

The king shook his head, but his eyes were warm. "You started them out there a moment ago, and I wish you every success in continuing."

A memory shook her. "I don't think I want too much success, thank you very much."

"What do you mean?"

"How do you think da Baneza got to be the way he was? Too much success. His Power gave him an advantage over everyone, and he developed the opinion that he was someone special, that he had the right to more and better than anyone else. Kitten made me aware of that danger."

I don't think there's much danger.

"Well, if you ever think I'm acting self-indulgent like that again, I hope you will let me know."

I hope you will gain the maturity to know without any help from me.

The king laughed. "Well, maybe I need some of the same. But I'm the king. I'm supposed to be better than everyone else. How can I avoid it?"

"I think it might be helpful if you marry the right wife, your Majesty."

They were startled by a deep, heartfelt laugh, so unlike Jesco's usual bark. "You've had it now, your Majesty."

"What do you mean, Jesco?"

"I mean you'd better say good-bye to your independent life. Once Eirlin decides you need to get married, you're doomed."

"So, who have you lined up for my consort, Eirlin?"

"Your Majesty! Jesco was only joking."

"I assume Lord Ostersund has appraised you of the extent of my talents? I have never heard a joke that was more earnest in my life."

"Well, we have to pardon Jesco. He's family."

Jesco put an arm around Wynna's shoulders. "And I ducked your tricks, too."

"Which neatly ducks the question. Who?"

She regarded her monarch for a moment. "I did have a thought, actually."

"I tremble in anticipation."

"My favourite patient is coming along very well."

Tyrbrand raised his eyebrows. "Cuquita da Launca? You can't be serious!"

Eirlin portrayed nonchalance, ticking points off on her fingers. "She has the right bloodline, the right contacts. She and her family are poised half-way between the warring parties. The war within herself has given her a unique perspective. She is beautiful, and intelligent..."

The Magician raised a cautioning hand. "Don't forget, 'and everyone is deathly afraid of her'."

"That isn't such a bad quality in a queen...all right, maybe not as afraid as that. But give me a few more months with her. You'll see."

"I have all sorts of faith in your abilities, Eirlin," Tyrbrand indicated the king with a formal gesture, "but his Majesty also needs an appropriate mother for his heirs."

"I refuse to discuss a patient's condition, but I will assure you that Cuquita's problems were created by the same situation that has torn this realm in two. I cannot allow you to blame her character or her heritage for this situation. I have every confidence in her recovery." She grinned. "And we haven't really decided whether Sensitivity can be inherited."

"Pardon me if I reserve the right to wait and see."

"Of course, your Majesty. I didn't mean..."

The king laughed. "Of course you didn't. Who would have the temerity to tell King Vetrorillo of Inderjorne whom he will wed?"

Only Eirlin the magical Matchmaker.

"That's quite poetic, Kitten. Is that you, Eirlin? The Magical Matchmaker?"

"It sounds completely sappy, but I think I prefer it to some of the things she calls me, your Majesty."

41.   The Final Healing

The Magician looked around the infirmary ward. "So what is it you want me to see?"

"This is a very delicate operation, Tyrbrand. I want you to watch Fang work, and I want Kitten here to help in case there is any problem with Fang."

Little Tooth has learned a lot. I am not worried.

Eirlin raised her eyebrows to the Magician.

Don't be so surprised. I always knew he had potential.

The Magician grinned, and Eirlin led him into a small private room at the end of the ward. Taresita was sitting propped up with pillows, a slight frown on her brow. Eirlin laid the Sword across her lap, and the girl caressed the jewel in her hilt. Kitten sent her a cheerful purr.

"So, how is my favourite patient doing today?"

"I'm being very patient, Healer Eirlin." The good side of the little girl's face turned up in a beautiful smile.

"Yes, you are, and today your patience is going to be rewarded. Today, we are going to fix that face of yours."

"Will it hurt? It hurt awful when I got it."

Eirlin put an arm around the slim shoulders. "Not anything like it. What I'm going to do is I'm going to put you sort of to sleep, but not really. It will be like you're having a nice dream." She laid the girl back on a single pillow and signaled Tyrbrand to sit on the other side of the bed. Their minds met, and they began to explore the patient.

The pain is yours to deal with, Kitten.

Yes, Healer.

"What is going to happen in the dream is that you're going to meet someone. Someone very nice, whom you are going to play with."

The little girl's voice sounded drowsy. "That's nice. Who is it?"

"It's going to be a puppy. Do you like puppies?"

"Oh, yes...like puppies." The eyes closed and the girl's hands fell to her sides.

Eirlin took Fang out of his sheath and held him delicately in her fingertips, as one would a fine paintbrush.

"Are you ready to meet him?"

"...puppy...?"

"That's right. You're going to meet the puppy. Now, he's going to want to lick your face. I know, because he always does that. Is that all right?"

The girl giggled. "...tickles..."

Are you ready, Fang?

Readyreadyready, Eirlin.

The Healer laid the tip of the Scalpel gently against the skin at the edge of the scar, and began to draw it, ever so slowly, down beside the wound, talking as she worked.

"Now this puppy's name is Fang, and when he meets a new person he likes very much, he gets a little silly, and sometimes he nips a bit. Don't worry, he won't really hurt you, but he has very sharp little teeth, and he doesn't know how strong he is. Can you feel that?"

"...silly puppy...doesn't hurt...not much..."

Tyrbran leaned forward, ready with a towel to mop up the blood as the keen blade sliced through the flesh.

Don't worry, there won't be much. He closes off the blood vessels as he goes.

Impressive.

Just keep watching, Magician, and see what you have wrought.

She finished the first cut and started at the top again, removing the scar tissue unerringly, leaving the healthy flesh intact. When the scar was gone, she laid the blade flat against the girl's face, moving him slowly down the wound.

All clean, little one?

Clean, clean, clean, Eirlin.

"Good. He doesn't see any blight. We can sew it up, now."

She pulled a single hair from her head and draped it along her arm.

Look carefully, my darling.

She lined the Scalpel up with the hair, and slid him slowly along it. As the blade passed, the hair lifted to brush its edge.

Clean, clean, clean, yes, yes, clean, clean.

"Tell me he's not singing."

"Quit complaining. You taught him."

"What's he doing?"

"I'm not sure, exactly. He says there's 'worms' on the hair, and he has to clean them off."

"Worms?"

"I can't get a straight answer, but he won't let me use the hair until all the 'worms' are gone."

Clean, clean, clean the worms. Eat them up, Yum!

"He seems to be enjoying himself, anyway."

"It's all a game to him, Tyrbrand. I hope some day he will take it more seriously."

He is only a ki...I mean a puppy, Eirlin. I'm sure I was like this once.

Both Eirlin and Tyrbrand chuckled.

What is so funny?

"The idea of you being this silly."

Yes. I know it's hard to believe, but we were all young at one time. Except perhaps the Magician. I think he was born wise.

I make no such claim even now, Cat.

All clean. Clean, clean, clean.

"All right. Now watch this, Tyrbrand. Put your hand on Kitten's hilt and use her senses."

The Healer set the end of the hair near the top of the gaping wound and laid the point of the knife over it. A miniscule drop of blood formed, and the hair slipped into the skin. Kitten could sense the tiny muscles beneath the skin moving and contracting, and the hair slowly emerged from the skin on the other side of the wound. Pulling the hair through with a pair of tweezers and alternating sides with the Scalpel, the Healer neatly knitted the edges of the slash together. When the hair became too short to work with, she pulled another from her head and repeated the process.

"If you keep this up, you're going to go bald."

She chuckled absent-mindedly as she concentrated on her work. "I only use hair on facial cuts. Good old linen sewing thread is good enough for everywhere else."

"That is incredibly fine work. I don't know how you do it."

She flashed a direct glance at him. "Woman's work. Sewing. No problem at all."

He chuckled and went back to watching her.

"Now we come to the part I wanted you to see."

"You mean this was all just routine?"

"The corner of the mouth is the real problem."

"Yes, it's all slack. What can you do about that?"

"Do you see what these are?" She indicated, through Kitten's senses, the fine white lines that permeated the flesh.

"I've seen them before. When we worked on Jesco."

"Yes. Do you remember, Kitten told you to follow them up to his head, to the part of the brain that controls the heart?"

"That's right. And I could keep his heart beating."

"It seems these little lines are how the brain sends messages to the muscles, telling them to work or relax. See how these are cut?"

"Yes. One side of the wound is all slack, and the other side was puckered up by the scar."

"The scar was in the way, so the messenger lines couldn't heal back together. So we removed the scar, and then we heal up the lines, and maybe, just maybe, she will get her old smile back."

"...puppy? Where's puppy...?"

"He's right here, dear. He wants to lick your face one more time. Don't talk, now."

Very carefully, the Healer worked, healing the tiny filaments, smoothing the skin. Then she was done. She sat up straighter, met the Magician's eyes.

"What do you think of that, Smith? Have you forged a wonder, or not?"

He smiled warmly. "I'm not taking all of the credit."

"...puppy...nice puppy...pat the...ow!"

The little girl's questing hand had found the Scalpel, and a fine line of blood ran across her finger.

No! No! Little girl hurt! No! No! No! No cut! Never hurt! NO, FANG! NO!

Eirlin clamped a hand around the wounded finger. "Quick, Kitten. This is why I wanted you here. Calm him down! Tyrbrand, keep her asleep."

Easy, Little Tooth. Easy, now. The girl is fine. Eirlin will fix it.

Never hurt! NO! BAD FANG! HURT GIRL!

FANG! You will listen to me! Listen! She is fine. Kitten laid down her most reassuring purr. *All is well, Little Tooth.*

HURT...hurt...fine? Girl not hurt?

She is just a little girl, and she made a mistake. It wasn't your fault.

Fang not bad?

"No, Little Tooth. You didn't do anything wrong. See? Eirlin is healing the girl's finger, and you can help. See, the Magician is helping. The girl sleeps.

"Thank you, Kitten. You see how it is, Tyrbrand. He is so powerful, but so unpredictable."

The Magician's eyes glowed. "But that is wonderful! Look at her face. It is so smooth. Eirlin, you have worked a miracle!"

The Healer sighed. "We have worked a miracle, Tyrbrand. It took all four of us. Now let's give the young lady a touch of energy to help her heal. You all know how. Just a little, Fang. She is very young."

Happy, happy girl. Beautiful face, soft as mother's fur. Happy, happy...

"That's enough, dear one."

Happy, happy...

There was a moment of warm contentment. Then the Magician began to withdraw his hand. "Well, we're all hap..."

"No, Tyrbrand, not yet." She clamped her free hand on his. *Now, Kitten.*

"What...?"

Through the weakened defences and down into the open mind she plunged, brushing aside the Magician's futile protests.

"Kitten, what do you see?"

The Magician is not well.

What? I'm doing fine. Get out of there, Kitten!

"Tyrbrand, I am sorry to use this moment to intrude, but you are even worse than I feared."

I am doing much better...

"Kitten?"

Look inside yourself, Magician. What is this? Here and here? What is all that, torn and broken?

The Magician made a half-hearted attempt to pull himself away, but the Healer's hand and the Sword's mind were more than a match for his waning powers.

Tyrbrand, why didn't you let me help you? You need Healing.

I am healing. I'm getting stronger every day.

Certainly. Like this little girl's face was. Torn, twisted, and maimed.

I...

Hush, now. There is no hurry. We can discuss it later. Right now, Kitten and I have work to do. Sit still.

I...

Sit still, my dear. We are getting good at this.

Fang help.

Not this time, dear one. It's better if you just watch. You have been a very good boy today and you get to rest as well.

Fang watch. Help Smith.

That's right. You watch us, and we will help the Smith. We are Healers and that is what we do.

She laid the Scalpel on the bed and reached with her free hand to caress the Magician's worn face. *Now, let yourself go, Tyrbrand, just like Teresita did. Trust me. Trust Kitten. No harm will come to you here. Relax, and sleep. Relax and sleep.*

Be at ease, Magician. Eirlin and I are here. This is the time when you do not need to be alone any more.

His head slowly drooped until he was lying across the bed. As Eirlin shifted the girl's slight body to make room, the tiny hand dropped across his hair.

"...nice puppy..."

I don't think we'll tell Tyrbrand about that.

He would make a fine dog. If you like dogs. I don't mind dogs. Not the nice ones.

That's very broad-minded of you, Kitten. Now let us be quiet and work.

Yes, Healer.

See that? The twisted part, all frayed and breaking?

Yes. You can Heal that, can't you?

I think so. Hold back the pain for him... Thank you... just there, and there... look at that!

That looks much better, Eirlin. Say, what about over there?

Kitten, we don't go to that part of his mind. It is private.

Just thought you might want to know...

Well, I don't want to know. Come back over here. This needs to be smoothed out.

Yes, it does.

There. That's better.

Well done, Healer.

Yes, I think it is. He will heal on his own, now.

And we can always come back and help some more.

If he will let us.

I think the Magician has learned something.

I hope so. Let us give him strength.

There was a long, peaceful moment, and Kitten basked in the warmth of it. The fact that she was giving, not taking the energy did not seem to matter.

I think we should stop now, Eirlin.

What? Oh, yes, I suppose we should.

Eirlin.

Yes, Kitten?

Swords are not supposed to meddle with the emotions of their Hands.

I can see why that would be a good idea.

But you are not my Hand...

So you are going to meddle? Shame on you, Kitten!

...because he is a very nice Magician, and he needs you very much...

He needs a Healer.

You know, I like Ecmund's way of getting ideas across to people.

What way is that, Kitten?

Paddling their backsides with the flat of his sword.

"Kitten! You wouldn't lower yourself."

Ah, the sacrifices we make for those we love.

Eirlin's mind firmed. *You will not meddle, Kitten.*

I already have. It didn't work. I will now remove myself from this conversation.

Kitten! You're pouting.

I am merely refusing to waste my energy on a lost cause.

So you consider me a lost cause, do you?

Lost, stupid, and useless.

Kitten!

Well, maybe not so useless. Little Tooth needs a Hand. I suppose you'll do until someone better comes around.

Well, if you're going to be insulting...

Oh, that wasn't insulting. You want insulting? I'm sure I can come up with something appropriately cutting.

Eirlin suppressed a laugh. *Kitten, you're just teasing me, aren't you?*

This is far too serious for teasing. Wake the Magician up and tell him you love him.

Kitten, I can't! I must be careful. I don't know if it's love.

Phtt!

I don't!

Too late. I woke him already.

"Eirlin, Kitten, I'm sorry, I didn't mean to eavesdrop, but you were sending rather loud messages. As usual."

The Healer snatched her hand from the Magician's grasp, red suffusing her face.

She blushes rather easily, doesn't she, Magician?

"Yes, and quite becomingly, don't you think?"

Probably not. It's just the strange bond that isn't love that makes you think so.

"Kitten, you stop it."

No. Talk to him. Out loud. That's what you're supposed to be so good at. So talk.

Eirlin glanced around, indicated the sleeping girl. "This is not the time or place."

Then make one.

The Magician smiled and rose, stretching as if after a long sleep. "Yes, Eirlin, we must do that."

Eirlin stood as well, hiding her confusion in the quiet bustle of removing her equipment from the bedside table. Before she left, she laid a hand on the brow of her patient, smiling softly. Then she turned out the door.

As they entered the larger ward, Tyrbrand took her hand and tucked it comfortably under his arm. His elbow touched Kitten, and they shared a wordless smile.

Eirlin glanced up at him, pretending she didn't want to smile as well. "You are both just too smug to bear."

"You'll get used to it."

* * *

Brought up in a logging camp with no electricity, Gordon Long learned his storytelling in the traditional way: at his father's knee. He now spends his time editing, publishing, travelling, and writing fantasy and social commentary, although sometimes the boundaries blur.

Gordon lives in Tsawwassen, British Columbia, with his wife, Linda, and their Nova Scotia Duck Tolling Retriever, Josh, whose personality bears no resemblance to that of any character in this story, because while the book was being written he grew up.

Mostly.

More from Gordon A. Long

At <smashwords.com> and <amazon.com>:

"A Sword Called...Kitten?" (First book in this series) Romantic comedy with an edge.

"Out of Mischief" World of Change 1
"Into Trouble" World of Change 2
"Mountains of Mischief" World of Change 3

"Why Are People So Stupid?" Light social commentary with a point.

Look for Gordon's books, selected reviews, and other writing at <airbornpress.ca>

Check out his opinions on people in general at the Are We Stupid? blog. <airbornpress.ca/arewestupid/blogweb/index.php>

Find his reviews and his ideas on writing at Renaissance Writer. <airbornpress.ca/writing/blogweb/index.php>

www.ingramcontent.com/pod-product-compliance
Lightning Source LLC
Chambersburg PA
CBHW070218260626
47160CB00002B/596

9780992124304